"Federation vessel, this is Terok Nor.

I am Major Heslo Artun of the Bajoran Militia and interim commander of this facility. I offer greetings on behalf of the Bajoran Republic." Despite his words, Picard noted a stiffness to his tone, as though he were reciting a script written for him and which he read under protest. Plainly, Heslo was not excited about this meeting.

Picard moved to stand closer to Data. "Major, I'm Captain Jean-Luc Picard, commanding the Federation *Starship Enterprise*. It is a privilege to speak with you today."

"Our sensors show you are on approach to Bajor, Captain. We request that rather than assuming orbit over the planet, you alter your course to dock at the station." As before, Heslo's demeanor was not rude, but instead hewing to strict formalities.

Picard said, "We are happy to follow whatever procedures you've established, Major. It was my understanding that the conference would be held at your government's primary capitol building."

"First Minister Kalem has directed a change of venue," replied Heslo. *"He feels that the station provides a more . . . appropriate . . . backdrop for the topics to be discussed."* The major offered the slightest hint of emotion by cocking his left eyebrow, which only served to draw further attention to the scar on his forehead. It convinced Picard there was more in play here than a simple change of setting.

Doubting Heslo would be willing to entertain further questions, Picard instead said, "Very well. We will adjust our course accordingly."

"Thank you, Captain." Heslo nodded. *"Our docking control officer will transmit pylon and mooring instructions. Terok Nor Operations, out."* Without waiting for a response, the Bajoran severed the communication. The viewer's image returned to that of Bajor. Still dominating the center of the screen, the planet now was larger than it had been before.

"Not exactly rolling out the red carpet for us, are they?" Riker's expression told Picard his first officer was not complaining but making one of his normal frank assessments.

STAR TREK™
THE NEXT GENERATION

Pliable Truths

Dayton Ward

Based upon *Star Trek* and
Star Trek: The Next Generation
created by Gene Roddenberry
and
Star Trek: Deep Space Nine
created by Rick Berman & Michael Piller

G
GALLERY BOOKS

New York   London   Toronto   Sydney   New Delhi   Bajor

G

Gallery Books

An Imprint of Simon & Schuster, LLC
1230 Avenue of the Americas
New York, NY 10020

First Gallery Books trade paperback edition May 2024

GALLERY BOOKS and colophon are registered trademarks of Simon & Schuster, LLC

Simon & Schuster: Celebrating 100 Years of Publishing in 2024

For information about special discounts for bulk purchases, please contact Simon & Schuster Special Sales at 1-866-506-1949 or business@simonandschuster.com.

The Simon & Schuster Speakers Bureau can bring authors to your live event. For more information or to book an event, contact the Simon & Schuster Speakers Bureau at 1-866-248-3049 or visit our website at www.simonspeakers.com.

Interior design by Kathryn A. Kenney-Peterson

Manufactured in the United States of America

Library of Congress Cataloging-in-Publication Data is available.

ISBN 978-1-6680-4641-8
ISBN 978-1-6680-4642-5 (ebook)

*Dedicated to
my wife and children*

HISTORIAN'S NOTE

The events of this story take place in the year 2369, soon after Captain Jean-Luc Picard's capture and torture at the hands of the Cardassian interrogator Gul Madred (*Star Trek: The Next Generation* "Chain of Command"), and before Starfleet's assuming tactical control of the Cardassian space station Terok Nor and establishing a permanent Federation presence in the Bajor sector (*Star Trek: Deep Space Nine* "Emissary").

A lie runs until it is overtaken by the truth.
—Cuban proverb

STAR TREK™
THE NEXT GENERATION

Pliable Truths

1

—

Emerging from the tunnel while balancing the oversized rock on his shoulder, Panat Hileb noted the thin sliver of orange sky separating the sun from the distant horizon. The horn declaring shift change was imminent, he knew, but any pause of work before that welcome sound brought with it the promise of swift punishment. Having seen others suffer for such a lapse, Panat did not break stride or spend any time appreciating what was a breathtaking view.

With just enough purpose to avoid provoking the guards, he shuffled from the tunnel entrance and past other workers on his way to the nearby mining tram, where he tossed the rock into one of the bins that still had room. In response to his action, the car shuddered where it sat hovering on its antigravity sled just above the flattened path that served as a service road leading to and from the mine. Knowing a fellow laborer was right behind him, Panat turned and headed back toward the tunnel where more rocks awaited. One constant about this work detail was that there were always rocks waiting to be removed from the mine for transport to the nearby quarry, which was little more than a refuse pit.

And a graveyard, Panat reminded himself. *Filled with bodies of those our oppressors no longer found useful.* It also included workers who slackened their efforts before the end of their scheduled work period.

Clearing rubble from the mine's work areas was one of the cruelest labors demanded by the Cardassians running the prison colony. Inside the mine, other Bajorans drudged through the arduous task of extracting uridium ore from the planet's depths. That valuable mineral, once separated from the surrounding bedrock, was placed in containers for transport to a location unknown to Panat and the other workers. None of the Bajorans knew if the ore was refined here or placed aboard cargo freighters bound for a processing facility on another world.

One more mystery for Panat and his fellows, along with not knowing the planet's name, location, or strategic value. Were they near some boundary separating Cardassian territory from that of an interstellar neighbor or rival? Despite the best efforts of the intelligence-gathering network threaded through the Bajorans, such information remained closely guarded secrets, which to Panat made sense. Assuming one was able to call for help, it was an all but useless effort when there was no way to know where to summon assistance.

Proceeding to the mine entrance, Panat made eye contact with other forced laborers. Some of them were friends, others he knew only by name. It was a matter of degrees; in a place like this, all who shared the same plight were colleagues, companions, and—when the time was right—comrades-in-arms. While they were here to serve their overlords, all the laborers also shared the desire to be rid of the Cardassians. Even for those like Panat, born during the Occupation, they longed for freedom.

One day, he mused. *One day, hopefully the Prophets will help our people.*

He noted the lengthening shadows stretching across the ground ahead of him as well as the surrounding canyon walls at the mine's entrance, which was cut into the face of the hillside as part of a larger excavation effort completed earlier in the year. The shadows at this time of day told him the days were getting shorter. Soon, the temperatures would begin to cool, and even here in the planet's temperate zone, another winter would make its presence felt.

Assuming you live that long.

"Step with greater purpose, friend."

He heard the comment, uttered in a quiet tone, from his left, and he looked up to see Ranar Ehu walking past him while carrying his own large piece of stone. Like Panat, he wore tattered clothes made from scraps of cloth and other materials provided by the Cardassians with irregular frequency or which he had scavenged or fashioned from discarded clothing. His hair, once dark and long, had gone gray and was thinning on top, and what remained was secured at the back of his neck with a strip of cloth. They had not known each other before being shipped to this planet but had become close companions in the years since. They shared many of the same interests from their lives before being transported here from Bajor. This included a fondness for the outdoors, a love of music and the arts, and constant plotting to undermine their oppressors.

With a small, guarded smile, Panat nodded at him. "All of my steps are with purpose." It was an innocuous response to an innocent salutation, which of course carried great meaning for those Bajorans who, like him and Ranar Ehu, participated in the resistance effort on this world.

Born during the Cardassian Occupation of Bajor, Panat had been content to do what he considered necessary to survive and keep his aged, frail parents safe. That meant enduring much hardship and sacrifice, doing as he was told by those who subjugated Bajor. It was not an ideal existence, but he could secure his parents food, shelter, and medication, and for a time that satisfied Panat. All of that vanished one horrific night when a Cardassian security detail descended on Panat's village in the Lonar Province, killing anyone they considered a waste of resources. His parents vanished in a hail of disruptor fire.

Panat was still reeling from the shock of their deaths when he was put aboard a transport ship and brought to this forsaken planet. From his first moments, he had sought out any Bajorans who might be part of the resistance movement he knew was gaining momentum on the planet of his birth. It had taken nearly a year before Ranar approached him and brought him into the fold, beginning their friendship and their partnership in arms.

And now we toil by day, and plot by night.

Indeed, Panat and Ranar, along with other trusted members of the Resistance, convened at irregular intervals after the work detail's return to camp and before curfew. They discussed possible disruptions. Given the isolated nature of the forced-labor camp and the relatively small population of Bajorans—fewer than two hundred, by Panat's count—doing anything too drastic would leave them no room to hide among the population. This abundance of caution forced them toward smaller acts that on the surface did not point to insurrection. Sabotaging equipment was a common ploy, though even that had to be done with care and proper timing. The same was true with finding methods of interrupting the workflow in a manner that did not arouse suspicion. Then there were the more challenging acts, such as eliminating one of the guards.

If things went according to plan, that would happen here, today.

The horn sounded, echoing off the hillside and making every worker look up from whatever task had consumed them. Those still carrying rocks to the tram continued forward, looking to add their final burden of the day to the bin.

"Finish up," said one of the Cardassian guards, Lubak, an older trooper whose disinterest had long ago become evident. His command was not a harsh order but a simple recitation of a directive given at this time every day. "Put those last rocks on the tram and get in line."

Rumors around camp held that Lubak had been passed over for promotion enough times that he was resigned to completing his term of required military service in as expedient and uneventful a manner as possible. To his credit, he had chosen not to take out his frustrations on the Bajorans, instead doing only the minimum necessary to maintain order and efficiency while overseeing their work. Like Panat, many of his fellow Bajorans knew Lubak's apathy was their good fortune, and therefore conducted themselves in a manner that would not cause trouble or otherwise draw the ire of more attentive and less benevolent guards.

Many of the other guards on the detail appeared to be of similar mindset. There was no denying this was tedious duty, perhaps punishment for infractions real or perceived. Deviations from the normal schedule of activities consisted in large part of accidents or a laborer suffering from exhaustion. Otherwise, most days followed a routine. Repetition, Panat knew, begat boredom, which in turn bred inattention. Sabotage was most effective when it could exploit that laxity in a fast, decisive, and even violent manner.

Changing direction so that he now proceeded toward the rally point where the laborers formed columns for marching back to camp, Panat cast a quick glance toward the front of the tram where another trooper, Locin, stood watching the daily ritual play out. As Bajorans brought the day's last chunks of rock to drop into those tram cars that still harbored room for additional debris, the Cardassian pulled a device from a holster on his equipment belt. He pressed a control on the unit and the tram's internal power systems activated. Utilizing antigravity plating, the entire set of twelve cars rose to hover less than a meter above the ground, emitting a low-frequency hum as it idled while awaiting further instructions. Under normal circumstances, whoever controlled the tram could send it on its programmed course with the touch of another control. Panat had seen the exercise play out on uncounted occasions over the years.

Today, however, the tram did not wait for that command. Instead, it lurched forward without warning, proceeding not at its normal, near-walking speed down the worn service path but accelerating as it altered direction toward Locin. With no time for him to move out of its way, the tram's front end slammed into him at waist level, knocking him backward and off his feet. Tumbling to the ground, he had no chance to scramble for safety before the tram hit him again, this time striking his head and pushing him back to the dirt before all twelve cars glided over him. The sound of Locin's death scream echoed off the canyon walls as the antigrav plating exerted force downward, keeping the tram above the ground while crushing the Cardassian to pulp.

Instead of stopping, the tram shot across the path and over open ground before slamming into a pile of oversized boulders. The collision caused the other cars to decouple, sailing off in different directions to either smash into the canyon walls or tumble into the ditches on either side of the pathway. Several of the Bajorans and even a pair of Cardassians, all clueless to the reality of what had just happened, stared in disbelief at the scene unfolding before them.

"Help!" Panat yelled, playing his part as a distressed Bajoran witnessing a traumatic event. "Guards! Help!" He knew there would be no helping Locin, but he had to play out the scenario the same way as those laborers who had not known this was coming. Running to what remained of the guard, Panat confirmed he was dead, likely before the tram had even finished its work. In a surprise bonus, his control pad had also been destroyed by the force of the tram's antigravs. There would be no examining the unit to see if it had suffered any tampering. Panat knew that it had, but even that contingency had been anticipated.

"What happened?" The question was loud and forceful, uttered by another Cardassian, Glinn Irvek. An officer in charge of the working detail as well as the guards assigned to oversee it, he was younger than several of the troopers around him, and prone to callousness and even brutality when it suited him. Panat and others had learned to give him a wide berth whenever possible, but even that was sometimes insufficient to avoid the glinn's wrath.

Pushing his way past Bajorans and a pair of guards, Irvek stopped near Panat and beheld for himself Locin's ghastly remains. "Who saw this?" He turned, his eyes boring into Panat with growing fury, and he even moved his right hand to rest on the sidearm holstered on his hip. Panat, who from the moment he and Ranar had hatched this scheme knew quick and severe retribution might be a possibility, braced himself for whatever might come next, but Irvek's hand was stayed by another voice.

"I saw it, sir," said Lubak, his voice carrying past Bajorans who moved out of his way as he approached. "Trooper Locin activated the tram as he does each day, and it ran him over."

As if exerting physical effort to tear his eyes from Panat, Irvek turned to his subordinate. "You're saying this was *his* fault? He did this to *himself*?"

Exhibiting the experience and wisdom of a seasoned soldier, Lubak replied, "I can't assign fault, sir. All I know is that there was no one on or near the tram when he activated it."

"Sabotage, then." Snarling as he glanced once more to Panat, Irvek said, "Get the workers into formation." Before Panat could move, the glinn pointed a finger at his chest. "You." He shifted his aim to Ranar, who stood at the forefront of the gathered Bajorans observing the scene. "And you, collect Locin's remains. Leave so much as a stray drop of blood on the ground and you'll die the same way he did." He glared at Lubak. "Watch over them."

They waited while another Bajoran retrieved a cadaver transport container from the supply building near the mine's entrance. He offered it to Panat before Lubak ordered him back to the formation of laborers gathering on the service path under the watchful eye of other guards.

Is Irvek going to kill them?

The question hung in Panat's mind, and he waited to see if the glinn might order his troopers to execute the entire work detail. Standing orders at the camp called for the immediate execution of any Bajoran found to have assaulted any Cardassian. Such drastic action had not occurred for some time, but it was not out of the question. When he first arrived here, a guard might kill a Bajoran for the feeblest reason. Laborers at that time were as expendable as they were replaceable, and it was not uncommon for the Cardassians to make an example of a hapless worker, often an elderly prisoner or some other, weaker member of the population. Panat had noticed that the guards never targeted anyone who could still provide manual labor. Likewise, he was aware that new arrivals to the camp had slowed as time passed. This corresponded with a subtle yet distinct change in how the garrison treated them. Punishments grew less severe except in the most egregious of circumstances, at least as defined by the Cardassians. So far as Panat knew, it had been over a year since any new Bajorans had been brought to the planet. What reason would the Cardassians have not to replenish the workforce?

With this in mind, Panat dismissed his worrisome thought. Still, there was a distinct chance Irvek would find or invent a justification to punish someone from the work detail. He would deem it necessary to set an example, or to remind the workers that disobedience carried penalties even though he possessed no evidence for misconduct. Such things were not needed when one carried the power of life and death over those under him.

Sunlight grew weaker with every passing moment as Panat and Ranar set to work collecting the trampled remains of Locin's body. Under Lubak's watchful eye, they exercised care in placing the remains into the cadaver pouch. Without gloves or other protective equipment, the task was even more gruesome thanks to the blood and other bits of bone, skin, and destroyed uniform that soon covered their hands and clothing. In keeping with Irvek's instructions, they also collected bloodstained rocks and loose dirt, placing these into pockets on the pouch's exterior. Ranar sealed the pouch, and they both stood to face the guard.

"Take . . . him . . . to Glinn Irvek's vehicle," said Lubak. Rather than conveying anger or impatience, the guard's mood seemed even more sober than it had been before the incident. He pointed toward the armored skiff parked outside the supply building. The antigrav vehicle was of the type preferred by the officers among the camp's garrison.

Shouldering their grisly burden, Panat and Ranar headed off in that direction. Without looking too obvious, Panat cast a look over his shoulder to confirm Lubak was not following them but instead had joined other guards in organizing the formation of Bajoran workers.

"You think he was pondering the idea it could just as easily have been him?" asked Ranar. "Accidents happen, and so on."

Panat shifted his part of the cadaver pouch on his shoulder. "I'm guessing all of the guards are thinking that." He also knew that Irvek and others were considering the possibility that Locin had not fallen victim to a tragic accident.

They would be right, of course.

"He got what he deserved," said Panat, remembering to keep his voice low.

Known for his excessive cruelty toward the elderly and his wanton advances toward many of the Bajoran women, Locin's fate had been decided four months earlier. It had come after the unnecessary execution of an older worker who had stumbled and fallen while loading tools onto a cart. One of the tools had landed on Locin's foot, and despite not causing injury, the Cardassian had erupted in fury at the perceived disrespect. He had beaten the old man senseless, cracking his skull along with several ribs, causing internal damage and bleeding. Even if the camp doctor had been able or willing to help, the worker's injuries were too severe, and he died within moments. The murder had stirred many of the Bajorans, coming within a hairsbreadth of triggering a riot. Only the other guards, including one or two appalled by Locin's actions, kept the situation from spiraling out of control. Resentment persisted for days afterward, to the point the trooper was assigned to other duties away from Bajoran work details.

That changed a month ago, when Panat saw him awaiting the arrival of the primary shift at the mine. Perhaps those in charge of deploying the individual garrison members thought enough time had passed and the workers were too exhausted to mount any sort of protest, but from the moment Panat laid eyes on him, he vowed Locin would pay for what he had done. That pledge set off a flurry of planning between him and Ranar, who harbored feelings even stronger than Panat's.

The plan required enlisting the assistance of another Bajoran, Yectu Sheeliate, a technician assigned to the camp's maintenance facility where care and repair of the Cardassian garrison's vehicles and equipment was conducted. Her skills had been vital in programming the viral code ported to the tram's onboard computer when it was brought in for its regular maintenance check. Panat did not understand everything about what she did, but she had modified the tram's systems in such a way that it had carried out its redefined purpose, homing in on the signal emitted only by Locin's control pad and not another guard's, then wiping all traces of any software changes from its onboard memory once the attack was over.

Yectu Sheeliate had accomplished her sabotage weeks earlier, then set a delay into the software to ensure a gap of time following its last maintenance check before the scheme was put into motion. If and when the tram was subjected to an investigation to determine the cause of its apparent malfunction, the Cardassians would, according to Yectu, find nothing out of the ordinary. It would appear Locin's death was caused by his own error with his control pad. A wrong button pushed or a command entered by mistake. The only accurate part of that assessment would be that the trooper had indeed brought about his own demise, in a manner of speaking.

Only as he and Ranar moved to take their place in formation with the others did Panat realize that the second shift of Bajorans had not yet arrived. Under normal circumstances, that detail would be on-site and ready to take over from the first shift with only a minimal amount of time and work lost during the transfer. Looking up the service path in the direction he would expect to see the incoming formation, Panat instead saw nothing. Neither did he hear the telltale signs of a large group on the march.

"Something's happening," said Ranar, echoing Panat's own thoughts. "Or, happened."

Instead of replying, Panat glanced around the formation, counting the Cardassians. Nineteen guards including Glinn Irvek. The twentieth guard, Locin, accounted for everyone. Rather than their full attention being on the working party, several of the guards were talking among themselves, and Panat could read troubled expressions on some of their faces. Punctuating the hushed, indecipherable whispers were occasional glances toward the Bajorans. A couple of the guards fidgeted with their disruptors or rifles. After a few moments, Irvek stepped away from his subordinates and waved in the direction of the service path.

"Back to camp," he snapped, his irritation almost but not quite hiding something else. Was it concern? Panat could not be sure.

As the Bajorans, organized into two columns, began their slow shuffle back to the dismal outpost that was their only home, the glinn shouted again in a louder voice. "Now."

Panat exchanged glances with Ranar. Whatever had occurred, it was unexpected and unwelcome, but what did this mean for him and his fellow Bajorans?

One way or the other, he expected the answers would not be long in coming.

2

Despite already losing count of the times he had read it, Gul Havrel once more regarded the decrypted message displayed on his desktop workstation. The labor camp overseer knew staring at it would not cause it to change, but he still could not believe what the words conveyed.

```
FROM CENTRAL COMMAND: BY ORDER OF DETAPA COUNCIL,
OCCUPATIONAL FORCES OF THE CARDASSIAN GUARD ON BAJOR
ORDERED TO IMMEDIATELY COMMENCE WITHDRAWAL ACTION.
    REMOVE ALL EQUIPMENT, WEAPONS, AND OTHER MATÉRIEL
DEEMED SENSITIVE FROM ALL PLANETSIDE FACILITIES AS
WELL AS TEROK NOR. ABANDON ALL OTHER ASSETS INCLUDING
INFRASTRUCTURE. CRADIS PROTOCOLS ARE NOW IN EFFECT.
    ALL BAJORAN NATIONALS ARE NO LONGER UNDER CAR-
DASSIAN AUTHORITY. ALL NATIONALS LOCATED OFFWORLD
ARE TO BE RETURNED TO BAJOR OR ALLOWED TO DO SO ON
THEIR OWN. RETURN OR SURRENDER TO PROPER AUTHOR-
ITY ALL BAJORAN HISTORICAL AND CULTURAL ARTIFACTS.
CEASE ALL EFFORTS TO PURSUE RESISTANCE TARGETS. TAKE
NO FURTHER AGGRESSIVE ACTION AGAINST BAJORAN AND
OTHER CIVILIANS UNLESS NECESSARY TO DEFEND PERSON-
NEL AND SENSITIVE MATÉRIEL. PLANETARY EVACUATION TO
COMMENCE IMMEDIATELY. ADDITIONAL TRANSPORT ASSETS
EN ROUTE.
    ABANDON TEROK NOR.
```

"Has this message been verified?" asked Glinn Trina, Havrel's adjutant and second-in-command of the labor camp and its tenant facilities.

With a sigh, Havrel replied, "I confirmed it three times. The ciphers used to encode and decode it are legitimate. This is an official directive from the council, with concurrent authentication from Central Command."

The decree, phrased as it was, sent a shock through Havrel. Across the width and breadth of Cardassian military forces, those charged with overseeing any aspect of the occupation of the Bajoran people were being told that operation was concluded. While Bajor was the epicenter of this extraordinary reversal on the part of the council, it would have repercussions throughout the region. Bajoran citizens served as forced labor on more than a dozen planets within the boundaries of Cardassian territory. The council's order called for their return to Bajor.

Such a command from the Detapa Council was as astonishing as it was unprecedented. Havrel could not recall a similar instance of the civilian government exerting this degree of control over military forces. While it was enshrined in law that the Cardassian Central Command answered to civilian authority, the reality of the relationship between the two entities was much more complicated. Havrel reasoned that whatever had brought about this momentous decision, it must have direct impacts on both parties, perhaps even forcing them to work together despite the barely restrained contempt in which each side often held the other.

But what of us? The question taunted Havrel as he considered his current situation, governing a labor colony on a world that officially did not exist. As he sat here in the private office of the modest home he maintained just outside the confines of the labor camp for which he served as gul, he was already considering the impacts both immediate and enduring that would affect the inhabitants of this remote planet far from the Bajor sector, including himself. Just in this room alone were pieces of Bajoran art and sculpture acquired over the course of his career. The council's orders with respect to such items came as a disappointment. Did they truly expect him to part with the collection he had spent so long acquiring? How would they know if he obeyed the directive? What were the penalties for noncompliance? After all this time, such a rash decision seemed unfair.

"Gul?"

It was Trina, and only then did Havrel realize he had been lost for a moment to his own thoughts. He turned from the workstation to face his aide.

"What did you say?"

His expression one of concern, Trina replied, "I'm sorry, Gul. I was asking if you wanted me to activate our withdrawal protocols. There is much work to be done if we're to secure operations and ready the laborers for transport to Bajor."

"Indeed," said Havrel. Tapping a control on the workstation, he called up the colony's schedule for the day. Only then was he reminded that nightfall had come, and the shift changes for the uridium mine and the disposal quarry had already taken place. Rather, they would have taken place if Trina had not already taken the initiative of sending word to the security details responsible for moving the groups of Bajoran laborers to and from the work areas. The glinn had ordered the guards to cease shift change and return all of the workers to the camp. Havrel could not fault the junior officer's initiative. Under normal circumstances, his order would have been the correct procedure. The problem was that Trina had no reason to suspect the circumstances now facing them were anything but normal.

"Signal the guards to direct the second-shift laborers to start." When Trina regarded him with confusion, Havrel added, "It will be some time before we're ready for transport offworld. They may as well remain useful while we wait. Additional uridium is always desirable, after all. Maintain our normal daily schedule for the time being." To his own ears, Havrel thought his explanation a weak cover story, but if his counterpart thought something was amiss, he chose not to show it.

Trina replied, "There is the matter of the accident at the mine, sir."

It took an extra moment for the comment to register, and when it did Havrel chastised himself. How could he have forgotten that already? Was the message from Central Command of such importance that it pushed aside even a moment's reflection on the loss of one of his soldiers from something as senseless as an equipment accident?

"They're bringing the remains back here, yes?" he asked.

Nodding, Trina replied, "Yes, Prefect. I've already ordered an investigation, but witnesses at the scene indicate the tram somehow malfunctioned. There was no one on or near it when he activated it, and there are no obvious signs of anything unusual."

"Have the maintenance staff inspect it. If it was mechanical or some other error, I want the cause identified. Have them go back through the maintenance logs and determine if any Bajorans worked on it recently." He knew the engineers charged with maintaining the camp's vehicles and equipment used Bajoran laborers who demonstrated useful skills in any number of areas. While there were always rumors of resistance efforts among the worker population, no real, irrefutable evidence of any such activity had ever been discovered here. Havrel knew that might only mean any actual perpetrators were good at avoiding detection. Vigilance was therefore necessary, but given the new orders from Central Command, he wondered if all of this would be moot in a very short time.

Trina moved away from Havrel's desk, tapping the communicator on his left wrist and opening a channel to the officer in charge of the security details to pass on Havrel's instructions. He was pacing near the office's door when it slid aside to reveal Ijok, one of the six Bajorans detailed to Havrel to maintain his house and the surrounding grounds, prepare his meals, and see to other duties and needs as directed. She and the others all worked under the watchful eye of Zajan and Decar, a pair of older Cardassian women who served as supervisors of the staff as well as being Havrel's personal assistants. Ijok stood in the doorway carrying a tray with a bottle of *kanar* and two glasses along with a small covered dish.

"Good evening, Prefect," she said, waiting for Havrel to direct her to enter. "When you did not partake of your evening meal, I thought—"

"Yes, yes," said Havrel, waving her in. "Thank you." He pointed to a small table to the right of his desk where she knew to place the tray. "Duty called once again, my dear. I hope you did not go to much trouble preparing tonight's offering."

Nodding in deference to Trina as she strode past him, Ijok proceeded toward Havrel. "No trouble, sir," she said, as Havrel expected she would. Leaving the tray on the table, she retreated from the desk and clasped her hands behind her back, as was expected from Bajorans working in proximity to any Cardassian. "Do you require anything else?"

Havrel noticed the look on Trina's face before replying, and as he did so he gestured to his adjutant. "Prepare something for Glinn Trina. We may be working late into the evening." After Ijok nodded and excused herself from the office, he waited for the door to close before regarding the other officer. "Something troubles you?"

"The guard commanders are confused about the abrupt

changes to their orders," said Trina. "Part of that is my fault, Gul. I acted without first consulting you."

Waving away the comment, Havrel made a mental note to come up with an explanation for the reversal of Trina's instructions to the guards. For now, the need to continue extracting uridium from the mine would suffice. Instead, he said, "That wasn't what I meant. You seem to have concerns about Ijok."

Clearing his throat, Trina replied, "Not her specifically. At least, not at this time. I'm thinking of the Bajorans in general. I know you've made a point to treat them well, but you do seem to provide an even greater latitude for those assigned to serve you."

"I don't do so lightly." Havrel rose from his chair and stepped around his desk, ignoring the meal and the *kanar*. Those would have to wait, he decided, as there were more pressing matters now demanding his attention. Gesturing for Trina to follow him, he moved from the office and outside the chalet serving as his home, heading for the labor camp's perimeter fence and the entrance reserved for him. Away from the house, he said, "If you mean I grant them a degree of trust, you'd be correct. Ijok and the others had to earn the right to work under Zajan and Decar."

"Still," said Trina, "it seems dangerous to risk allowing them to work in such close proximity. Do you not worry about one of them trying to poison your food or kill you in your sleep?"

Havrel laughed. "That's why I have Zajan and Decar, both of whom I've known since I was younger than you are now. I have complete faith in them to oversee the workers they lead." Far more than simple assistants or housekeepers, the women also were veterans of the Cardassian Guard, having left the military some years earlier after serving on Havrel's staff at a prior duty station. Upon learning of their retirement, Havrel invited them to come work for him directly, and they had accepted his offer. They were a luxury for someone of his rank and station, and one for which he did not mind paying to ensure his home enjoyed a level of civility and security he might otherwise have forgone at a remote posting.

The guard assigned to the small outbuilding near the entrance entered the code to deactivate the gateway positioned between two posts that along with dozens of others formed the force-field barrier surrounding the labor camp. The trooper nodded in greeting to Havrel and Trina as they passed through before reactivating the electronic barricade. Now inside the camp, Havrel continued walking in the direction of the two-story building that served as the outpost's headquarters. Three larger structures bracketed the command post, one to either side and the third behind it, each serving as barracks for the enlisted guards along with individual quarters for the officers. Buildings behind those housed equipment, vehicles, and supplies as well as maintenance, training, and recreational facilities for the guard complement along with a small hospital. An expansive open field separated this portion of the camp from the pair of buildings used to billet the Bajoran workers. Guard towers placed around the camp's perimeter kept watch over the grounds, with a garrison of sixty troopers divided into shifts and scattered around the base itself to protect infrastructure and pay closer attention to their Bajoran charges.

Havrel watched as the columns of laborers from the primary shift at the uridium mine and disposal quarry during daylight hours, having already entered the camp via a different gate, were now organizing into a formation on the field. There they would undergo the first of two counts between now and just before their nightly curfew. The days on this planet were just under thirty intervals in duration, divided in half between the two shifts. Each shift spent twelve intervals at work and twelve under curfew, with the remaining periods devoted to transport to and from work areas as well as meals and hygiene here at camp.

"Prefect," said Trina as they entered the outpost's headquarters, passing the guards on duty there. "Should we not be redirecting the workers toward activities needed to support our own departure?"

It was a valid question Havrel would expect his adjutant to ask. Still, he could not help exhaling with consternation. "I'm afraid it's not quite that simple. In fact, I think it's well past time you learned just how complicated our situation is here in our own little private paradise." He smiled as he said the last part, underscoring the irony of describing their home in this way. The planet was unremarkable in most respects. It did possess a temperate climate, but its more picturesque regions were well away from the camp, the location of which had been dictated by a need for proximity to one of the world's richer uridium deposits. Rather than lush forests or calming beaches, the outpost instead was surrounded by austere, uneven terrain tucked between a pair of low-rise mountain ranges. While practicality was the primary reason for the campsite, the area did own its share of secrets.

Proceeding to his office, Havrel waited for Trina to enter behind him before closing the door. "Computer, activate security protocol Vinalu Cradis One Four."

In response to the command, Havrel heard a series of locks engage, sealing the room's door and windows, leaving him and Trina alone in the well-appointed office. A subdued hum from the room's far end accompanied a portion of the back wall sliding aside to reveal a compact two-person field transporter.

"I don't understand," said Trina, his expression turning to one of confusion as he watched the process play out. "A hidden transporter? For escape?"

Although Havrel laughed at that, the reaction was not spurred by amusement. "How I wish it were that simple."

"Cradis." Appearing to consider this for a moment, Trina said, "That word was in the message from Central Command.

'Cradis protocols are now in effect.' That part of the message was meant for us, wasn't it?"

"In a manner of speaking, yes." Havrel waited for Trina to join him on the recessed transporter pad before touching a control on the vestibule's wall. There was the usual fleeting moment of disorientation as everything faded in a shower of golden light and the view of his office beyond the vestibule disappeared, to be replaced heartbeats later with the sight of a much larger chamber.

"Where are we?" asked Trina.

Havrel exited the transporter alcove into another office, this one possessing more luxurious furnishings. In addition to an expansive workspace, there also were quarters for him on those occasions when duties required him to be here rather than the camp's official headquarters. Turning as Trina followed him, he caught the look of confusion on the younger officer's face.

"Welcome to the real reason for our presence on this world."

The office's door slid aside, and Havrel stepped out onto a raised walkway running along the second story of a nondescript building to survey the immense underground cavern in which he now stood. High ceilings rose and curved up and over a collection of buildings not unlike those of the labor camp. One- and two-story structures flanked enormous warehouses, and there were signs of activity around the buildings as Cardassians—some in military uniforms but far more wearing utilitarian work clothing, laboratory attire, and even environmental equipment—exited or entered the various structures.

"What is this place?" asked Trina. "It's bigger than the camp. Where are we?"

Havrel replied, "Deep beneath the camp." He gestured toward the cavern ceiling. "One of the reasons for its location was this cavern as well as providing an entrance to the uridium deposit in close proximity. There were other areas in and around the region that encompassed the vast mineral repository which in reality would have made a more attractive place to establish the labor camp. However, they did not offer the advantages of a suitable subsurface environment in which to establish this facility." He smiled. "The entire complex is powered by geothermal energy thanks to natural wells located beneath us. Down here, we're totally independent from the camp, and completely undetectable."

Making no attempt to hide his disbelief, Trina said, "This activity has been here the entire time?"

Once again, Havrel smiled. "This planet's only use to Cardassia is its location. The uridium we mine could be obtained from other systems closer to the homeworld, but the camp's presence offers a plausible reason for our being here in the event it's ever discovered by an adversary."

Confusion replaced skepticism on Trina's face. "It was my understanding that this planet's location is classified."

"Far more than that, my friend," said Havrel. "You already knew this world has no name. It's only given a number in our databases. Should an adversarial power ever gain access to our stellar cartography models and data, they'll discover it listed as uninhabited and incapable of supporting life." He smiled again. "Indeed, when you and everyone else assigned to camp were given your orders, your posting was listed for a completely different planet. So far as any official records are concerned, this planet doesn't exist."

Trina said nothing for a moment, choosing instead to stare at the scene before him. There would be many questions, Havrel knew, most of the sort he had asked upon arriving on this world. At first, he had thought he was being penalized for some unknown infraction that had angered some superior officer, immolating his career in the Cardassian Central Command and banishing him to this distant, all-but-forgotten rock to serve out his punishment running a mining camp. Only after meeting the officer he was sent to replace was the truth explained to him. Far from being castigated, he had been entrusted with a very singular responsibility.

"There are secret installations on numerous worlds," said Trina. "Including Cardassia Prime. Why the extraordinary measures for this place?"

Havrel replied, "It's by no means unique. You are correct such facilities exist elsewhere, and neither you nor I are ever likely to see them. The success and continued prosperity of the Cardassian people lies in how well they can be protected by those of us who commit our lives to their security. To achieve and maintain that security, we must sometimes carry out tasks others might consider extreme or distasteful." He gestured to the sprawling underground settlement before them. "Such work is conducted here, and it must be protected at all costs." Reaching over to Trina, he placed a hand on the younger officer's shoulder. "Come. I'll show you what I mean, so you can understand the importance of what occurs here beneath a thick, warm blanket of secrecy."

Once more, he considered how he and his adjutant differed. Trina was young, and much closer to the beginning of his career than the end. Because of that, he still harbored a great deal of the optimism expected from junior officers who had not yet been exposed to many of the harsh realities that came from service to the Cardassian people. His head doubtless swam with the platitudes instilled during his training at the military academy, where young men and women were molded into instruments for the Cardassian Central Command, to be used, exploited, and discarded as they saw fit.

We are all but tools, Havrel reminded himself.

Shaking his head, Trina said, "Prefect, if secrecy is so vital to the success of whatever you're about to show me, then why risk it by bringing Bajorans here?"

"They are unaware this place exists." Havrel learned that when taking command. The labor camp on the surface was an almost perfect screen for the activities taking place far beneath their feet. So far as they knew, they had been interned on yet another planet to exploit its natural resources for the good of the Cardassian people. "The Cradis protocol is a directive from the Obsidian Order. It directs me to ensure we relocate this facility without ever exposing its presence, or leaving behind any trace it was ever here. None of the Bajorans will ever know. They will die here."

3

—

Entering the transporter room, Captain Jean-Luc Picard nodded to the lone ensign standing behind the control console. Her posture stiffened upon his arrival, and he noted the young woman's attempt to conceal her anxiety. He recognized her as a recent assignment to the *Enterprise*, but he could not recall her name.

"Ensign . . . ?" he prompted.

The woman somehow managed to stand even taller as she replied, "Ensign Lindsey Bridges, sir. I came aboard two weeks ago."

The captain nodded, now remembering her name along with the excerpts he had read of her understandably thin personnel file while reviewing the new arrivals. "My recollection from our initial meeting is that you requested this posting."

Bridges smiled, pleased to be remembered. "Yes, sir. Competition for the *Enterprise* is fierce, but you know that."

"Indeed. You managed to arrive at a rather interesting time, all things considered."

Picard conceded his comment was an understatement, given the excitement surrounding the ship's recent mission while under the temporary command of Captain Edward Jellico during his absence. Pushing away those memories before they had a chance to manifest, he instead took a moment to appreciate the feeling of normalcy that came with speaking to a member of his crew. He understood the expectations and reasonable tension a young officer might experience coming face-to-face with their commanding officer while carrying out their duties. With a crew the size of the *Enterprise*'s, it was not unusual for a new ensign to go weeks, months, or longer without ever seeing their captain after their brief welcome aboard.

"I hope you're settling in well enough."

Nodding, Bridges replied, "I am, sir. Thank you." When she smiled this time, it was all Picard could do not to return it. "You've likely heard this a hundred times, but I'm excited to be here. This is a dream for me." As if realizing she might be breaching protocol, she cleared her throat and composed her expression. "I'm sorry, sir."

The captain schooled his features to remain impassive, despite his amusement at the ensign's obvious nervousness. For a moment, it usurped his own unease. It was rare for him to harbor such feelings, but the circumstances surrounding this particular meeting were anything but ordinary. He thought he was prepared for this visitor, only to realize he was beginning to experience misgivings.

Lindsey Bridges was helping him. With all he had endured in recent weeks, Picard found himself comforted by this casual, even mundane encounter with the ensign, someone at the beginning of their career and with an entire galaxy awaiting them. It reminded him that he once was an anxious young ensign, driven to carry out his duties to the best of his abilities while avoiding any embarrassing mishaps in front of his commander.

Was it really *so long ago?*

Finally offering a small smile of his own, Picard replied, "No apologies necessary, Ensign. We're glad to have you aboard."

Her confidence restored, Bridges nodded before a signal from the transporter console got her attention. Checking her readings, she said in a controlled voice, "We're being hailed by the *Gorkon*, sir. They're ready for transport."

"Make it so, Ensign. Energize."

Picard had just enough time to pull down and straighten the front of his uniform tunic as a shower of energy appeared in the transporter alcove, within seconds coalescing and solidifying into the form of Vice Admiral Alynna Nechayev.

"Admiral," said Picard, straightening his posture, "welcome back to the *Enterprise*."

A trim, even petite woman several years his junior, Nechayev's narrow, angular features gave her an almost hawklike appearance, an effect only intensified as she regarded Picard with piercing eyes he knew missed nothing. Despite her intimidating demeanor, which she used to great effect when the need arose—or when it suited or even amused her—Nechayev's expression softened upon seeing Picard.

"Hello, Jean-Luc," she said, stepping down from the transporter platform and extending her hand. "It's good to see you." As they shook hands, Nechayev placed her other hand on top of his, and he felt the slight extra pressure as she regarded him. "How are you feeling?"

Caught off guard by her gesture, and understanding the unspoken subtext behind her question, Picard replied, "I'm fine, Admiral. Thank you for asking." Uncomfortable with the exchange in the presence of Ensign Bridges, he gestured to the exit. "Thank you for taking the time to meet with me personally." With a final nod to Bridges, he fell in step beside Nechayev as they made their way from the transporter room.

The admiral said, "Considering the gravity of the situation and the other factors in play, I felt an in-person meeting was best for all involved."

Approaching a turbolift, they entered and Picard said, "Observation lounge." As they began ascending through the ship's upper decks, he returned his attention to Nechayev. "How was your trip from Starbase 375?"

"I'd say it was uneventful, but I'd be lying." For the first time since Picard had known her, he observed her releasing a tired sigh. "I've spent the last thirteen hours reviewing more status reports than my last month as a ship captain. The past week hasn't been much better. This business with the Cardassians leaving Bajor is causing no end of headaches at Starfleet Command. I thought we were past the worst of it when they pulled most of their forces from that sector in their misguided attempt to seize the Minos Korva system and we pushed them back. We're trying to game out every possible scenario for what it means, not just for how their withdrawal affects the Bajoran sector as well as the surrounding region but also for how we deal with them going forward."

Picard nodded. "I've been reading the reports. To say it's a complicated situation is an egregious understatement."

The turbolift halted, and Picard allowed Nechayev to exit the car first before catching up to her in the corridor. They said nothing else during the short walk to the observation lounge located behind the *Enterprise*'s main bridge. After procuring Earl Grey tea for the both of them from the room's sole replicator, Picard offered one to the admiral where she had taken a seat near the end of the curved, polished conference table. He noted that she seemed to have conspicuously left open the chair at the table's head for him.

"I'm going to hazard a guess you didn't come all this way from Starbase 375 just to brief me on the Bajor situation," he said, taking the seat nearest to Nechayev.

As she often did, the admiral offered a small smile that communicated she knew far more than she might say aloud. Taking a sip of tea, she placed the cup back in its saucer before replying, "You guess correctly, Captain. You've read the reports, so you know the situation on Bajor is fluid, to say the least. Their resistance movement, which gained momentum after the bulk of

Cardassian forces were redeployed to the border, internal squabbling on Cardassia Prime, and the concessions we were able to force them to make following that business near Minos Korva have the Cardassians completely pulling the plug on their occupation of the Bajorans." She sighed. "We have their civilian leadership to thank for that. They really stuck it to their military's Central Command."

"Internal squabbling," repeated Picard. "The civilian Cardassian government doesn't typically have that level of authority over their military forces."

Nechayev said, "Times appear to be changing, at least in the short term. That means new headaches for Starfleet as we try to keep tabs on everything they're doing in response to this upheaval. But it also means an opportunity for us to do right by the Bajorans, who as we speak are still coming to terms with the quantum shift their society is experiencing. That's before we consider the impact of the Cardassian withdrawal. They're leaving as quickly as ships can arrive to retrieve them, but they're not going quietly."

"I saw those reports as well." Picard grimaced, recalling the litany of unsettling data points those accounts contained. "Environmental damage, an escalation of violence against the Bajoran people, and other acts of sabotage both on the surface and the Cardassian mining station orbiting the planet."

Nechayev said, "If they can't take it with them, the Cardassians are doing everything they can to render it inoperable or otherwise useless to the Bajorans. In a few extreme cases, they've even planted booby traps they know will cause injury or deaths." Speaking of such acts seemed to be inflaming the admiral's temper, but she held herself in check. "A number of these efforts have been discovered and neutralized, and of course the Cardassian officials blame the activities on 'rogue operators' disobeying the orders of their Central Command. While they're being difficult with the Bajoran government, they *are* responding to Starfleet requests to keep their people in line. Because of this, the Bajorans have grudgingly requested our assistance to mediate the process as it continues."

"A Starfleet presence in the Bajor sector?" Picard could not keep the look of surprise from his face. "The Cardassians will love that."

"I suspect they'll have a rather broad spectrum of feelings once they find out I plan to send you to oversee the process."

Pausing in the act of lifting his cup, Picard regarded the admiral with surprise. "Me?"

"I'll admit I was reluctant to consider this option, given your recent . . . experience . . . with the Cardassians," replied Nechayev, her expression softening. "But an officer of your stature and diplomatic prowess is exactly what's needed to help advise the Bajoran government through this very delicate situation."

"Given his own recent successes against the Cardassians," said Picard, "Captain Jellico seems like a more logical choice."

He tried not to dwell on the fact it was while Jellico commanded the *Enterprise* that his fellow captain had completed the difficult task which had earned him well-deserved praise from Command. Nechayev had given his ship to Jellico after selecting Picard along with Doctor Beverly Crusher and Lieutenant Worf to conduct a covert mission on Celtris III—a planet just across the border separating the Federation from Cardassian space—after obtaining intelligence that a metagenic device was in operation there. In reality, the Cardassians engineered the entire affair after discovering Picard was considered an authority on such weapons, with the aim of enticing him to investigate so he could be captured and interrogated about Starfleet defense strategies for the Minos Korva system.

Nechayev said, "Captain Jellico is one of the most formidable tacticians I know. He was the right person for the situation along the border and forcing the Cardassians to capitulate to our demands, but what's now required on Bajor is a defter touch. They're demanding reparations from the Cardassians even as many in the upper echelons of their Central Command are already attempting to downplay their actions—crimes, really—that occurred during the Occupation."

Picard grimaced at the report's usage of such bloodless terms as "alleged improprieties" and "unsanctioned activities," supposedly committed by individuals acting outside the boundaries of authority rather than being part and parcel of what was daily life on Bajor for five decades. "History will not be kind to the Cardassians, to be sure. Or to us, for that matter."

Finishing her tea, Nechayev replied, "I know you believe the Federation didn't do enough to assist the Bajorans during the Occupation. I sympathize, but we were bound by the edicts of the Prime Directive."

Once more, Picard felt emotions stirring within him, and again he prevented them from undermining his bearing. "We were committed to the military mission against the Cardassians while at the same time turning a blind eye to their numerous war crimes, proven and otherwise." He caught himself, clearing his throat. "I apologize, Admiral. It's just that for the first time last year, I saw with my own eyes the true plight of the Bajoran people, at least those fortunate enough to escape their homeworld and seek safe harbor elsewhere." Along with Ensign Ro Laren, he had visited Bajoran refugee camps in the Valo star system. "Perhaps if we'd taken a more active role assisting Bajor and other worlds affected by Cardassian oppression during the war, things might have turned out differently for them."

"I agree," said Nechayev. "Now we have an opportunity to right some of the wrongs perpetrated against the Bajorans. For this process to work, the Cardassians must abide by the stipulations to which they agreed. This means a peaceful withdrawal from the Bajor sector while respecting the Bajorans' cultural heritage and property. It also includes the release of any and all Bajoran prisoners and laborers, no matter where they're being held. Holding the Cardassians to these agreements is a challenging proposition, to say the least, but I know you're the right person with the right temperament to see it through."

Leaning forward in her chair, the admiral rested her forearms on the conference table and regarded Picard with an intense gaze for a moment before saying, "Given everything you've recently been through, Captain, I don't like having to ask you to do this. I wouldn't do it if I didn't think it was absolutely necessary, but I am *asking* and not ordering you to consider taking the assignment."

Picard said nothing. The memories of what he had endured on Celtris III at the hands of Gul Madred, his Cardassian inquisitor, remained raw. His private—and ongoing—conversations with Counselor Deanna Troi in the wake of the incident had been helpful, and while the physical pain he had suffered was gone, the emotional scars would be a long time healing. On a personal level he would prefer to have no contact with any Cardassian or anything involving them. He also knew that facing off against those who sanctioned his torture, even if they had no actual participation in those acts, would be a form of therapy. Holding them accountable for their treatment of the Bajorans was important, but he could not deny his own stake in how the events might unfold.

Still, a question plagued him, one he dared not speak aloud. Could he keep his personal feelings at bay while acting in the best interests of the Bajorans and the Federation?

There's only one answer, he mused. *Otherwise, you need to recuse yourself.*

"It would be my privilege to represent the Federation, Admiral. I accept the assignment."

Nechayev eyed him for a moment, her expression softening just a bit. "I know you're still recovering from your ordeal, and while I'm a firm believer in getting back on the proverbial horse after you've been thrown, I'm not completely heartless." Then she smiled. "Despite my reputation."

For the first time since her arrival, Picard felt himself beginning to relax. "Rest assured, Alynna, I will carry out my duties to the best of my abilities. You have my word."

"Good." Nechayev nodded in satisfaction. "Your word means more to me than similar pledges by other officers." She rose from her seat, prompting Picard to stand in deference before she extended her hand. "Good luck, Captain. We're all counting on you."

Picard took her proffered hand. "Thank you, Admiral."

At the edges of his consciousness, twinges of doubt lurked.

4

———

At the center of the observation lounge's curved conference table, a holo-projector displayed a computer-generated representation of a star system. Commander William Riker studied the fourteen planets orbiting a single star, taking note of the radiation field separating the sun's ninth and tenth planets.

"The Bajoran system," said Lieutenant Commander Data, who sat across from Riker and had provided the holo-projector. Reaching to the unit's base, the android pressed a control and the image zoomed inward to focus on the system's largest planet. It was a lush, blue-green world that to Riker looked very similar to Earth. Of course, the landmasses were different than those found on the planet of his birth, in size and shape as well as location.

"The B'hava'el system," said Ensign Ro Laren from where she sat to Data's right.

Turning in his seat to face her, Data asked, "I beg your pardon?"

"We call it B'hava'el, sir." Ro gestured to the holographic planet. "It translates more or less from our native language to 'Bajor' in Federation Standard."

Data replied, "That is not in our records, Ensign, but I will make the appropriate updates. Thank you." Returning his attention to Riker, he added, "Five of the system's fourteen planets are suitable for humanoid life without special provisions. The system's largest planet is also home to the Bajoran people, and—"

"Mister Data," said Riker, interrupting and perhaps avoiding altogether a detailed recitation on the history of the Bajoran system. "I'd like us to focus on the planet's current condition as well as that of its people, so we have as clear an understanding as possible of what we're likely to encounter when we arrive." He gestured to Ro. "You're the crew's sole Bajoran, so I thought your presence here and your firsthand knowledge would be appropriate with respect to our preparations."

Ro said, "Understood, Commander, though I'm not sure how useful I'll really be. I only lived on Bajor during my early childhood before I joined a Resistance cell and eventually got away from there. I moved between different refugee camps in the Valo system, where many of my people had fled to escape the Occupation. From there you know the rest of my story, sir."

Nodding, Riker opted not to continue that line of discussion. Ro Laren's past was an amalgam of strife, suffering, betrayal, and loss that no one should have had to endure at such a young age. Her career in Starfleet was marred by a series of disciplinary actions, capped off by a deadly away mission to Garon II while she was assigned to the *Wellington*. Her disobedience of her captain during a hostile situation on the planet resulted in confusion, leading to the deaths of eight of her shipmates. Court-martialed for disobeying orders, Ro received a demotion to the rank of ensign and incarceration at a penal colony, where she stayed until fate and circumstances brought her to the *Enterprise* a couple years later.

At that time, just the previous year, Riker along with Picard and a significant number of the crew objected to the idea, based on her court-martial conviction. But Ro had comported herself with distinction while helping to prove that Cardassians were behind a terrorist attack against a Federation colony which was being blamed on Bajoran Resistance fighters. She also helped to expose a backdoor deal involving Starfleet admiral Clifford

Kennelly, who promised to supply the Resistance cell weapons in exchange for preventing further attacks on Federation targets. Having committed a clear violation of the Prime Directive, Kennelly was court-martialed and to the best of Riker's knowledge currently occupied a cell at the same penal colony that previously housed the ensign.

Ro's experiences had hardened her, but to Riker's relief the changes were not permanent; not all of them, at any rate. He had seen the progress she had made since her arrival on the *Enterprise*. Her adaptability was a strength, even if her temperament still ran her afoul of superior officers, including Captain Picard and Riker on occasion. Despite this, the first officer as well as the captain agreed Ro Laren had potential; all she needed was the right environment and opportunity to grow. To that end, Picard had requested she remain aboard the *Enterprise*.

"What can you tell us about what we're liable to encounter once we arrive?" asked Riker.

Clearing her throat, Ro said, "I know the new government has asked for the Federation to mediate whatever discussions they're hoping to have with the Cardassians. I'm sure there are a number of Bajorans who'll be happy to see us, but that won't be true for everyone. To many Bajorans, Starfleet is another outsider coming in and taking control of *our* world and whatever resources it has left."

Data said, "Our stated mission is to assist the Bajoran Provisional Government in addressing their grievances against the Cardassians, and to assess the overall situation on Bajor with respect to humanitarian assistance going forward, so that the Bajorans can once again govern themselves."

"After fifty years, Commander, many Bajorans don't make distinctions between uniforms. Cardassian or Starfleet, it's all the same to them. There won't be a parade or any other warm welcome when we arrive. The new first minister might be genuinely happy to see us, but others in the government will be plying us with fake smiles and counting the minutes until we leave."

"I don't know that I'm worried so much about the first minister and other government representatives," said Riker. "What about the Cardassian station orbiting Bajor?" He remembered seeing the station's designation from a briefing memo he had read earlier in the day, but the name escaped him. "What's it called?"

Ro replied, "Terok Nor, sir. It's been there since the earliest days of the Occupation. It's basically a giant ore-processing plant where the Bajorans provided the forced labor."

"Terok Nor is a common Cardassian design, sir," added Data, "utilized in numerous star systems where the Cardassians have established a foothold with the intent of harvesting natural resources from selected planets."

"Sounds cozy," said Riker. "In addition to the security officers assigned to escort Captain Picard and his diplomatic team, Commander La Forge will be leading an engineering team to the station to assess its condition. With its existing orbital docking facilities, the Bajoran government wants to repurpose it for their own use, but early reports are the Cardassians are doing everything they can to make it unusable before they bug out."

Ro said, "Commander La Forge and his people will have their work cut out for them."

"I was informed before this meeting that we're getting some additional help. The *Oceanside* is en route with additional engineering personnel as well as a medical team to partner with the detail Doctor Crusher is putting together." In addition to helping out with Terok Nor's engineering woes, the Provisional Government had also requested assistance evaluating a handful of medical facilities on the planet's surface. According to the report Riker had seen, everything from hospitals to crude aid stations were in use, though he noted the overall number of patients was very low. The Bajorans wanted to relocate those patients along with matériel and personnel from the makeshift field hospitals to more permanent structures, which would be furnished with equipment provided by the Federation to supplement those items the Bajorans already possessed.

At first, Riker was surprised by the rerouting of the *California*-class vessel to the Bajoran system. Such ships were usually dispatched to worlds with which Starfleet had recently made first contact. Their list of duties and priorities were well regulated, to minimize the potential for damaging relations with a potential ally and possible future Federation member. On the other hand, those crews had acquired a reputation for their adaptability and ability to respond quickly to changing and even chaotic situations. Riker likened them to the Starfleet Corps of Engineers, detachments of which served aboard *Saber*-class starships and operated under a mission profile not dissimilar to the one given to "second contact" teams.

Data said, "There is also a contingent of Bajoran engineers and others, previously on the station, who have chosen to remain aboard, until relocation and resettlement options are finalized. Reports indicate many of these citizens possess considerable technical expertise about the station and its onboard systems that Commander La Forge may find useful."

"Assuming the Bajorans want us there." With a nod toward the holo image between them, Ro added, "Bajor has supplied forced labor to the station for decades. At first, they were confined to those areas supporting uridium ore–processing operations, but over time some workers demonstrated sufficient engineering aptitude to assist in maintenance and repairs across the station. Parents passed down their knowledge and skills to their children so they could take over when they were old enough." Her expression hardened. "It wasn't about helping the Cardassians, but rather simple survival. Workers with skills were valuable commodities and received better treatment and privileges than those easily replaced. Why risk a Cardassian life making a dangerous repair when you can send a Bajoran?"

"And it's not as though the Cardassians didn't see the bigger picture," said Riker. "Their forces were outnumbered, the only cards they had to play were threats and rewards. Happy workers— or at least those who don't suffer unnecessary mistreatment—are easier to control."

"Not every Cardassian got the message," replied Ro. "There was no shortage of Cardassians who saw the Bajorans as slaves to be worked to death." She paused, and Riker noted how her gaze shifted to the conference table's polished surface for a moment before adding, "Or otherwise abused in whatever way they deemed fit or entertaining, just because they could."

"It would make sense for Bajoran Resistance fighters to find ways to exploit the situation for their own benefit," said Data. "Placing agents in positions of trust aboard the station would almost certainly provide opportunities for all manner of disruptive acts."

Now a small smile teased the corners of Ro's mouth. "That's a very polite way of putting that, Commander. There are plenty of stories of the Resistance carrying out attacks on station personnel and infrastructure. Not all of them were successful, and regardless of the outcome a number of Bajorans were executed, with or without trial. This included killing innocents as a way of trying to convince the Resistance their actions would only bring more suffering for their fellow Bajorans."

"I've read accounts of some of the Resistance's activities," said Riker. "To say the Cardassian threats weren't a successful deterrent is a hell of an understatement."

Ro nodded. "When you're fighting for your family, your way of life, and your entire world, all bets are off, sir. Life under Cardassian rule was one of eventual extinction. There are many among my people who think the luckiest of us died early on, or at a young age if they were born after the Occupation began. The threat of suffering and death became less and less of a deterrent as time passed because it was a facet of everyday life. You're reduced to just existing, and counting the days until death finally comes. You decide to make a choice, but there was ever only one option." She shrugged. "It's easy to commit to the cause when you literally have only your life to lose."

Riker suspected that after the Bajorans' years of living either in fear or determined resignation, this perspective was the obstacle the Federation would have to overcome if it ever hoped to have an open, honest relationship with the Bajorans. These people had been through hell, and they had no reason to trust or even welcome outsiders who had stood by, hidden behind rules and regulations, and watched as an entire civilization was subjugated.

"That the new Provisional Government's reached out is a good sign," he said. "I'll admit I was surprised by it."

Data offered, "The government's new first minister likely understands and appreciates what a Starfleet presence in this region signifies with respect to providing assurances to the Bajoran people that the Cardassians will no longer be a concern."

"That doesn't mean he trusts us, Data." Riker knew little about Kalem Apren, the man elevated to lead the Provisional Government. His first act was to order the cessation of all hostilities. It was obvious Kalem was still trying to get his feet under him, navigating the proverbial minefield while trying to serve as an example.

And hoping not to appear weak, mused Riker.

"You can bet any skepticism he harbors toward Starfleet and

the Federation is shared by a significant percentage of my people, sir," Ro added. "Earning Kalem's trust could pose a serious challenge."

"It is just the first thing we will need to accomplish if we are to convince the Bajorans that a permanent Starfleet presence in the Bajor sector is a benefit for all concerned," said Data.

"Hearts and minds." Riker grunted in mild amusement at his own comment. "It's definitely the first order of business. If anyone can forge that relationship, it's Captain Picard."

5

—

Hand over hand, Panat Hileb descended the makeshift ladder into the narrow tunnel that extended down from the barracks lavatory through the building's foundation and the soil and rock beneath it. The only illumination in the access chute was from whatever escaped from the narrow opening above him, which was being concealed by fellow prisoners. Panat heard the faint sound of plumbing fixtures being returned to their normal positions, once more hiding the tunnel's entrance beneath the lavatory's waste-extraction system.

Not the most dignified way to die if you fall, thought Panat as he continued his descent, now enveloped by utter darkness.

The tunnel had already been carved out years before his arrival at the camp, the ladder he navigated consisting of metal rods formed into U shapes and driven into the bedrock. The tunnel as well as the intricate means of disguising its presence was just one of numerous extraordinary accomplishments of unknown Bajorans who had preceded him as inmates here. That it had never been discovered amazed him.

Other hideaways had been found by guards carrying out surprise inspections, including several created for the express purpose of being uncovered. They gave the troopers something they could point to as proof they were doing their duty. Wiser minds, well before Panat's internment, concluded that conforming to the camp's rules without even minor attempts at disruption would engender its own form of suspicion. If every Bajoran presented themselves as a model inmate, the Cardassians would likely assume there must be illicit activity taking place. Better for the laborers to offer the occasional misdirection in the hopes of keeping their overseers distracted from those things that needed to remain concealed.

Counting the rungs, he reached thirty-three before his left foot felt solid ground. Still unable to see anything, he stepped off and turned before reaching out and rapping his knuckles on the metal panel he knew was there. He tapped out the memorized pattern of knocks—two, pause, three, pause, one, pause, two—and waited. After several seconds, a section of the panel slid away and he was blinded by an intense white light.

"Clear," said a disembodied voice from the other side of the panel before Panat heard several bolts being undone and the entire metal sheet was removed to reveal an opening through which he could crawl. No sooner was he through the opening and into the larger cavern than a pair of Bajorans were fastening the panel into place. His eyes still adjusting to the increased light level, he heard a voice call out to him.

"Hileb," said Yectu, and Panat turned to see his friend, a middle-aged Bajoran woman, smiling at him from the makeshift worktable running along the nearby rock wall. Dark hair, cut short for practicality rather than style, framed a narrow face highlighted by lines and creases that told her story. Like everyone else in the camp, Yectu wore her years in servitude within every wrinkle along with roughened hands and disheveled clothing. Captivity and the brutality she witnessed, if not experienced firsthand, had not dimmed the intelligence and determination Panat saw in her eyes. He also could tell from her expression that something was afoot—something he doubtless would find interesting.

"Sorry I'm late," he said, dusting off his shirt. "The count was delayed again."

He knew there was no need to explain further. For everyone in the camp, their every activity revolved around the counts held multiple times each day by Cardassian troopers charged with direct oversight of the laborers. Although times varied by small intervals, the guard detail still carried out most counts on a somewhat predictable schedule. With the day divided between two shifts of laborers working in the mines, there were occasional overlaps. Laborers working on the second shift came back at sunrise. Counts at the mines usually bracketed meal breaks, then their return to camp, and a final count before curfew went into effect.

While random counts still occurred in the middle of the night, they did so with far less frequency than when Panat had first arrived. There was occasional conversation among the prisoners as to whether this meant the Cardassians had lapsed into routine and complacency, or whether they might be playing some sort of extended ruse in the hopes of exposing any schemes. Because of this and other uncertainties of the guards' behavior, strict precautions and discretion were practiced by nearly every member of the camp's detainees.

Yectu gestured for him to join her at the worktable where she spent most of her time down here. It consisted of what Panat knew was an outdated computer workstation she had salvaged from the refuse and repaired, along with a data-storage module of similar vintage. Both devices were wired to a portable generator also requisitioned from oblivion after being discarded by the camp's maintenance staff. The unit provided power to the lighting hung around the cavern, which was perhaps half the size of the barracks building he had called home these past few years.

"Where's Ranar?" asked Yectu.

Pointing upward, Panat replied, "Keeping watch. I decided it was best that we not have too many people down here, just in case

the guards get jumpy and pull a surprise inspection or search."
With the lighting, he could see two more Bajorans, Drizu and
Kijam, working at the cave's far end. Their attention was on some
other bit of electronic flotsam Yectu had without doubt fashioned
from whatever scrap materials and tools she had been able to collect over the past months and even years. The cave was a veritable
treasure trove of such artifacts, discarded or forgotten by their
Cardassian hosts and scavenged by members of the camp population to be repurposed as appropriate. "We probably shouldn't stay
down here too long either. Just in case."

Nodding in agreement, Yectu said, "This won't take long.
And you're right about the guards. They've been on edge."

"Just like the past several nights," replied Panat. "They haven't
been talking among themselves on our way back from the mine.
Whatever happened that night, it definitely has them rattled, but
none of our spies around the camp have been able to turn up anything." He then tapped Yectu on her shoulder. "That reminds me.
This is the first time I've seen you since the 'accident' with the
mining tram." Had it already been nearly a week since Trooper
Locin's untimely demise? "I'm sure you've heard, but it looks to
have worked perfectly. He never saw it coming, and none of the
other guards seemed to suspect a thing. They weren't saying much
about that either."

"There were some rumblings in the maintenance shop that
evening," replied Yectu. "They had the tram brought back for inspection, and so far they've found nothing that makes them suspicious." She shrugged. "More suspicious than normal, that is."

Panat said, "If they haven't found it by now, then they'll probably never find it. Too bad for Locin. No hero's funeral for him."

"Good riddance," replied Yectu. "I'm only sorry we couldn't
have taken out more with him." Before Panat could say anything,
she held up a hand. "I know. Anything more and it wouldn't have

looked like an accident. Patience, deliberation, focus." She smiled. "Just spare me the lecture, is all I'm asking."

Panat nodded. "That seems fair."

Waving to her computer terminal, Yectu said, "Besides, that's not why I wanted you down here." She tapped one of the workstation's interface controls and the terminal's display activated, taking an extra moment for the image on its screen to coalesce into a message rendered in Cardassian text. "Gul Havrel received this that first night while you were still out at the mine." The script was a jumble of letters, numbers, and symbols, indicating an encryption scheme at work.

"You intercepted his message traffic?" Panat regarded his friend with disbelief.

Yectu grinned. "Right off his own terminal."

"How in the name of the Prophets did you manage to—" Shaking his head, Panat let the rest of the question die in his throat.

Maybe it's better if I don't know the details.

Oblivious to his concerns, Yectu replied, "You can thank Ijok. She's been our contact inside Havrel's home and offices for a few years, but we've only used her on very rare occasions due to the risks involved. I recently gave her a shielded data transceiver to plant in Havrel's quarters, but we have to be careful since there are rumors he orders routine sweeps for covert surveillance and other intelligence devices."

"He thinks we're spying on him?" asked Panat.

"Possibly." Yectu shrugged. "But I think he's just paranoid about one of his subordinates trying to undermine him."

Panat chuckled. "Not out of the question, but how does Ijok keep from being discovered?"

"It's embedded in the serving tray she uses to bring him meals in his office. It has a short range and operates on a low-power frequency well below those scanned by Cardassian comm systems.

She only leaves it in there until he's finished eating, then removes and hides it before transferring the data rod through the camp network to me."

"The camp network," repeated Panat. The association of different prisoners acting as couriers of one sort or another was the lifeline of the intelligence-gathering and -distribution apparatus for the camp's Resistance members. Information transferred by word of mouth as well as on everything from data rods to encrypted notes scratched on innocuous items like clothing, tools, and even food was key to remaining apprised of various happenings involving their Cardassian overseers. Due to the inherent nature of such activities, couriers operated in near isolation from one another, in cells of two or three in order to minimize impact should they be discovered and interrogated. A capture took place not long after Panat's arrival, costing the lives of the courier and one other Bajoran. There had been heated investigations and searches for accomplices in the days afterward, but as far as Panat knew, no one else had ever been discovered.

"We've only tried this three times before," said Yectu. "The message traffic Gul Havrel receives is pretty straightforward." She began tapping controls on her computer terminal, her attention on the screen. "Nothing that might attract undue attention from someone eavesdropping, but the night everybody started getting agitated? Havrel received a message with a different encryption algorithm. It took me until tonight to crack it."

On the screen, Panat watched the jumbled characters rearrange themselves into something he could recognize as actual Cardassian text.

Panat moved closer so he could read the official-looking message, his eyes widening with the first sentence. "They're withdrawing from Bajor?"

"The Occupation is over," said Yectu. "Even as we speak, the Cardassians are withdrawing or at least preparing to withdraw."

Reading the words for a second and then a third time did little to convince Panat it was genuine. "But why? It makes no sense for them to do something so drastic or with little or no warning. Cardassians never do *anything* drastic without warning."

"It might have something to do with what happened in the Minos Korva system," said Yectu. "Some of the guards in the maintenance bay were talking about that. Apparently an attack group was set to invade the system, but they were stopped by Starfleet." She shook her head. "From everything I know, it was the first time the two went head-to-head since their war ended. Maybe it made the Detapa Council reconsider a few things."

Panat said, "If what you're saying is true, then the Federation may have influenced the Cardassians to pull out of Bajor. What would make them do that? They've never taken an interest in our situation before."

"Times change, my friend."

Still staring at the screen, Panat said, "This means we could be going home." Even as he said the words, he saw Yectu's expression change as she pointed to another part of the message.

"Cradis protocols are now in effect," she read aloud. "I've heard that term before, when I was at the Wupen labor camp on Sartana V."

"I know that camp," said Panat. "It doubled as a forward operating base for Obsidian Order agents."

"Right," said Yectu. "*Cradis* is a term I heard one of their agents use when they were discussing how to eliminate another camp on the planet's far side. Apparently, it was being used as a testing facility for various projects that would've been considered war crimes if they ever came to light." Panat watched her expression harden. "Outlawed weapons. Genetic research. Experimental surgery. Prisoners held without due process or trial. Torture and murder. All of it supposedly against Bajorans and other subjugated peoples as well as Cardassians classified as political prisoners or criminals." Once more, Yectu pointed to the screen. "Someone issued a Cradis protocol against that camp. From what we could tell, it meant disbanding it and leaving no trace. The buildings, the labs, the prisoners, everything. All of it was gone, like it never existed."

That the Cardassians might be engaged in activities which would, if discovered, provoke condemnation from other interstellar powers was not at all hard to imagine. That did not surprise Panat. "So, it's a covert message to anyone involved in similar efforts to dissolve those projects before returning home?"

Drizu shook her head. "They included a reference to Cradis protocols in the message, but the headers I decrypted indicate this was sent directly to Havrel from Central Command. It was meant for him, specifically."

"You're saying there's something here, on this planet, that might be governed by Cradis protocols?"

"It'd be the only reason for Havrel to receive such a directive," replied Yectu. "Whatever it is, and if they're following the same protocols, he's been ordered to move or destroy it before they pull out of here and leave no trace."

Panat felt a chill course down his spine. "That likely means eliminating witnesses, or even anyone who might have knowledge of the planet, even if they weren't involved in whatever the Cardassians are doing here." He locked his gaze with Yectu's. "That means us."

"Exactly," said Yectu. "Whatever it is they've got here, I have no doubt he'd murder everyone in the camp to protect the secret. That's what a Cradis protocol means."

The thought of the Bajorans who might die here, far from home, and those who might still wonder whatever became of them infuriated Panat. To survive everything the Cardassians had thrown at them while enslaving them on this planet, just to die for the sake of expedience?

No, he decided. That would not happen. At the very least, it would not happen the way Gul Havrel, the Central Command, or anyone else might envision.

"We need to find out what they're protecting," he said, his voice hard.

Yectu replied, "Even if we did, what then? We don't even know where we are!"

"Then we find a way to tell someone where we are." Panat's mind raced with possibilities. There had to be a way to avoid dying here, alone and forgotten. "Even if we can't expose them or destroy what they're doing, we can fight. After all of this, I'm not going to just stand around and wait for them to murder us all."

If he was going to die, then Panat would die in the company of as many Cardassians as he could take with him.

6

Retrieving his tea from the replicator, Picard maneuvered to the sofa in his ready room where Beverly Crusher awaited him, teacup in hand.

"How are you feeling today?" she asked after he had settled himself on the couch.

The captain held his teacup just above its accompanying saucer, halting the motion of bringing it to his mouth before replying, "All things considered? Very well, actually."

"What about last night? Any trouble sleeping?"

Sipping his tea, Picard placed the cup back on its saucer and rested it on the nearby side table. "I'm happy to say I slept soundly." He paused, drawing a deep breath. "I awoke rested, which to be honest surprised the hell out of me."

"That's good to hear." Crusher smiled.

Long ago he had mastered schooling his facial expressions to affect an air of calm confidence, but Picard knew better than to try with the doctor. Even without the Betazoid empathic abilities of Counselor Troi, Crusher still possessed an equally keen perception and an uncanny knack for reading people. He was certain the doctor would detect any deception, which was fine, as he had no desire to lie to her. Beverly Crusher was one of the very few people on his ship with whom he could be absolutely open and frank about any topic.

It was Crusher who had assisted him as he sought emotional stability following his intense mind-meld with Ambassador Sarek.

The meld was performed to help the renowned Vulcan ambassador stabilize his emotional control so he could carry out an important diplomatic meeting with representatives of the secretive Legaran race. In the aftermath of his capture and assimilation by the Borg Collective, Picard had once again leaned on the doctor as he struggled to reacclimatize himself with his own individuality. In her own quiet way, Crusher helped him come to terms with the tremendous guilt he felt at being used by the Borg to attack and destroy the Starfleet armada during the Battle of Wolf 359. Recovering from the horrors of that experience was an ongoing process, though time had helped.

She also had been instrumental in helping him realize the positive effects of the alien probe that had placed him in a coma. Picard awakened to discover he had only been unconscious for a mere twenty-five minutes, but to him it felt like he had spent decades living the life of Kamin, a member of a long-dead race, the Kataan. Only he remembered the Kataan civilization, lost over a thousand years ago. With Crusher's assistance, Picard came to understand how it had changed his outlook and improved his existence.

Seize the time. Picard recalled the earnest advice he, as Kamin, had given Meribor, Kamin's daughter, as she grappled with a decision about marrying. *Live now. Make now always the most precious time. Now will never come again.* The legacy and memories of the Kataan people demanded nothing less. They had proven invaluable during his imprisonment on Celtris III. When the pain had become too much to bear, he retreated to the small, warm home he had shared with his—with *Kamin*'s—wife, Eline, and their family. He had used a number of mental tricks in order to prevent Gul Madred from pushing through his resistance in order to crush his spirit. Despite his efforts, Picard had to admit that the Cardassian interrogator had come dangerously close to breaking him.

"Jean-Luc?"

Looking over to Crusher, Picard saw her staring at him and realized he was lost within his musings, as happened when he allowed Kamin's memories free rein.

"I'm sorry. I was . . . just lost in thought for a moment."

Her brow furrowing, Crusher asked, "Thinking about Celtris III again?"

Picard nodded in agreement. Her exceptional skills had healed his physical injuries and treated the ailments stemming from the dehydration and lack of nutrition, but he still felt a precarious balance when it came to his psychological health. On an intellectual level, he knew every facet of Gul Madred's treatment of him was calculating and deliberate, with its incremental, relentless breaking down of mental and emotional barriers. Madred had already extracted any useful information within the first hours of Picard's imprisonment thanks to a variety of psychotropic drugs. Everything that came afterward stemmed from the Cardassian's sadistic need to defeat his adversary on every possible level.

"I'd be lying if I said those events aren't still disconcerting." Retrieving his cup, Picard took a sip before realizing the tea had gone cold. He grimaced as he placed it back on the table. "On the other hand, I haven't dreamed about them in several days."

Crusher said, "On this mission, you'll be meeting with Cardassians. That may trigger those same feelings and memories, even when you're dreaming."

Picard frowned. "There's not much to be done about that." Forcing a smile he knew would not convince Crusher, he added, "The show must go on, as they say."

To her credit, the doctor did not call out his strained attempt to lighten the mood. "I know you've made considerable progress coming to terms with what happened to you. To be honest, I expected nothing less of you, not after everything you've gone through."

Setting aside her own tea, Crusher shifted her position on

the couch so that she could reach out and take his hands in hers. "That . . . inner strength of yours has always been one of your greatest assets, Jean-Luc. It's what's convinced you that you're up for this assignment. Maybe you view it as a way to test yourself— to confront those responsible for the treatment you received."

"You believe I wish to stare into the face of my adversary," said Picard, his voice low as he contemplated Crusher's stark assessment. He nodded. "You're right. On some level, I need to see how this will affect me going forward, and the only way I know how to do so is to face it head-on." Pausing, he released a small sigh. "Otherwise, I'll never be sure."

His assimilation by the Borg still haunted him. He recalled how, nearly two years after that horrific event, he had stared into the face of Third of Five, the drone renamed "Hugh" by La Forge. An away team had discovered him beside a crashed Borg ship and brought him back to the *Enterprise* for study. Picard had at first seen the drone as nothing more than something he might exploit. His chief engineer proposed creating a piece of software to be introduced to the Borg by Hugh. It would act as an invasive virus propagating though the entire Collective via their interconnectivity and possibly disabling every Borg drone. With the program ready to implement, the captain realized he could not go through with it, as he and many of the crew had come to see Hugh as an individual. Returning Hugh to the crash site, Picard wondered if the drone's experiences might be imparted to all Borg in those few brief seconds before he was re-assimilated. There was a chance, however slight, that this momentary awareness of his individuality could have an effect on the Collective.

It is inevitable that the Borg will cross our path again, Picard thought. *Only then will we know if we—and Hugh—had any lasting effect.*

The doctor released his hands, and he said after a moment,

"This isn't like my experience with the Borg. They're an implacable single entity devoid of emotion. The Cardassians are individuals with a broad spectrum of feelings, beliefs, and ideals. We know, from experience, that not all Cardassians share the same outlook of their civilization's place in the interstellar community. There are those who would vociferously protest what was done to me and what other Cardassians have done to Bajor. Do their voices not have value? Should I not attempt to see past my own experiences and look for common ground? Isn't that one of the Federation's guiding principles?"

Crusher regarded him, her expression sympathetic, then professional. "You're saying you accepted this assignment to uphold and demonstrate Federation values?"

"I suppose I am," replied Picard, "but also my own. We'll be sitting across from representatives of a society very much at odds with ours. I need to demonstrate, to them as well as myself, that I will not be deterred from the duty I've done my best to carry out every day of my adult life. If I'm no longer capable of that, then I'm doing a disservice not only to myself but to the crew I command and the citizens I've sworn to represent and defend."

For the first time since their conversation began, Crusher offered a small, understanding smile. "*That* is the Jean-Luc Picard I know. You may not realize this, but it's the first time I've actually heard you sounding like your old self since you came back from Celtris III."

Before Picard could object, she raised a hand. "I don't mean while you're on the bridge or carrying out your duties. You're much too disciplined and proud to ever allow personal feelings to influence you." She gestured to the room around them. "I'm talking about how you speak to me. I know you have your doubts, Jean-Luc, but I know you well enough to understand the depth of your resolve. I know you have it within you to win the argument you're currently waging with yourself. You'll do what's right just as you always have, for yourself and for the crew, for the Bajorans, and even for the Cardassians."

Realizing his body had tensed, Picard schooled himself to relax. "Thank you, Beverly. That means a great deal."

Crusher's smile faded. "I need you to remember not to push yourself too hard or set unrealistic expectations. We know from experience how shrewd and manipulative the Cardassians can be. They'll want to establish dominance in those meetings. Captain Jellico understood this."

"He was the right person in that moment," said Picard. "His approach to negotiation stemmed from a more martial, tactical perspective, seeking avenues of attack in response to Cardassian methods. It was an effective strategy."

"That was then, and this is now," said Crusher. "The situation on Bajor is different. The Cardassians will be looking to avoid losing face on an interstellar stage, and they'll worry about being cornered." Once again, she smiled. "You're an accomplished diplomat, but they'll almost certainly know what you went through on Celtris III. Expect them to try exploiting it."

Nodding in agreement, Picard replied, "I fully anticipate them trying to use that should discussions become heated. I'm hoping to avoid that."

"All I'm saying is you should be prepared," said Crusher. "Expect the unexpected, as they say."

"I fully intend to." Picard forced a small smile. "After all, the unexpected is one of the reasons why we're out here."

Even as he spoke the words, he felt a vestige of doubt, and he was sure Crusher sensed it.

7

—◆—

Turning from the oversized screen set into one bulkhead of the engineering section's main work area, Lieutenant Commander Geordi La Forge removed his VISOR. That simple action halted the direct and continuous flow of visual information from the prosthesis to his brain, and he saw nothing. He stepped over and laid the device on the master situation table occupying the center of the room. With both hands free, he was able to rub the sides of his head just above the VISOR's neural connection points implanted in his temples. As the discomfort began to fade, he sighed with momentary relief.

The headaches, a minor yet constant presence from the moment he began wearing the prosthesis when he was just five years old, was something La Forge normally ignored. They worsened when he was tired or overworked, and as the *Enterprise*'s chief engineer, there were far too many days when that was true. It was not uncommon for him, once alone in his quarters, to seek solace in the unrelenting darkness that over time had become the gift offered by his blindness.

Without his VISOR, his other senses took over as La Forge had learned to let them. He heard conversations between members of his engineering staff, the soft tones of keys and other controls being manipulated on the room's various consoles and workstations, and underscoring all of that was the constant, steady pulse of the ship's warp core. In fact, he was sure he detected a minor warbling from it, deciding it sounded like a variance in one of the antimatter flow regulators. He was sure the deviation was still well within safety limits, but La Forge preferred everything in line with Starfleet specifications, except in those rare instances where experience and circumstances had shown him a better way. Once La Forge applied his modifications, he always made sure to submit a detailed report to Starfleet explaining his changes and suggestions for updating the specs. To date, none had been refuted or denied.

"Geordi."

La Forge heard the approach of Lieutenant Commander Data, and was in the process of retrieving his VISOR before the android spoke. Fitting the device across his eyes and feeling the connectors at his temples take hold, he waited the extra heartbeat as the influx of visual information from across the electromagnetic spectrum resumed. He turned toward his friend, noting the aura the VISOR presented as an interpretation of the energy that powered him. Everyone La Forge encountered possessed their own unique radiance, and he used them to identify individuals from one another. This allowed him to pick out people he knew from crowds as efficiently as a sighted person.

"Are you feeling all right?" asked Data.

Nodding, La Forge blew out his breath. "Yeah, I'm just tired." He gestured toward the wall monitor he had been studying. "I've been going over the technical schematics they sent us, hoping to have a handle on what we'll be facing when we arrive at the station." He shook his head. "What a mess that thing is."

Displayed on the screen was a series of technical schematics for Terok Nor, the Cardassian space station orbiting Bajor. A circular outer ring connected to a smaller yet bulkier inner circle via hull sections that also acted to support three pylons that extended above and three below the ring. They curved inward, suggesting a crablike life-form. The station was designed to accommodate orbital docking of ships of varying size, which La Forge determined also included the largest Federation starships while supporting a population of nearly seven thousand people. The facility was massive.

The bulk of internal space within each of the station's three pylons was devoted to the processing of uridium ore extracted and transported from the planet below. The foremost points of upper and lower pylon also served as a docking port for larger vessels. Additional spaces along its outer "habitat ring" supported the processing effort while also providing docking access for smaller vessels. The station's operations and control, including its main computer, were located in the central core. An odd design, different from the space stations La Forge was familiar with, it appeared cold and uninviting. The longer he stared at the schematic, the more intrigued La Forge became with the station.

Data said, "It is my understanding Cardassian construction methods are rather efficient, with respect to design and resources, particularly with respect to their ships and space-based installations."

"Efficient by Cardassian standards," La Forge replied. There was a cold, almost ruthless competence to their construction techniques. Perhaps this was an outgrowth of the Cardassians, who seemed to place a premium on such concepts. "But there's more to it than the differences in design methodology."

"I have reviewed the formal request for assistance by the Bajoran Provisional Government," said Data, "along with the status reports sent by the current leader of the team overseeing the transfer of the station's operational control from the Cardassians to the Bajorans."

Nodding, La Forge said, "Someone realized that over forty years of Occupation had produced people who learned how to maintain and repair many of the onboard systems." The engineer suspected any expertise obtained was in spite of the Cardassians, but it stood to reason anyone forced to work within the ore-processing plants or any of the areas supporting those systems picked up some knowledge from their overseers. "I doubt there are many Bajorans who understand the station's computer or command and control systems."

"I have studied Cardassian computer hardware and software design as it relates to this class of space station," said Data. "I believe I will be able to work with the onboard systems in a manner sufficient to assist in the transition."

La Forge tapped on the screen and several areas of the schematic illuminated in red, indicating several different areas across the station. "According to the early reports, the Cardassians sabotaged a number of onboard systems and broke whatever they could before leaving. We'll need teams to deal with the station's infrastructure, everything from power distribution, environmental controls to the replicators, and waste extraction. They even damaged several of the docking ports. The latest report says the Bajorans on-site will have those fixed before we arrive."

He stared at the diagrams and their status updates for another moment before adding, "I've done comparative studies of Cardassian ship and support-systems design. I know enough to get in and get my hands dirty, but this will be slow going."

After standing silent for a moment, Data said, "Geordi, I have reviewed the *Enterprise* personnel files. There are seven crew members whose records include interactions with Cardassians, or their technology as a consequence of their service during the Federation-Cardassian War. Foremost among these individuals is Chief Petty Officer Miles O'Brien."

La Forge was aware of O'Brien's record of Starfleet service and that he was a veteran of the war, having seen combat on numerous occasions prior to joining the *Enterprise*. His technical expertise was also impressive, earning high marks while attending Starfleet's engineering school for enlisted personnel when he was seventeen. As a chief petty officer, O'Brien oversaw a team of noncommissioned officers who maintained the ship's twenty transporter rooms and attending systems, reporting directly to the transporter systems officer. La Forge had often inspected the work while it was underway, and O'Brien was always there, sleeves rolled up, hands dirty, and head and arms sticking into the bowels of a console or crawling through a Jefferies tube.

This team also crewed the transporter rooms, and La Forge had noticed when he became chief engineer that O'Brien scheduled himself for this duty whenever senior staff required transport, regardless of the hour, as well as whenever high-ranking officers or visiting dignitaries came aboard. Chief O'Brien conducted himself by that time-honored axiom of leading from the front and by example, and his personnel evaluations were always exemplary in all categories.

"It looks to me like the chief is criminally underutilized," said La Forge. "His qualifications and experience should have earned him a commission a long time ago."

Data replied, "I believe he is someone who prefers to work 'in the trenches,' as I have heard him say. A commission would almost certainly reduce the opportunities for hands-on work. He may be content with his role as a noncommissioned officer. Regardless of rank, someone possessing his experience and years of service is unquestionably an asset. This would seem to be especially true given the number of variables we are likely to encounter while conducting repairs on Terok Nor and assisting the Bajorans to return the station to full operational status."

"Absolutely," said La Forge.

"What could possibly be so interesting?"

Miles O'Brien glanced up from his desktop terminal to see

his wife, Keiko, standing on the other side of the desk. Then he realized her hair was down, resting on her shoulders rather than pulled back into the ponytail she normally wore while working in the *Enterprise* botanical sciences labs. That led him to noticing she had changed out of her work clothes in favor of a cobalt-blue silken robe tied at the waist. When had this transformation occurred? Glancing at the terminal's chronometer, O'Brien saw that it was now nearly 2130 hours, and he had been staring at the technical diagrams sent to him by the *Enterprise*'s chief engineer for nearly two hours.

Blinking several times in rapid succession, O'Brien replied, "I'm sorry, Keiko." He looked around the room before asking, "I missed Molly's bedtime, didn't I?"

"Afraid so." Keiko tilted her head toward the doorway leading to their daughter's bedroom. "I read her the story she likes, but she told me she likes the way you read it better."

"That's because you don't provide the sound effects. Or the music."

Keiko laughed. "I'll work on that." Gesturing to the terminal, she asked, "What's so interesting?"

"Commander La Forge picked me for a repair team to work on the Cardassian station. He sent me the specs for it." He swiveled the terminal so she could see its screen. "It's been a long time since I worked with Cardassian technology, but they don't tend to change things that often."

Studying the diagrams for a moment, Keiko said, "That doesn't look like anything I've ever seen before."

"It may not have all the bells and whistles of Starfleet systems, but it works." In his varied experiences with them, O'Brien observed that Cardassians preferred to stick with proven designs and methodologies when it came to technology. At first it seemed odd to him, given how much of their civilization's resources were devoted to their military and their ability to wage war. Then he recalled from his studies of ancient Earth history how the great military powers of the world had created scores of weapons and machines for conducting battle in the air, the skies, and the oceans by sticking to straightforward designs that could be mass-produced in rapid fashion. With that in mind, it was easy for O'Brien to track the common threads through to present-day Cardassian technology, which was rooted in designs first conceived decades and even centuries ago. Good news, considering the assignment he was preparing to undertake.

"You're really into this, aren't you?" said Keiko, smiling as he perched herself on the corner of the deck nearest his chair. "Are you that anxious to get off the ship?"

Smiling, O'Brien replied, "You know, even with what it suffered during the Occupation, Bajor is supposed to have some beautiful forests and jungles, and an abundance of diverse plant life. I bet if you asked your department head, you could get permission to beam down while we're working on the station. I bet Starfleet would love some kind of updated site survey, since the Federation has already offered to help repair the planet's environmental damage."

"That's a good idea," said Keiko. She glanced at the computer screen once more before adding, "You seem pretty excited by this assignment."

O'Brien shrugged. "It'll be a nice change of pace. Transporter systems duty isn't exactly crackling with excitement." He smiled. "Avoiding excitement is the point."

"There's more to it than that, isn't there?" When he did not respond, Keiko said, "I know you've been thinking about a change for a while now. Are you getting bored with Starfleet?"

"Bored?" O'Brien shook his head. "No." He paused, glancing toward Molly's room. "It's just that I've been thinking a starship in deep space isn't the best place to raise a child."

"Have you thought about talking to some of the other parents?" asked Keiko. "Maybe Doctor Crusher can offer guidance on being a Starfleet parent from a mother's perspective." Then her eyes narrowed. "Maybe Worf can offer you fatherly advice."

The unexpected comment caught O'Brien off guard, and he could not stop the laugh that escaped him. "That'd be something, wouldn't it?" The moment passed. "But seriously, Molly deserves a life that's stable, and maybe not so . . . dangerous?" Thinking back to the occasions when the *Enterprise* had encountered a threat to the safety of the ship, O'Brien blew out his breath. "And to be honest, a change like that might be good for us. Something a bit more routine, with regular hours and more time for vacations."

"You're not serious," said Keiko. "I'd never ask you to do something like leaving Starfleet."

Leaning forward in his chair, he placed his hand on her leg. "You don't have to. I've been thinking about it for a while, and I had to remind myself that I've been in Starfleet for almost twenty-five years. That's a career, especially for a noncom like me. I can put in for retirement and we can start a new chapter somewhere else. Anywhere you and Molly want to go."

"And what will you do?" Keiko placed her hand atop his. "I know you, Miles Edward O'Brien. You'd be climbing the walls and pulling out your hair inside of a month."

"I'll find something to do. *We'll* find something to do, *together*." Before Keiko, O'Brien had never contemplated leaving Starfleet. Even after a war and all its lasting impacts, this was the only life he had ever known, and he had seen no reason to give it up, but things now were different. He had other considerations and priorities beyond his own aspirations.

Keiko said, "I know this couldn't have been an easy thing for you to consider, and I love that you'd walk away from Starfleet for us without hesitation. I know you're still mulling it over, and you can have all the time you need to reach a decision. Whatever that is, just know that I love you." She pointed to the computer screen. "How about this? We wait until after this next assignment, and then talk about it some more. Deal?"

"Deal." Twisting his hand underneath hers, he laced his fingers with hers and offered a gentle squeeze. "Thanks, Keiko."

Tugging on his hand, she pushed herself from the desk and moved to sit on his lap before wrapping her arms around his shoulders. "You're very welcome, Chief. Now, may I remind you that our daughter is sleeping soundly in her bed and we have the rest of the evening to ourselves?"

"Is that right?" O'Brien slid his arms around her waist. "Whatever will we do?"

Keiko smiled. "You'll think of something." Then her smile faded. "But no music. Or sound effects."

8

Even with the thick carpeting beneath his feet from where he sat in the bridge's command well, Picard felt the shift as the *Enterprise*'s massive engines disengaged and the vessel dropped out of warp speed. On the main viewscreen, he watched as distant stars, portrayed as colorful streaks passing to either side as the ship tunneled through subspace, retreated back to their normal appearance as remote pinholes in the opaque backdrop of space. After more than forty years spent in the company of those same stars, the transition to and from warp speed was still one of those things that brought him comfort. He had always felt at home aboard ship. It was here, among the stars, that he truly felt alive.

"We are secure from warp speed," reported Data from the flight controller's station, situated between Picard and the main viewer.

Sitting to Picard's right, Commander Riker ordered, "Proceed on to Bajor. Full impulse."

It was during this exchange that Picard noticed Counselor Troi. Seated on his left, she silently regarded him, with the slightest hint of a knowing smile teasing the corners of her mouth. The captain knew she had sensed his emotional shift. She seemed pleased that he had allowed himself this fleeting bit of peace.

Duty first, Picard reminded himself.

It was not chastisement, but instead a simple clarification of priorities. Troi must have understood his intention, as he caught her subtle nod before they both returned their attention to the viewscreen.

Now visible and growing larger with each passing second was a planet, a blue pearl emerging from the darkness, and as the *Enterprise* drew closer Picard noted five small moons orbiting it. He could also make out a smaller object even closer to Bajor than its natural satellites. "Magnify," he called out.

Lieutenant Jae, the officer at the operations station, tapped a control on her console and the image on the main viewer jumped forward, bringing Bajor into full relief. Parked above the planet in geosynchronous orbit was a dull metallic construct.

"Terok Nor," he offered, regarding the Cardassian space station with a critical eye. Despite it being the epitome of practical Cardassian design prioritizing function over form, Picard appreciated the station's odd, even foreboding beauty.

"Captain," said Lieutenant Worf from the tactical station above and behind Picard. "We are being hailed by Terok Nor's operations center."

Rising from his chair, Picard stepped toward the viewer. "Onscreen."

The image of Bajor and the station disappeared, replaced by the face of a Bajoran man. Cropped black hair framed his narrow, angular face, and he wore the uniform of an officer in the newly established Bajoran Militia. His otherwise humanoid features were accented by the subtle creases across his nose. A scar on his forehead intersecting his left eyebrow suggested to Picard that he, like a significant percentage of Bajorans filling the militia's ranks, had served in the Resistance movement, bringing with him hardwon skills and experience.

"Federation vessel, this is Terok Nor station operations. I am Major Heslo Artun of the Bajoran Militia and interim commander of this facility. I offer greetings on behalf of the Bajoran Republic."

Despite his words, Picard noted a stiffness to his tone, as though he were reciting a script written for him and which he read under protest. Plainly, Heslo was not excited about this meeting.

Picard moved to stand closer to Data. "Major, I'm Captain Jean-Luc Picard, commanding the Federation *Starship Enterprise*. It is a privilege to speak with you today."

"Our sensors show you are on approach to Bajor, Captain. We request that rather than assuming orbit over the planet, you alter your course to dock at the station." As before, Heslo's demeanor was not rude, but instead hewing to strict formalities.

Picard said, "We are happy to follow whatever procedures you've established, Major. It was my understanding that the conference would be held at your government's primary capitol building."

"First Minister Kalem has directed a change of venue," replied Heslo. *"He feels that the station provides a more . . . appropriate . . . backdrop for the topics to be discussed."* The major offered the slightest hint of emotion by cocking his left eyebrow, which only served to draw further attention to the scar on his forehead. It convinced Picard there was more in play here than a simple change of setting.

Doubting Heslo would be willing to entertain further questions, Picard instead said, "Very well. We will adjust our course accordingly."

"Thank you, Captain." Heslo nodded. *"Our docking control officer will transmit pylon and mooring instructions. Terok Nor Operations, out."* Without waiting for a response, the Bajoran severed the communication. The viewer's image returned to that of Bajor. Still dominating the center of the screen, the planet now was larger than it had been before.

"Not exactly rolling out the red carpet for us, are they?" Riker's expression told Picard his first officer was not complaining but making one of his normal frank assessments.

Troi said, "The Bajorans will have no end of doubts about our intentions. Many will be wary, and with good reason. After all they've endured, trust is a commodity they'll extend only when they feel it's warranted."

"Can't say I blame them," replied Riker. "What do you suppose Heslo meant about First Minister Kalem considering Terok Nor a better setting for the conference? My gut tells me something's up."

Considering the question as he returned to his seat, Picard said, "It could be something as simple as wanting to offer the Cardassians a setting that puts them more at ease and therefore more agreeable reaching consensus."

"I didn't sense anything overt from the major," said Troi. "A bit of smugness, but it's possible that's a simple outgrowth of the confidence he and other Bajorans might be feeling now that the tables have turned in their favor. It's reasonable to assume the Cardassian delegation will attempt to act as though they're not affected by the change in the status quo, but they'll be sitting across from people they once tyrannized, who are now in a position to make demands of them they may not wish to grant. I suspect egos will flare."

Picard recalled from his review of Kalem Apren's biographical summary that before the arrival of the Cardassians, he had served as junior minister of the planet's Hedrickspool Province. During the Occupation, he relocated to the Kendra Valley, working as an arbiter to settle disputes between Bajorans in Kendra Province. Kalem had sought out the position of first minister for the new Bajoran government. It was unknown how Kalem felt about the Cardassians who had oppressed his people for over forty years. Surviving the Occupation was a feat in and of itself. It was well documented that in the takeover's early days, Cardassian forces made a point of executing leaders at all levels of government to make clear to all Bajorans who now ruled them. How he had escaped was a mystery, though no mention was made if he had collaborated. Was this gamesmanship designed to annoy the Cardassian delegation?

From his station, Worf reported, "We are receiving instructions from Terok Nor docking control." Tapping additional controls on his console, the Klingon placed one hand on the station's curved railing. "I am routing them to Commander Data."

What he needed was more information, Picard decided. He would have to be on his guard to make sure the conference did not deteriorate into chaos. There was too much at stake, for the Bajorans as well as the Federation and—he conceded—even the Cardassians.

Picard sat in silence, watching as Data maneuvered the *Enterprise* into position beside one of Terok Nor's upper docking pylons. The station was massive, its outer mooring areas able to accommodate the *Galaxy*-class starship with more than enough room for other vessels of equal size to utilize the other two upper pylons.

"Docking maneuver complete," reported Data, his fingers moving across his console with unmatched dexterity. After a final look to Lieutenant Jae, who nodded in confirmation, he added, "Mooring clamps are attached. All systems at station-keeping mode."

"Thank you, Mister Data." Rising from his chair, Picard looked to Riker. "Well done."

Picard knew his first officer was a stickler for detail when it came to bridge personnel being proficient in a number of areas that included docking operations as well as separating and reconnecting the *Enterprise*'s primary and secondary hull sections. These and related exercises were a frequent element of training simulations Riker required on a continuing basis for all conn and ops personnel. Even Data took part in the drills despite his expert piloting and navigation skills, doing so as a benefit to the other officers with whom he might be assigned to bridge duty.

"Mister Data," said Picard. "When is the *Oceanside* due to arrive?"

Without having to consult his console, the android replied, "Seven hours, thirty-four minutes, sir."

Nodding in approval, Picard looked at Riker. "You have the bridge, Number One," he said before glancing at Troi. "The counselor and I have some final items to address before we meet with First Minister Kalem."

Riker replied, "Understood. Geordi will likely want to get over there with his team as soon as he gets the go-ahead. Doctor Crusher is finalizing her preparations for the medical team she'll be leading on the surface." He turned to face Worf. "Begin enhanced security on all airlocks. Lieutenant, you'll command the first security team we take over."

Before the Klingon could reply, Troi said, "Captain, after giving this some thought, Mister Worf believes it might be better if he remains on the ship."

"Oh?" Picard shot a quick glance in Worf's direction before returning his gaze to her. "For what reason?"

"Given the state of the Bajorans, a Klingon—another race still remembered for their conquering ways—might do more harm than good at this early juncture."

Considering her comments, Picard asked Worf, "Lieutenant?"

The security chief straightened his posture. "Sir, I did express these concerns to Counselor Troi."

"Captain," added Troi, "it's a valid observation, given the evolving situation on Bajor post-Occupation."

"I commend your thoughtful analysis, Lieutenant." After a moment, Picard ordered, "Very well. Number One, I know you were planning to oversee our efforts on the station and the surface from the *Enterprise* while Counselor Troi and I attended the conference. Mister Worf will take the conn, allowing you to carry out your duties on-site."

"Very good, sir," said Riker.

Satisfied with the new arrangement, Picard returned his attention to the main viewscreen, Data had adjusted the image to provide a view of Terok Nor from the *Enterprise*'s vantage point, with the ship now moored. Even from this angle, the size of the station remained impressive, the sight made even more grand by the curvature of Bajor just visible in the screen's lower-left corner.

Taking in the scene, Picard allowed himself a moment of satisfaction. He had always personally disagreed with the Federation's policy of not assisting the Bajorans. His recent meeting with Nechayev was one of the very few times he had allowed himself to voice his true feelings, rather than fuming in silence at the narrow-minded interpretation of the Prime Directive. Wanting or expecting the Bajorans to offer them absolution was naïve, at worse arrogant. The path to forgiveness would be long and fraught with obstacles, tests, and judgment.

It was time for the Federation to walk that path.

9

—•—

After curfew, the barracks' doors were secured from the outside, and shutters closed over the windows. Inside, observers were posted near each door and window, listening for signs of guards or anyone else who might be approaching. Two more were up in the roof, accessed via a trapdoor hidden behind a recessed lighting panel in the ceiling. There, Ranar and another lookout huddled in the dark, and by accessing the ventilation ducts that ran the length of the building they could use the flues at either end to keep watch over the compound outside. The vantage point near the barracks' front looked out over the center of camp, the most likely direction from which a guard might come. The main lights had been extinguished, leaving only smaller ones above the exits as well as the doors leading to the makeshift kitchen, lavatory, and showers. Except for the small handheld lights carried by several of the Bajorans with whom Panat shared living quarters, the barracks was dark.

Scattered around the edges of the common room, groups of prisoners engaged in normal conversations mixed with the occasional louder outburst. There was a buzz in the air that to anyone outside who might be listening sounded like the usual sort of interaction between people who worked and lived in constant proximity to one another. While there was truth to that, the background chatter also provided sound camouflage for Panat and a smaller group of twelve Bajorans who huddled on the floor near the center of the building's common room.

"Keep the lights low," warned Panat. From where he lay on the floor, he caught sight of a wayward beam that interrupted his hasty briefing. In response to his instruction, those wielding the lamps assumed positions similar to his, keeping the illumination inside the circle of inmates gathered at the center of the room. This prevented any telltale light flashes from escaping between seams in the doors or windows and possibly attracting unwanted attention from outside. The lights were fashioned from handheld units and other devices purloined from the camp's equipment bays or scavenged from the refuse. Rather than attempting to hide these, the prisoners instead left them where they could be discovered without effort, passing them off as reading lamps whenever they were found by guards conducting inspections. As the years passed and incidents involving the small lights presented themselves, most of the guards relaxed their rules on this and other lesser infractions. There might be the occasional guard who would confiscate them as a means of demonstrating his authority, but for the most part the Bajorans were allowed these minor comforts.

However, Panat knew they could not afford to arouse suspicions or do anything to provoke interruptions.

"You now know everything I do," he said in a low voice, after completing his description of what Yectu had shown him in the workspace hidden below the barracks. He studied the faces of the gathered inmates, many of whom looked back at him askance. It was a lot to absorb in such a short amount of time, but time and opportunity were precious commodities in this place. No one had the luxury of being able to contemplate long-term planning. There were only those moments, infrequent and unpredictable though they may be, that might present an opening to act against their overseers. Was this one of those occasions? Could they seize upon the mysterious information they had collected, and somehow turn it into an advantage? Barring that, could they at least make life more difficult for the Cardassians? Without more information, there was no possible way for Panat to know.

He asked for a show of hands, and aside from Yectu and one other person, no one in their group had heard the term "Cradis" used in any form here or anywhere else before.

"Meeju," said Yectu, gesturing to the younger woman who had raised her hand. "Where did you hear it?"

"In the officers' quarters," replied the other Bajoran, her voice almost a whisper. "We were completing our laundry tasking for the day. Glinn Trina and another officer were talking." Meeju crab-walked toward the empty circle at the center of the group. "Trina mentioned the word in the context of being an active protocol. I don't think he'd heard the term before."

Yectu shook her head. "Unless he'd had reason to interact with the Obsidian Order for any length of time, there's no reason for him to have heard it. The same's true for Gul Havrel. He's certainly not an agent, so perhaps he answers to them, at least in some respects."

"Did Trina say anything else?" asked Panat.

Frowning, Meeju replied, "He didn't offer specifics, but it was obvious he was uneasy. I have to wonder if he was even aware of whatever the protocol involves until now."

"If Havrel is overseeing or even just protecting some kind of top-secret project," said Yectu, "then information about it would be compartmentalized to an extreme degree. Anyone not directly involved wouldn't be briefed on it. It's possible none of the guards would be aware of it either."

Panat shifted his body, trying to find a more comfortable position on the floor. "So we're saying there's a separate group of Cardassians? Engineers, scientists, soldiers, and whoever else they need. People we've never seen, and not connected to the camp in any way?"

"Probably," replied Yectu, gesturing to indicate the group. "As for the rest of us, we're just laborers, right? Mining uridium for transport somewhere else. Anybody watching us would see the same mind-numbing routine. That's our life, day after day. Nothing out of the ordinary, especially for the Cardassians. We make a perfect cover for some kind of clandestine activity they don't want anyone to know about."

"And it's not as though it'd be hard for them to be here without our knowing," said Panat. "Nearly the entire planet beyond the camp perimeter, the mine, and even the quarry is a potential hiding spot, if you think about it."

Yectu held up a hand. "But we *have* heard there are areas all over the planet where large concentrations of mineral deposits interfere with sensors."

Nodding, Panat said, "Has that ever been confirmed? After all, it's not as though any of us have access to sensor equipment."

It was Meeju who answered, "I've never heard anything specific, but Trina and some of the others have occasionally complained about how sensors don't always work in the mining tunnels and shafts. Usually, they're in the midst of investigating possible new veins and deposits, and they end up having to send a team into the new areas to survey things firsthand."

"There are no transporters," said Panat. "At least, none I've ever seen. It always made sense they wouldn't have them, or at least easy access to them, or shuttles, in the event of a prison uprising. We still outnumber them." Havrel and his troops worrying about a possible rebellion among the inmate population was a valid concern, but to Panat it sounded worse in theory than actual application. The Cardassians held all the weapons. Even if any prisoners managed to get their hands on any small arms, they would be grossly outgunned by the guards.

Yectu replied, "But if there *is* something else going on here that rises to the level of employing Cradis protocols—something the Cardassians want hidden at all costs—it'd be another reason to keep the planet isolated."

"If they're going to this much trouble, it must be pretty terrible," said Drizu, who like Panat returned to camp after long days spent in the mines to devote many of his evenings to monitoring the Cardassians and scheming ways to undermine them. "Some kind of illegal weapons technology, or something else to inflict on people like us. If they've been given orders to move it off this planet, they're not going to leave us alive. Even with the declaration from the Detapa Council ordering the release of all Bajorans, they're not going to let us return to Bajor and risk any of us saying anything, whether it's to our own government or Starfleet or whoever we could once we got back."

Panat wondered how long it might take someone to arrive at the same conclusion. "You're right. The best we can hope for is they take us with them to wherever they establish a new location for their project, but if I were placing bets?" He paused, eyeing each of his companions for a moment. "We're already dead. It's just a matter of time."

"Why not just kill us now and get it over with?" asked Meeju.

Yectu replied, "We're still pulling uridium from the mines, so I guess there's that, but there really is another thing to consider. The Cardassians have benefitted from our labor for decades. They're not going to be happy about giving that up, and we've all heard stories of Bajorans—men, women, even children—who've gone missing after some Cardassian takes an interest in them. Do we really think there won't be those who opt to skirt the order about returning us to Bajor?" She shook her head. "Mark my words. People will disappear during this. Maybe they'll be declared dead, if any sort of information is provided at all. Meanwhile, they'll be taken back to Cardassia Prime or some other planet deep in their territory and forced to live out their lives in servitude. By the time anyone figures out there are Bajorans unaccounted for, it'll be too late."

"Not me," said Meeju, her voice hardening. "I'll die first."

Panat understood and sympathized with her declaration. He knew she, like Ijok and a few other Bajoran women, was assigned to housekeeping duties for the Cardassian detachment's officers' quarters. That their job also meant seeing to other needs of those officers, Panat tried not to think about. Instead, he focused on how Ijok, Meeju, and others exploited their masters' appetites against them at every opportunity. As distasteful as it might be, it served the Resistance. His first impulse was to exploit that weakness one last time.

"Or," he said, "we kill them first." That earned him a dozen faces staring at him with varying expressions of disbelief. His friends even spent a moment exchanging glances with each other before returning their attention to him.

"You can't be serious," said Drizu, the first to break the silence.

Panat nodded. "I am serious. If they're going to kill us, then we have nothing to lose by trying to take out some of them before they get us. That said, it doesn't have to be like that. At least, not yet. Even if we can't save ourselves, maybe we can do some good before our time's up."

Yectu, now starting to smile, said, "You mean sabotage?"

"Whatever they've got here," replied Panat, "I'm guessing it'd make a lot of people upset if it was exposed or compromised in any way. Maybe destroying it earns the Cardassians some well-earned scrutiny from the Federation, or whoever forced them to pull back from Bajor." His initial instinct was to avoid doing anything that might be construed as helping the Federation. Considering everything they—representing hundreds of worlds supposedly committed to the ideals of peaceful coexistence and mutual cooperation—had failed to do while the Cardassians plundered Bajor and its people, the idea they might be an ally never seemed possible.

He knew of one person who had somehow found a way to see past their hatred of the Federation. How long had it been since his first meeting with Ro Laren, who like him had endured life in various refugee camps in the Valo system? Cruelty had already visited her when they crossed paths at a camp on Valo II. As a child, she had lost her father to brutal interrogation and torture at the hands of the Cardassians. After doing what was necessary to survive, Ro had escaped the camps and done the unthinkable: joined Starfleet. Was she still wearing their uniform?

"If we can hurt them here," said Yectu, "there's no way to know what benefit it might have. There's a chance no one will ever know we were here or did anything."

Panat said, "We'll know."

"For as long as we live, that is," added Drizu. His cynical attempt at humor was enough to elicit small laughs from the rest of the group. "Okay, then," he said after a moment. "What do we do?"

"We need more information," said Panat. It was with great reluctance that he turned his gaze to Meeju. "By whatever means necessary."

Nodding, the younger woman replied, "I understand."

"You won't be alone," said Drizu. "Kijam is also detailed to the officers' quarters. He can work with you, figure out a strategy."

"I've done it before," said Meeju, her voice firm. Looking to Panat and Yectu, she asked, "What do you need?"

Panat said, "Whatever you can learn about what they're hiding, and where."

"I'll make contact with Ijok through the network," added Yectu. "I think with a bit of work and luck, I can get deeper into

Havrel's data files. With time, I may even be able to worm my way into the camp computer system's main memory banks."

"Be careful with that," said Meeju. "If they've activated an Obsidian Order protocol, that likely extends to the computer system as well. They may be monitoring for signs of intrusion. If they find out we're sneaking around in there—"

"They'll likely kill us all." Panat released a deep sigh. "So I'd appreciate us doing our best to avoid that."

Murmurs of agreement filtered back to him before he ended the meeting. Panat gave the signal that their larger circle of protectors could begin the process of modulating their conversations and other raucous behavior should any guards be listening.

The more he considered their situation, the more Panat convinced himself the likelihood of any Bajoran leaving this planet was negligible at best. As he saw it, this understanding left him and his companions with two options. They could wait to die, or they could do something that allowed them to face death on their own terms.

Panat hated waiting.

10

—◆—

Terok Nor was beautiful in its own way, Riker decided.

From the moment he passed through the umbilical passageway linking the *Enterprise* to the station, he found himself taken by the facility's architecture and design. There was an emphasis on utility and efficiency, such as in those areas devoted to cargo handling, ore processing, and the comings and goings of vessels. It was not until moving away from those sections that a visitor began to see the obvious care and even artistry that went into creating the spaces where the station's inhabitants spent a significant portion of their time. Nowhere was this more evident than the Promenade, the hive of activity that was Terok Nor's central core.

"Wow," said La Forge as he and Riker along with Doctor Crusher surveyed their surroundings. "This is like something you'd see in a market square somewhere."

High curving walls rose two stories from the Promenade's main level forming the dome Riker knew served as the space-side hull of the station's outer ring. A second level was stacked above, linked to the outer walls by several connected walkways leading to shops as well as oversized viewing ports set into the bulkheads. From where they stood, Riker could see storefronts and other spaces to his left and right, lining the main walkway that curved away from him in both directions. To his left, he saw sections of a metal fence being dismantled, affording access to space he assumed was meant only for merchants or offices.

"That section once was for Bajorans," said Crusher. "According to the briefing, this part of the station was cordoned off, and they were forbidden to enter this area."

Riker asked, "Who ran these shops?"

"The Bajorans had their own in the cordoned area," replied Crusher. "Over there, it was either Cardassians or whoever was willing to pay for space." She indicated to their right, which to Riker seemed to take up a far greater parcel of space than surrounding establishments. "Ferengi, for example."

"That's Quark's Bar."

Riker turned toward the new voice coming from behind them to see a humanoid representing a race he had never before encountered. Tall and lean of build, the new arrival appeared to be male, but Riker was forced to admit he was going just by the voice he had heard. He was dressed in a brown-and-tan uniform that looked similar to but not exactly like those of the Bajoran Militia. His dirty blond hair was slicked back away from his face, which was so smooth Riker at first wondered if it might be a mask.

"Commander Riker, I'm Odo, chief of station security. Major Heslo apologizes for being detained in the operations center, as he's finalizing preparations for the arrival of the conference delegates. He asked me to greet you in his place." His arms behind his back, he made no effort to extend a hand in greeting. "He also asked me to assist with showing your people where they'll be working while they're here, at least at the beginning." While Odo did not come off as rude, there was no warmth to his greeting, and Riker sensed the security chief would rather be anywhere than here.

Opting to keep things professional as well as amiable, Riker introduced La Forge and Crusher before replying, "It's good to meet you, Mister Odo. Thanks for meeting us."

Turning his attention to La Forge, Odo said, "You'll probably want to see Ops before you get started in the engineering spaces, Commander. I can take you there once we finish down here."

The chief engineer nodded. "I'd appreciate that. Thank you."

Unable to resist, Riker said, "I'm sorry, but I'm afraid I don't recognize your species."

"That's all right. I don't recognize my species either."

Without elaboration, Odo indicated for them to follow him as he began walking down the Promenade in the direction of the bar, which Riker could see had to be the center of activity in this part of the station. He guessed its array of tables, bar space, and gaming areas allowed for at least a hundred patrons, and he spotted spiral staircases leading to areas on the second level that allowed for more. As they passed the establishment, Riker noted that the majority of tables and bar stools were unoccupied. A broad-shouldered Lurian, his narrow, oversized bald head poking out from the dark jumpsuit he wore, sat alone on a stool near the entrance, while a pair of Ferengi worked behind the bar.

"Pretty quiet around here," said Riker.

Odo replied, "It's early. A number of the merchants gave notice they were closing their shops. They figure with the Cardassians leaving there wasn't much point to staying."

"Really?" asked Crusher. "I would've thought their leaving might attract renewed interest or attention."

"There is some of that," replied the security chief. "Some Bajorans are applying for space. There are also a number of quarters on board that were already unoccupied or else abandoned by the Cardassians. Major Heslo's staff is working on a plan to make those living areas available to those who wish to work or live on the station."

Crusher said, "From the reports I've read, homelessness is rampant on Bajor."

"Some of that is being alleviated by the Cardassian withdrawal." Odo punctuated his reply with a grunt of obvious irritation. "Of course, they couldn't just leave without causing more trouble on their way out. Many of the outposts and other facilities that once housed Cardassian troops have been ransacked or destroyed. They didn't do any further damage to Bajoran cities and settlements, but that still leaves thousands of people without homes."

"Starfleet is already moving to address that," said Crusher. "The *Oceanside*'s primary role will be taking point on the relocation efforts. Temporary housing to begin with, followed by repairs and expansion efforts to existing communities and infrastructure. It'll take time, but the Federation is committed to providing as much aid as possible for as long as it takes."

La Forge added, "Other ships with additional supplies are also heading to Bajor."

"There are many Bajorans who don't want you here," replied Odo. "In their eyes, living under Starfleet rule doesn't sound better than under the Cardassians."

"Understandable," said Riker. "All we can do is demonstrate our intentions through action and hope for the best."

Again, Odo offered a low grunt, which the first officer already equated with a cynicism that might very well be the security chief's default. "Asking for hope from a people who've had it quashed for over four decades might be a wasted endeavor, Commander. First Minster Kalem seems optimistic, and it's fair to say he's not alone."

"You're advising us to manage our expectations," said Crusher.

Odo nodded. "Always a sound strategy."

Ready to get past pleasantries—real or otherwise—Riker looked around the Promenade. "We know there are still Cardassians aboard the station. Where are they?"

Odo said, "Billeted in quarters on the habitat ring. After the initial problems some of them caused, I thought it best to keep them segregated as we began receiving Bajoran refugees from the surface. We'll try to keep them out of trouble until transports arrive to take them back to Cardassian space."

Satisfied the security chief had things under control, Riker said, "We should continue the tour. If the Bajorans see us working instead of just standing around, that might help our case."

"I thought standing around and talking was standard Starfleet procedure," replied Odo, but when he did so he smiled in a way that Riker took to mean the humanoid was giving him grief.

"Not until you make admiral," said Riker, offering his own smile. "Until then, they actually expect us to work for a living." When Odo grunted this time, it was with obvious humor, and his smile widened.

Riker and his colleagues let the mysterious humanoid take the lead as they began a tour of the Promenade. As they walked, he took note of several Bajorans wearing militia uniforms, and posted in pairs at various points along the curving thoroughfare.

"Your security people?" he asked as he moved to walk alongside their guide.

Odo nodded. "Yes. All of them are essentially new recruits, former members of the Resistance who accepted offers to join the militia. All of them are too young to have known a time before the Occupation, and for many the Resistance was the only form of stability or even family they've ever known. Now that the Cardassians are leaving, they're finding themselves without a cause."

"There seems to be a lot of them here," said Crusher. "Are you expecting trouble?"

"With the conference taking place on the station, I thought it prudent to increase the number of officers patrolling the common areas." Odo gestured to a pair of Bajorans they passed. "There's still friction between the Bajorans and those Cardassians still here and on Bajor. Even with what are supposed to be strict orders to abide by the terms of withdrawal, not every Cardassian is going quietly. I expect there to be a few incidents before they're all gone. Until that happens, a palpable security presence will help."

Riker could not fault the security chief's logic. He was about to say so when he saw Odo's expression sour as something caught his attention a second before a question echoed across the Promenade.

"Constable Odo, you're not scaring off our new guests, are you?"

Riker turned at the sound of the high-pitched voice to see a Ferengi making his way in rapid fashion from the large bar toward them. His bold, multicolored jacket was at odds with the station's drab motif. Riker noted that he was not sporting a headpiece to cover the back of his oversized, hairless skull, as was usually worn by the Ferengi. His large ears, pronounced brow, and jagged teeth did not make him appear menacing but instead a dealer or salesman of questionable character, and therefore consistent with every other Ferengi the first officer had ever encountered.

Quark, he reasoned.

"What do you want now, Quark?" asked Odo, confirming Riker's suspicions. The security chief sounded like he might be ready to punt the Ferengi bar owner out the nearest airlock.

Advancing to within a few paces of the security chief, Quark waved one hand above and behind him toward the overhead, and Riker followed the gesture as he seemed to point toward an area above the bar on the Promenade's upper level.

"My holosuites are offline. *Again.* That's the third time this week. Do you have any idea how much these interruptions are costing my business?"

Odo seemed unmoved by the Ferengi's problem. "We're operating at reduced power, Quark. You and every other merchant on the Promenade were warned this would be an issue until repairs to the central power core are completed. Until then, essential systems take priority."

"My holosuites *are* a priority, Odo." Then, as if noticing Riker and his colleagues for the first time, Quark shifted his stance to face them. "And now Starfleet is here, ready to rescue us from financial ruin." He placed his two wrists together, his hands forming a U. "I am Quark, proprietor of Quark's Bar, this station's premiere dining and entertainment establishment. You're from the *Enterprise*? All that time spent in deep space, surely you understand the need to unwind, relax, and enjoy yourselves while escaping all the pressures and demands of duty. What you seek, I can provide."

"But it'll cost us," said Riker, unable to suppress a smile.

"Of course." Quark's reply was matter-of-fact. "Why else would I be here?" He gestured past them toward his bar. "While *you're* here, I hope you'll consider spending some of your time *and* latinum with us."

Riker said, "I'll discuss authorizing shore leave for our off-duty personnel with Captain Picard. I'm sure he'll be open to the idea, time permitting, of course."

"I wouldn't dream of doing anything to interfere with the important work you have to do here, Commander." Eyeing Odo, Quark added, "Including getting my holosuites back online."

Excusing himself from the conversation, the Ferengi turned and headed back to his bar, and Riker could not stifle a chuckle as he watched him leave.

"Persistent, isn't he?"

Odo replied, "You have no idea, Commander."

Despite his initial judgment, Riker decided this Ferengi was different from others he had encountered. He appeared more polished when it came to the art of the deal, which made sense for a provider of leisure and entertainment. Riker figured his customer base up to this point likely consisted of freighter crews, Cardassians, and anyone else who was not Bajoran. With the promise of a regular Starfleet and Federation presence, to say nothing of the other ship traffic that would attract, Quark likely knew he would have to further his efforts to appear welcoming.

All while generating a nice profit, Riker mused. Of course, this assumed the Ferengi did not elect to close his business and seek opportunity off the station.

La Forge asked, "How serious is the situation with primary power?"

"The Cardassian engineers decided to commit a little sabotage on their way out," replied Odo. "I suspect they don't possess the same skill as Starfleet engineers, but they know enough to break something for effect. As part of their initial withdrawal, the Cardassians made sure to remove munitions as well as key elements of the fire-control system. They also made off with numerous computer components, supplies, and even pulled power relay junctions, optical data network routers, and processing hubs, leaving the station to run on substandard backup systems. Four of the six reaction chambers powering the station's fusion reactor are offline. A contingent of Bajoran engineers is working on the problem, but they're running into difficulties. Familiarity with Cardassian technology varies, and usually stops at knowing just enough to sabotage it."

"A pretty steep learning curve, then," said La Forge. "I've been studying the schematics, and a few members of my team have experience with Cardassian technology. I think we'll be able to get on that right now. With Major Heslo's permission, of course."

Odo said, "You'll have to forgive him, Commander. He's been dealing with all manner of problems from the moment he accepted this assignment. Bringing order to the chaos of the Cardassians pulling out would be hard enough without the other obstacles they're throwing up. He's had crews working a task list around the clock, including overlapping fourteen-hour shifts. So, additional people who can be available to work on the more serious problems would be welcome."

"Fourteen hours?" asked La Forge.

"Bajor's day is based on a twenty-six-hour clock." Crusher asked, "I'm guessing that means the station follows the same schedule?"

"That's correct, Doctor," replied the security chief. "I've heard it takes some getting used to, but I also hear Starfleet prides itself on its adaptability."

"We'll manage," said Crusher. "Have the reactor issues affected the station's medical facilities?"

Odo replied, "There's an infirmary here on the Promenade, and emergency aid stations in each of the pylons. Those were used to deal with injuries in the ore-processing areas, but don't expect much from them. Cardassian medical technology isn't as advanced as the Federation's."

"Not to mention the Cardassians probably didn't put a high priority on avoiding workplace accidents," said La Forge.

"I'd like to have a look at the infirmary so I can make an initial report," said Crusher. "I know the *Oceanside*'s medical team will be overseeing any upgrades, but the sooner the better."

"We'll stop there before heading to Operations," replied Odo.

They were approaching the last of the metal fencing that served as the Promenade barrier. Riker noted the Bajoran working party charged with dismantling the final components, and another crew beyond the barricade taking on the task of removing trash and other debris cluttering the deck in that section. Still others worked on installing lighting panels in nearby bulkheads and storefronts, bringing illumination and life to what Riker suspected had been, until recently, a much less inviting area. He took the workers for civilians, as none of them wore militia uniforms, and he also caught the looks of interest, skepticism, and suspicion on several of their faces.

"This area was a ghetto," said Odo. "One of the first things Major Heslo ordered was to get rid of the barricades and open up the entire Promenade. With this and making large portions of the living quarters available to Bajoran nationals who might want to work and live here, he's moving fast to demonstrate the station's no longer under Cardassian control."

"I bet some of the Cardassians still here aren't thrilled," said La Forge.

Odo grunted again. "Do they teach understatement at that academy of yours, Commander?" Despite the obvious poking question, the humanoid still affected a wan smile. He paused, regarding the workers. "Under Cardassian control, this station was a microcosm of what life was like for Bajorans. They existed to serve their masters for as long as they were useful. Forced labor, servants." He stopped himself, as though reluctant to finish; when he did his expression turned sour. "*Companions*."

"You mean comfort women," said Crusher.

"Not exclusively." Odo shook his head. "From my understanding, most were treated well. That often extended to better living conditions or care for their families."

Crusher's voice turned hard. "It's still exploitation."

"Absolutely," said Odo. "Bajorans have been exploited in every way you can imagine, Doctor, along with a few you should never have to contemplate. They've emerged from under the shroud of subjugation, most of them for the first time in their lives. Earning their trust will be a tall order." His expression softened as he regarded Crusher, before turning his attention to Riker. "For their sakes, I honestly hope you can do that, Commander."

The first officer nodded. "As do I, Mister Odo." As he saw it, there was only one thing to do. "We should get started."

11

—

"I hope you'll find this satisfactory, Captain," said Major Heslo Artun, standing at the wardroom's entrance and allowing Picard and Troi to enter first. "It's the largest meeting space on the station, and the most well appointed. The station commander and his senior staff typically used it for meetings and meals as well as social and ceremonial functions." Walking past a pair of *Enterprise* security officers standing outside the wardroom entrance, the major stepped into the room and allowed the doors to close behind him. "We had to do some quick repairs to make it presentable. A few Cardassians decided to have one last wild party here before leaving the station. I'll spare you the details, but let's just say it was definitely not a formal or solemn occasion."

Picard allowed himself a small, knowing smile as he surveyed his surroundings. Old habits made him treat the room like any other he might enter for the first time, subjecting it to a critical eye as he inspected every detail. To him, it appeared clean and orderly, with no signs of whatever revelry or debauchery that may have taken place.

"Whatever you did, Major," said Troi, "it looks very inviting. I'm sure First Minister Kalem in particular will appreciate your efforts."

"As do I," added Picard. "Most excellent work, Major."

His eyes fell upon the narrow, elongated hexagonal table that was the room's centerpiece. Its internal illumination along with the elaborate, decorative lighting panels positioned along the interior bulkheads gave the room an almost regal air. The table was flanked by six high-backed chairs on each side, with matching seats at each end. Dominating the exterior bulkhead on the table's far side were five oversized circular viewing ports affording a breathtaking view of Bajor. Due to the station's rotation, the planet appeared to be moving slowly from left to right, already disappearing past the rightmost portal to offer an unfettered vista of open space.

"We received the dietary information sent from your ship, Captain," said Heslo. "I was told you have a particular fondness for a certain Earth tea. I've asked for that recipe to be added to the replicator menu as soon as possible."

"That's very thoughtful of you, Major. Thank you." Picard noted the major's demeanor was much warmer and more welcoming than displayed during their earlier interaction. Wearing what Picard suspected was a newly acquired or replicated red-brown militia uniform, Heslo, like most Bajorans, also displayed an elaborate *D'ja pagh* on his right ear, its silver chain suspended between a clip attached to the ear's upper cartilage and a stud affixed to its lobe. Given the harried nature of the assignment he'd accepted, he appeared unruffled and almost pleasant to be around.

Troi said, "Major, I understand you've been dealing with a number of issues since taking command of the station." She gestured to the room around them. "I must say I admire your ability to balance so many competing priorities." Her approach had an immediate effect on Heslo, as Picard observed him relaxing just the slightest bit as the hint of a smile seemed to play at the corners of his mouth.

"I appreciate you saying that, Commander. I don't mind admitting it's been a lot. The Cardassian withdrawal has not been without incident, the havoc they wrought on their way out, for one thing. Overseeing repairs and upgrades to various onboard systems and other support infrastructure is proving to be a challenge for us, but we're getting through it. There's also the matter of finding places for people to live." Heslo gestured around them. "The station affords quite a number of accommodations, but it's not enough for everyone looking for even temporary shelter. A number of people have inquired about opportunities to work on the station, and we're reviewing those requests and offering billet space for anyone who wants to live here as well."

Picard said, "My first officer has briefed me on the situation. Beyond whatever supplies and personnel from the *Enterprise* we can provide to help, I've also authorized him to investigate any other means of offering assistance to you and your staff."

Drawing himself up, Heslo nodded. "Thank you, Captain. I must also apologize for my conduct during our earlier conversation. I hope you'll excuse it as coming from a flawed, tired man in dire need of a good night's sleep. Your people have been nothing but forthcoming since your arrival, and I'm grateful for your assistance."

"It's obvious you're no stranger to managing multiple, competing priorities," said Troi. "What did you do before joining the militia?" Picard detected the unspoken qualification to her question. The counselor was broaching what in all likelihood had to be as sensitive a topic for Heslo as it would be for any Bajoran.

The major picked up on this as well. "I was a school administrator during the Occupation. We did what we could to make life as normal as possible for the children. The Cardassians charged with overseeing our province left us alone for the most part, as we tried to avoid their notice."

"You were also a member of the Resistance," said Picard. He recalled the very slim file on Heslo. "Talk about balancing priorities."

For the first time, Heslo offered a true smile along with a knowing nod. "I had to be cautious. Anything I did that might link me to the Resistance would also endanger innocents, especially the children in my schools."

"What was your role in the Resistance?" asked Troi.

Heslo replied, "I was an intermediary for passing messages and other information. One of our most effective defenses was in how we organized into cells. Small groups, no more than six people in each cell. That way, if someone was captured or discovered, they could only betray a very limited number of members if questioned or tortured. I had contacts for assistance, but I just transported information from one drop point to another."

"That sounds dangerous," said Picard.

"It was. I would be alerted for a pickup, with instructions on where to deliver it. Mostly handwritten notes in one of several codes we developed over the years, but there were also occasional data rods or memory slips stolen from the Cardassians. Those were among the more valuable packets I delivered. The process could sometimes take several days, owing to the measures I took to ensure I wasn't being monitored. More quickly if time was a concern, of course, but in general I elected to move with deliberation to avoid detection."

Troi said, "I'm guessing at least some couriers were discovered."

"A few." Heslo's gaze shifted from her, and he cast a look over her shoulder as though looking for someone through one of the viewing ports. He held that look for a moment before returning his attention to the counselor. "A friend of mine . . . She was a teacher at one of the schools in our province." When he paused again, Picard saw the pain in the other man's eyes. "They came for her one day. I never saw her again. That I'm standing here talking to you is enough for me to know she never told them about me or the others in my cell. Thirteen years, and every day since then I wonder what she endured to protect me." Then his tone hardened.

"I also wonder how things might have been different if the Federation had done *anything* to help us."

The rebuke hung in the air between them for a moment. Despite his composure, there could be no mistaking the palpable grief and anger Heslo harbored. Who could blame the man for his feelings and disposition? Still, Picard sensed something else. Was it a simple desire to be heard after being forced to remain silent for so long?

"I am very sorry for your loss, Major," the captain said. "I can't begin to understand how you must feel, not just for your personal suffering but also that of all your people. I know how that must sound in light of everything that's come before, and decorum forbids me from commenting upon the decisions of my superior officers and the civilian leaders. All I can offer is that *I* am here, *now*, and it is my duty to ensure Bajoran interests are properly represented at these negotiations."

Heslo cleared his throat. "Again, I offer my apologies, Captain. I didn't come here today with the intention of speaking to you as I just did. I'm aware you took this assignment from your superiors despite your own personal history with the Cardassians. I also know you've spoken before of your feelings with respect to Bajor and the Occupation, and I've been told you personally wanted the Federation to do more. There are those among my people who won't fully grasp what that means—not without some persuasion—but I assure you I do. I'm grateful you're here now."

"No apologies, Major. Let us both look forward, together." He extended his hand, and with no small measure of relief, Heslo shook it.

The wardroom's door opened to reveal another pair of *Enterprise* security officers flanking a Cardassian dressed in the uniform of a military officer. Tall and lean, his black hair was swept back from his narrow, angular face. Dark eyes peered out from beneath his pronounced brow, sweeping the room in that manner common to seasoned, battle-tested soldiers. Picard recognized him.

"Gul Dukat," he said, clocking Heslo's own expression of surprise. It was obvious Dukat was the last individual the major expected to see. Until very recently, this officer had served as prefect overseeing the Occupation forces on Bajor and here on Terok Nor. Picard understood Dukat had been ordered back to Cardassia Prime after being relieved. On an unrelated noted, Picard marveled at Dukat's resemblance to Gul Macet, commander of a Cardassian warship the *Enterprise* had encountered two years earlier. Nechayev had confirmed the two were related in some unspecified manner.

Dukat made a show of offering a slight introductory bow at the waist. "Captain Jean-Luc Picard of the *Starship Enterprise*. This truly is a momentous occasion. Of course I'm familiar with you and your exploits going back a great many years, and now you command the pride of the Federation Starfleet." He turned to Troi. "Commander, it is a pleasure to make your acquaintance as well."

"Gul," said Troi, and Picard caught the disdain lacing just that one word. "I can sense your pleasure."

Rather than being embarrassed at her veiled callout of whatever emotional reaction he might be having, Dukat offered a wide smile. "So I've heard."

Deciding he disliked this particular Cardassian on principle, Picard forced himself to remain composed. "I was not aware you'd be attending these proceedings."

With a smug smile, Dukat replied, "I must confess I hadn't anticipated taking part, but we Cardassians are creatures of duty. We follow the orders we're given." He held out his hands in a manner Picard decided was as irritating as his smile. "Besides, how often does one get to meet a genuine hero of the Federation?"

Picard acknowledged the disingenuous comment with a polite nod. It was almost certain the withdrawal had cost Dukat standing within the Cardassian Central Command, so for what reason would he be here now? If Heslo's reaction was any indication, Dukat's presence here had been unanticipated by the Bajorans. But the confidence—even arrogance—Terok Nor's former commander exuded only solidified Picard's hunch that his joining the diplomatic entourage was a calculated decision. Someone had decided his presence might throw a measure of imbalance into the discussions, as Kalem and his delegation were forced to sit across a table from the one individual most responsible for their people's subjugation.

We'll just see about that, Picard decided.

Everyone turned at the sound of the doors opening to admit another pair of security crew members entering ahead of an older Bajoran man dressed in elaborate civilian attire consisting of a blue silk shirt under a black jacket with matching trousers. He appeared middle-aged, or at least comparable to that for a human. Thinning gray hair framed an angular face accented with deep lines and piercing blue eyes. He made eye contact with Picard.

"Captain," he said, entering the room and extending his hands. "I am Kalem Apren, first minister to the people of Bajor." With both hands he cradled Picard's own. "It is a genuine pleasure to finally meet you."

Picard replied, "The pleasure is mine, First Minister." After pausing long enough to introduce Troi, he continued, "The Federation is grateful you asked for our assistance in this matter, and I'm honored to act as their representative during these proceedings." Casting a wary eye toward Dukat, he added, "It is my hope we can address each of your concerns in a manner beneficial to all Bajorans."

Releasing Picard's hand, Kalem beheld Dukat. "So, you are the face of the Cardassian Guard for these discussions."

Affecting an air Picard suspected was well practiced, Dukat replied, "Central Command thought it appropriate I attend. They recognize my value to these negotiations."

"Perhaps they can explain it to us," said Heslo, making no effort to hide his disdain.

Rather than reply, Dukat smiled before moving away from the group toward the replicator set into a bulkhead at the room's far end. "Major, I don't suppose you remembered to stock *kanar*?"

Before Heslo could reply, Kalem chose that moment to assert his own authority. "Major, you've done a remarkable service to me, readying the venue for our discussions. I greatly appreciate your efforts and those of your staff."

With introductions complete, Picard turned to Winona Bailey, the officer assigned to lead the current security detail. "Thank you, Ensign. Your team may take your posts." In response to his command, Bailey gestured for her three companions along with the two officers already in the room to take up their assigned equidistant positions around the room's perimeter. From those points, they would be able watch over the entire room in the event anything untoward occurred. By mutual agreement, it was decided *Enterprise* security personnel would remain inside the wardroom during the discussions, after Major Heslo expressed concerns about Bajoran Militia members taking matters into their own hands with respect to the Cardassian delegation.

Heslo's communicator pendant sounded, and he tapped it. "Heslo here."

"*Major,*" said a woman's voice over the open channel. "*Enterprise security officers are escorting the rest of the Cardassian delegation to the wardroom.*"

"Understood. Thank you." Severing the connection, Heslo

turned to Kalem. "First Minister, if you'll excuse me, I'll meet the delegation outside and escort them in."

Kalem nodded, and the major exited the wardroom. The minister led the *Enterprise* officers over to a viewport. "I know we'd originally planned for the conference to take place on Bajor, Captain, but I thought it important to set a certain tone for what's to come. After decades of occupation, my people and I now find ourselves at the beginning of a new era. Before we can move forward, there are a number of issues we must navigate. I suspect the Cardassian delegation will challenge us at every turn, but it is my intention to communicate to them we are no longer their servants." He indicated the wardroom and—by extension—the rest of the station with a sweeping gesture. "Just as this station is no longer theirs to control, neither are my people or even these negotiations."

"Of course, First Minister," replied Picard. "It's my duty here to ensure both sides are heard in a manner that is constructive while ensuring your very legitimate grievances are addressed."

While he anticipated at least some parley with the Cardassians to secure any concessions, Picard had no intention of giving them any room to treat the first minister or any other Bajoran as they had during the Occupation. He knew the decision to withdraw from Bajor, coming from the Cardassian civilian leadership, had to have sent shock waves through the Occupation forces as well as their larger military apparatus. This, on top of the shame they had suffered thanks to Captain Jellico's actions during the Minos Korva incident.

Troi said, "First Minister, based on my past interactions with Cardassian negotiators, we can expect at least one member of the delegation to try demonstrating they still retain a degree of influence over your people."

"I wouldn't expect anything less, Commander," replied Kalem. "The history of each of our respective civilizations is replete with examples of former oppressors having to face reprisals from those they had once subjugated. Accountability can feel like tyranny when one has evaded the former for so long a time."

It was obvious Kalem intended to play on the new dynamic between Bajorans and Cardassians to the maximum, doubtless buoyed by knowing the Federation had a vested interest in seeing Bajor emerge from the shadow of its decades-long persecution. Bajorans waited with anticipation to see just how much the Cardassians would be held to account for their actions. Further, there were as-yet-uncounted Bajorans who had managed to escape the planet over the years, or perhaps were born elsewhere after their parents or grandparents fled to seek refuge wherever they could find it. Those people also longed to return to the world they still considered their true home.

With all of that at the forefront of his mind, Picard knew his duty was to afford Kalem the opportunity to leverage his opportunities while keeping a tight rein on the conference's direction. He was sympathetic to the first minister's position, but the captain could not allow the discussions to deteriorate to a point they no longer served a constructive purpose. Although the Cardassians may have been forced to withdraw from the Bajor sector, it would be foolish for Bajorans or the Federation to think the Cardassian Union would not continue to influence interstellar affairs in this region for the foreseeable future.

How far that influence extended might well be decided in this room.

Once more, the wardroom's doors slid aside, revealing Major Heslo. Behind him was a Cardassian male with deep lines in his face and streaks of gray highlighting his otherwise silken black hair. Unlike the cumbersome armor Picard associated with members of their military, the new arrival instead wore a dark gray suit consisting of trousers and shoes along with a jacket featuring a high collar. Given the flared neck bone structure connecting the typical Cardassian's head and shoulders, Picard found this tailoring choice unusual. So far as he could tell, the suit possessed no ornamentation or accessories of any kind. Entering behind him was a female Cardassian, dressed in a similar ensemble though her jacket's collar was low enough to expose her throat. Picard also noted she appeared much younger than her counterpart.

"Gentlemen," said Heslo. "Allow me to introduce Commissioner Wonar and Arbitrator Ilson of the Cardassian Diplomatic Service." To the Cardassians, he said, "Delegates, this is First Minister Kalem Apren, leader of the Bajoran Provisional Government, Captain Jean-Luc Picard, commanding officer of the Federation *Starship Enterprise*, and the ship's counselor, Commander Deanna Troi."

Wonar bowed his head. "It is a pleasure to meet with you today. First Minister, I offer greetings from the Detapa Council, and wish to communicate the chairman's fervent desire that these proceedings prove beneficial to both our peoples."

"Welcome to Bajor, Commissioner," said Kalem. "And to Terok Nor. It is my hope that our discussions are as amenable as they are productive."

Looking to Picard, Ilson said, "Captain, your reputation precedes you. It is an honor to make your acquaintance."

Not bloody likely. Despite the thought and being on edge thanks to Dukat, Picard forced himself to remain poised as he replied, "Thank you, Arbitrator." He gestured to Troi. "Commissioner, on behalf of Commander Troi and the United Federation of Planets, thank you for coming. It is *my* privilege to be present at what promises to be an historic occasion."

"We are still awaiting the arrival of Kai Opaka and the commander of the Bajoran Militia, Colonel Novari," said Kalem. "I believe their individual perspectives will be quite valuable during our discussions." He indicated the wardroom table where Dukat had already claimed the seat at its near end, and an elaborate bottle of dark liquid—presumably *kanar*, a popular Cardassian liquor—along with a glass. "Before we begin the official proceedings, I thought we might enjoy a first meal together, unless you prefer to dine in your quarters?" Picard was surprised by the proposal, given the first minister's earlier comments about asserting control. Could this be a ploy to place the Cardassians at ease before lowering the proverbial boom? Or perhaps Kalem was hoping to avoid a confrontation?

This should be rather interesting, he decided.

12

—

Hands clasped behind his back, Gul Havrel stood before the viewing port separating the laboratory's control room from the specimen ward. Six examination tables were arranged side by side along the wall to his left, each visible through the transparent material of their respective collapsible cleanroom shelter. Each table faced a counterpart, likewise shrouded, on the room's opposite side. Inside each shelter, computer and other equipment positioned behind the table monitored the patient lying on it. Five Cardassians, each wearing an environment suit, moved around the room, carrying padds they used to interface with the computer equipment overseeing each specimen.

Every patient was a Bajoran.

Men and women, young and old. Naked and held in place by restraints securing each limb and with another across their forehead. While a few appeared healthy—with the factors of malnutrition, dehydration, and poor hygiene considered—most suffered from a host of maladies. These ailments could be identified by variations in skin coloring or the blood exiting through every orifice. From where he stood, Havrel could see that two of the specimens, both adult males, possessed empty sockets where their eyes had been.

"An infection that feeds on ocular tissue?" asked Glinn Trina from where he stood just behind Havrel, who could hear the apprehension in the younger officer's voice.

"To begin with," replied Havrel, recalling the same report

his second-in-command had to read prior to their arrival. "Eyes, along with other soft tissue and cartilage. That usually means ears and noses, along with other . . . external anatomy . . . before attacking internal organs. The heart and brain seem to be the most resistant, at least in Bajorans. There hasn't been an opportunity to test the protocol on other species, but I'm told that is being considered once our relocation efforts are completed."

Trina asked, "Are we safe?"

"Relax, my friend," said Havrel. "There are four redundant safeguards in the event of a breach." Then, because he could not resist, he turned from the viewing port and added, "Besides, if anything does get out, there's a self-destruct system in place that will destroy everyone and everything in this entire cavern. You'll never feel a thing."

His expression turning apprehensive, Trina replied, "That is . . . reassuring."

That evoked a laugh from Havrel before he returned his attention to the laboratory. "Worry not, Trina. Once the doctors in there finish collecting their final data, this room and all of its contents are scheduled for sterilization. It will likely be completed before midday."

"We're not taking the . . . specimens with us?" asked Trina.

Havrel shook his head. "No. The research teams have gathered as much useful information as they can from this group. The test conditions under which they've been operating can be re-created easily enough. Besides, there are the obvious safety and security concerns to consider." He gestured to the viewing port. "We certainly don't want anything like this getting out prematurely." When Trina said nothing, he turned to his deputy. "Something about this troubles you?"

Looking around the room as though to ensure their conversation was not being overheard, the glinn replied, "Gul, I understand why weapons of this sort are created, and that they represent an added layer of security for the Cardassian people. However, I've seen how you treat other Bajorans. You are generous, even kind. You are not like other senior officers with whom I've served, and I admit I find that sort of benevolence . . . refreshing."

"You wonder how I'm able to do that while overseeing experiments like these," said Havrel. When Trina nodded, he added, "For me, the distinction is simple. The people in the room before you are either criminals or were already diagnosed with terminal medical conditions."

Trina asked, "They volunteered to be test subjects?"

"Of course not." Havrel almost laughed at the younger officer's naïveté. "They simply were of no other use. Why waste already limited resources feeding and housing them when they can instead provide a greater service?" Turning from the port, he left the laboratory technicians to their work and headed into the connecting hallway as Trina followed him. "Verify with the research teams that they remain on schedule. Our preparations for departure must be completed within the next five days." According to the communiqué he received this morning, a flotilla of transport vessels was being dispatched; they were coming from Cardassia Prime. The next several days would not be restful.

And once we've completed those tasks with such hurried determination, he thought, *we will stand by and wait for the wheels of leadership and bureaucracy to turn ever so slowly.*

Trina fell into step next to Havrel as he exited the passage and into the larger cavern that housed the bulk of the underground facility's footprint. "It will be done, Gul. All sections report they are also on schedule."

"This includes the genetic research teams?" asked Havrel.

"As they were the smallest group and with the least amount

of equipment and staff," replied Trina, "their preparation efforts are nearly complete."

Noticing the glinn's pause, Havrel prompted, "And their test subjects?"

The younger officer cleared his throat. "Already eliminated, Prefect."

"It's for the best," replied Havrel. "Theirs is a controversial field of study." Genetic manipulation and engineering had long been a subject of great contention among different interstellar communities. The aim was to find a way to enhance and improve the quality of life for Cardassian people, but experimenting on non-Cardassian subjects would of course invite denunciation in the strongest terms. The Federation would be an outspoken critic. Its banning of the practice predated even that august body's founding. Havrel knew the consistency with which it observed, circumvented, or even outright ignored such laws was at best selective. Still, such hypocrisy would not stop Federation leaders from denouncing the practice. That the test subjects participated without their consent made the situation even more difficult.

These are the concerns of my superiors, thought Havrel, though he was well aware exposure of this facility and its activities would implicate him as much, if not more so, than those whose orders he followed.

"What of the military weapons group?" he asked.

Trina replied, "Also on schedule, Prefect."

Havrel nodded, satisfied for the moment. In addition to their computer and holographic equipment, the weapons research team also had several prototypes in varying stages of development and construction. None of the weapons could be tested here. Exercises would take place at other locations far from this world; distant, uninhabited planets and moons where the results of their testing could remain undetected. Several weapons outlawed, or at least viewed with disdain by a number of adversarial powers, remained on-site. The existence of three weapons—subspace mines and two different mass-dispersal biowarfare agents—were outlawed by many interstellar rivals.

The weapons, along with the teams responsible for their creation, would be the first things transported to the evacuation fleet. There was no doubting the Federation would take an interest in their activities if they ever came to light. If all went according to the plans of those in the leadership, the Federation and others might well experience firsthand the effects of such weapons.

Again, those are not my concern, he reminded himself. *For now, I have but one mission.*

The two officers said nothing more about the work taking place in the cavern as they returned to Havrel's office via the hidden transporter alcove. Exiting the camp through the perimeter fence and returning to his home, Havrel directed Trina to an empty chair positioned before his desk before signaling his assistant, Zajan, that he would be expecting his midday meal in short order.

"Prefect," said Trina after he had settled into his chair. "I have done my own calculations, and I believe the transports' maximum speed indicates they won't arrive here until several days later than previously estimated."

Havrel could not help the laugh that escaped his lips. "If there's anything from which one can take comfort, it's the consistency and the unerring inefficiency of the Central Command."

His second-in-command seemed taken aback by the comment. "With all due respect, sir, should one not exercise caution when making such statements? The Central Command's reach is very long, as is that of the Obsidian Order."

"On that, we agree," said Havrel. "But I think they would deem this planet unworthy of their time and attention. Indeed, if the council had not elected to withdraw from Bajor and sever all connections to the Bajorans—the publicly acknowledged ones— it is entirely likely you and I might have remained here, all but forgotten." He turned to face his second-in-command. "But that is the price exacted for carrying out one's sworn duty."

That seemed to put Trina at ease, and the young officer nodded in apparent agreement. "I do *feel* similar frustration from time to time, Gul. However, I also feel I have not earned the right to express such opinions aloud. After all, I do not wish an errant comment, spoken in a moment of frustration or simple exhaustion, to be interpreted as disloyalty."

Havrel smiled, reminded of Trina's short duration of service. He had not yet had sufficient time to acquire the cynicism of veteran soldiers such as himself.

"My young friend, there are many things you learn once you are far from military academies and books filled with customs, courtesies, and protocols to be observed lest one demonstrate a monumental disrespect toward our long history and enduring traditions." Rising from his chair, Havrel held up his hand and pointed to the ceiling. "Keep this in mind: There has never been a Cardassian who wore the uniform of our military who did not indulge in the time-honored practice of complaining about those over them. It is the soldier's inalienable right to espouse such objections. Of course, they must also learn to exercise sound judgment when giving voice to such grievances."

Now it was Trina's turn to smile, and the glinn even laughed. "Another lesson not taught at the academy."

"Indeed." Settling back into his seat, Havrel directed his second-in-command to follow suit. Both officers had been here since well before sunrise, coordinating their efforts to oversee the preparations for withdrawing assets still located far beneath the camp. There remained much to do.

The door to his office slid aside to reveal Ijok, carrying a tray with a covered dish. Havrel waved her in, and Trina understood his time with the gul was at an end for the time being. Rising from his chair, the glinn regarded his superior officer.

"I will provide an updated status later today, Prefect," he said, and Havrel noted how he couched his statements while the Bajoran woman was in earshot.

"Excellent. Thank you, Trina."

As Trina exited the room, leaving Havrel alone with Ijok as she placed the tray near his desk, he could not help asking her, "My dear, would you say you are treated well?" The woman froze while standing within his reach, her expression betraying her uncertainty for a fleeting moment, and he guessed she wondered whether this might be some form of verbal trap. "Do not be afraid. I am genuinely curious."

She seemed to steel herself before answering, "Yes, Prefect. I am treated well. Thank you for asking."

"Given a choice of returning to your homeworld or remaining in my employ," he said, "which would you choose?" As he spoke, he could not resist tracing his finger along that portion of her forearm left exposed by her tunic's shortened sleeves. "What if I told you I could promise you a life of comfort, free from the trappings of this place or anything like it, and all I would ask in return is that you serve me with the same loyalty you've always shown?"

It was not a noble question. One of the thoughts that had plagued him since receiving the relocation order from Central Command was what to do with his collection of Bajoran artifacts and the cadre of Bajoran women in his immediate employ. If the council's directive to return the art and sculptures was absolute, perhaps they might allow him to keep Ijok and the others?

No links to this place, he reminded himself. *A pity.*

Clearing her throat, Ijok said, "I've never seen Bajor, Gul. All I've known is this life. You've treated me . . . very well from the first day I came to work for you. I'm grateful you consider me worthy of the honor you propose."

Havrel saw the tremble in her slight form, and understood it. While others might enjoy playing cruel mental games with the laborers in their charge, it had never been something that appealed to him. He recognized the bravery this woman showed with her honest answers to his questions. It was just one of her many qualities he found alluring.

"Tell Zajan I'd like to see you after I finish my meal," he said, having no need to explain further. He knew the head housekeeper would ensure Ijok was ready when he called on her. "And think about what I've asked you. We can discuss it later."

Fatigue beginning to take hold of him, Trina entered his private quarters and allowed the door to close behind him. Only then did he allow himself to breathe a sigh of relief. The scenes to which he had borne witness in the underground cavern lingered. What troubled him was not the cruelty visited upon those Bajorans unfortunate enough to serve as test subjects, but instead the casual indifference with which Havrel and others seemed to regard the entire affair. That it was wrapped in a veneer of concern for the security of the Cardassian people unsettled him.

Was this the level to which a great society had fallen? Trina did not consider himself naïve or a fool. He understood the need to exhibit strength and supremacy in the face of those who would undermine the Cardassian way of life. What he had observed— was it a sign of strength or something far more sinister?

Then there was Gul Havrel, who seemed determined to exist within a body of ethics that was fluid at best. In other officers, Trina might have attributed Havrel's actions to ambition, but it was not that simple. The gul was as concerned about his personal status as he was the successful relocation of the facility hidden deep beneath the camp. Aside from the few Bajorans who worked in his home, he seemed ambivalent toward the rest of them in his charge.

Trina did not consider himself an expert on interstellar law or even the laws of the Detapa Council. It seemed to him as though its directive and Havrel's intentions were in conflict. The order to return or release all Bajorans and their cultural property seemed simple, with no room for interpretation. Did the "Cradis protocols" mentioned in the message received by Havrel provide cover for deviations from what appeared to be explicit instructions? The gul believed it did, or was that merely his own interpretation? By following Havrel's orders, was Trina obeying the law, or breaking it?

This was far too much for a junior officer to consider, he decided.

He was in the midst of removing his uniform's heavy armored tunic, leaving him still clad in his form-fitting black undershirt, when his door chime sounded. Setting the tunic on the small desk that served as his quarters' workspace, he called out, "Enter."

The door slid aside to reveal Nesha standing in the corridor. As was normal for the Bajoran, he wore a brown tunic and matching pants, doubtless crafted from whatever material was supplied to the laborers. At first glance, he appeared plain and unremarkable, with his hair kept back from his face and held in place by a dark band. Trina noted he was carrying a basket with the items he often used to clean his quarters and those of his fellow officers.

Trina saw past all of that.

"Good afternoon, sir," said Nesha in greeting as he awaited permission to enter. "I didn't realize you would be here at this time of day." He indicated his basket. "I'm scheduled to clean your quarters now, but I can come back when I'm not disturbing you."

Trina smiled, recognizing the attempt at formality for the sake of others, Cardassians and Bajorans alike, who might hear him. "No, do it now so you won't disturb me later."

Stepping inside, Nesha allowed the door to close behind him before placing the basket on the floor near the room's front wall. "I apologize for the confusion, sir."

"Not your fault," he said, turning back to his desk. "I did not expect to be here." His computer workstation's screen was deactivated, and there were no padds or other sources of information that might be compromised by unauthorized access. Stepping closer, he made a casual motion to ensure the drawer was locked, and verified the control pad in the desktop was deactivated. There was nothing here for him to hide from curious eyes; no clues about any of the work he still needed to complete.

"Where should I begin?"

Nesha was standing just behind him. Trina felt hands begin to slide around his torso, before moving under his shirt to rest against his skin. He closed his eyes and released a contented sigh, allowing himself to relax against the body pressing into his back.

Work could wait.

13

—

Arvada III.

It was Beverly Crusher's first thought as the transporter beam released her and she beheld the surface of Bajor. Gone was the cool, computer-controlled environment of the *Enterprise*, replaced by a warm breeze wafting across the forested glade before her. Situated on a rise forming a bend in the Yolja River, the area offered a view of the fast-moving water; Crusher could hear it playing off rocks partially submerged in the river. Trees flanked the clearing in the other directions, tall enough that their canopies provided partial cover from the midday sun.

What should have been a scene of utter tranquility was one of despair and sadness as the doctor's gaze fell upon the site of the makeshift field hospital.

It was almost like a memory emerging from the depths of her mind and given worldly form. At least, that was the sensation washing over her. Three large tents sat at the center of the haphazard formation of prefabricated as well as pop-up emergency shelters, cargo containers, and other detritus at the improvised encampment. Most of what Crusher saw carried a Starfleet insignia stenciled or otherwise emblazoned somewhere, but there also were boxes and crates marked with Bajoran symbols and text. Farther downstream, Crusher's eyes followed a trail through the trees to another, larger clearing where even more of the temporary shelters stood or were in the process of being erected.

Bajorans as well as others in Starfleet uniforms moved with

varying degrees of purpose between both areas, and down the trail connecting them. From one of the tents, two Bajorans wearing medical smocks carried a stretcher between them, transporting a patient to one of the adjacent tents. No sooner were they clear of the opening than a second pair of orderlies bearing a litter of their own moved another patient into the tent. Crusher could sense a pall of tension, anxiety, and even pain lingering in the air around the camp. Watching the activity around her, she could not keep visions of a similar settlement from rushing to the forefront of her mind.

A decrepit shelter, now serving as a first-aid station. People lying on cots and stretchers or just on the floor, others sitting beside them or hovering over them in a bid to render help. Moans and other sounds of suffering, overwhelming in the confined space.

Beverly, a mere child, running to keep up with Felisa Howard, her maternal grandmother, as the woman rushed between patients trying to assist those who called out. The precious few doctors are overwhelmed.

"Beverly." Nana is calling her, reaching with an outstretched hand. "Come here." Her grandmother is handing her a bandage and directing her to stand by her side. "Place the thick part on his leg, and tie it the way I showed you."

Small hands trembling, Beverly does as instructed, wincing as the man on the cot grunts in pain as the bandage tightens around his leg. A red stain appears in the middle of the cloth, already growing in size as she finishes tying the knot.

"Nana," she says. "What about the skin healer?" She makes a gesture with her hand, mimicking her holding the device she's seen her grandmother use to fix cuts and bruises when Beverly hurts herself while playing.

Working on another bandage she's affixing to the hurt man's stomach, Nana replies, "There aren't enough of them to go around, sweetheart. We just have to make do until it's our turn."

"Can we give him something to help him feel better?" Beverly asks when the man moans again. "Medicine?"

A frown turns down the corners of Nana's mouth. "There isn't enough of that either." Then she looks up. "Remember those blue and purple plants I have growing in my garden? On the trellis, with the long stems and seven petals? They smell like lemon?"

"I thought the yellow ones smelled like lemon," Beverly says, but Nana shakes her head.

"Not those. Don't touch those without gloves, honey. Just the purple ones. Run back to the house and bring as many as you can. Bring them all, along with my bag with the other herbs and plants I picked this morning. Run, Beverly, as quick as you can."

With purpose, Beverly runs out of the tent, past the hurt people waiting to be helped. Friends from school. Their parents. That nice old man who lets her pick tangerines from the tree in his backyard and is now holding a bloody rag to his head. His wife, crying. She can't—

"Doctor Crusher?"

Startled from her reverie and annoyed for allowing the momentary distraction, she turned to see Ensign Alyssa Ogawa regarding her with a concerned expression. She doubtless had noted the way the doctor had frozen after getting her first look at the camp.

Not the first time you've seen this, Crusher chided herself. Focus.

"I'm sorry, Alyssa. I was just . . ." Crusher stopped as she caught sight of the other nurses and orderlies from her staff who had accompanied her to the surface. Directed by Nurse Ogawa, they were proceeding toward the aid station. Shaking her head, Crusher cleared her throat.

"Old memories."

Nodding in understanding, Ogawa asked, "Childhood memories?" The nurse knew her; there would be no fooling her. Crusher had told her about living on Arvada III, along with some—but not all—of the struggles they had faced on that ill-fated colony world. It had been her maternal grandmother, who had adopted her after she lost her parents, trying to forge a life on a world far away from the bustle of Earth and other Federation worlds. For a time, it was an idyllic place to live, play, and grow up, and Nana had been at the center of it all. The few memories Crusher retained of her mother and father were faint and fleeting, but Felisa Howard had always been a steadfast presence in her life.

That reminds me, Crusher mused. *I need to send her a message. It's been too long. Even longer since I last visited.*

The Caldos colony, where she and Nana had relocated after escaping Arvada III, was still the elder Howard's home, but it was not in the *Enterprise*'s assigned sector. Traveling home to see her grandmother would require an extended leave for Crusher to make the journey and be able to stay and enjoy herself. The thought was indeed appealing, but such things would have to wait. More pressing concerns demanded her attention.

With Ogawa walking beside her, Crusher made her way to what she figured to be the provisional hospital's main area. There were both Bajorans and Starfleet personnel coming and going from the tents and adjacent prefab huts, including members of her team who had already thrown themselves into the fray. They moved with an unmistakable urgency, but there was something off about the scene before her. She saw no bloodied wounded waiting on stretchers or sitting or lying on the ground outside the aid station, and no nurses or orderlies racing between waiting patients while assessing their condition. She knew the medical team here was facing not combat wounded but simpler maladies. Here were Bajorans and Starfleet engaged in the time-honored practice of caring for the sick and injured, and there did not appear to be any pressing or catastrophic injuries requiring transport to sickbay.

Small favors, Crusher decided.

As she and Ogawa approached what was labeled as a command post, the heavy curtain serving as a door moved aside and a lean Denobulan male stepped outside. He wore a black Starfleet utility jumpsuit with blue shoulders and the rank pips of a commander. His long brown and gray hair was pulled back from his face and secured in a ponytail. He paused seeing Crusher and Ogawa, and when he smiled his narrow face seemed to stretch and widen.

"Doctor Crusher?" he asked. When she nodded in reply he extended his hand. "I'm Doctor Tropp from the *Oceanside*. Your reputation precedes you. I'm happy to finally meet you in person."

Shaking his hand, Crusher introduced Ogawa before gesturing to the hospital tent. "You've already met some of my people."

"They didn't waste any time getting to work," replied Tropp. "We can worry about getting to know each other better if we get a chance, later on."

Ogawa said, "Doctor, your team seems to work fast. You did all of this in just the past three hours?"

Again, Tropp's face spread into a wide smile. "That's what we do, Ensign. The *Oceanside*'s mission profile is designed around fast action. Get in, get it done, and get out. Hopefully, we'll leave things better than we found them." His expression turned more somber. "We're normally sent in to follow up after first contact.

So, we're usually the first beings a newly contacted civilization sees when they're introduced to the technology and other materials we've been authorized to share." He waved a hand to indicate the camp. "Then there are the less pleasant assignments."

Crusher and Ogawa followed Tropp as he led the way to the larger tent at the center of the compound. "I have teams at three other locations, setting up sites like this one at or near what was until recently forced-labor camps." He pointed to a low rise behind the thicket of trees and the other set of shelters being constructed there. "The Abonti camp is farther down the river. We opted to put our command post here, upriver, because there's a lot of runoff from the camp's water and waste-extraction systems. The Cardassians didn't put a high priority on their environmental impact."

"I've read the reports," said Crusher as they approached the tent. "When you're strip-mining the planet for anything and everything you can carve out of it, fresh air and water fall by the wayside."

"Are you using the old labor camps?" asked Ogawa.

Slowing to a stop, Tropp turned and nodded. "Unfortunately, yes. Housing. There are thousands of Bajorans without homes. Those the Cardassians labeled as criminals made up the bulk of the camps. Cardassians employ a very broad means of defining lawbreakers, and those sentenced to the camps lost everything. Relocating and resettling everyone will take months if not longer, but for now the camps are better than nothing. The Starfleet Corps of Engineers will be sending ships and detachments to help with rehabilitating homes and villages around the planet, or creating new settlements. Whatever it takes, for however long it takes." He smiled again. "Part of me wishes I was still an engineer so I could hang around and help with that."

Crusher asked, "You were an engineer?"

"Oh, yes," said Tropp. "But it was long before either of you were even born. I joined Starfleet as an engineer, and along the way I received training as a medic. The ship I served on was sent on missions where help from Starfleet Command or other ships wasn't an option. It was while helping with a humanitarian aid mission that I realized I preferred medicine to engineering. I changed specialties and went back to school. Got my medical degree in 2278 and have been practicing ever since."

"You have to love that Denobulan life span," said Ogawa.

Tropp replied, "One hundred eighty-four, next month."

They continued to the aid tent and Tropp pulled aside the door flap, holding it for Crusher and Ogawa to pass through. Inside were four rows of cots running the length of the shelter, twelve to a row. Every cot was occupied, along with an additional bed tucked into each of the four corners. Nearly every patient appeared swaddled in bedclothes, and Crusher saw many of the cots had been fitted with portable warming units. Behind each patient's head was a small, field-deployable version of the medical monitors used in the *Enterprise* sick bay. Moving between the different beds were members of Tropp's team as well as several Bajorans, most of them wearing some version of medical smock or overalls.

"We were told you were dealing with a lot of patients," said Crusher. "The reports indicated a variety of injuries sustained either from working in the camps or abuse by the Cardassians. And a form of blood poisoning?"

Tropp gestured toward the patient ward. "At first we were getting patients from all over. We established a routine, sending the physical injuries and other non-life-threatening cases to other sites, and those presenting with the infection are here." As though reading the meaning behind Crusher's and Ogawa's troubled expressions, he added, "Whatever it is, it's not contagious. We ruled that out right away."

Allowing herself a sigh of relief, Crusher asked, "You're saying you still haven't identified it?"

"Not yet." He motioned for them to follow him as he cut a path between the first two rows of cots. "We think it's ingested, something in the food or water. We're just getting started on identifying a source." As they passed from cot to cot, Tropp indicated different patients. "The Bajorans who set up this camp were inundated with patients from all over the place. Different camps, different provinces, so we're not sure where exactly to start looking."

Ogawa said, "It could be from any or all of the camps."

"Or none," replied Tropp. "It's an alkaloid poisoning of some kind. Its effect on a person's bloodstream is dramatic, but whatever's causing it has eluded us."

Crusher paused at one cot near the end of the second row, stepping around its portable monitor to study its readings. The first thing she looked for confirmed her suspicions about the warming units even though the outside temperature was mild and it was stuffy here in the tent.

"Reduced body temperature," she said. "Almost hypothermic. That's a definite symptom of some forms of alkaloid poisoning. Elevated heart rate? Even for a Bajoran these readings are troubling."

Moving to stand next to her, Ogawa pointed to another reading. "Dehydration and what looks like borderline malnutrition."

Tropp said, "Many patients can't hold down any food, and some are expelling waste at an alarming rate. We're trying to compensate with intravenous fluids and dietary supplements administered directly to the stomach. It's an uphill battle, but we're finally starting to gain some traction. We've been analyzing blood samples from every patient to see if any of our traditional blood-poisoning remedies can treat it, but so far we've had no success."

Ogawa asked, "It's only affecting Bajorans?"

"Yes," replied Tropp. "No humans or Denobulans are at risk. We're still screening other species based on who's down here from the *Oceanside*, and we'll expand that to include the *Enterprise* teams."

"If it's something in the food or water," said Crusher, "we need to isolate that."

"Agreed. We've placed a moratorium on all water sources and any food native to the planet. Crews up on the *Oceanside* are replicating food and beaming down field rations and replicators as fast as they can."

"We can help with that," said Ogawa. "I'll notify the *Enterprise* to coordinate with the *Oceanside*'s captain and see what they need from our end."

Crusher asked, "Have you started backtracking these patients to see where they came from?" As Tropp nodded, she waved away her own question. "If it's a contaminant, we'll have to check them all, just to be safe. Start with the camps, and move to nearby villages and provinces." Then, remembering what Tropp had said before, she pointed downriver. "Water and waste treatment facilities. It could be something there."

"Exactly my thinking," said Tropp. "We just didn't have the people to do all of that while helping establish shelters and field hospitals along with treating patients."

Turning over all of the competing priorities in her mind, Crusher was organizing her action plan. Tropp was on the right track, but needed more hands on deck to attack the problem from different points. The *Enterprise* crew could do that. She needed to brief Captain Picard and get his approval, but she knew he would place his full faith in her proposed actions.

"All right, then," she said. "Let's get to work."

14

—

"... we have endeavored to adhere to the directives as put forth by the Detapa Council and the Central Command," said Commissioner Wonar. "Our forces on Bajor are continuing to withdraw our people and equipment as quickly as possible. We have done our part to honor the terms, but your people are determined to frustrate our efforts."

Picard studied Wonar, who sat at the wardroom table's far end. At the other end, First Minister Kalem had listened with rapt attention to the Cardassian delegate for the twenty-five minutes it took for him to recite his list of grievances, real and imagined. This gave Picard ample opportunity to study the conference participants. Counselor Troi was on his right, and Kalem on his left. Kai Opaka Sulan, Bajor's acknowledged spiritual leader, was seated across from him. In keeping with the tenets of her faith, she wore formal robes of a silklike purple fabric, accented with a brightly colored sash hanging from her left shoulder. Her hair and the sides of her head were concealed beneath an elaborate headpiece made from the same material as her robes, leaving only her ears visible, and the ornamental *D'ja pagh* affixed to her right ear. Next to Kai Opaka was Colonel Novari Jahn, commander of the Bajoran Militia. Across from the Bajorans at Wonar's end of the table were Arbitrator Ilson and Gul Dukat.

"Agents of the resistance element which has acted with near impunity for years continue to harass our soldiers," droned Wonar. "Meanwhile, you seek yet more concessions, as your militia continues to hold innocent Cardassians in custody, First Minister. We cannot have a constructive dialogue while this and other provocations continue. Would you not agree this must be discussed first?"

Kalem had remained silent, never once attempting to raise an objection or question a single point Wonar presented. Only now, when the commissioner appeared to have finished this latest soliloquy, did the minister speak.

"No."

The blunt reply elicited an audible gasp from Arbitrator Ilson, causing Picard to glance in her direction. This allowed him to catch Gul Dukat's faint sardonic grin. It lasted a heartbeat before the Cardassian schooled his features.

Clearing his throat as he glared at Ilson, Wonar asked, "Minister?"

"I said no, Commissioner. Your concerns are worthy of discussion, and we'll get to them in due course. On the matter of persons being held, I wish to remind you of the need to ascertain to the greatest extent possible the current status of all Bajoran citizens in Cardassian custody on worlds other than Bajor. We know that many have been taken over the course of the Occupation, forced to labor for your people's various ends."

Ilson replied, "We are aware of your wishes on this matter, First Minister, but given the amount of time that's passed, I should advise you that it will be difficult."

"I've observed Cardassians to be fastidious recordkeepers," said Kalem. "I understand your hesitation. We realize a great many of these unfortunate souls are likely dead. However, completing such an accounting is one of our priorities. There are far too many families on Bajor with unanswered questions about loved ones, and only the Cardassians can provide the answers."

"I can forward this matter to our superiors," said Wonar.

"Perhaps Central Command can offer insight into this matter." To Picard, the offer sounded sincere. "In the meantime, what of our people who remain in detention?"

Kalem replied, "Those members of the Occupation forces currently in custody are being treated far better than any Bajoran prisoner who lived under Cardassian rule. They will continue in our custody until I deem it appropriate to transfer them to your care."

Wonar's dissatisfaction was evident, and the captain half expected the commissioner to launch himself at the first minister. Instead, he coolly asked, "May we know the nature of the offenses these individuals allegedly committed?"

"They were apprehended for not adhering to the directives put forth by your council and the Central Command. Namely, plundering Bajoran personal property as well as significant cultural items."

In a most condescending tone, Ilson asked, "Can you be more specific?"

Kai Opaka quietly replied, "Family heirlooms and other items of personal value. Art, sculpture, historical documents and artifacts. Since the earliest days of the Occupation, irreplaceable treasures have long been taken at the whims of our former oppressors. Many of your people act as if they were entitled to loot and pillage Bajor one final time."

Leaning forward in his seat, Dukat said, "What you describe are the unsanctioned actions of willful individuals intent on personal enrichment."

"As *you* say," Kalem replied. "Others are in custody for the violence they carried out against Bajoran citizens."

"I'm sure they acted in self-defense," said Dukat. "I've seen reports of citizens attempting to take the law into their own hands, hoping to exact retribution for perceived slights."

"Perceived slights?" Colonel Novari grunted in obvious contempt. "An interesting turn of phrase." To Picard, he pointed out, "Cardassians have elevated euphemisms to high art, Captain."

Dukat replied, "Every story has two sides, Colonel. The simple fact is nothing in the council's orders or instructions from Central Command endorses such actions. Whatever offenses those in custody supposedly committed, they were undertaken without the consent of their superiors."

"As presented," said Opaka, "that statement is true. Consenting to their illegal activities would be a hazardous practice. One cannot deny the actions undertaken before our eyes, and I'm not talking about today or the past few days, Gul Dukat. We are on a space station your people put above my world for the sole purpose of expediting the exploitation of Bajor. This is not a perceived slight, Dukat. Do not dishonor those who lived and died under you by pretending you have no idea what I'm talking about."

Rather than appearing upset, Dukat regarded her with cool detachment. "Are you implying the Central Command, or perhaps even the council, approves of what you're insinuating?"

"I thought I made it clear I wasn't insinuating anything," said Opaka, and Picard watched her eyes harden. "With the exception of First Minister Kalem, you and I know better than anyone in this room the fluid nature of your relationship with the truth." She paused, her eyes moving to Wonar and Ilson before adding, "I hope this isn't indicative of how these discussions will be conducted."

Picard stood up. "I believe a brief recess is in order. We've been here a while, and we still have a great deal to discuss. It's in *all* our interests that we remain focused." Looking between Kalem and Wonar, he asked, "Gentlemen?"

The Cardassian diplomat's jaw tightened before he nodded. "Yes, Captain. That is acceptable."

"Yes, Captain," added Kalem. "A most excellent idea."

After agreeing to resume the talks in twenty minutes, Wonar and Ilson, under escort from two *Enterprise* security officers, proceeded from the wardroom to other quarters that had been set aside for their personal use. Rather than accompanying them, Dukat remained at the table until they were gone, then with a silent smirk, he rose and crossed to the table of food and beverages at the room's far end.

Unbelievable arrogance, Picard decided, watching as a pair of security guards remained nearby, staying close but trying not to appear obvious they were there to keep watch on the Cardassian.

Standing at the head of the table, First Minister Kalem said, "I apologize for my temper, Captain. I said I would not allow the Cardassian delegation to thwart our attempts to speak to our concerns, but I did hope the conversation would remain constructive."

"They're seasoned diplomats, First Minister," replied Picard. "Doubtless accustomed to exchanges, heated and otherwise." After glancing to where Dukat busied himself at the refreshments table, he added in a lower voice, "Remember, they have orders from their superiors. They've been instructed on what they will agree to, as has been decided by the Detapa Council. Don't expect them to make it easy. They'll huff and growl, but they know the Federation will hold them to account."

Keeping his voice low, Kalem replied, "I'm quite familiar with the Cardassian propensity for dramatic flair, Captain. That includes Dukat."

The captain glanced past the first minister to where the gul, glass in hand, was now moving to the viewing port at the room's far corner. Dukat took up a position before the window and appeared to contemplate the passing view of Bajor as Terok Nor rotated on its axis. Watching this unfold, Picard wondered if the act was deliberate. Based on what he knew of Cardassian physiology, their hearing was no sharper than other humanoid species, and less acute than humans and Bajorans. This, too, could be an element of whatever he was trying to affect.

"He worries you," said Kalem. "I have experience with Dukat. I learned to be wary whenever he was around. He used to present himself as a benevolent ruler, but make no mistake; he is as ruthless as every other Cardassian. Perhaps even more so."

A recent memory welled up inside him, and Picard forced it down. "I've . . . met a few Cardassians. They are formidable adversaries, but we must not lose sight of the goal. With all due respect, First Minister, my job is to see to it the Bajoran people endure no further maltreatment, from Gul Dukat or anyone else. I have no desire to undermine your authority, sir, but we must do what is necessary to keep these negotiations productive."

For the first time, Kalem offered a small, knowing smile. "I appreciate your candor, Captain. I think I can sympathize with your difficulties. I was afraid you might attempt to take over the negotiations rather than act as the mediator you've been to this point, which is why I was more forceful with my remarks in the beginning. I did not expect you to exercise such restraint. You possess many admirable qualities, including integrity. Many Bajorans have come to believe that is not a Federation trait."

"I would hope to prove them wrong, sir," said Picard.

Kalem regarded him for another moment before replying, "Achieving that will be a challenge, but I believe you could prove me . . . prove all of us wrong." Then his eyes narrowed. "Start with Kai Opaka."

Across the room, Picard saw Opaka engaged in a quiet conversation with Counselor Troi. He indicated to Troi with a nod, and she excused herself. As she walked toward him, Picard watched the Bajoran religious leader look around the wardroom.

Her gaze lingered a moment on Dukat with what Picard took to be derision before exiting the room.

An excellent strategy, Picard mused, wishing he could avail himself of a similar maneuver.

"Captain?" asked Troi as she approached.

"Counselor," Picard spoke in a low voice, "what is your assessment of our progress? How are our guests feeling?"

Matching his volume, Troi replied, "The commissioner and arbitrator are very confident. They've managed to parse their words so they don't come across as lying. But I can sense something else. I don't know that I'd call it deception, but there is an intent to manipulate the discussions."

"I'd be surprised if they didn't know of your abilities." The Cardassians would be aware of her due to the recent run-in with the *Enterprise* and discussions with Captain Jellico in which she had taken part. Neither Wonar nor Ilson had made a point of mentioning it, which was interesting, but Picard chalked it up to a larger strategy being employed by the Cardassian delegates.

"What about Gul Dukat?" he asked, glancing to where the former prefect stood at the viewing port.

Troi frowned. "Definitely conflicting emotions. The confidence and arrogance we all see feel normal for him. He's comfortable being in control, and presents himself in that way even if it eludes him. He's putting on a front of self-assuredness, but I feel a sensation of disgrace. He doesn't want to be here."

"You're an empath," said Kalem. "Are you able to get all of that just from being in the same room with him?"

Shaking her head, Troi replied, "No, First Minister. It's partially a reading of his emotions, but Starfleet was able to provide information about Dukat and his time as prefect. Based on their assessment, the current circumstances have undoubtedly cost him standing with the Cardassian Central Command."

"And yet they sent him to participate in these negotiations," said Picard.

"His presence is sure to unsettle some of the Bajorans on the station," Troi offered. "I spoke with Mister Odo, the station security chief. He told me there were several Bajorans who saw him arrive. If there was one person the Bajorans would want to see brought to justice, it's Dukat."

Picard noticed the gul appearing to appraise Troi from across the room. Dukat's expression was neutral, but there could be no mistaking the manner in which he looked at her. Picard felt his bile rising at the casual disrespect shown toward a member of his crew. Then Dukat caught the captain's hard glare and held up his glass before returning his attention to the window and its view of the world beyond the station. Only then did Picard close his eyes.

"'O gentle son, upon the heat and flame of thy distemper, sprinkle cool patience.'"

"Captain?"

It was Troi, and Picard's eyes snapped open. Only then did he realize he had spoken the *Hamlet* quote aloud. How had he allowed his emotions to control him to such an extent? Shaking off the momentary lapse, he cleared his throat.

"My apologies, Counselor." Dismissing the last of his errant thoughts, he said, "Please notify Lieutenant Worf to work with Major Heslo about increasing our security coverage on the Promenade. I don't wish to overburden him, but we need to maintain order during these discussions." He knew the major as well as the station's interesting, enigmatic security chief, Odo, were concerned about someone seizing an opportunity to seek vengeance against Dukat or any Cardassian. They had already instituted protocols that kept all but authorized personnel away from this area of the station. An enhanced Starfleet presence in the station's main thoroughfares would help to mitigate any potential risk.

Picard heard the wardroom doors open behind him, and he saw Troi's eyes widen.

"Captain—" she began, before another voice interrupted her.

"Captain Picard, how wonderful it is to see you again."

The words, that tone—*that voice*—cut into him with the speed and precision of a finely honed blade. Before he even realized that he was moving, Picard turned. Every fiber of his being screamed to do anything but stand here in this room.

Accompanied by two *Enterprise* security officers, Gul Madred stood smiling at him.

No, Picard corrected himself as he noted the new insignia on Madred's uniform, identifying him as a legate. A promotion.

"What is the meaning of this?" asked Dukat, stepping away from the port and striding toward the legate. "Madred? Why was I not informed you would be joining us?"

Picard felt his heart racing. His mouth had gone dry. With his hands behind his back, he clenched them into fists. He willed himself not to react in any outward manner at the new arrival. Only his eyes moved, tracking Madred as the legate entered the room. For the first time, Picard realized he was taller and more muscular than Dukat. They wore identical uniforms, but there was no mistaking Madred was the senior officer. Picard's eyes met his, and Madred held the captain's gaze even as he spoke to his fellow Cardassian.

"I'm a soldier, Dukat," he said, in that aloof manner Picard remembered so well. "I go where I'm told. I was ordered to assist in the important work taking place here." Then came that sinister smile Picard still saw in his nightmares as Madred stepped up to him and Kalem. "Imagine my surprise, Captain, when I learned you were overseeing these negotiations on behalf of the Federation."

Picard, fighting to maintain his bearing, said nothing. If

Madred noted his reaction, he chose not to acknowledge it. The Cardassian turned to Kalem.

"First Minister, it is an honor to make your acquaintance."

"Legate," said Kalem, "would you do me the honor of explaining who you are and why you're here?"

"As I said, sir, my superiors directed me to attend these negotiations." Turning to Dukat, Madred said, "Commissioner Wonar and Arbitrator Ilson speak on behalf of the Detapa Council. The Central Command is not confident *their* interests are being adequately represented."

Taken aback by the blunt response, Dukat said, "This is the first I'm hearing of this."

"Yes," said Madred, "they asked me to tell you when I arrived." From a pocket of his uniform, he extracted a green data rod and proffered it to his counterpart. "Your new orders, Dukat. I'm told it contains everything you need."

Feeling as though he had gained a semblance of control, Picard glanced to Troi, who was studying him with unguarded concern.

"This is completely inappropriate," said Dukat, his voice wavering in obvious anger and embarrassment as he snatched the data rod from between Madred's fingers. "I intend to contact Central Command to verify this for myself."

Madred glowered at him. "Central Command's verification is included. You may certainly contact whoever you wish to seek independent confirmation." He paused, and when he spoke this time it was in that low, ominous manner that made Picard's blood run cold. "But do it elsewhere. You are no longer required here."

Stunned into silence, Dukat looked around the room and took in the expressions of everyone observing his dressing-down.

"Very well," he said, his voice low and his tone defeated. "I will contact Central Command and seek clarification."

"Excellent," said Madred, who had turned and was now walking to the food and beverage table as if dismissing the entire interaction. Dukat glanced one final time at Picard and Kalem before pivoting on his heel and storming out of the wardroom.

"Captain," said Troi as the doors closed, "are you—"

"Not now, Counselor," he ordered.

Helping himself to a glass of *kanar*, Madred stared right at Picard and raised his glass.

"Now then, what should we talk about?"

15

—

Man, I'm tired.

The thought all but consumed La Forge as he and Data emerged from a turbolift onto the Promenade.

"I feel like I've been run through a transporter during an ion storm," he offered, blowing out a breath. Using the sleeve of his Starfleet utility uniform, he wiped sweat from his forehead, and saw dust and lubricant gel on it. "Join Starfleet, see the galaxy. It'll be fun." Data looked at him with a bemused expression, and the chief engineer could not suppress a small chuckle. "Sorry, I'm a little punchy. It's been a long time since I put in a day like these last two."

"Geordi," Data replied, "I have seen you work far beyond the human limits of endurance in order to address a pressing engineering or technical problem. Indeed, it has been my experience that you work harder than anyone under your supervision."

"I can't ask anyone reporting to me to do anything I'm not willing to do."

"Of course," replied the android. "Setting an example. It is one of your many qualities and a characteristic of effective leadership, as I have seen you exhibit on multiple occasions."

La Forge smiled. "And sometimes that means you get dirty, right along with everyone else."

The hours spent working inside Terok Nor's vast maze of maintenance conduits, access crawlways, and service panels had been an invigorating change of pace. Their work over the past thirty hours had returned two of the four inactive fusion chambers of the station's main reactor to limited service. La Forge had a team of his engineers running a level-1 diagnostic one last time before making them available for mainline use. This still left two chambers to repair. The station working with two-thirds of its power-generation ability was an improvement from when the *Enterprise* team had started. Barring incident or something unforeseen, he estimated the remaining two reaction chambers would be online by this time tomorrow.

And that, gentlebeings, he mused, *is how we do that.*

Tackling a complex technical problem always energized him, and this station was one gigantic technical problem. *No, it's more than that.* The station was an evolving series of smaller challenges, all linking together to form the larger, more complex challenge facing them. It was a massive hairball, as Miles O'Brien had so eloquently put it during one of their inspections.

"I'll tell you one thing these days have been good for," said La Forge as he and Data weaved in and around some Bajorans and Starfleet personnel of assorted species from the *Enterprise* and the *Oceanside*. "I'll never complain about all those rules and regulations for maintaining systems aboard the *Enterprise* ever again. To say Cardassian standards for this sort of thing are lacking is a serious understatement."

He caught Data regarding him with puzzlement before asking, "But you authored some of those rules and regulations. Seven have been adapted by Starfleet for use on all our starships."

La Forge could not help laughing. "That'll teach me to be so conscientious." He looked around the Promenade. It was not as crowded as it had been the previous evening. The engineer realized the raised lighting levels, intended to mimic sunlight at this hour on Bajor's surface, succeeded in disorienting him. Having lost track of where they were on the large thoroughfare, he began searching for familiar signs or indicators of their present location.

La Forge was hungry, and he had only allowed himself thirty minutes for a midday meal before returning to work. Eating here on the station would be faster and easier than going back to the *Enterprise*. Several of the storefronts along the Promenade advertised the promise of restaurants, a small grocer offered different cuisines, and a deli specialized in Klingon dishes. The very thought of that made La Forge's stomach lurch, and he was relieved to see it, like many of the adjacent shops, was still in the process of preparing to open. There was Quark's Bar, but La Forge wanted something quick and without the noise in the establishment that plainly was the beating heart of this section of the station.

Data pointed up to where the wide corridor curved to their right. "There is a replimat."

"Works for me."

Making their way along the Promenade, La Forge was able to admire the odd blending of form and function typifying Cardassian architecture and design. Bold, curved columns towered above them, accented by colors and artistic designs that evoked an aesthetic like those cultures on ancient Earth. This was accented by the obvious examples of technology: overhead illumination, lighting panels set into bulkheads and columns, viewscreens, and the omnipresent hum of the station's main reactor. It was, La Forge decided, an unusual and yet striking blend of artistic expression and technological advancement.

He heard voices coming from around the bend that drifted across the Promenade. Without thinking, he hastened his pace, falling in step with Data. They negotiated the curve in the main corridor to find three Bajorans, all dressed in loose-fitting clothing consisting of brown or tan fabrics, attacking someone. They had no weapons, just their fists and feet finding their target, who was dressed in a dark suit. He was on the deck rolled into a ball while covering his head with his hands. Other Bajorans were watching the fight, keeping their distance. A few people in Starfleet uniforms were trying to push their way through the growing crowd.

"Hey!" La Forge shouted. "Move aside!" With Data leading the way, they cleared a path through a dozen civilians. The assailants ignored La Forge and continued their attack.

With just enough force to get his point across, La Forge pushed aside several gawkers and moved to the closest attackers, arresting the Bajoran's next punch by grabbing his raised left arm at the wrist. Shocked by the abrupt interruption, the Bajoran attempted to break free. At the same time another took a swing at Data with his free hand, but the android easily deflected him.

"Data!"

La Forge reached without thinking across to his hip where under other circumstances a phaser might have been holstered. The station's chief of security, Odo, had instituted a new order forbidding weapons on the Promenade except for *his* officers.

Damn it!

Data retained his hold on the first Bajoran even as he parried a punch thrown by one of his companions. Planting the palm of his left hand into his assailant's chest with just enough strength to knock him off balance, the android sent the man tumbling backward off his feet before stumbling and falling to the deck.

"That's enough!"

The shouted command came from one of two Bajorans wearing militia uniforms, each brandishing a phaser while ordering onlookers to move aside. They shouldered their way through the crowd that had gathered to watch the fight. Seeing a third Bajoran assailant trying to run, La Forge grabbed him by his collar before subduing him in a defensive hold that would, if sufficient time passed, render the man unconscious. He was relieved of that burden by another pair of militia members arriving on the scene.

"Are you all right?" one of the officers, a woman, asked La Forge.

The engineer nodded. "Yeah." Before she could inquire about Data, he added, "He's fine too. Trust me." La Forge knew she likely had no idea who his friend was.

Pausing as though to assess the android, the Bajoran officer replied, "Yes, I can see that." She observed as her companions took the three attackers into custody. "Take them to Security. Odo will want to question them." Satisfied that her people were following her orders, the woman returned her attention to La Forge. "Thank you for your assistance."

"No problem." He looked past her to see Data tending to the man who had been attacked. Only then did he realize it was not a Bajoran who had been targeted, but a Cardassian. "Oh, man," he said moving forward to assist his friend. Was this a member of the delegation meeting with Captain Picard?

"You," said the Bajoran security officer, her voice dripping with contempt as the Cardassian, with Data's proffered hand, regained his feet. He made a show of straightening his disheveled clothes, which were now dusty, before using both hands in an attempt to smooth his hair. He had wide eyes that moved in rapid fashion as though assessing everything around him. At first, La Forge thought the Cardassian might be scared, but his mannerisms reflected something else. This was not fear, the engineer decided.

He's scanning for other threats, the way a soldier might.

Clearing his throat, the Cardassian bowed his head toward Data and La Forge. "Thank you for your assistance, gentlemen."

He attempted an air of confidence, but La Forge could tell he was still rattled as he directed his attention to the Bajoran officer. "For what it's worth, Lieutenant Cebal, their attack was unprovoked on my part."

"I don't know if I'd go that far," replied the woman. "They're Bajoran. You're Cardassian. Around here, that's enough. You might consider moving your business to another location. I can recommend a good airlock if you're having trouble making a decision."

Before the Cardassian could say anything else, Cebal turned and departed, and her subordinates followed her toward what La Forge knew was the station's security office. That left the Cardassian, who was now alone with the two *Enterprise* officers and a dwindling collection of Bajoran onlookers. A pair of militia members were standing some distance away, near the replimat. *No dinner*.

"I expected a cold welcome," said the Cardassian. "I thought with the station having new owners, I'd still be offered at least a measure of grace."

Eyeing him with skepticism, La Forge said, "You're not like any Cardassian I've met before. Who *are* you?"

"His name is Elim Garak."

Startled by the new voice, La Forge turned to see yet another Cardassian standing in the middle of the Promenade walkway. This new arrival exuded a palpable confidence, and La Forge noticed how those few Bajorans still in the immediate vicinity gave him a wide berth. Only the pair of security officers who stood in front of the replimat watched this new arrival with focused intensity. Whoever this Cardassian was, he was someone the Bajorans wanted to avoid.

"Dukat," said Garak, "I honestly thought it would be a bit longer before our paths crossed again." Even he seemed put off by *this* Cardassian.

"How fortunate for me that we meet one last time, so that I get to see how far you've truly fallen. Garak's Clothiers?" Dukat looked past Garak toward the shop behind him, which bore the owner's name.

Straightening his posture, Garak replied, "A good tailor is an asset to any well-dressed individual, Dukat." He paused, eyeing his rival's uniform. "Perhaps I can offer you a wardrobe upgrade for your trip home."

Dukat smiled. "Another time. I am proud to wear the uniform of my people. They honor me by allowing me to wear it and serve them. That was once true of you, Garak. Don't you miss that feeling of purpose, of pride?" He gestured to the storefront. "I doubt you'll garner the same level of appreciation by making clothes for your betters."

"Providing a needed service and doing it well is always reason for purpose and pride, Dukat. The nature of that service is irrelevant, so long as genuine effort is devoted to the task."

What is with *these two?*

Watching the interplay between them, La Forge could see it was but the latest in what had to have been a long-running feud, with Dukat and Garak doing their best to outmaneuver each other in this battle of wills and words.

"Excuse me," said Data, stepping into the fray with an innocence and naïveté that was unique to him. "Mister Garak, are you not leaving the station with the rest of the Cardassians?"

It was Dukat who replied, "Lieutenant Commander, Garak may present himself as a simple tailor, but rest assured he is far more than that. Or, rather, he used to hold that distinction." The gul held up a hand to offer a dismissive wave. "The details are unimportant, but suffice it to say his presence on Cardassia Prime or indeed anywhere within the Cardassian sphere of influence is no longer welcome. His usefulness to our people has ended, leaving him to wander the galaxy in search of anyone or anything that might offer him refuge." He made a show of looking around the Promenade. "I'll be leaving soon, Garak. Bound for the world you can never again call home. Knowing that warms my heart."

"Interesting," said La Forge, "my understanding is you're only leaving because they bounced you out of the negotiations." He had seen the updates on the ongoing discussions. Having decided Dukat was being too insufferable, he could not resist a verbal jab.

Seizing the opening La Forge provided, Garak said, "No doubt he's being recalled to answer for his abject failures as prefect of this station and Bajor, to say nothing of the embarrassment he's caused all Cardassians now that the full truth of the Occupation is beginning to emerge. Central Command does not take kindly to such things, Dukat, and I suspect the Detapa Council will have something to say about all of this. I'm only sorry I won't be able to observe it for myself." When he smiled, there was no warmth. La Forge thought Garak resembled a predator, watching with satisfaction as its prey became mired in a trap.

For his part, Dukat seemed to take the rebuke in stride. "Those in the halls of true power know that the decision to withdraw from Bajor was not because of me. This was the will of the council, to which we as soldiers are beholden. I did my duty to the best of my ability. While I expect no honors or rewards, I anticipate my devotion to serving the Cardassian people will be appropriately recognized."

Is he kidding? La Forge almost asked the question aloud.

"At the very least," Dukat continued, "I'm going home." He paused, looking around the Promenade once more. "A part of me will always be here, infused within the walls of this station as a constant reminder to those we tried to help. Perhaps the Bajorans, with their newfound confidence, might seek humility before they take their first steps into their new future." With a glance to La Forge and Data, Dukat smiled again. "Maybe they, or even Starfleet, might one day seek out my guidance."

"An unlikely prospect, sir," said Data.

La Forge added, "But we'll be sure to keep you in mind."

"I have no doubt that you will." Dukat turned to Garak. "Will you remain here, a traitor in exile? Or will you run, seeking a place to hide from the Obsidian Order when they inevitably decide to deal with you in the manner you so richly deserve?" His expression hardened. "When that time comes—and it *will* come, Garak—my only hope is that I'm able to witness it."

Garak replied, "I'll be sure you're sent an engraved invitation."

With a final grunt of what La Forge supposed was satisfaction, Dukat nodded to them before taking off down the Promenade, his Bajoran security escorts falling in behind him.

"He doesn't like me very much," said Garak. "Does he?"

"It would appear not, sir," Data replied.

"That was weird," said La Forge. "Are you actually planning to stay here?"

"The station commander has approved my request to open a shop. I'm surprised he did, given the general feelings toward Cardassians. However, I was never directly involved in the Occupation. The Bajorans' animus toward me, while certainly understandable, is misplaced."

La Forge replied, "Good luck convincing them."

"My dear commander," said Garak with a broad smile, "that's one of the things I do. Persistence is an admirable trait in a tailor, after all. Good day." With that, he turned and headed into his shop.

After he was gone, Data said, "A most interesting individual."

"Yeah, he's something, all right. Whatever's going on between

Garak and Dukat, I don't want to be anywhere near them when it boils over."

La Forge's stomach growled, reminding him that he was hungry and he now had very little time to do something about it. The engineer sighed in resignation.

Back to the grind.

16

—

Pulling on his shirt, Nesha regarded Trina's sleeping form. The Cardassian officer faced away from him beneath a heavy blanket. He had not stirred, remaining all but insensate as Nesha rose from the bed and dressed himself. While some might find the scene pleasing, Nesha did not.

So peaceful, he thought. *So vulnerable.*

This had been his second visit in as many days, but Nesha harbored no tenderness with respect to Trina. This was in service to the greater good, and there was no question he could kill the Cardassian with no regrets. He could do it now. While the glinn had taken the precaution of securing his weapons—a sidearm and a pair of knives—in a locked safe, his quarters still offered a number of options if Nesha chose such action. It was but further proof that the glinn lacked any appreciable field experience. Anyone subjected to that reality, to say nothing of any form of ordeal that challenged one's survival, would have developed a keen sense of their surroundings that would transcend sleep. It was a survival instinct shared by those who had seen combat.

So easy.

Nesha realized he not only was contemplating the Cardassian's death at his hands, but without conscious thought he also had identified the items he might use to hasten the glinn's demise. The cleaning materials in his basket presented obvious choices. Everything from writing to eating utensils to the decorative sculptures on the desk and shelves to the very bedclothes offered possibilities.

It had not always been this inviting. Bajoran women and men assigned to the upkeep of the camp's officers' quarters had to earn the trust of their Cardassian overseers. Working under the guidance of the Cardassian stewards, they went about their duties: preparing meals, cleaning individual billets as well as the common areas, doing laundry, and performing any tasks assigned to them. During Nesha's visits, insinuating himself into the daily routine of cleaning up after Trina and his fellow junior officers, he did nothing beyond what he was instructed by the stewards. Gul Havrel must have issued directives for the treatment of the Bajorans working in these capacities, as Nesha could recall only a single instance of an officer abusing a laborer. That action brought swift punishment, and so far as Nesha knew, the young Cardassian never repeated his actions.

The success of long-term clandestine surveillance hinged on the Cardassians becoming comfortable with, even apathetic to, the presence of the Bajorans laborers. Covert observations were made when they went about their assigned tasks. The key was to do nothing that might draw undue attention. If one of them saw or heard something they considered of possible value to the Resistance, that began an intricate, methodical process of relaying information to a designated contact, who in turn forwarded messages back to the other insular cells. Meanwhile, Nesha and his fellow Bajorans went about their days and nights, observing but saying or doing nothing to upset the careful balance of trust and indifference.

Still, the urge to act was powerful.

Nesha held no particular contempt for Trina. The glinn had never mistreated him or any other Bajoran, so far as he knew, but he was still part of a larger entity that had imprisoned and exploited Bajorans. Nesha envisioned a day when he no longer answered to anyone under threat of punishment or even death. If achieving that goal meant removing those like Trina whose mere existence perpetuated the oppression of his people, Nesha was prepared to do just that.

But he would have to wait.

Carrying out the cleaning tasks that were his reason for being here, Nesha managed to avoid disturbing Trina's sleep. This included removing the makeshift transceiver he had placed in his quarters during a previous visit. As Yectu had assured him, the unit remained undiscovered while secured to the underside of the glinn's bedframe. Its short range and low power had required its positioning in proximity to the desk and its workstation. Hiding it inside one of the containers of cleaning products was a practiced move.

At this time of day, there were fewer officers milling about the barracks, giving Nesha the opportunity to exit the billeting area and carry out a few other tasks required of him as part of his daily work. The troopers posted as guards or assigned to patrol the compound on foot gave the Bajorans a wide berth so long as they appeared to be working. Nesha knew the guards took greater notice of the Bajorans assigned to the officers' quarters, so it was incumbent to avoid doing anything that might attract excessive attention.

He carried out the remainder of his duties before checking out with the stewards. Released from his obligations for the time being, Nesha made his way toward the Bajoran barracks. Only then did he notice there seemed to be a higher level of activity in the compound than was normal for this time of day. Nesha realized many of the people he passed were assigned to the primary labor shift at the mine. Had he lost track of time? A glance to the horizon told him sunset was still at least an hour away. Was something amiss?

Approaching the barracks, he saw Panat Hileb and Yectu

Sheeliate standing at one of the wash troughs outside the barracks. Yectu was using a wire brush to scrub at a stain marring an article of clothing, while Panat worked to clean a large pot Nesha knew he used whenever he prepared a stew. Without hurry, Nesha crossed to the trough and took up a position on its opposite side before opening one of the spigots. Water began pouring into his trough, and Nesha proceeded to wash his hands, glancing around to verify no guards were in the immediate vicinity.

"I didn't expect to see you here this early," he said.

Panat smiled. "We go where we're told." Running the pot under the spigot, he said, "There was a cave-in. No one was hurt, but an entire section of tunnel collapsed. The supervisors ordered the secondary shift to bring the equipment needed to dig it out. They're doing that tonight." He sighed. "And so, we get a rare, brief reprieve."

Halting the interminable mining operation for any reason was a major change of routine. Nesha was amazed Gul Havrel had not kept the primary shift there to dig. It was an unusual deviation from the gul's behavior. Something out of the ordinary was happening.

"What are you doing later?" Nesha asked, keeping his voice low, while employing the code that meant he had something to share away from watchful eyes.

Yectu shrugged without looking up from her scrubbing. "Depends. What did you have in mind?"

"I've got that thing. It's from our friend, I have no idea if it's anything you can use."

Panat replied, "Maybe we'll take a look at it later, but we might not need it after all."

Shutting off the spigot, Nesha shook most of the water from his hands before patting them dry on the legs of his pants. In as casual a manner as he could muster, he moved around the trough and affected a smile for the benefit of any nearby guards. Through his teeth, he muttered, "Tell me you did what I think you did."

"I did what you think I did." Yectu was now taking a particular interest in the stain on what Nesha saw was a shirt.

Stunned by this development, Nesha looked around again before dropping all pretense. "You're inside their system?"

Yectu paused, glancing around before replying, "Havrel must have left the workstation in his quarters logged in before going to bed. I had all night with a direct connection. The first thing I did was clone the user profile for one of their computer technicians and mask it so the system automatically erases the new profile's activity log as I work."

"You tricked the system into thinking you're a Cardassian?" asked Panat.

"Basically. With the system removing all traces of my activity, the only thing anyone will see, if they do an audit, is whatever the tech does. I'm essentially invisible."

They said nothing more as Panat took a rag to drying his pot and Yectu finished her attempt to wash her shirt. Nesha waited while they gathered the rest of her things, then they walked together toward their barracks.

Speaking softly, Panat said, "We're in trouble. The Cardassians are protecting a terrible secret. It's literally beneath our feet."

Nesha could not believe what he was hearing. "You're serious."

"Oh, yes." Keeping her voice low, Yectu added, "They'll kill all of us to keep what's down there from being discovered."

Feeling more exposed as they walked across the open compound toward the barracks, Nesha asked, "What do we do?"

"Even with the order to release all Bajorans held in camps on other planets," Panat replied, "Havrel has no choice but to eliminate all of us. It's the only way to ensure the security of the protected program before they move it."

"They won't take us along?" asked Nesha. "We've been free labor for decades. Why stop now just because they made an agreement? If everyone thinks we're dead, they'll never come looking for us."

"No matter what happens to us," said Yectu, "we have to let someone know we're here and what's happening."

Panat said, "Now that we have access, we're going to craft a coded message. Yectu will make sure it's hidden within a batch of outgoing communications traffic. After that, all we can do is wait."

"Wait?" Nesha was dumbstruck. "To die?"

"We may have to wait to see if anyone hears our call for help," said Panat. "But I have no intention of sitting idle. If I'm going to die here, I'm going to die fighting."

"May the Prophets help us," Nesha said as the trio arrived at the door to their barracks. "We have to pick our moment. The instant we do anything, the Cardassians will act. The question is, how do we know when that moment is?"

Panat's response was cut off by a commotion from behind them. Turning, Nesha saw three Cardassian troopers converging on a lone Bajoran man. He was young and carrying some sort of container, falling to the ground as he was struck by a baton wielded by one of the guards. His container went tumbling across the dirt as the trooper's two companions, their own batons drawn and swinging, began pummeling the Bajoran about his back and legs. All around the compound, other Bajorans were watching. Nesha saw other Cardassians moving in, drawing batons and disruptor pistols preparing for other prisoners' reactions.

"Stop! Please! I didn't do anything!"

The man's cries for mercy went unheard as the guards beat him for several more seconds. His muscles tightening, Nesha did not realize he was beginning to move until he felt a hand on his arm. He turned to see Panat's eyes boring into his own.

"No." Panat's gaze flickered to the infuriating scene playing out before them.

Although he knew his friend was right, Nesha understood the warning just as he knew others were at this very moment schooling other prisoners not to intercede. A group response from the inmate population would only benefit the Cardassians, giving them justification to start killing everyone in sight. Would Gul Havrel allow that, even now?

"We have to wait," said Yectu, her voice low and shaky as she choked back tears.

The beating ended, and the Bajoran man lay facedown in the dirt. Nesha could see he was still alive, though he was bleeding from his head and his left arm lay at an abnormal angle. One of the troopers reached for the man's container and opened it, extracting some smaller package Nesha could not identify.

"From the gul's private stores," said the trooper. With a leering grin, he turned to the beaten prisoner. "Is this your way of telling him you don't appreciate the food he provides you?"

"For that?" asked Yectu, making no effort to hide her disgust. "All of that, over a *zabo* steak?"

Panat grunted. "You know how Havrel loves his personal luxuries."

Two of the troopers hauled the Bajoran to his feet. The man cried in pain as one of the guards grabbed his injured arm. The third guard pointed to two other Bajorans standing nearby.

"You. Carry this imbecile to the infirmary." As the prisoners hastened to comply, the troopers fell into step behind them, escorting the Bajorans to the camp's small and unimpressive medical facility. The remaining onlookers were left to stare at each other with expressions of disbelief, fear, and anger.

Nesha asked, "Think he'll survive the night?"

Blowing out her breath, Yectu replied, "I doubt it."

"There's nothing we can do for him," said Panat. "We need to think bigger. I'll start a message. Yectu, be ready to send it."

"Do you really think anyone will get that message?"

Panat frowned. "Maybe." He looked to Yectu. "Perhaps if we can add something that might attract attention."

"What do you mean?" asked Nesha.

"I'm going to reach out to an old friend."

17

—

Despite their best efforts, Doctor Crusher could still feel the sense of despair lingering in the air of what had once been the Singha labor camp.

"Smaller than the others we've seen," she said, holding a hand to her forehead in an attempt to shield her eyes from the late afternoon sun. All around her, buildings that once housed Bajoran forced laborers stood silent. On the other hand, facilities constructed for the Cardassian occupational forces were proving quite useful. A few had been repurposed as billeting for Bajoran refugees, and her counterpart from the *Oceanside*, Doctor Tropp, had taken over one building. He turned it into a larger and better-appointed version of the field hospital near what had been the Abonti camp. There was room for equipment and treatment facilities and, as it turned out, more patients.

"We're expecting another group within the hour," said Tropp as he guided Crusher and Keiko O'Brien on a brief tour. "For now, the Cardassian facilities are our best option for treating as many patients as we can. In addition to whatever's contaminated the water and food supply, we've got the usual assortment of injuries—broken bones, lacerations, and so on—along with malnutrition, severe dehydration, and diseases of every sort." The Denobulan stopped his walking dissertation and turned to face Crusher and O'Brien. "There are also more severe cases like cardiac events and a couple of strokes. I've sent those patients to the *Oceanside*, where my staff can give them better care. The stroke victims are responding well to treatment, and I'm optimistic they can make a full recovery."

Crusher asked, "What can the *Enterprise* do?"

"You're already doing it." Tropp's smile stretched his face, but Crusher saw the fatigue in his eyes. "Our workload has been cut by more than half since your people started helping. You've got a top-flight staff, Doctor. You should be proud."

Unable to keep from beaming at the praise, Crusher replied, "Believe me, I am."

Tropp said, "They're doing such a good job, they've freed you to do what you came here for." Turning his attention to O'Brien, the doctor extended his hand. "We've not been introduced. I'm Doctor Tropp, chief medical officer of the *Oceanside*."

"Keiko O'Brien, mission specialist, botany." She shook his proffered hand. "Doctor Crusher thought I might be able to help with the investigation."

"Another set of eyes and skills is always welcome." Tropp's eyes narrowed in evident curiosity. "You're not Starfleet?"

O'Brien shook her head. "No. I'm married to someone in Starfleet. He's not an officer." She leaned forward. "To hear him tell it, being enlisted is much more fun, though I have to wonder if he's thinking that right now."

"Your partner is Chief O'Brien?" Tropp smiled again. "I've heard stories about him. He's a skilled technician in his own right, and can apparently hold his weight in beer without flinching."

"Sounds like the chief," said Crusher. She knew of the transporter officer's penchant for relaxing with a drink after his duty shift. She recalled him discussing the replicated version of a beer he had chosen, complaining how the beverage's synthehol component could never re-create the taste of a fine Irish ale.

"Oh," said O'Brien, "that's Miles, all right."

Tropp said, "He sounds like he'd fit in aboard the *Oceanside*.

Perhaps I should find a way to meet him before our two ships part ways."

Leading the way through the makeshift hospital, the doctor indicated another, larger building toward the compound's far end. "That structure serves as the camp's facilities control center. In addition to housing the power generators and infrastructure for computers and communications, its lower level is devoted to extracting water from an underground river that runs beneath the camp." He pointed to the north. "The river originates up in the mountains, dropping to the lower elevations before running through fissures and into underground chasms on its way down here. The Cardassians constructed a collection and filtration system on the same level. The water is then pumped into the camp's distribution system."

"It's online?" asked O'Brien.

"No." Tropp shook his head. "As a possible contamination issue, it was deactivated. We've transferred potable water from the *Oceanside*, and of course we now have replicators online in the hospital as well as the buildings that house refugees."

Crusher said, "According to your initial report, a number of patients sent to your field hospital were interned here."

"That's correct," replied Tropp. "We conducted preliminary tests of water samples taken from the springs once we thought it might contain a toxin or something else that might be linked to the alkaloid poisoning. Our science officer can cover a lot of areas, but we don't have a botanist on the *Oceanside*."

"It's a good thing I brought my secret weapon," said Crusher, nodding to O'Brien. While the *Enterprise* crew did have botanists, a check of the ship's personnel told her Keiko O'Brien had the most experience, so Crusher had obtained the captain's permission to use her.

O'Brien said, "If there are particular types of vegetation

present in large quantities, especially any that produce variations of persistent carcinogenic alkaloids, for example, where the water is being fed from the spring into the camp's water system? That might be a cause. We'll need to get samples."

"I can assign you a guide to take you inside the facilities control center and lead you to where the springs are tapped," said Tropp as they arrived at the hospital.

Entering the building, Crusher was struck by how modern this setup appeared. Patient beds of the sort she used in the *Enterprise* sick bay filled the ward, and she saw no empty beds. It was like the Abonti camp, with patients everywhere as overtaxed Bajoran and Starfleet personnel moved back and forth in a desperate attempt to render aid.

"It's worse here," said O'Brien.

Tropp sighed. "Yes. Based on everything we've been able to piece together, this site is one of two that could be the origin point. If there's an answer to be found, this is the best place to start."

"We just need our guide," said Crusher. Her attention was divided between the conversation and the pain and suffering around her. Every impulse commanded her to care for these patients.

They're dealing with it, she reminded herself. *You can help more of them by finding whatever's causing this.*

"Doctor Beverly Crusher. Keiko O'Brien." Tropp was gesturing toward someone behind them. "Meet your guide, Kira Nerys."

Crusher turned to see a young Bajoran woman with shoulder-length red-brown hair, dressed in simple tan pants and a maroon shirt that appeared at least one size too big for her. The series of five small, horizontal ridges creasing the bridge of her nose drew Crusher's gaze to the woman's large, dark eyes, which were intently studying her. Her shirtsleeves were rolled up to her elbows, exposing toned forearms that told the doctor this was someone accustomed to manual labor. There was no mistaking the determination and even anger in the eyes that peered back at her. *Or is it something else?*

Crusher extended her hand to Kira. "Pleased to meet you, and thank you for agreeing to help us."

Her expression remaining unchanged, the woman offered, "We were instructed to provide assistance." Just before Crusher could pull her hand back, the woman took it, after which she held it for a moment as though unsure what to do. She then released her grip before dropping her arm to her side. "Sorry. I'm not that familiar with human customs."

"There's a learning curve," offered Tropp. "My apologies, Nerys, we've all been too busy for etiquette classes."

O'Brien said to Kira, "The last thing we want to do is take you away from patient care. We're grateful for your assistance. If we can find the source of the contamination, developing a treatment will happen quickly." Then, to Crusher's surprise, Keiko added, "May we address you as Nerys, or do you prefer—"

"Kira." As the word left her mouth, she frowned in obvious regret. "I'm sorry. I meant . . . people usually just call me Kira."

Crusher said, "Kira it is, then." Sensing the woman's obvious discomfort as they exited the hospital and proceeded toward the facilities control center, she said nothing. As they walked, she became aware of the number of Bajorans scattered about the compound. Many were assisting the *Enterprise* and *Oceanside* medical teams, while others were simply standing or sitting, clustered into small groups, but Crusher also noticed individuals off by themselves. Some of the groups were animated, speaking in unguarded tones while laughing or perhaps airing a grievance. Many of those sitting alone were eating or reading. In a few cases, some were lying stretched on the ground, basking in the midday sun. Crusher wondered if they were contemplating life with a level of freedom they had never known.

Kira Nerys had almost certainly been born during the Occupation. A majority of the planet's population were on the brink of facing an existence they may not even have allowed themselves to dream could come to pass. Now here they were, being thrown headfirst into the deep end of the pool of independence and self-determination. There was every reason for the Bajoran population to fear what they had to view as the vast unknown.

"Kira," said O'Brien as they closed in on the facilities building. "Are you familiar with the water-delivery system?"

"Somewhat," replied Kira. "I was brought to the Singha camp when I was a child. When I was old enough, I worked as an apprentice with the men and women who maintained the water system. I was a runner more than anything else, delivering tools or messages to the different workers. It was a lot better than hauling uridium out of a mine, but eventually I gave it all up."

"To do what?" asked O'Brien.

Kira shrugged. "Join the Resistance and learn how to fight the Cardassians." She stopped herself from saying anything else, and Crusher noticed the sudden pall that seemed to fall over their conversation. "The knowledge I gained working here gave me an advantage in planning and carrying out sabotage and making the Cardassians miserable."

"There probably aren't many who know the inside of that building and what's underneath it better than you."

"A lot of people knew a lot more than me," replied Kira. "But most of them are dead, thanks to the Cardassians."

Crusher offered, "We're sorry for everything you went through."

"*We're* sorry you didn't do anything to help." Kira's retort came almost on top of Crusher's last words. She held up her hands. "That was out of line. I hope you understand that while there are a great many Bajorans who are happy to see the Federation and

Starfleet assist with rebuilding, there are almost as many who'd prefer you just leave."

O'Brien began, "But—"

"I know," said Kira. "The Cardassians left us in a bad way, and here you've come to our rescue. After over forty years of fighting our own battles with no hope of anyone ever coming to help us, we're self-sufficient. Even with the environmental issues the Cardassians left us, I'd like to think we'd find a way." She gestured around. "After all, this is *our* world."

"We understand your hesitation," said Crusher, "and I for one understand your anger. All I can say is we're here, and we want to help."

Kira nodded, but it was a short, perfunctory motion. "I've learned a few things about humans, including various adages and maxims you sometimes use. Tropp taught me one I really like." Her expression turned hard. "Actions speak louder than words."

Nodding in understanding, Crusher knew Starfleet and the Federation had a long path to travel in order to earn the trust of Kira and all Bajorans.

That journey started right here, right now.

18

—

"Reparations? First Minister, you cannot be serious."

Commissioner Wonar almost punctuated his statement with a laugh before Picard watched him choke it back while attempting to maintain his composure.

"Surely," said Kalem, "your superiors on the Detapa Council did not send you all this way to speak to us without raising the possibility?" The first minister was far better at schooling his expression than the commissioner. "After everything that was taken from the Bajoran people in service to the Cardassian Union, they're owed recompense."

Arbitrator Ilson replied, "It is worth noting, First Minister, that the Bajoran people welcomed us with open arms all those years ago."

Wonar added, "She is correct. There was a time when our two peoples existed peacefully with one another. I understand you may not know about that period, but it did happen. It is a matter of record."

"Whose record?" asked Troi.

The arbitrator glared at her. "Are you accusing us of lying?" Instead of waiting for the counselor to reply, Ilson glowered at Picard. "We find the presence of a Betazoid at these proceedings inappropriate, Captain. It's obvious she's reading our thoughts and relaying that information to you."

"And you believe she's doing that telepathically?" asked Picard. "I'm afraid I don't include mind reading among my own skills or talents, Arbitrator."

Troi said, "I can sense emotions, but I cannot read minds. Your thoughts remain your own."

"Having one's emotions read is disconcerting," said Ilson. "We request she be removed from these discussions."

"Your request is noted," replied Picard. "Denied."

Fuming, Ilson asked, "May I ask why?"

"Because she is my trusted advisor. Commander Troi stays." Picard had decided this was one of those times when he needed to assert himself to keep the situation from becoming heated yet again. Looking at Wonar, he said, "For the sake of expediency and decorum, let us just say your version is an interesting interpretation of the events that transpired."

"I believe there is a proverb or axiom from your culture, Captain," said Legate Madred, speaking for the first time in the current session. Picard noticed that neither Wonar nor Ilson was comfortable with this development. For his part, Madred seemed amused by the entire affair. Leaning forward so he could rest his forearms on the conference table, the legate smiled at Picard. "'History is written by the victors.' Have I quoted it accurately?"

Picard smiled. "Well enough. I'd be remiss if I didn't point out the quote has been appropriated, misattributed, and cited ironically by several individuals throughout our history. That said, the overriding sentiment it's meant to convey remains consistent."

"Consensus at last," said Madred. "There may be hope for us after all."

"It's no surprise that victory over an opponent allows one to craft whatever version of facts they feel best serves them," said Picard. "It could be as complex as the history of one civilization's subjugation of another, or as simple as determining how many viewing ports are set into that bulkhead." He pointed to the quintet of windows dominating the wardroom's far wall before leveling his gaze at Madred. "Are there five ports, or only four?" Picard watched with satisfaction as the Cardassian's smile faded, replaced by a look of irritation before Madred leaned back in his seat.

Rather petty on my part, Picard conceded to himself. *But damn, it felt good.* A knowing look from Troi only reinforced his thought.

"Similar sentiments on history and those who craft it are certainly relevant to these proceedings," said Kalem. "Commissioner, I do not deny our peoples once existed in harmony with one another, for a time. This, despite the obvious differences in our cultures. Would it surprise you to learn there are a great many Bajorans who, even after all that has transpired, wish to see that harmony restored?"

This seemed to take Wonar aback, but Picard thought he covered his reaction well enough. "I would indeed, First Minister, but I also find it heartening."

"That is the resilience of the Bajoran people, Commissioner," said Kai Opaka. "One of the greatest sins you committed against us was to diminish us to the point we questioned our faith. You forbade us from embracing those beliefs, and you imprisoned our spiritual leaders for preaching the word of the Prophets. We lost our connection to them, and we might well have lost our souls, until it became evident we were being tested. Only by fighting for our faith could we earn back our bond with the Prophets. Many—though not all—rediscovered our capacity to forgive."

Wonar replied, "I must say, Eminence, your words are truly inspirational. They give me hope that our peoples can work together to put the mistakes of the past behind us and forge a new future together." Picard could not tell if the commissioner was being sincere, or if this was the polished delivery of a savvy diplomat. He suspected the truth was somewhere in the middle.

"If our people are destined to find harmony and create that new future," said Kalem, "we must remember and be honest with one another. It is in that spirit that I sit before you today, asking all Cardassians to hold yourselves accountable for your actions against my people. If you can find it within yourselves to do so, then perhaps we have the foundation of an enduring harmony."

"And if we can't?" asked Madred, earning a look of disapproval from Wonar.

Unperturbed by the legate's question, Kalem replied, "Then the future the commissioner envisions will not come to pass."

He seemed prepared to offer a rebuttal, then Wonar stopped, and Picard noted how he exchanged glances with Ilson before he said, "This seems an appropriate time to end our discussion for the day. I propose we resume this exercise tomorrow morning." Before Kalem could respond, the commissioner pushed himself from his seat and made his way to the door, leaving Ilson to hurry after him.

Rising from his chair, Madred offered a sardonic smile to Picard. "I find discussions of this sort stimulating and refreshing. Wouldn't you agree, Captain?" He paused a moment before walking out of the room.

"An interesting exchange, to say the least," offered Kalem as he rose to his feet. "I wonder how long he'll make us wait tomorrow morning?"

Beginning with the first session, Wonar had made a point of being late on his arrival or when returning from recess. Picard knew this was a tactic employed by negotiators of every stripe since time immemorial in a quest to assert dominance over their opponents. He was immune to the ploy, having learned long ago to exercise patience; often this infuriated the other party. But Picard was not the one doing the negotiating. He could advise Kalem, hoping to shield him from the worst of whatever games Wonar played. The Bajoran leader had been unflappable, but Picard would be hard-pressed to say any progress had been made.

Madred.

As Kalem and Kai Opaka moved away from the table to speak in private, Picard turned his chair to face Troi. "Counselor, what do you make of . . . Gul Dukat's replacement?"

"His presence here is unexpected, and unwanted," Troi replied. "I sense irritation and doubt directed at him from both Wonar and Ilson. As for Madred, he seems to be enjoying the discussions, but especially whenever tensions rise." She paused before adding, "I also sense his particular fascination with you."

"That doesn't surprise me," said Picard. "It's obvious his participation is calculated. But that would mean someone in authority knows about our recent . . . encounter, and made the deliberate choice to send him here without first informing anyone. Logical, given the effort expended to lure me to Celtris III."

The Cardassians, as part of their planned invasion of the Minos Korva system, knew the *Enterprise* would lead any Starfleet response to an attack. They believed Picard possessed detailed knowledge of every strategy to defend against them, therefore questioning him was of paramount importance. One of the flaws in their thinking was that Picard had no such knowledge. That sort of information was compartmentalized and protected until such time as he had a need to know, and only then would it have been dispatched to the *Enterprise.*

Another flaw in their scheme was selecting Madred to conduct the interrogation.

In a lower voice, Troi asked, "How are *you* feeling?"

Drawing a long breath, the captain then exhaled it. "I'd be lying if I said his being here hasn't had an effect. At first it was a visceral reaction, but the dynamic here is . . . much different from Celtris III." He could not help the memory flash of Madred's office, dark and foreboding, and the words of his tormentor as his clothing was cut from his body.

From this point on, you will enjoy no privilege of rank, no

privileges of person. From now on, I will refer to you only as "human."
You have no other identity.

Hung from restraints in the middle of the room, like a trophy on display. Torture inflicted by a device surgically implanted in his body. The pain continuing even after Madred knew he possessed no useful information, inflicted for his captor's amusement as he worked to shatter Picard's mind and spirit.

"Captain?"

Picard opened his eyes, realizing he had fallen into the memory. He looked down to see his right hand rubbing his left wrist, recalling the ache of skin rubbed raw from the restraints. He struggled for several seconds to bring his pulse down.

"I'm sorry, Counselor."

Troi regarded him with concern. "But if we need to take some time—"

"No." The response was curt. "No," he repeated, this time in a softer voice. "I appreciate your concern, Deanna, but that would send the wrong signal."

Troi said, "To Madred?"

"And to whoever is responsible for him being here. It seems obvious to me the Cardassians are engaging in these discussions as a way to appear conciliatory. They know the Federation is watching, and that we're planning an extended, increased presence in this sector. Anything that might derail that process benefits them." Picard leaned closer to her. "Nothing must be permitted to jeopardize our standing. Not now, when we're only just beginning to make inroads with the Bajorans. We've already failed them in so many ways. I do not wish to do so again. I cannot allow the Cardassians to think they've succeeded."

Her eyes locking with his, Troi asked, "No matter what it might do to you?"

It was a valid question, and one she was required to pose. Her willingness to challenge him was just one of the reasons Picard wanted her here. She was his constant reminder to check in with himself, and to gauge his own feelings.

"I have no intention of allowing things to get out of hand," he said. "I'm counting on you to help me if I fail to see the warning signs." While Madred might be an adroit manipulator, Picard was confident Troi would see through any scheme he might be employing, either against the Bajorans or Picard.

Footsteps coming toward them made him look up to see Kai Opaka approaching. She paused a few paces from them, her hands clasped before her.

"Captain, may I speak with you?"

Rising to his feet, Picard replied, "Yes, Eminence. By all means." Troi acknowledged him with a quick look before stepping away toward Kalem. "How may I help you?"

"It occurred to me that with the formal discussions occupying so much of our time, I had not yet had the opportunity to thank you for overseeing these proceedings."

"It is my privilege, Eminence. On behalf of the Federation, I wish to formally thank you for inviting us. I feel there is much we can learn from one another."

"As do I, Captain." Settling into Troi's chair, Opaka waited for him to retake his seat before saying, "I understand you have a Bajoran serving aboard your ship."

"Ensign Ro Laren," replied Picard. "Thanks to her, I've come to know and appreciate a great deal about your people, including the knowledge that I have more to learn."

Opaka said, "The praise of a superior officer is not to be dismissed." Then, a small smile tugged at the corners of her mouth. "I understand she had to work to earn your confidence."

It was now Picard's turn to smile. "She made a rather memorable first impression, but she comported herself with distinction.

I saw her potential, and I thought the *Enterprise* was the right place for her. Ro accepted my offer to join my crew, and she has continued to work hard at putting her mistakes behind her."

"It is fortunate she had someone like you watching out for her," Opaka said. "I don't know if another would be as quick to take a chance on someone with her past."

"I believe in second chances if at all possible," said Picard.

"As do I," replied the Bajoran leader. "That is what I see here: a second chance for both our peoples." She then leaned closer. "There is something else, Captain. Something about you. I sense you are troubled in the presence of the Cardassians, and especially Legate Madred. You two obviously have a past." As Picard spent a few moments offering a distilled, sanitized version of his ordeal at the hands of the Cardassian interrogator, Opaka reached out to take his hand in hers.

"I have experienced my own pain at the hands of the Cardassians. My son was part of the Resistance." She faltered, casting her gaze downward before adding, "And it cost him his life."

Picard gripped her hand. "I am so very sorry, Eminence."

Blinking several times in rapid succession as though trying to force away hurtful thoughts, Opaka replied, "And I am sorry for you, Captain. I hope your wounds, physical and otherwise, heal soon."

After a moment with them both spent in silent reflection, she said, "You strike me as a person of strong character. I hope you are but one representative of many who hold similar values. My people desperately need help."

"I'd like to think I'm a fairly ordinary example of what the Federation can offer you, Eminence. I understand how difficult it must be for Bajor to ask anyone for help, let alone us. However, it's my sincere desire that we can help you move past the wounds your people and your world have suffered."

Opaka smiled. "You are very perceptive, Captain. This is difficult for my people. After all, the Cardassians introduced themselves with an offer of help."

"Eminence, it is my goal to demonstrate just how much our values differ from those of the Cardassians."

"We shall see, Captain. We shall see."

19

So far as Miles O'Brien was concerned, after a long day there was nothing like hoisting a pint at a good pub. Ten Forward on the *Enterprise* was decent, and O'Brien certainly had no complaints about the service or what he imbibed, but the lounge's atmosphere was too subdued.

The bar at the center of Terok Nor's Promenade level, on the other hand, had potential.

O'Brien heard the low buzz of multiple conversations blending together as he approached the bar's entrance. He could see patrons standing or occupying stools at the bar that was the establishment's dominating feature. Others were seated at tables arranged around the main floor. The clientele was a mix of Bajorans as well as Starfleet. O'Brien noticed the Bajorans seemed to be keeping to themselves. Despite a few exceptions in the form of a shared smile or a raised glass, there remained a subtle segregation.

It was early for this particular bar, O'Brien suspected. Crew members from the two ships would likely be coming in due course. Shift change had just taken place. It was not a raucous place by any measure, but the bar's overall vibe appeared to a positive one. The lone exception to the frivolity permeating the establishment was the bulky Lurian sitting by himself at the end of the bar closest to the door. He looked to have been perched there well before O'Brien's arrival, and the Lurian seemed to have a fresh beverage held in one of his oversized hands.

A regular, O'Brien decided.

"Miles."

Surprised by the familiar voice, O'Brien smiled as he turned to see Keiko walking toward him. He was going to meet her, with outstretched arms, but she pulled back at the sight of his uniform.

Regarding him with mock disdain, she giggled. "What did you get into?"

O'Brien looked down at the black utility jumpsuit, its shoulders and upper torso colored mustard to identify him as part of Starfleet's operations division. The gray undershirt was a bit snug around his neck, and he found he needed to roll up its sleeves along with the jumpsuit's when he got warm. Dust and some spots of green goo added to his disheveled appearance, but to him it was proof of a hard, productive day's work.

"Occupational hazards," he said as Keiko leaned in for a kiss. "What are you doing here?"

"I knew you'd be off duty, so I thought it'd be a nice change of pace to eat someplace that's not our quarters or Ten Forward."

"Where's Molly?" asked O'Brien, suddenly realizing he had no idea what time it was. "I didn't miss bedtime again, did I?"

Shaking her head, Keiko said, "The nursery. She'll be fine for an hour while we eat, and you'll still be able to read her story tonight."

"I like your thinking." O'Brien felt bad whenever he missed story time.

That sentiment had only deepened thanks to what he had witnessed while working on Terok Nor. The station had become home to hundreds of Bajoran refugees, freed from the various forced-labor camps scattered around the planet. This included dozens of orphaned children, now billeted in quarters and supervised by a cadre of Bajoran caregivers. A great many more remained on the planet, housed in temporary camps established by teams from the *Enterprise* and the *Oceanside*. Finding or providing housing for every displaced Bajoran would take months, but it was the children that worried O'Brien.

It'll work out, he told himself. *It has to.* The idea Starfleet or the Federation would fail at such an important mission was impossible for him to fathom. *We'll make it work.*

"Miles," asked Keiko, "are you all right?"

Realizing his expression must be showing his concerns, O'Brien forced a small smile. "I'm sorry. I was just . . . thinking about something." He did not wish to burden her. Instead, he gestured toward Quark's Bar. "Want to see what's on their menu?" The differences in their palates had become a running joke between them, and he expected Keiko to balk at the suggestion. She instead surprised him by shrugging.

"Why not?"

They entered the bar, and O'Brien scanned the room for an empty table. Before they could even find seats, he caught sight of Commander Riker standing at a gaming table in the rear of the establishment. He realized what the *Enterprise*'s first officer was doing, and indicated for Keiko to follow. Riker saw their approach and nodded in recognition.

"Chief," he said, "how go the repairs?"

"It's a challenge, but we'll get there, sir."

Riker smiled as Keiko moved to stand beside her husband. "Good evening, Mrs. O'Brien."

"Please," she replied. "Keiko."

"Only if you call me Will." He returned his attention to what O'Brien now recognized as a dabo table as the wheel at its center started to spin. It appeared similar to roulette, which he had played a few times. Overseen by a Ferengi dealer, this version of dabo consisted of three concentric circles, each featuring thirty-six symbols of varying colors. The circles rotated independently of one another, with the outer and inner rings spinning clockwise while the middle ran counterclockwise. The chief noted that Riker had placed slips of gold-pressed latinum on a number from each of the three circles. After a moment, the wheels began slowing before coming to rest and highlighting their respective winning numbers.

"Did you win?" asked Keiko, evoking a chuckle from Riker as the dealer relieved him of his latinum strips.

"I'm afraid not." Shaking his head, he said, "My first time playing, and it shows." He gestured to the gaming table. "I haven't won a single round all night. I need to quit while I'm behind."

"On the contrary, Commander Riker."

O'Brien turned at the sound of the new voice to see a garishly dressed Ferengi moving toward them. He extended his hands in a welcoming gesture, and O'Brien assumed he was the bar's owner.

"Welcome to Quark's," he said before making a show of bowing to Keiko. "It's nice to see someone with at least a hint of fashion sense." He offered a dismissive wave to Riker and O'Brien. "Starfleet really needs better tailors."

Keiko, not missing a beat, asked, "I thought Ferengi liked their women without clothes?"

"Who doesn't?" replied Quark, earning a scowl from her before he turned back to Riker. "Commander, you've comported yourself admirably. I encourage you to continue playing to your heart's content." Clasping his hands together before him, the Ferengi's smile seemed to grow wider. "As a token of my appreciation and in consideration for your wounded feelings after such a tremendous loss, I'd like to offer you a ten percent discount on your next drink."

Riker grunted. "Your charity knows no bounds, Quark."

His expression turning dour, the Ferengi replied, "Charity? Commander, this is a family-friendly establishment. I'll thank you not to use such unseemly language here." The Ferengi stepped closer to Riker and leaned in. "Tell me, are the rumors true? I've heard Starfleet is petitioning the new Bajoran government to assign a permanent crew here on the station. If all Starfleet officers play dabo as well as you do, Commander, I'll finally be able to buy that moon I've always wanted." Without waiting for a response, Quark turned and slid back through gaps in the crowd in the general direction of the bar.

"Glad I could help," offered Riker to the Ferengi's retreating back.

Watching Quark leave, O'Brien said, "Quite the charmer."

Keiko replied, "As long as you have credits to spend."

Riker stepped away so another player could take his place. "Time for me to get back to the ship." To O'Brien, he said, "Chief, Commander La Forge tells me you've been a tremendous help getting the station's systems back online. He says you're a natural and mentioned if you ever wanted to pursue a commission, you could probably be a chief engineer on a starship in a couple of years."

Pride swelled within O'Brien as he absorbed the first officer's praise, made all the better by having Keiko hear it. "Thank you, Commander. I appreciate that. I guess I just like getting my hands dirty."

Riker smiled again, gesturing to O'Brien's uniform and its evidence of his day's work. "I can tell. Enjoy your evening. You've earned it. Just avoid the dabo tables."

After he left, Keiko's expression was one of unabashed admiration. "Well, look at you, Mister Big Shot Engineer."

Feeling a bit self-conscious about the compliment he had received, O'Brien replied, "Well, this big shot engineer is hungry and could use a drink."

The *sem'hal* stew was awful, Elim Garak decided, wondering at the same time how such a thing could even be possible. One of his favorite childhood meals, the stew's greatest appeal was that it far exceeded the deceptive simplicity of its ingredients. His mother had made it for him more times than he could remember, during that innocent, even naïve period when he considered his life to be ordinary.

Back when you knew nothing, he reminded himself. *About anything.*

Testing another spoonful of the stew, Garak blanched at its taste, which he found almost insulting to his dear mother, to say nothing of being an affront to his taste buds.

How had the replicators managed to produce such a foul concoction? He knew Gul Dukat had favored the dish, and that was more than enough of a reason to ensure Terok Nor's food preparation systems included the recipe. Garak figured this latest in a spate of admittedly minor issues was one component of the larger problems plaguing various systems around the station, many of them doubtless caused by deliberate acts of sabotage carried out by Cardassians prior to their evacuation. He could understand the troopers breaking items and equipment the Bajorans, or even Starfleet, might find useful, but to defile the sanctity of one of the things the station offered in the way of comfort and luxury bordered on criminal.

I suppose it beats the food in prison, mused Garak as he contemplated the bowl of disappointing *sem'hal* stew before him growing colder with each passing moment. He was about to resign himself to finishing his meal when he detected the sound of footsteps approaching him. Any lingering desire he may have had for the stew vanished when he looked up into the face of his visitor.

"This is interesting, meeting you here," said Madred.

Placing his spoon next to his bowl, Garak clasped his hands on the table. "It was my understanding that being forced into exile meant never having to see people I don't like. Leave it to Central Command to fail at something so simple."

Dressed in his legate's uniform and wearing the smug expression that had always made Garak want to wipe it off in a hail of disruptor fire, Madred gestured to the table's empty chair. "May I—?"

"No." Garak made no attempt to stand. Doing so would signal to Madred that he felt intimidated by his arrival, and he needed to make a display in order to defuse such a notion. Remaining seated and keeping his voice level, he said, "I'm simply particular so far as with whom I share my meals. I'm sure you understand."

If he was put off by the comments, Madred gave no sign. "Indeed I do."

As Garak expected, he sat in the chair in a transparent attempt to assert dominance. In predictable fashion, he made a show of looking around at the other tables in the replimat area, most of which were empty save for a few Starfleet personnel. Those Bajorans who had been there when Garak arrived had made a point to leave. As such, there were few within hearing range, so their conversation could proceed without eavesdropping.

"I must say, this choice of life path is rather surprising," said Madred after a moment passed in silence. "I would have thought someone with your talents, reputation, and contacts would be spared from an existence such as this."

Garak forced himself to swallow another spoonful of the dreadful *sem'hal* stew, without offering any sign of his disdain for his visitor and what the replimat had foisted upon him. He kept his gaze on Madred, who seemed to be watching him with detached fascination. They both knew how this game was played. Likewise, each knew their rival was more than up to the task of employing these tactics as part of a larger, deliberate campaign to elicit reactions of impatience or frustration.

"Congratulations on your promotion," said Garak after a moment. "I have no doubt it was well earned. But I wonder about the disparity in recognizing you so soon after your rather egregious misstep on Celtris III." A momentary flicker in the legate's eyes told him he had struck a nerve, but Madred covered it well enough. When he smiled this time, Garak could tell it was forced.

"Central Command is nothing if not perceptive." Madred held out his hands. "For example, they're able to discern between an honest mistake made in the midst of a fluid, even chaotic situation from actions undertaken with the intent to disrupt or even sabotage respected leaders. And the ramifications of undermining orders and even policies championed by those to whom we pledge our loyalty."

Like a knife fight between two skilled practitioners of the deadly combat art, Garak knew that he and Madred were circling each other, looking for an opening that might allow a figurative blade to slide between a pair of proverbial ribs.

"Oh, come now." Garak leaned closer. "We both know this isn't the first time you've fallen victim to your own folly. The reports were sealed, but we know what really happened when you *interrogated* the son of that council member after accusing him of espionage. The entire reason you were sent to Celtris III in the first place was your inability to control your sadistic instincts. An innocent man died while in your charge."

For the first time, Garak saw Madred's jawline tighten. "He was not innocent. He was a spy, turned by Starfleet in an attempt to infiltrate the council and disrupt it from within."

"Never proven," replied Garak. "You ignored the recommendations of those with knowledge of the situation. Why? Because you hoped to show yourself worthy to those who could advance you within the ranks."

Madred started to reply, but caught himself. Instead, he studied Garak for a moment before leaning closer. "It was you, wasn't it? You're the one responsible for my reassignment to Celtris III."

"You credit me with far more influence than I ever enjoyed," replied Garak. In point of fact, he had recommended to his superiors that Madred be removed from his posting and punished. The decision to send him to the distant outpost on Celtris III was a favor by someone within Central Command. Garak reasoned the action was to protect Madred by removing him from the hierarchy's easy grasp. It had to be someone who had sanctioned his actions while trying to expose the council member's son. Everyone involved was spared the short-term embarrassment until time passed and tempers cooled. All that was required was for Madred to conduct himself in a manner that did not draw any more attention of a potentially embarrassing nature.

A good plan, reasoned Garak, *until it was implemented*.

Still clueless as to the truth, Madred said, "I don't pretend to understand the inner workings of the Obsidian Order, but even I know their agents operate with great impunity."

"If I had been responsible," said Garak, "do you really think I would have allowed what you did on Celtris III to go unanswered?"

"Given your status as an exile," said Madred, "you can't possibly know what transpired. Unless, of course, all of that is simply fiction."

Ignoring the comment, Garak said, "You allowed your ambitions to undercut Central Command. Torturing Picard for your personal satisfaction after you knew he possessed no information regarding Minos Korva was your undoing." Now it was his turn to lean closer. "You are very intelligent, Madred. I've never believed otherwise. You're always looking for a means to climb higher within the command structure, but I must warn you, it will inevitably put you at odds with those already occupying the higher perches you seek."

Madred settled back in his chair, affecting a relaxed air. "Are you telling me you never considered ways to advance your own career?"

"Better to be seen as useful," replied Garak, "even indispensable to those in power. Such individuals grant tremendous latitude so long as their requests and desires are met."

"And you squandered the very privilege you once enjoyed." Madred sighed. "Even with the setbacks I suffered, it seems my supposed failures are of a minor consequence compared to how you and even this station's former prefect fared. My . . . interactions . . . with Captain Picard have convinced Central Command this conference presents a means to redeem myself and further our ongoing interests with Starfleet and the Federation."

Garak almost laughed, but held himself in check. "The more likely explanation is that you are momentarily useful to these proceedings solely for the impact you may have on Picard. If I were you, I'd manage my expectations."

Rising from his chair, Madred regarded him for a moment before replying, "Meanwhile, you should consider your own path."

Picking up his spoon, Garak made a show of eating another bite of the now-cold and even more offensive stew. "It remains foremost on my mind, Legate."

He watched as Madred turned and exited the replimat, strolling as though he was without concerns until the curve of the Promenade took him out of sight. Only then did Garak drop the spoon for the final time.

Redemption, he mused, well aware of where he stood with those responsible for his exile. *An amusing notion.*

20

The previous day had proceeded more or less according to the plan. Therefore it made perfect sense to Geordi La Forge that in the early hours of this new day things were going straight to hell.

"I think this is it, Commander," guessed Ensign Sonya Gomez, whom La Forge had tapped to accompany him. With an equipment bag matching the one he carried slung over her left shoulder, Gomez led the way down yet another of Terok Nor's byzantine service corridors. She had paused before an access panel set into the curved bulkhead.

"MacDougal to La Forge," said the voice of the *Oceanside's* chief engineer, over the open communications frequency. *"According to our scans, you're in the right place."*

"We're at the access point, Sarah," replied La Forge. "Are you still picking up the power fluctuations from the ODN relay hub at this location?"

There was a pause before MacDougal said, *"It's intermittent, but still there. Using the algorithm Commander Data created, we're also tracing similar readings to and from a dozen other hubs scattered across the station."*

With Data's assistance, MacDougal was overseeing several investigation and repair teams dispatched from her ship and the *Enterprise*. She was directing these efforts from the central engineering section located in Terok Nor's lower core. This morning they were running down and addressing a small but mounting series of issues related to the station's vast optical data network. It sounded like a logistical headache.

La Forge knew his counterpart was up to the task. He had experienced Sarah MacDougal's proficiency as a chief engineer firsthand, during her brief tenure aboard the *Enterprise*, which coincided with his first year aboard the newly constructed *Galaxy*-class vessel. She had been with the ship just before its official commissioning ceremony, and along with three peers oversaw the vessel's state-of-the-art engines as well as numerous onboard systems. At the time *Enterprise* had the latest advances in Starfleet technology and ship design. Having excelled in his engineering classes at Starfleet Academy, La Forge had always considered chief engineer as a possible career path. Despite being assigned to flight operations on the bridge, he continued to train across multiple departments. As cross-training was one of Captain Picard's expectations for junior officers, La Forge spent the better part of his first year aboard the *Enterprise* learning from MacDougal and her colleagues. After the ship's first year in deep space, MacDougal and the others were transferred, while La Forge received a promotion and reassignment as the *Enterprise*'s chief engineer.

I can't believe it took me so long to figure out what I really wanted.

At the access panel, Gomez was now using her tricorder to transmit the proper security code to release the hatch's magnetic seal. No sooner did she key the sequence than the lights in the passageway began to flicker in a chaotic rhythm.

"I don't think it's supposed to do that," said La Forge, suppressing a sigh as Gomez attempted the procedure for a second and third time. Her efforts did manage to change the pattern with which the lights blinked. Gomez held up a hand to shield her eyes, and even with his VISOR to shield him from the worst of the effects, La Forge still found the experience irritating.

"Just out of curiosity," he said, "try sending the code to lock it."

Gomez started to protest, then shrugged. "Why not?" Tapping a control on the tricorder's compact interface, she aimed the device at the hatch and once more pressed the activation key. The corridor lighting stabilized to something approaching normal, but the hatch remained sealed.

Shaking his head in disbelief, La Forge was already regretting answering Data's hail at what had been an unholy hour of ship's night. "I have absolutely no idea why that worked."

"Progress," said the ensign, holstering her tricorder before sliding her bag from her shoulder. From the satchel she extracted a palm-sized P-38 magnetic lock interface and pressed it to the access panel. She keyed the small control pad set into the unit's face, and after a moment La Forge heard the sound of the hatch's seal releasing.

"There we go," she said. "If that hadn't worked, I was going to have to go hunting for a crowbar."

"You mean you don't carry one? I thought I taught you better than that." La Forge smiled to emphasize his mocking tone, recalling how she had been a nervous wreck upon her arrival aboard the *Enterprise* four years earlier. Despite a few mishaps, Gomez had worked hard and applied herself, overcoming her initial anxiety and clumsiness to become one of his best engineers.

The two of them worked together to pull the access panel aside, revealing a crawlspace. Peering inside, La Forge noted the conduit's accumulation of dust along with its very limited illumination.

"Are those . . . droppings?" asked Gomez, exchanging the P-38 for a flashlight from her bag, which she then slung back over her shoulder.

"I wouldn't doubt it. You've heard the reports about the voles, right?"

Gomez scowled. "Voles?"

"It was in our briefing packet." La Forge's study of the station's technical schematics detailed the existence of what was labeled as a "vermin pacification system." Unable to resist, the *Enterprise* chief engineer discovered the station had at some point—or, more likely, multiple points—been subject to an infestation of voles, a species of rodent-like creatures. Indigenous to Cardassia Prime, they had a reputation for finding their way into cargo shipments and eventually onto space vessels, which likely explained their presence here. La Forge had heard about sightings of the small yet irksome creatures in less trafficked areas of the station.

"There have been reports of voles chewing through power and ODN cabling," he said, "and even pulling isolinear data rods from their slots on various equipment and either destroying or making off with them."

"Could they be the cause of these power fluctuations?"

La Forge shrugged. "From what I've seen of this place, I'm not ruling anything out." He moved to the conduit's opening. "The report said they like dark, quiet places. You know, like Jefferies tubes, or whatever the Cardassians call these things."

Sighing, Gomez used her free hand to tussle her dark, shoulder-length hair. "I guess that shower was wasted."

"Probably." Steeling himself for the clouds of dust he was about to unsettle, La Forge hoisted himself into the conduit, which like the Jefferies tubes on the *Enterprise* was large enough that he could at least crawl on hands and knees. His VISOR saw to it he did not need a flashlight, the prosthesis filtering through the entire electromagnetic spectrum to present him with an unfettered view of the tunnel ahead of him. "How far is the hub?"

Gomez, crawling into the conduit behind him, replied, "About fifteen meters. There should be a bend about halfway there."

"I see it." La Forge noted and then tried to ignore the obvious signs of vole activity here, including tufts of hair, droppings, and what appeared to be bones and other remains of those members of the vole contingent that had proven ill-equipped to survive. What he did not see were any obvious signs of chewing through any of the power or ODN conduits routed along the crawlspace's ceiling or its bulkheads. Making his way to what had to be the relay hub ensconced within a protective shell, he observed no obvious signs of voles—or anything else—attempting to gnaw their way into the compartment.

What his VISOR did reveal to him, however, was an intense shimmering he long ago had come to associate with the signal traffic produced by optical data technology as it routed tremendous amounts of information at the speed of light.

"Wow," he said, more to himself than Gomez or anyone else, but MacDougal still heard him through the open comm channel.

"Something wrong, Geordi?"

Shifting his body so he could sit cross-legged in the conduit, La Forge had to slouch to keep his head from smacking the low overhead plating. "This hub is doing some serious work. Even without a tricorder, I can tell there's a lot of data being routed through this location. A lot more than most of the hubs I've inspected."

It operated on the same basic principles as the ones that drove Federation and Starfleet versions. Still, he knew there were variations unique to Cardassian ODN systems laced into its computer network hardware and software design methodology. So far, most of what La Forge had seen told him Starfleet's processes were superior, but given the station's immense size and the fact that the technology powering it was decades old, it remained an impressive feat of engineering. That still did not explain the amount of activity he now saw, which was at a level he might expect from Terok Nor's main operations center or central computer core, or perhaps to a lesser extent the entire Promenade. Given the location of this hub and its adjacent access space, there was no major piece of station infrastructure to account for the data load this relay was processing.

"*Once you verify its internal sensors are back online,*" said Mac-Dougal, "*I can run a diagnostic from here. That should tell us why the network is routing so much information down there, and from where.*"

Moving to sit beside La Forge, Gomez said, "I'm glad I don't have to explain to the Cardassians or the Bajorans or anyone else the reason the replicators or thermostats aren't working is because of an ODN junction on the opposite side of the station from their quarters."

"I'm betting the sonic showers and toilets being out of commission isn't making for a fun stay either." La Forge undid the fasteners on the hub's protective cover.

Gomez added, "And random comm traffic piped in at all hours? That's just rude."

The spate of malfunctions had begun just after Terok Nor's midnight—based on Bajor's twenty-six-hour day. In addition to plaguing various private quarters, the issues also were targeting areas of the Promenade as well as support areas with no apparent pattern, rhyme, or reason. All signs pointed to an error in the station's vast computer network, and Data had spent the hours subjecting the entire system to a rigorous level-1 diagnostic, while he scanned millions of lines of computer code rendered in no fewer than seven different Cardassian computer programming languages. The android's ability to focus on a daunting yet mind-numbing task cut down a search that might have taken days to four hours. Only then had he opted to awaken La Forge and other humanoids who required sleep, deploying them to different points around the station to investigate the anomalies that appeared to originate with dozens of disparate ODN relays.

Hampering efforts was the increasingly annoying fact that some of the reported irregularities could not be substantiated or traced. This gave rise to what MacDougal called "boojum hunts," or quests to track down what ended up being nonexistent or "phantom" problems. Despite being dead ends, they still demanded time and resources to inspect and rule out each one, while irritating those charged with carrying out those tasks.

After pulling the outer panel free to expose the relay's inner workings, La Forge retrieved the tricorder from the holster on his right hip and opened it. "Let's see what this tells us." Scanning the relay produced one quick and obvious result. "Sarah, you were right," he said, raising his voice for the sake of the active comm channel. "The internal sensor was offline." It took him a moment to find the control to reactivate that feature. "Does that make a difference?"

MacDougal replied, *"We're getting readings again, Geordi."*

"If only all the repairs could be that easy," said Gomez.

"No kidding." Studying his tricorder's readout, La Forge examined the relay's array of isolinear data rods, cylindrical secondary data-storage devices similar in form and function to the processing chips used in Federation and Starfleet systems. After a moment, a change in the readings made him frown, and he took a closer look at the array of data rods, arranged in four rows of ten. Each rod, secured in its own slot in the relay's interface, was formatted to hold instructions and system files configured to support this particular relay's specific, dedicated functions. They also were designed with easy replacement in mind, allowing the unit to devote its smaller internal processor to the information being routed to it with greater speed and efficiency.

"Sonya," he said, "do you see this?" He pointed to the third row of rods, and Gomez leaned closer to look.

"Hey, one of these things is not like the others."

All of the relay's data rods were a uniform amber color with a white endcap, except for one capped in red. "There's nothing that says this is wrong," said La Forge. "The white labels indicate hard-coded engineering instructions stored on the rod, which are the type normally used in systems like these where they rarely need to upgrade the baseline software. Red is usually reserved for temporary storage like code patches and library computer extracts." Raising his voice, he asked, "Data, are you there?"

"*I am still here with Commander MacDougal, Geordi.*"

"Can you check the maintenance logs to see when this relay was last serviced?"

The android replied, "*Stand by.*"

From his own satchel, La Forge retrieved a Cardassian data reader. He then extracted the incongruous data rod from its port and inserted it into the reader. "It's encrypted," he said as he observed the reader's scan of the rod's contents. "But there's a time stamp indicating it's less than a week old."

"*Geordi,*" said Data over the open channel. "*Maintenance logs indicate that relay junction was last serviced two months ago.*"

La Forge exchanged worried looks with Gomez, who asked, "You know what that means, right?"

"Yeah." The *Enterprise* chief engineer nodded. "This was deliberate."

From his combadge, MacDougal said, "*If this is supposed to be sabotage, it seems pretty silly.*"

"Or it's just the beginning."

21

—

Stepping out of the turbolift, Picard realized it had been forty hours since he last set foot on the *Enterprise* bridge.

Almost at once, he felt at ease as he took in the familiar sights and sounds. He had always thought of a starship's engines as its heart, but Picard considered the bridge its nerve center. As a young officer assigned to flight controller duties, he had always felt as at home on a ship's bridge as he did in the stellar cartography labs. It was not until standing night watch duty as an ensign aboard the *U.S.S. Reliant* that he sat for the first time in the bridge's command chair. That was when he realized it was where he belonged. Every subsequent action, decision, duty assignment, and choice of ongoing study was aligned toward the goal of commanding a ship of his own.

"Captain," said Riker, and Picard pulled himself from his brief reverie.

He turned to see his first officer standing with Lieutenant Worf and Ensign Ro Laren at Science II, one of the bridge's rear stations. The Klingon was as stoic as ever, but Picard could tell that Ro seemed to be struggling to keep her own emotions in check.

"You asked to see me, Number One?" asked Picard, moving from the turbolift alcove to join his officers.

Riker nodded. "Yes, sir. An ensign working in the communications section was conducting efficiency checks of the subspace relays in this region. All of the message traffic she analyzed was routine in nature, except for one transmission that stood out from the rest."

"Stood out?" Picard asked. "In what way?"

Riker looked to Worf, who said, "It was a short-burst transmission, sir, attached to what we're certain is a Cardassian message. The communications ensign thought it was encrypted and ran every cipher we have, but she could not crack it. Then she tried running it through the universal translation matrix, and that did not work."

"Are we sure it isn't garbled or some sort of subspace static or artifact from another message?" asked Picard.

Speaking up, Ro replied, "Oh, it's garbled, sir. Deliberately."

"I don't understand," said Picard.

Ro replied, "It's a code, sir. One created by a Bajoran. Two Bajorans, actually. I know this because I made it up with a friend of mine when we were children."

Picard did not even bother trying to hide his astonishment. "And you recognize this code from a message piggybacked onto a Cardassian transmission? You're certain?"

"Yes, sir." Ro crossed her arms, casting her gaze downward for a moment, and Picard sensed she was recalling something unpleasant. "Remember the refugee camp we visited last year on Valo II? When I lived there as a child, I befriended a Bajoran boy, Panat Hileb. We played with other children, and one of our games was creating puzzles and codes to communicate with each other in a way we thought could fool the adults around us. It's basically a series of mispronouncing words and inverting syllables." She smiled, but Picard saw it was without humor or joy. "Not very sophisticated."

"And you're sure it's this same code in the transmission?" asked Picard.

Ro replied, "Yes, sir. Once I realized what I was hearing, I pieced it together."

Looking to Riker, Picard asked, "Do we know where the message originated?"

The first officer shook his head. "No, sir, not yet. I've already instructed the communications section to trace the signal to its point of origin. As it was a Cardassian transmission, it didn't follow the standard protocols we use to carry out similar traces, but initial analysis suggests the original message was intended for a straightforward delivery to Cardassia Prime."

"Do we at least think it could have originated in Cardassian space?" asked Picard.

"It's the most likely conclusion, sir," said Ro. "Our subspace relay happened to be positioned in such a manner as to allow interception."

Picard said, "That might prove helpful in back tracing."

"It's a little more complicated than that, Captain," replied Ro, and Picard's concern grew with each passing moment as the ensign explained the message's contents and how it described the plight of her friend Panat Hileb. The unknown number of Bajoran nationals being held prisoner on an unnamed planet was troubling enough. Adding to that the idea of a troubling secret the Cardassians seemed determined to protect at all costs only made the situation even more dire.

When Ro paused her recitation, Picard asked, "You're certain this person sent the call for help hoping you would somehow receive it?"

"Yes, sir. My name is embedded as part of the message. I'm convinced it's from him." Ro paused, shaking her head. "I have to say, sir, I thought he was dead. I haven't seen Hileb since I left Valo II, and we lost track of each other in the years after that. I never knew what happened to him. I guess we know now."

Picard processed this revelation, shaking his head in amazement. "It was quite a gamble on his part, hoping you'd somehow find it."

Worf replied, "It is rather astute. This person likely knew that Starfleet listening outposts and subspace relays regularly monitor Cardassian communications passing through Federation space. The process was accelerated thanks to routine maintenance checks on that specific relay." He nodded in obvious respect. "I admire the ingenuity of those responsible for engineering this feat."

Allowing himself a small smile, Picard said, "They're certain it's because of this hidden facility that the Cardassians will never release them."

"Leaving no trace seems to be the operative phrasing, Captain," said Ro. "If Hileb's right about what's there, the Cardassians could be in violation of any number of interstellar treaties. Outlawed genetic engineering, illegal weapons research, and that's before whatever they face for violating the terms of the withdrawal agreement. I have no doubt the Cardassians will murder every last Bajoran there if it means keeping their secret." Her expression hardened. Without going into great detail, she described what life might be like for any Bajorans spared death on the planet only to spend the rest of their lives in servitude to Cardassian masters while officially being listed as missing or dead. As he listened, Picard felt his jaw clenching in mounting anger, which he forced himself to keep at bay.

"The message provides no coordinates," said Riker. "According to Ro, the Bajorans have no idea where the planet is located, or even if it has a name or stellar cartography designation. The only information we have is that a group of Bajorans, acting as part of the Resistance movement, were able to determine the protected facility must be moved, as the planet's location is now considered too near the Federation border."

"A shift in territorial lines," said Picard, considering that notion in light of recent developments in Cardassian-Federation relations. "There was no formal altering of territorial boundaries, but the Cardassians were determined to annex the Minos Korva system." The system, now a mere four light-years from the current border, would be viewed by the Cardassians as a security concern. A Starfleet observation outpost placed in that vicinity might be in position to detect activity related to this planet. Could that have been the real reason for threatening to attack and occupy the system?

Minos Korva, thought Picard. *Merde.* "The Cardassians can't hide an entire planet."

"No, sir," said Ro. "But they can alter star charts, redact any mention of location or identifying characteristics, and prevent anyone traveling to or from the planet from accessing any navigational information."

Worf added, "Based on what we know of Cardassian military activities, I believe they would refer to such a world in casual terms as a 'ghost planet.' If it does appear on any official star charts, it may well be listed as uninhabited or otherwise unsuitable for supporting life."

"All right, then let's start with that," said Picard. "Review all star maps of that area, with an emphasis on planets inside Cardassian territory that are less than ten light-years from the Minos Korva system." It was a hunch but, given the circumstances, it was one he felt comfortable playing.

Riker said, "Ensign, assuming we can find the origin point, what about composing a message to send back? Let your friend know we heard him and we're figuring out what to do next? They may be able to provide more information."

"I'm a bit rusty, but I can try," said Ro. "They may not have a means of monitoring communications. If the Cardassians discover it and find a way to translate it, that may scare them into executing their prisoners."

Turning from the workstation, Picard paced down the ramp on the bridge's starboard side. He moved to stand in front of the conn and ops stations, his attention on the main viewscreen as he took in the image of Bajor. From the *Enterprise*'s vantage point docked at Terok Nor, the planet looked serene, even welcoming. There was no way to see from this distance the pain and suffering inflicted over four decades on this unassuming world and the people who called it home. The idea they still had to face the cruel reality of just how malleable the Cardassians viewed truth and honor stoked Picard's anger. Even now, as they labored to push off the heel of subjugation.

"There's also the matter of the conference," he said. Turning from the viewscreen, he regarded his officers. "We cannot allow it to be disrupted. Even as we investigate this message, we must continue the proceedings. If we say or do anything that might alert the delegation we know something is amiss, it could doom the Bajorans on that planet." That was a good enough reason to determine the mysterious world's location as rapidly as possible.

"If things are moving as quickly as Ro's friend indicates," said Riker, "there may not be much time to mobilize a response. Doing this without tipping our hand means carrying on just as you have."

Picard said, "Indeed, but we still have options. Number One, you'll take the *Enterprise* to the Minos Korva system. So far as anyone is concerned, Starfleet has just reported a malfunctioning subspace relay station in that sector and ordered us to investigate. We're at a critical point of negotiations, and I cannot leave. But I have a capable first officer." He offered a wry grin. "Continue your efforts to trace the signal to its point of origin."

"What about Commander La Forge and his engineering team?" asked Worf. "Or Doctor Crusher and her team on the surface?"

"Mister La Forge's efforts are bearing fruit," replied Picard, "but there remain a number of technical issues demanding his attention." His chief engineer had already reported the series of odd glitches that had begun plaguing the station overnight, along with his evidence that these were deliberate acts of sabotage. La Forge had shared his concerns, mirrored by Picard, that these annoying yet minor malfunctions might be a precursor to a more aggressive undertaking. There was no solid proof linking the difficulties to any Cardassians, or any individual who had already departed the station.

"Doctor Crusher and her team are having a positive impact on the refugee situation. For the Bajorans' sake, both groups will continue with their activities. Given the precarious nature of the negotiations, any whiff of what we're doing may derail the entire process."

Stepping toward the tactical station, Riker leaned one hand on the curved console. "Sir, if there *are* Bajorans on a planet just over the border, and the Cardassians suspect why we're really there, they'd likely kill all of their prisoners before we could ever get close enough to rescue them."

The idea of igniting another interstellar incident between the Federation and the Cardassian Union did not sit well with the captain. Both sides were still feeling around, after the incidents in the Minos Korva system. He knew better than to think the Cardassians would forgive Captain Jellico or Starfleet for how they were embarrassed.

All while you were Madred's guest.

The thought emerged from the depths of Picard's consciousness alongside a vision of the legate, who was now in the midst of tormenting him in a new way. He drove the errant notion back, forcing himself to keep his attention on the matter at hand.

"Are we going after them?" asked Ro. "Crossing the border—"

"Is something we'll have to consider," said Picard. "Our first priority is verifying your friend and the other Bajorans are still alive and that planet's location. Wherever they are, the Cardassians are protecting something. Let's find out what that is. It may provide leverage if we end up confronting the Cardassian government directly about their violating the withdrawal terms."

Supporting the Bajoran government while it negotiated an equitable agreement for the suffering caused by over forty years of Cardassian occupation was vital. Exposing illegal Cardassian weapons research and development initiatives, on the other hand, was fraught with danger. Whatever happened in the coming days here on the station as well as in or near the Minos Korva system could determine the course of interstellar relations in this sector for years to come. All of it hinged on whether his crew was better at exposing secrets and threats than their Cardassian counterparts were at protecting them.

It's always a game with the Cardassians, Picard reminded himself. *Always.*

22

—

The water reached to her shins and required her to roll up her trouser legs to avoid soaking them. Her surroundings reminded Beverly Crusher of the days she spent playing in and around the shallow, slow-moving stream that ran behind the house where she lived with her grandmother. She would while away hours searching for rocks to add to her collection, fascinated by the rich mix of stones with their different textures and colors. The flat, shiny ones were always fun to find, and once Nana taught her how to skip them across the water, finding more became a moral imperative. They would often try to see who could get a rock to skip the farthest or the most times in a single throw. Nana always beat her, but there was the one time when she—

"Doctor Crusher?"

Looking up at the sound of her name, Crusher saw Keiko O'Brien regarding her with an expression mixed of equal parts confusion and amusement. She stood a few meters from her, pants legs likewise rolled to a point above her knees to keep them dry. Around them, the sloping terrain of adjacent hills rose above and away from them, framing the stream that coursed in lazy fashion through this small canyon. Trees grew in abundance here, towering overhead but not so high that they blocked the afternoon sun. At another time and under different circumstances, the idyllic scene would be perfect for a picnic, a lazy day spent relaxing with a book, or even a romantic getaway.

Save it for shore leave, Doctor, she thought. *There's work to be done.*

"I'm sorry, Keiko," she said, offering a sheepish smile. "I was lost in thought. This place reminds me of where I grew up."

The two women continued their slow walk down the center of the shallow stream, moving southward to where a fork in the river sent water into the underground system that fed the Singha labor camp. Searching for any clues to the source of the contamination afflicting Bajoran refugees, they had already walked the route coming upstream, starting at the point where the river descended beneath the surface. Sensor scans from the *Oceanside* determined that most of the subterranean area between here and the camp did not allow space to move about. Anyone caught in the current and sent tumbling into the underground passage would almost certainly drown. That left areas in closer proximity to the camp and its water-filtration and -distribution system, or something upriver. While minute traces of what they categorized as an alkaloid poisoning had been detected in the water feeding the camp, neither woman had been able to identify it based on what was known of Bajor's biodiversity.

All of that effort left them one place to investigate, and they were standing in it.

Walking with slow, deliberate movements through the water, a tricorder held in her right hand, O'Brien asked, "The Caldos colony, wasn't it?"

Crusher nodded, the very name evoking pleasant childhood memories. "Beautiful forests, rolling hills and distant mountain peaks, lakes and rivers and streams like this one. I spent a lot of time outside when I was a kid."

"You liked getting dirty, didn't you?" asked O'Brien, adding a wry grin to punctuate the question.

"My grandmother was a practitioner of holistic medicine.

She spent years studying the local plant life and figuring out which possessed medicinal qualities. It was a habit she picked up before we moved to Caldos, and it came in handy a few times. Other colonists would come to her for a remedy to treat this or that. She's the main reason I became a doctor. She keeps talking about writing a book documenting everything she's learned over the years."

Her attention divided between the conversation and her tricorder, O'Brien said, "So, no modern technology?"

"We had our share," said Crusher. "It wasn't forbidden, per se, but those who lived there made a conscious choice to limit its influence to varying degrees. Many of the colonists built their homes by hand or farmed without mechanical equipment, not because they were forced to but because they enjoyed the lifestyle."

O'Brien frowned. "I like the idea of eschewing technology, but that sounds like a lot of work."

"Don't worry," said Crusher. "We had computers and access to entertainment and news. We weren't hiding from modern society, but rather setting firm boundaries on how much it could encroach upon our daily lives. It was nice to sit and relax at the end of a hard day, enjoying a meal by the fire in our yard overlooking the stream." Her eyes narrowed, and she cast a mischievous expression toward her companion. "And I don't mind saying there's nothing quite like a warm bath outside by a roaring fire, with a bottle of wine in easy reach." O'Brien's laugh echoed off the sloping canyon walls, triggering a responsive giggle from Crusher.

"This place reminds me of where I grew up, too," O'Brien said. "The foothills near Mount Hanaoka where I lived with my parents in Kumamoto. We typically got a lot of rain there, so everything was green and lush."

Crusher said, "I've never been to that part of Japan. I visited Tokyo on vacation with my husband when we were first married.

I attended a few conferences at the Daystrom Institute on Okinawa. We also hiked the Sabō Trail to Mount Haku. Warm baths outside by the fire with wine work wonders after that too."

Before she could respond, O'Brien's tricorder beeped and she stopped walking. Holding the device before her, she began turning in a slow circle. "The tricorder just picked up something." Without waiting for Crusher to answer, she moved to the stream's far side and bent closer to the water, using her free hand to reach for something beneath the surface. When she stood up, it was while holding a yellowish-white plant with broad leaves and a long stem.

"There are traces of the alkaloid here."

Despite knowing whatever afflicted the Bajorans could not be transmitted without ingesting the water, Crusher still felt a sudden bout of self-consciousness regarding their current surroundings. "You're sure?"

"It's the same trace readings we found back at the camp." O'Brien held out her tricorder for Crusher to see, and the doctor nodded in agreement. "But stronger here."

Holding the waterlogged plant while subjecting it to the tricorder's scans, O'Brien said, "The readings we got at the camp were enough to tell us something was off, but this is a better sample." Then she frowned. "Beverly, it's not native to Bajor."

"Are you sure?"

"I ran a cross-check, based on what's loaded to my tricorder. I'd need to compare these scans against what the *Oceanside* crew's catalogued since they arrived, but I'm almost certain whatever's doing this isn't indigenous to the planet."

Crusher pointed to one of the readings. "Hang on. Enhance that." As O'Brien manipulated the tricorder's controls, the unit's compact display zoomed in on one of the scan readings. "That sequence of amino acids. Look at its breakdown."

Holding the tricorder closer, O'Brien said, "Tri-tyrosine, and something that looks like histidine and lysine. It's almost a perfect balance." She looked up. "The odds of that occurring naturally are—"

"Are next to impossible." Crusher blew out her breath in astonishment. "Keiko, I think you just found the answer."

Instead of being pleased with herself, O'Brien's worry seemed to deepen. "We may have found it, but we need proof." She held up the soggy plant. "We need the source."

"I thought the yellow ones smelled like lemon," Beverly asks, but Nana shakes her head.
"Not those. Don't touch those without gloves, honey."

Pointing to the tricorder, Crusher said, "Let's start asking uncomfortable questions."

Picard gripped the conference table, locking his feet around the legs of his chair to keep from floating out of it, only to realize the chair was beginning to move.

Dammit. These malfunctions, or glitches, or whatever they might be, were already becoming ridiculous. Around the table, Picard saw that everyone—Counselor Troi, First Minister Kalem, Kai Opaka, Legate Madred, and the two Cardassian intermediaries—were mimicking his movements in increasingly futile attempts to maintain their positions and their dignity. As for himself, Picard was comfortable in null gravity. Decades of space travel had inured him to its effects. Troi and Madred likewise seemed at ease, but the Bajorans and other Cardassians were having a tougher time.

"Troi to La Forge," said the counselor after reaching with a slow, deliberate movement to tap her combadge. "We could use some assistance in the wardroom. The artificial gravity seems to have stopped working."

Over the open channel, the *Enterprise*'s chief engineer replied, *"We just saw that, Counselor. Give us a minute to run it down."*

The interruption was but the latest in the series of setbacks La Forge and his people along with Chief Engineer MacDougal and her team from the *Oceanside* had been chasing for the better part of a day. It seemed as soon as one problem was identified and corrected, two more sprang up in its wake. Station residents contended with nuisance issues like nonfunctioning replicators and turbolifts, but the glitches had moved to safety features being deactivated at airlocks and docking ports. Major Heslo had already ordered those entry points taken offline, so they could only be opened manually lest a random computer instruction vented the Promenade or some other populated area to space. Heslo and his people were also locked out of the station's main operations center thanks to another wayward computer command, forcing them to work out of an auxiliary control space in the lower computer core, not far from where the Starfleet engineering teams were concentrating their efforts.

That all of this might be the product of sabotage made the situation all the more troubling.

Picard felt his stomach lurch, a telltale sign that gravity was returning. This sensation was followed by his feet settling back to the deck, allowing him to release his death grip on the edge of the conference table. Around him, he saw the other conference attendees as well as their chairs returning to the floor. Other evidence of the impromptu encounter of weightlessness was all around them, in the form of padds, plates, food, and other miscellaneous items dropping after being given free rein to roam the room.

"La Forge to Troi. Everybody okay up there?"

"We'll pass on lunch," said Picard. "But otherwise we're all right, Commander." He waited until everyone at the table affirmed his statement with nods and gestures—Madred with a grunt of disapproval. "Thank you for the expedient remedy. Picard out."

At the table's opposite end, Commissioner Wonar said, "A most unpleasant way to begin the day's discussions, Captain."

"My apologies, sir," replied Picard, resettling himself in his chair and pulling down on the front of his uniform tunic. "Our people continue to deal with a spate of malfunctions like these. They haven't yet had much success identifying the source of the trouble, but I'm confident they'll do so in due course."

Next to Picard at the head of the table, First Minister Kalem said, "I find it curious these incidents began only after the Cardassians ceded control of Terok Nor to Bajor."

"Perhaps your people aren't adequately skilled to operate this station," said Madred. His expression was one Picard had taken to envisioning beneath his boot.

"A possible explanation," replied Kai Opaka, "but an unlikely one, given your people forced my people to maintain this same station for decades."

"My friends," said Picard, holding his hands above the table before him. "This is not a path toward conducting a productive conversation. We still have matters of great import to discuss."

"The captain is quite correct," said Kalem. "Perhaps we should move on to other topics. For example, I am quite intrigued by the findings of the Starfleet medical teams, who appear to have identified the source of the ailment afflicting a great number of Bajorans." The first minister turned a withering gaze first upon Madred before moving to focus on Wonar and Arbitrator Ilson.

Picard forced himself not to react to the first minister's unexpected revelation. He had informed Kalem and Opaka about

Doctor Crusher's findings just moments before the current session began. There had been no time to provide full context or meaning to what Crusher and Keiko O'Brien had discovered on the surface. He had not expected Kalem to toss it in the Cardassians' faces in such blunt fashion.

As though sensing his growing alarm, Troi shifted in her seat to face Kalem. "Sir, if we could just—"

"I'm grateful to the efforts your people have expended on our behalf," said Kalem, holding up a hand. "I am the leader of the people now plagued by this issue, and it is my duty to be their voice as we seek explanation and recompense."

"What are you suggesting, First Minister?" asked Wonar.

The Bajoran leader held out his hands. "I should think it obvious, Commissioner. The compound used to poison our water supplies is artificial in nature and not native to our world." His hands turned to fists as he laid them on the table. "Your people introduced this contaminant as a means of further antagonizing the Bajorans they can no longer control."

"That's quite an accusation," said Ilson. "I would suggest taking care not to—"

Kalem's voice took on an edge. "I would suggest you remember you are guests here, Arbitrator. This station, this planet, *and my people* are no longer yours to control. I further suggest you contact whoever it is that provides you direction for these discussions, and seek additional instructions. Reaching an understanding and an accommodation *before* we find the proof of Cardassian misdeeds would be beneficial to both sides, wouldn't you agree?"

Before anyone could respond, Kalem rose from his chair. "Our business here is concluded for the day. Commissioner, I await any updates you may receive from your superiors." He looked to Opaka, who stood and followed him out of the room, leaving Picard and Troi to stare at the trio of Cardassians at the table's opposite end.

"That was certainly unexpected," said Troi.

Wonar said, "Was it, though? This all feels like a coordinated attack between Bajor and the Federation against the people of Cardassia, Captain. Is that what you wish me to convey in my next report?"

"Convey whatever you wish." With nothing left to discuss in the Bajoran leaders' absence, Picard got to his feet. "In the meantime, I would consider the first minister's proposal. If it's determined Cardassians are responsible for what is happening on Bajor and *on this station*, rest assured the Federation will hold your government responsible."

"Just as it has during our time on Bajor?"

Silence hung in the wake of Madred's statement. When no one answered, he added, "We both know of the Federation's ability to remain detached from matters it does not wish to recognize. I suspect this conference will end up representing nothing more than another iteration of the attitude that august body has spent generations refining." Then he smiled. "I must thank you, Captain. It's been quite some time since I was this entertained."

23

—

The room possessed no furniture except for the single chair in which Gul Havrel sat. A single lighting panel set into the center of the ceiling was the sole illumination source. Other than the prisoner—who wore wrist restraints attached to a retractable metal rod descending from that same lighting panel, holding his unclothed form upright while he balanced precariously on the balls of his feet—Havrel was alone.

As expected, Trooper Arrir had cried out in pain with every blow, and even pleaded for mercy while steadfastly denying the accusations Havrel leveled at him. He bled from a number of small, thin lacerations across his body, more than the prefect had even bothered to count, courtesy of the combat knife that was the sole item Havrel had brought into the room with him. The cuts were inflicted to induce pain and, in theory, incite cooperation rather than seriously wound. If he allowed it, a medic would need only a short time to administer treatment and perhaps a stimulant to foster accelerated blood production in the trooper's body.

Havrel had not yet allowed such measures.

Rising from the chair, he held up the knife in his right hand so Arrir could see it. Despite his obvious pain and fear, the young Cardassian followed the blade's movements with widening eyes, doubtless imagining where his superior officer might apply it next.

"Your user profile was employed to access the communications system," said Havrel, for the fourth time since this session began. Or perhaps the fifth. Had he lost count? He surprised himself at his lack of attention to detail, then excused it due to the current situation. "You attached an encrypted data string to an outbound message packet. I applaud your ingenuity, as it was all but imperceptible. I did not know they taught such skillful trade-craft at the school where you received your training. Your service file does not list an aptitude for such clandestine talents. What other special gifts do you possess that you deem unnecessary to share with those to whom you answer?"

He punctuated the question by drawing the blade's tip across the trooper's bare chest. This time, the cut was deeper, eliciting a guttural moan of agony as the prisoner gritted his teeth to keep from screaming. When he stepped back to admire the new inci-sion, Havrel watched the thin line of dark blood leaking from the fresh wound, converging into a single stream that coursed down Arrir's torso before dripping to the floor. For his part, Havrel was both surprised and disappointed that it was the first wound to produce that amount of blood. Were his emotions beginning to slip from his control? Might now be a good time for a respite?

No. Something about Arrir's responses made Havrel question his prisoner's guilt. On the other hand, he was not yet convinced of the trooper's innocence. He could remedy all doubt by calling for the camp physician and having him administer the medica-tions necessary to compel the prisoner's truthful answers to all questions put to him. So, why did he not do that?

You may not be sure what he is, thought Havrel, *but you're also not certain what he isn't.*

"Who was the intended recipient of your message?" he asked, just as he had previously done three—definitely four—times. On this iteration, he offered an addendum. "Are you an agent, sent to spy on this camp, or perhaps on me?" He stepped closer, raising the blade so it was level with Arrir's eyes. "Were you dispatched by the Obsidian Order?"

The trooper's expression changed from one of pain and fear to utter surprise, and his body began to tremble at Havrel's approach.

"The Obsidian Order?" Arrir nearly choked around his reply. "I have never encountered anyone from the Order, or if I have, then I did not know it. Why would they waste time with me? I'm a simple soldier."

A soldier assigned to technical and administrative tasks, Havrel reminded himself. Not a combat trooper or even a prison guard. On the one hand, his official assignment seemed like an ideal cover for an agent conducting clandestine activities. His duties would allow him access to the very tools required to send the message attributed to him.

On the other hand, Arrir's reaction to Havrel's accusation was so quick and so raw that the prefect was convinced it could not have been a performance. For certain, it was not the response of someone trained in the art of resisting interrogation and even torture, as he knew agents of the Order received. This was good, Havrel decided, for if he was wrong about Arrir, then he would have much for which to answer.

Or would you?

The question lingered in his mind, even as he knew the Cradis protocols under which he now operated also afforded him a great deal of latitude. This qualified autonomy extended to his ability to exercise judgment and initiative in the interests of maintaining operational security for the project. Havrel did not need explicit instructions for what he could do to protect its secrecy, as the simple invocation of the protocols came with automatic granting of that authority. Even the Obsidian Order was required to observe the conventions when such action was implemented. Barring anything egregious or that carried the risk of exposure and therefore public embarrassment of the Order, Central Command, or even the Detapa Council, the chances of Havrel being punished or even questioned for his actions taken to safeguard the project were low.

Assuming anyone finds out what happened here.

"Let us begin again," he said, returning his attention to the stricken trooper. "The system administrator's investigation revealed your user profile created and dispatched the message. According to her, you did a remarkable job concealing evidence of your activity. It took her quite some time to identify the source of the anomaly in the access logs she found by sheer happenstance. We have her attention to detail to thank for her discovery, along with her concern that we may have an enemy in our midst. Are you that enemy? What was the message's content? An activity report? A scathing indictment of our operation here? What could possibly be so interesting that it required you to go to such lengths to communicate with your mysterious correspondent?"

When he again held up the blade, Arrir flinched. In fact, it was the first such reaction from the trooper since being brought into the room. He had endured being escorted in by the pair of guards along with the humiliation of being stripped and suspended from the ceiling. Even when some of the cuts from Havrel's blade produced audible reactions, Arrir's body had not wavered or fought the mistreatment as he continued denying knowledge of any wrongdoing. Now Havrel saw a fear in the trooper's eyes that was more visceral than his previous responses.

"I told you, Prefect. I don't know about a message." The reply was weak, and almost inaudible. "I don't have authorization to use the communications array. I've never been granted that level of access." His arms grew taut as he sagged against his bonds, the weight of his body now supported by his restrained wrists as his chin all but rested on his chest. "Ask the administrator to audit my profile. She will see the truth."

In point of fact, Havrel had already requested such an audit, which he knew required an extensive review not just of the individual being investigated but also the entire system responsible for granting and controlling access to various areas of the camp computer network. He did not pretend to understand the complexities of such things, preferring instead to leave those and other mundane tasks to those who demonstrated the appropriate proficiency. Still, there was something to the way Arrir pleaded. Was he merely confident his cover could withstand such targeted scrutiny, or might he be telling the truth?

Regardless of the answer, the central problem remained: A message had been sent. Its contents and recipient were unknown. Security had been compromised. The ramifications of that breach were unknown, and could be escalating even as he stood here, seeking answers from someone who appeared to possess no useful knowledge.

Cradis protocols were of no help in this instance. Havrel knew he required guidance.

"You saw him?"

Huddled in the workspace beneath their barracks building, Panat watched Meeju nod in response, and he noted the haunted look in the woman's eyes.

"They took him to the infirmary," she said. "His uniform was missing. They covered him with a blanket, but I could see he had cuts all over." She gestured with her hands to indicate her own body. "He wasn't beaten. This wasn't a fight. He was tortured."

Leaning against her workbench, Yectu said, "Somehow, someone discovered his credentials were used to access the communications array."

Panat asked, "You couldn't have cloned a profile with the necessary clearances?"

Eyeing him with an expression bordering on contempt, Yectu replied, "There are only five people with that clearance. If I'd used one of their profiles, it would've been discovered even faster."

"I know." Panat offered a grim half smile, knowing how difficult it had been for his friend to do what she had managed to achieve. With the tools at her disposal and the restrictions under which she operated, getting the message out at all was nothing short of a miracle. It was not unreasonable to assume someone with comparable skills and better resources might discover what she had done. "And it doesn't matter. You accomplished what we needed you to do." Yectu had dispatched the message he had crafted for Ro Laren. Would someone—some Starfleet vessel or outpost—intercept the missive and route it to her, wherever she might be? Only as he struggled to translate the message into the code he and Ro had created as children did he consider the possibility she was no longer in Starfleet or, if she was, that she might not be in a position to act on the message in a timely fashion. That had not dissuaded him, and now it no longer mattered. His plea to her was out there, traversing the stars. There was nothing more for Panat and his friend here to do, except wait.

But not wait to die, he reminded himself.

"If Havrel let the trooper live," he said, "then he's probably doubting his involvement. They're going to start tearing the computer system apart, looking for the source of the infiltration, so maybe it's a good thing you didn't clone one of the more prominent profiles."

Yectu said, "I didn't say I didn't do it. I said I didn't *use* it."

Frowning, Meeju said, "Wait. You *did* clone another profile?"

"I cloned them all. Twice, actually." Before Panat or Meeju could ask, she added, "In case something like this happened. In fact, I set it up so that anytime one of their system administrators finds and removes a cloned profile, two more are generated to take its place. I inserted a self-replicating code fragment that executes, then deletes itself after every operation, but not before generating a new iteration that routes to another part of the system. Even if they find and delete profiles, my code is still active, detecting any trace activity and moving to stay ahead of it. The only way they're getting rid of it is if they flush the entire system and restore from a protected backup."

"Which they might not be able to do while they're in the midst of all this preparation to abandon the planet," said Meeju. "That's evil."

Yectu shrugged. "Thank you."

"It's not the computer system we have to worry about," said Panat. "Havrel knows someone is working against him. He's already ferreted out the obvious culprit and likely figured out that trooper had nothing to do with it. He has to keep looking."

"As paranoid as Cardassians can be," said Yectu, "and with the secrecy of the project still a concern, he'll start with anyone who has access to the system in any way." She sighed. "For the moment, that rules out any Bajorans, but he's not stupid. He'll get to us, eventually."

Panat said, "But we've still got some room to maneuver. On top of this, he still has to finalize the relocation operation, and keep anyone not briefed into the project from finding out about it. We already figured that's why he's maintaining the mining schedule. If he breaks from the routine, then we know something's up, and why."

A soft yet insistent knock echoed on the panel leading out of the dugout and into the ladder well.

"Time to go," said Panat. The rapping's pattern needed no explanation, and with Meeju's help he unsealed the panel, allowing Yectu to crawl through and begin ascending the ladder. With the panel once more in place, Panat followed her and Meeju back up to the barracks, emerging from the tunnel beneath the lavatory. Two of his fellow Bajorans were standing by to put everything back in place to disguise the hidden entrance. Panat saw Ranar waiting for him just outside the shower room.

"Surprise count," said his friend, holding jackets for the three of them. "Come on."

With a glance behind him to ensure the lavatory was ready for inspection, Panat along with Meeju and Yectu followed the rest of their barracks mates outside, falling into their assigned rows and columns so the guards overseeing the proceedings could get an accurate count.

"Another day," said a voice behind Panat. "Another count."

"At least they didn't wait until the middle of the night," replied someone else.

Taking his place in the formation, Panat glanced at Yectu as she fell in line to his left. "Coincidence?" he asked, keeping his voice below the volume of the prisoners' shuffling as they moved to their assigned positions in the group.

"Doubt it," said Yectu, facing forward rather than looking around.

Panat sighed. "Me too." He tried not to appear obvious as he watched the guards prowling around the formation's perimeter as though looking for a reason to mete out punishment on any of the prisoners. Something had them bothered. That much was obvious.

They were running out of time. He could sense it.

Ro, are you out there?

24

—

Will Riker watched the streaking stars recede to distant points of light as the *Enterprise* dropped out of warp. There was nothing remarkable about the image of space depicted on the bridge's main viewscreen.

Even as that thought occurred to him, the first officer smiled at the idea he could ever see space as anything but remarkable. Had he become desensitized to the idea of traveling between distant stars with greater ease than his ancestors had crossed Earth's oceans? What of the first humans who ventured forth to explore the other planets and moons in the Sol system? What was it like for that first human, Zefram Cochrane, to fly a ship faster than light itself? A beneficiary to all the struggles, tests, triumphs, and tragedies endured by those who had come centuries before he was born, Riker could never reduce the wonder to just another day at the office.

His commanding officer's ability to marvel, find poetry and stark beauty in even the most mundane things he might encounter was just one of the many things Riker admired about Jean-Luc Picard. While other first officers would have jumped at another assignment or even the opportunity to command, Riker harbored no regrets about his decision to forgo promotion and a ship of his own. He still had much to learn about being an effective leader, and the best example he had ever encountered normally sat in the chair Riker now occupied. Besides, being the first officer of the *Enterprise* was better than commanding any other ship in the fleet. Entrusted with a vessel that was the latest to safeguard a legacy dating back centuries was a high point of any Starfleet officer's career. From the age of wooden ships facing battle on the high seas to the first Earth vessel capable of exploring beyond the province of its own system and on to the exploits of every starship to bear its name, this *Enterprise* was a caretaker of legend. Starfleet had entrusted custody of that heritage to one of its finest captains, who in turn had once again placed the responsibility for its safe return to him.

So don't screw up, he mused.

"We're secured from warp speed, Commander," reported Lieutenant Jae, who crewed the flight controller's station in the absence of Commander Data. "We've arrived at the far boundary of the Minos Korva system." Rated for both the conn and ops positions, Jae was an officer who typified Captain Picard's preference for his crew continuing to train and gain experience across a broad spectrum of disciplines and duty assignments. It not only furthered their education and enhanced their chances of consideration for promotion and prestigious assignments, but this adaptability often came to the fore aboard a starship, where the situation could go from routine to chaos in seconds.

I should try to avoid that, thought Riker, even as his gut told him that more than likely would not be his option.

Pushing himself out of the command chair, he said, "Let's have a look around. Full sensor scan, Mister Worf."

"Aye, sir." The Klingon reported, "Long-range sensors detect a series of automated sensor buoys along the border."

Riker frowned. "Those weren't here during our last visit."

"No, sir, they were not. Scans detect no sign of ships. But that will not last for long." He looked up from his console. "Unless the ships are cloaked, we are alone."

Riker grunted. "Don't even joke about that." Though the *Enterprise* was a long way from any interstellar power known to employ cloaking technology, he knew better than to assume things could not go sour at a moment's notice. It would not be unlike the Romulans to send ships on covert missions into Federation space to poke around, but coming this far across the Neutral Zone would be out of the way even for them.

Again, he chided himself, *don't jinx it.*

"Ensign Ro," he said. "How far are we from the first subspace relay to pick up your message?"

Seated at the ops station in deference to Jae's seniority, Ro tapped the appropriate controls on her console to query the relevant information from the ship's computer. "Just under two light-years, sir. The relay is positioned at the halfway mark between the system's outer boundary and the Cardassian border."

"And how far to the next closest relay?"

The ensign replied, "Approximately two hours, twenty-one minutes at warp 5, sir."

"Approximately?" When Ro turned in her seat to regard him with a puzzled look, he smiled. "Sorry, I couldn't resist. I know not everyone can be Commander Data, but he does set the bar rather high."

Taking the joke in stride, Ro nodded. "Agreed."

Riker stepped forward to stand directly behind the two stations, resting his right hand on the back of Ro's chair. "All right, we've got our cover story in place. We're just a happy little starship on routine survey and repair duty." It helped that a check of Starfleet maintenance logs revealed the subspace relays in this region and in particular the one adjacent to the Minos Korva system were due for evaluation and possible upgrades. To any potential passersby, the *Enterprise* would look exactly like what it purported to be.

The plan submitted to him by Lieutenant Commander Leland Lynch, the acting chief engineer, included scenarios with the relays being brought into one of the ship's shuttlebays where they could receive legitimate upgrades and other needed maintenance. Lynch had even gone so far as to propose an alternative, more visible action involving an away team in environmental suits dispatched to carry out their work at the relays' respective locations while the *Enterprise* held station nearby. The elaborate ruses, complete with the authentic plans for servicing the relays, had been developed and submitted before Riker even had a chance to request them, impressing the first officer. Initiative went a long way toward counteracting any unexpected developments they might encounter.

Lynch had evolved and matured since his early days on the *Enterprise*, when he had displayed a tendency to butt heads with other members of the engineering staff and even annoy Captain Picard. When La Forge had been promoted to chief engineer, he took Lynch on as a personal project, helping the man learn to integrate into a team and not come across as standoffish. Whatever La Forge had done worked, as each of Lynch's subsequent officer evaluations were glowing.

"All right then," said Riker. "Let's start snooping. Mister Worf, how many star systems on the Cardassian side of the border are within our scanning range?"

Taking a moment to query the main computer, the security chief replied, "According to our star charts, there are three, sir. Two of the systems contain Class M planets."

Riker tapped the back of Ro's chair before pushing away from it. "Okay, so let's work with Captain Picard's theory about Minos Korva. If Starfleet were to put an observation outpost in this system, we know for sure they'd be able to see everything our scans are picking up, and more. If that idea has spooked the Cardassians, each of the three systems could be home to the planet we're looking for. Let's go hunting. Sensors, Mister Worf."

It took several minutes for the lieutenant to run a full sweep of the targeted star systems. Turning from the main viewscreen, Riker saw something was not sitting right with the Klingon.

"Worf? What is it?"

With a small yet still audible grunt of irritation as he continued to study the readouts on his console, the Klingon replied, "According to our scans, none of the Class M planets show signs of habitation. Indeed, there are no signs of any higher-order civilizations at all." His station chose that moment to emit a small string of tones Riker recognized as new information being routed from the *Enterprise*'s vast array of sensors. Taking a moment to consult the additional data, Worf shifted his stance, brow furrowed.

"Our scans do indicate signs of habitation on the third planet of what our star charts identify as the Satera star system. The sensors show it as Class M, but the charts show the planet is listed as Class T, incapable of supporting most humanoid life."

"Class T?" asked Ro. "A gas giant?"

Turning in her seat at the conn, Lieutenant Jae asked, "Do we think the Cardassians mislabeled a planet on the star charts and hoped no one would notice?"

"Of course they would," replied Ro, shaking her head in disbelief.

Riker had to admit the ruse, if in fact this was a hoax perpetrated by the Cardassians, was elegant in its simplicity. "It could work. The Minos Korva system is uninhabited, and close enough to the Cardassian border that civilian traffic gives this area a wide berth. Even Starfleet doesn't send ships out this way with any regularity. We rely on automated sensor drones to cover regions like this."

"The Cardassians would know this," said Worf. "They may have measures in place to defeat the ability of a sensor drone to scan across the border."

Ro said, "If that's the case, then why can the *Enterprise* do it?"

Contemplating the possibilities, Riker could come up with one plausible scenario. "Somehow, the Cardassians know the patrol routes of our automated probes in this sector. We're not scheduled to be here, so maybe we just got lucky."

Luck tended not to last, or it turned sour. The faster they could verify the presence of Bajorans in the Satera system and get out of here, the happier Riker would be.

"If the Cardassians are holding Bajorans there without having declared so," said Worf, "that is a violation of the withdrawal agreement. Expected behavior for Cardassians." He growled in obvious disapproval.

Riker said, "They think they're in the right when it comes to the Bajorans, but that's not even our biggest problem. If Ro's friend is correct and the Bajorans are in danger of being executed to protect Cardassian secrets, we can't stand by and do nothing."

Worf countered, "If we attempt a rescue mission, we could be responsible for triggering an interstellar incident. War, once again with the Cardassian Union."

Riker moved to stand between Ro and Jae, and he stared at the viewscreen. The planet that was the subject of interest was not visible, but it was there, taunting him. Could the Cardassians afford to have whatever secrets they were protecting exposed? Would any of that matter if a Starfleet vessel violated their border and carried out an unsanctioned mission against Cardassian forces? Would such action provide cover for burying the secret of that world? There also were the Bajorans to consider. If Riker seized the initiative and it all went to hell, would Starfleet have his back?

Don't screw up.

"Ro," he said, "maybe your friend can help shed some light on things. I think it's time we let him know we're in the neighborhood."

25

—

"Captain, you're allowed to call a recess."

Lost in thought, it took Picard a moment to realize Counselor Troi was talking to him. Embarrassed, he cleared his throat. "I apologize, Deanna. I'm not myself today."

It then occurred to him that he had said nothing to her during their walk to the wardroom. All he could recall was a perfunctory greeting after meeting her in the passageway outside their adjacent quarters. What had she just said to him?

"I was saying you don't need to wait for the first minister or the commissioner to request a recess." Keeping pace with him, she leaned closer, as if to make sure he was listening. "It's within the protocols for you to declare a recess for any number of reasons."

Picard said, "Is one of those reasons that a Cardassian intermediary captured and tortured me, and is now enjoying watching me as I relive that experience every time I look at him?" He glanced around to make sure they were alone.

To her credit, Troi took the serve and smacked it back across the figurative net. "That might fall under extenuating circumstances, such as requiring a visit to the lavatory or the Romulans declaring interstellar war. There might also be special dispensation for happy hour at that Ferengi's bar on the Promenade."

"Research that last one and get back to me."

He had spent the evening in private contemplation, ensconced in his temporary quarters attempting to lose himself in the pages of a book he had brought with him from the *Enterprise*. The book ended up holding little interest for him, and neither had the other tome he had packed as a contingency. There was nothing wrong with either volume, but they could not compete with the thoughts filling his mind. Despite multiple attempts, the Bajorans and Cardassians were as far apart now as they were when the discussions began. It was fair to say some of the demands levied by First Minister Kalem on behalf of Bajor leaned toward the extreme. However, his requests for assistance removing environmental hazards from the planet and a commitment to the return of Bajoran nationals and property taken offworld, as well as a full accounting for missing Bajorans and items, were reasonable.

As they turned a corner in the corridor, Picard said, "Have we heard from Commander Riker?"

Troi replied, "They arrived at the coordinates and are commencing repairs." Picard knew she was playing her role in the charade they had engineered to disguise the reason for the *Enterprise*'s departure. They had agreed not to speak of the ship's real mission anywhere on the station, in the event they were being monitored.

"They might return before we're done here," said Picard. "The Cardassians seem determined to downplay the lasting effects of the Occupation. 'Unauthorized deviations to the rules and regulations' is one excuse I recall."

Troi replied, "The one that irritated me was 'unsubstantiated indiscretions.' One has to wonder at their efforts to minimize what happened. Surely no one can accept something that's in direct contradiction to what they've seen and heard with their own eyes and ears."

"I assure you, Counselor," said Picard, "the capacity to craft a reality to suit one's worldview in order to avoid any responsibility for whatever horrible thing they have either enabled or incited is eternal." Even with their current efforts, the captain feared that how the suffering of the Bajorans had been ignored would remain one of the darkest chapters of Federation history.

His next thoughts were lost amid the sound and flash of the explosion.

White light flooded his vision, and he reached up to shield his eyes. Picard detected movement within or beyond the pale shroud that seemed to cover everything. Voices, muffled and indistinct, rang hollow in his ears. The white began to fade and figures emerged. His head throbbed with pain, and he sensed someone leaning close. Then he felt a hand on his chest.

"Jean-Luc, can you hear me?"

His eyes focused and he saw a wave of red before him, and he realized it was Beverly Crusher, leaning so close her hair was almost brushing his face.

He was lying on his back, instinct telling him to seek cover, and Picard attempted to sit up. That was a mistake, his body protesting the sudden movement. With a groan of pain, he let himself collapse back to a supine position.

"As your doctor, I advise against that for a few minutes."

Only then did Picard realize he was lying on some sort of bed. His vision, while still blurry, had refocused enough for him to see subdued overhead lighting set into the curved ceiling above him. It took him an extra moment to recognize the telltale signs of Cardassian architecture.

"Where am I?"

Returning to his side, Crusher leaned over so he could see her. "The station infirmary. You've been unconscious for nearly twenty minutes, but you don't have any serious injuries."

He blinked for several seconds, trying to clear his head. Then a single thought emerged from the others whirling in his head. "Deanna."

"I'm here, sir," said another voice, one he recognized for its soft, almost melodic quality. Troi added, "I'm fine, thanks to you."

Picard frowned. "Thanks to me?"

"You pushed me out of the way when the explosion occurred," said Troi. "We weren't close enough for serious injury from the blast, but a piece of debris caught you in the side of your head and you fell to the floor on top of me."

Gritting his teeth, Picard tried to remember, but there was a hole in his memory where that recollection should have been. He reached up to where his head hurt, expecting to find a bandage or blood or some other sign of injury, but he felt nothing.

"I already treated your wound," said Crusher. "I also scanned for signs of concussion or hearing damage, and you're fine. You'll probably be sore for a couple of days."

Finally able to arrange his thoughts into a useful order, Picard asked, "The explosion. What was it?"

"It was a bomb, sir," said Troi. "In the room set aside for the Cardassian delegation. We would have passed it on our way to the boardroom. If it had gone off just a few seconds later . . ." She let her voice fade.

Picard tried sitting up again, and this time he ignored his body's protests. "Was anyone hurt?"

Crusher replied, "Commissioner Wonar was in the room when the bomb detonated, and there was a Cardassian guard detail just outside. They suffered injuries and are being treated aboard the commissioner's ship, but Wonar took the brunt of the blast at close range. I got there as fast as they could beam me aboard, but it was too late. He never had a chance."

"But how—?" Picard stopped himself, a wave of dizziness

washing over him. Crusher moved to him with a hypospray and injected him; within seconds the unsettling sensations began to fade. He even felt a bit revitalized thanks to whatever she had given him. "How did someone get an explosive into that room? It was supposed to be secured, and guarded even when the commissioner wasn't there."

Troi said, "Major Heslo has the station's chief of security examining the scene with help from Commander La Forge."

A shuffling from somewhere behind him made Picard turn to see First Minister Kalem and Kai Opaka entering the infirmary, a Bajoran Militia security detail right on their heels. The Bajoran leaders wore matching expressions of shock and concern, and they made their way in hurried fashion across the room.

"Captain," said Kalem, extending his hands toward Picard. "Thank the Prophets. We were just informed of this unspeakable tragedy."

He took one of Picard's hands in both of his, and the captain could feel the first minister trembling in obvious worry. As for Opaka, at first she appeared to be her usual stoic self, but Picard could see the concern that also haunted her own eyes.

"First Minister," said Picard. "Eminence, given the circumstances, you may not be safe here. I'm compelled to ask that you both agree to let us transfer you to a safer location." He almost said the *Enterprise* before remembering his ship was not here. "Perhaps the *Oceanside*. I'm sure her captain will be more than happy to accommodate you."

Opaka replied, "We appreciate your concern for our safety, Captain, but our leaving the station would only send the wrong message, both to the perpetrators of this terrible crime and those looking to us for leadership and guidance."

"Further," said Kalem, "no matter who is responsible, it was an act of aggression upon our guests on our station. I cannot hide while others search for the guilty parties, and neither can I remove myself and leave others to shoulder that responsibility."

The dizziness was gone, and Picard was beginning to feel more like himself despite the muscle aches. Pushing himself from the patient bed, a move he made under Doctor Crusher's disapproving glare, he pulled down on the front of his uniform, which he now noticed was dirty and torn in places. "I can appreciate that. My primary concern is the blow it would be to your people if anything happened to you."

"Are you concerned about how any failure on your part to protect the first minister and Her Eminence might be perceived by the Bajorans, Captain?"

Although his body tensed despite his best efforts, Picard forced himself not to further react as he turned to see Legate Madred entering the infirmary. Another pair of Bajoran Militia members flanked him, but if the Cardassian took any notice of their presence, he did not show it.

"Madred," said Picard, keeping his voice neutral, "it is good to see you uninjured."

The legate made a show of putting a hand to his chest, though his face registered no emotion. "Captain, your concern is most touching. It is exactly what I would expect from a proper Starfleet officer."

Refusing to take the bait, Picard instead asked, "Where is Arbitrator Ilson? Was she harmed?"

"Like Legate Madred," said Troi, "she wasn't in or near the room when the explosive detonated. She's being questioned by the station security chief."

"When does the questioning expand to include Bajorans?" When everyone turned to look at him, Madred added, "Surely I'm not the only one who suspects this was the act of a terrorist.

There are Bajorans with significant grievances against my people, even if we disagree on the merits of their complaints."

To Picard's surprise, Kalem said, "The legate raises a valid point. This may be the work of a Bajoran, perhaps a former Resistance fighter or someone else seeking vengeance." He turned to Madred. "In the interests of continuing to advocate for my people, Legate, we pledge to assist in any way possible to help find and punish whoever is responsible. Despite our differences I still believe our discussions hold value. I sincerely hope we can find a way to forge a path ahead."

Madred said nothing at first, but his expression told Picard he had already made his decision and was waiting for a properly dramatic interval to pass before responding.

"To be honest," he said, "I was ready to end these negotiations, particularly in light of this indefensible attack upon one of our esteemed representatives. However, I have informed Central Command of this alarming incident. My superiors have instructed me to continue in Commissioner Wonar's stead. Arbitrator Ilson will remain, to assist me." When he paused, with a tilt of his head, his expression seemed to soften. "We all have our duty."

Excusing himself, Madred departed the infirmary with his Bajoran bodyguards in tow. The *Enterprise* officers exchanged surprised looks with Kalem and Opaka.

"That's quite a development," said Picard.

Crusher said, "I do not like that individual." She studied Picard. "All right?"

"Yes." Picard nodded. "I'm fine. Rather, I will be fine. We need to get to the bottom of this, and quickly." To Kalem, he said, "First Minister, it pains me to say this, but given the circumstances, we must consider the possibility this was the work of Bajorans."

Kalem's expression turned somber. "I agree, Captain. It would be foolish to rule out such a possibility. There have been other reports of Bajorans taking matters into their own hands against the Cardassians who've not left the planet or this station. My orders on this are very clear: such behavior will not be tolerated and the perpetrator will be punished."

Opaka said, "There is too much at stake, and we cannot allow our emotions to control us. We will work together to get past this, for the good of Bajor."

As the Bajorans left, Picard noted Troi watching them. "Captain, I sensed something . . . odd . . . from Madred while he was talking. It was a satisfaction—a sort of *perverse* satisfaction—with the turn of events."

"You think he was behind this?" asked Crusher, her eyes wide. "Really?"

"It wouldn't be the first time someone resorted to underhanded methods," said Picard. "It's more likely he's taking advantage of an opportunity to further his own interests."

"He's dangerous, Captain," said Troi. "Now that he doesn't have the commissioner to rein him in, he'll use this as a way of provoking you."

"We need to be careful, Jean-Luc," added Crusher, and he saw the genuine concern in her eyes. "*You* need to be careful."

26

———

No sooner did the transporter beam release her than Beverly Crusher felt herself enveloped by a profound chill. The sensation reminded her of walking into the large cooling unit at the back of her grandmother's lab where she stored various plants as well as seed and soil samples. The only sources of illumination were the lights worn by her, Keiko O'Brien, and Kira Nerys, strapped to their left wrists. The trio had activated them prior to transport, ensuring they did not materialize in total darkness. The effect of the limited visibility in the otherwise utter blackness was profound. Crusher could not help the momentary shiver coursing through her body, and rubbed her hands together for a moment before tapping her combadge.

"Crusher to *Oceanside*. Transport complete." She turned to see O'Brien and Kira standing behind her, and each indicated they were fine. "We're all here, safe and sound."

"Acknowledged, Doctor," said the voice of Captain Tamiko Hayashi, the *Oceanside's* commanding officer. After a moment, she added, *"According to our scans, you shouldn't be too far from the source of the readings."*

"We'll keep you posted," said Crusher.

Hayashi replied, *"We'll be here if you need us, Doctor.* Oceanside *out."*

Adjusting the sling of the satchel draped over her left shoulder, Crusher raised her arm and shone her flashlight's beam around their new surroundings. She could see and hear water seeping from countless fissures in the rock, running down a narrow, shallow stream that was all that remained of what she assumed was once a subterranean river.

"I'd guess the rerouting of the water into the camp affected its course down here," said Kira.

O'Brien stepped into Crusher's line of sight, her light playing off the nearby wall. "I can't believe this tunnel runs directly under the camp's water-management system, and no one ever noticed it before now."

"The Cardassians who built the camp likely knew about it," said Crusher. "They would've conducted site surveys and sounded the bedrock to make sure it could handle the stress of construction and if infrastructure needed extra support."

"It was likely Bajorans who built all of that," said Kira. "Overseen by their *benevolent* Cardassian overlords, of course."

When her tricorder beeped for attention, Crusher looked at the unit in surprise. "There's something down here. I'm picking up refined metals and indications of technology."

"Could it be mining equipment?" asked Keiko. "Or something left over from the original construction? They may have tossed rock debris and leftover materials down here."

Kira said, "That tracks with the usual Cardassian lack of concern for the environment. Given all the chemical and biological waste they tossed into our rivers, lakes, and oceans, it's no wonder the entire planet isn't in bed with whatever this contagion is."

The doctor's light was playing along the damp wall, but her attention was focused on listening for any sounds apart from the gentle litany of dripping water from multiple points all around her, and Crusher almost missed the irregularity on the stone in front of her. Catching herself, she pulled the light back, retracing her steps, until the beam shone on something out of place in an underground cavern.

"Have a look at this," she said, her voice echoing off the tunnel walls. She listened to the sounds of Kira and O'Brien sloshing through the ankle-deep water, their lights dancing along the walls and ceiling as they drew closer. With the three of them now standing together, they were able to combine their lights to get a better look at the wall.

"What is that?" asked O'Brien as she focused her light on a small circular cap, mounted to a portion of pipe embedded into the rock.

Shifting the satchel on her shoulder to a more comfortable position, Crusher eyed the valve. "About ten centimeters across. Maybe it's a valve of some kind?" Activating her tricorder, she aimed the device at the odd fitting, and the unit beeped within seconds. "Nine point eight centimeters. This is recent. Very recent. According to these readings, the hole behind this thing was cut no more than a few weeks ago."

"A few *weeks*?" asked Kira. "By whom?"

Frowning, Crusher replied, "The pipe is horonium, while the cap is a tritanium alloy. My readings indicate the metallurgy's consistent with Cardassian processing techniques."

"Who else?" asked Kira, before adding, "Actually, the more important question is, where does this thing go?"

Checking the readings on her tricorder, O'Brien replied, "The pipe extends upward through the rock at a ninety-five-degree angle for approximately fifty-two meters." She looked up from her readings. "That's the underground river running into the camp."

"That doesn't make any sense," said Crusher. "Opening that valve down here would send water shooting down into this cavern. The pipe's too small to effect any sort of efficient drainage or flood control."

O'Brien said, "Let's take off the cover and see?"

Expecting a fight to loosen the cap, Crusher was surprised

that she could turn it with just one hand and no effort. It only required a half turn before the cap came off in her hand, but no torrent of water followed.

"Look inside," said Kira, shining her light into the now-open pipe. "There's something in there. A tube of some sort."

Crusher reached into the pipe, her fingers playing across the edges of whatever was stored inside. She felt it give under her touch, and a clockwise turn freed it from whatever locking mechanism held it in place. What she extracted was a cylinder fashioned from a transparent polymer. A metal cap at the cylinder's forward end included a nozzle, whereas the opposite cap was heavier, suggesting internal components.

"It looks like a kind of injector system," said Crusher.

"Beverly," said Keiko, who was once again studying her tricorder, which had begun to emit an attention-getting beeping sound. "This is it. This *has* to be it. This is how they were contaminating the water. I'm picking up significant alkaloid residue that matches the samples we found. The concentration here is incredible. There's no way to mistake it for something else. *This* is it."

She pointed to the open valve. "The pipe's far end contains a mechanism to receive this cylinder. According to my tricorder readings, the cylinder is loaded with the alkaloid before sending it to the pipe's far end, where it positions itself inside that endcap. The valve at the other end opens up into the river under the water-management system. The nozzle in the cylinder ejects the alkaloid, and the empty cylinder returns to this point."

"That sounds like a pretty crude plan," said Kira. "This worked?"

Crusher said, "The simplicity works in its favor." She gestured to the valve. "Whoever did this was in a hurry. I'm guessing a drill took care of boring the conduit before the valves were applied.

It likely would've required someone to go underwater to set that valve into place, and the initial drainage down to here might explain the pools of water down here."

"That seems like an awful lot of trouble to poison people with something that isn't fatal," said Kira, before adding, "At least, it hasn't proven fatal *yet*."

O'Brien said, "It also seems like an awful lot of trouble to do from down here." She looked around the cavern. "That alkaloid could have been introduced into the water supply from anywhere along the river's natural route. Why here?"

"Easier to conceal the nature of the toxin?" offered Kira. "You said it's artificial and not native to Bajor. The obvious source is the Cardassians. They're not known for their subtlety when it comes to how they treat Bajorans. They'd rather just kill us outright, assuming they had no further use for us."

"But that's just it," said Crusher. "Whoever was behind this didn't do it to kill anyone. All it did was create a huge influx of patients requiring medical care." She paused, her thoughts locked in an internal struggle even as a single line of reasoning fought to separate itself from the jumble in her head. "A distraction. Drawing attention and resources to other areas. The field hospitals, the other labor camps, even Terok Nor, but why? There's still an entire hospital on the surface above us, filled with patients, and if we're right about all of this, then this is ground zero."

O'Brien replied, "*One* ground zero. Remember, Doctor Tropp said there were at least two. We haven't even examined that other location." She pointed to the cylinder Crusher still carried. "But if we find something like this there . . ."

"Then we've got a ball game," said Crusher. Opening her satchel, she placed the cylinder inside for safekeeping. "I'll run a full spectrum of tests once the *Enterprise* gets back." The current mission had scattered the crew and taxed the senior staff.

Commander Riker even had to rely on an assistant chief engineer and Doctor Selar.

"We've gotten what we came for," she said. "Let's call it a day and get out of here."

"Not so fast," said Kira. "There's something else down here."

Turning toward her voice, Crusher and O'Brien saw that the Bajoran woman had moved with surprising stealth to another section of the tunnel nearly twenty meters away. Crusher did not recall Kira making any sounds that might give away her position. Down here in near darkness, it was an impressive skill.

"You're very good at keeping quiet," she said as they joined her.

Kira replied, "A surprise attack is harder if they can hear you coming." She lifted her light to the cavern wall. "Look at this."

The last thing Crusher expected to see in the tunnel was a door.

"It's a recent installation," said O'Brien. "The tricorder can't scan what's behind it. According to these readings, that's solid rock there."

The door featured a handle, and Crusher reached for it. There was no resistance when she turned the handle, and she felt the latching mechanism disengaging as the door swung outward. A shaft of light emerged from the opening, widening as she pulled the door farther open.

"Look out!"

Crusher only had time to see the muzzle of the disruptor before she felt a hand on her arm, yanking her out of the doorway. She heard the sound of the weapon discharging and the electrical sensation playing across her exposed skin as an energy bolt screamed through the space where her head had been.

Off-balance, she tumbled into O'Brien, whose hand was still gripping her arm as they both fell out of the line of fire. She grunted in pain as her knee struck the cavern's unyielding rock floor. She heard another round of weapons fire, this time from behind her. A second shot followed, and as she rolled onto her back Crusher saw Kira advancing on the door, both hands gripping her phaser as she entered the room beyond the open entryway.

"Are you okay?"

It was O'Brien, her face a mask of concern. Before Crusher could respond, she saw Kira emerge from the doorway, still holding her phaser in her right hand.

"You're pretty fast with that thing," said Crusher, before grimacing at her sore knee.

Kira nodded. "Well, we weren't being quiet, so I settled for being ready."

"Fair enough." With O'Brien's help, she regained her feet, and they followed Kira into the room. Crusher froze at the entryway, feeling her jaw go slack in response to the sight before her.

"Oh my god," said O'Brien.

Cargo containers and crates of varying sizes filled a modest-sized chamber. Among the dozens of items not packed away out of sight were art pieces—sculptures, paintings, tapestries, jewelry. Haphazard stacking created voids and passages between the larger containers, which Crusher assumed contained a greater number of items similar to their visible counterparts.

"This is Bajoran," said Kira, her voice tight. "Stolen. I recognize pieces that went missing decades ago. We knew the Cardassians were looting, and whenever we found anything, we took it back. But we also knew they were shipping artifacts offworld, presumably to Cardassia." She shook her head, her expression one of disgust. "I guess that's what you do when you sell off your own civilization's cultural and historical artifacts to fund your military: go and take someone else's."

"I'm all for preserving history and culture," said Crusher, "but who did you shoot?"

Waving with her phaser, Kira led them deeper into the room and to the unmoving form of a Cardassian soldier slumped against one of the larger cargo containers.

"I only stunned him," she said, taking the moment to holster her weapon.

Crusher asked, "Any idea who he is?"

"Gul Tranar," said Kira. "Former prefect of the camp above us. I'm guessing he had plans for all of this, but they fell apart when the Cardassians were told to abandon Bajor. Even with the order to return any plundered artifacts, he probably would've gotten all of this offworld if the Federation hadn't decided to show up."

O'Brien said, "He cooked up a plan to poison Bajorans, and for what?"

"One more way to express displeasure at being forced to leave," said Kira. "Accountability feels like oppression when you've never been held to account."

"This should help the captain," replied Crusher. She knew Jean-Luc had been engaged in a battle of wills as he attempted to assist the Bajorans with their negotiations for compensation from the Cardassians. The discussions were hampered by the all-but-impregnable air of superiority that seemed to surround the Cardassian delegation. The tragic death of Commissioner Wonar, possibly at the hands of a Bajoran assassin, did not make the process any easier.

Gul Tranar and his secrets, on the other hand, might be just the thing to buy Jean-Luc some much-needed leverage.

27

—

Odo had heard all of the rumors surrounding the mysterious Cardassian with a secret past. He found them interesting and even a bit amusing, after a fashion. The idea that this unimpressive, unremarkable individual calling himself a tailor might once have been an agent for Cardassia's elite intelligence organization was intriguing. There were things about him that piqued Odo's curiosity and made him want to dig deeper into the dark corners of his life. What might he find? Who might he upset with his quest for truth? Would he be doing the tailor a favor by drawing attention to his presence on the station? Or would his actions merely serve to expedite his departure from the realm of the living?

These were the types of thoughts that occupied Odo's time, exercised his mind, and gave him a sense of purpose. If exposing Garak for the liar, spy, assassin, or whatever else he once might have been would protect the station, Odo would gladly sacrifice the loner to achieve that goal. He would derive no pleasure from it, but he was driven to the exclusion of all else to carry out the mandate given to him by Major Heslo: keep Terok Nor safe.

Well, he admitted to himself, *I might enjoy it. A little.*

At long last, the tailor shop's doors slide aside and the lights activated, revealing Odo's presence inside the establishment to its proprietor. To his credit, Garak managed to appear not at all surprised by his uninvited guest.

"Good morning, Constable." Garak made a show of looking around the room. "I'm not even going to bother asking how you managed to get in here without setting off the alarms. Let's just file that under the prerogatives of your position." He paused, studying Odo. "Is today the day you decide to rid yourself of that garish ensemble which does absolutely nothing to offset your unique complexion, let alone frame your head and neck in a respectable manner? A man with your physique would look more dignified with a high collar. Regal, in fact. I'm absolutely certain I can make it work for you."

Odo was already growing bored with this Cardassian's penchant for wordplay. "You know that's not why I'm here, Garak."

"I do?" The tailor's eyes widened in what presented to Odo as feigned confusion. Then his mouth opened in an expression of shock. "Wait. You're here about that unfortunate incident involving Commissioner Wonar."

"Let's just say you were the first person I thought of."

After it was determined the room had no damage to the point where it might pose a danger of explosive decompression, Odo and the *Enterprise*'s chief engineer, Commander La Forge, had subjected the room to a variety of scans using Starfleet equipment as well as a portable sensor unit Odo had found in the station's security locker. It was not nearly as sophisticated as La Forge's tricorder, much like Cardassian justice compared to the Federation's. Cardassian law simplified things by assuming guilt before the trial. Brutally efficient. Odo found it arrogant.

As Garak proceeded to go through the motions of preparing to open his shop for the day, Odo said, "The explosive was an interesting construct. It was built using components of both Bajoran and Cardassian design. The sort of thing you'd expect from the Resistance: using whatever parts they could find. It occurs to me you have as much reason as any Bajoran to kill Cardassians."

Garak paused in the act of dressing a mannequin, turning to face the security chief. "You honestly believe I would employ such a shoddy device in order to carry out a thoroughly incompetent assassination attempt?"

"Incompetent?" Odo scowled. "Commissioner Wonar might think differently."

"Perhaps," said Garak, "but Arbitrator Ilson and Legate Madred are still alive."

"Meaning?"

Rolling his eyes, the tailor replied, "If I was going to construct a device that implicated me as the prime suspect, I'd at least make sure it was worth my while. Killing one person is a waste of a perfectly good explosive."

Odo crossed his arms. "You seem well-versed on the topic."

"Look around you." Garak made of show of gesturing with his arms to indicate his shop and by extension the rest of the station. "I've lived here long enough to know how things work. No one hoping to carry out successful acts of terrorism is going to expend time and resources on a single soft target. There are several other more efficient methods. However, even as you pursue this hunch for the wrong reasons, you are overlooking one simple fact: The list of people with the knowledge to build that device is very long. It includes any Bajoran who fought in the Resistance who's still alive. It even includes you, Odo."

"And you," replied the security chief. "You do have a list of detractors, which so far as I know is every Cardassian currently drawing breath. It would make your life a lot easier if the more enthusiastic champions for your demise were no longer around. On the other hand, it all does make for an interesting cover story."

"Well," said Garak, "this does generate warm thoughts. I've given you my reasons for why engaging in an act as amateurish as that one would be a waste of my time. The fact that it would expose whatever ruse you think I'm employing is but another justification for avoiding something so stupid."

Now it was Odo's turn in this verbal sparring match. "There is one thing that separates you from most, if not all, potential suspects. We both know this tailor shop is just an act. You've been here too long and there are too many rumors about your past to dismiss them all. I pay attention when all of the noise sounds the same, even if it's produced by different sources."

Garak smiled. "Oh, yes. This notion of yours that I must be an agent for the Obsidian Order."

"Or some other intelligence entity," replied Odo. It was true that Garak had caused no trouble during his time on the station. At least nothing to which Odo could connect him; still, he did not understand why Gul Dukat had tolerated him, and why Major Heslo now allowed him to stay. Garak was a Cardassian, and given the current circumstances, ordering any and all Cardassians from Terok Nor seemed like a common-sense decision. Perhaps Heslo's replacement would have different thoughts on the matter. "If you are what you claim you're not, then you're smart enough to make it look like a sloppy attempt in order to throw off suspicion."

"I think that's a compliment," said Garak, his expression one of amusement as he picked up a jacket and crossed the floor toward a mannequin. "One I gratefully accept."

Odo said, "I'm also wondering if Wonar was your actual target, or whether you might have been after Madred."

The hesitation was fleeting, perhaps imperceptible to almost anyone else, but Odo caught it. Garak covered it well enough, continuing through the motion of dressing the mannequin with the jacket.

"Madred and I have crossed paths before," he said. "I won't deny it."

"You won't?"

"I mean, I could." His eyes widened in that manner Odo was beginning to find irritating. "I'm just not denying it right now."

"I saw you two in the replimat," said Odo. "It appeared rather animated, despite the remarkable self-control you both exhibited. Two professionals, keeping their emotions in check as they conducted business."

Garak smoothed wrinkles from the jacket before turning toward another suit and readying it for another mannequin. "A discussion about matters long past. We've settled our differences. At least I thought we did. He even provided me with a bit of useful advice for getting on with this rather challenging new phase of my life."

"Terrorism?" asked Odo.

"I was going to say exile."

"He seems like the sort of person someone might want to kill. Maybe not in general, but certainly you."

"My goodness," said Garak in mock surprise. "Such language, and impure thoughts." He shrugged. "Still, perhaps we did not leave things as I thought. With that in mind, tell me, Odo. Have you considered the possibility it was Madred who instigated this mess? He's the one with the most to gain from these negotiations. Removing Wonar allows him to take the lead in the talks, advocating not only for Cardassia but for his own advancement. Madred lost favor when he couldn't torture one Starfleet captain without botching it."

He held up a hand, pointing a finger toward the ceiling. "And as a bonus, he gets to implicate me and put me in your sights. Being the dogged, relentless purveyor of truth and justice that you are, perhaps Madred knows you'll devote your time to the obvious suspect who's standing right here in your midst, thereby ignoring whatever plans he may be putting into motion."

Before Odo could respond, alert klaxons began wailing both inside the store and out on the Promenade. Racing out of the shop, Odo saw the alarms were activated all through the concourse. He looked to the various viewscreens positioned on stanchions or mounted to bulkheads, but none of them were active. He tapped his communicator pendant.

"Odo to Operations. What's going on?"

The voice of Major Heslo burst from the channel. *"Odo, we've got a serious problem. The station is moving."*

It had been a long time since Miles O'Brien had seen so many status indicators flashing alert conditions at the same time. When that sort of thing happened, it was his experience that people were shooting at him, or his ship.

This was something altogether different.

Standing at one of the consoles in the auxiliary control center in the lower portion of Terok Nor's central core, Commander La Forge was doing his best to make sense of the Cardassian schematics flashing on the array of display screens and status monitors. Next to the console, a portable version of the master situation table in the *Enterprise*'s main engineering section had been programmed to handle a litany of translation duties so the Starfleet personnel could interact with the station's systems. O'Brien could see the unit was overtaxed.

"La Forge to all *Enterprise* and *Oceanside* personnel. Be advised the station is shifting out of its orbit. We're moving, and we're not in control."

"What can we do?" asked O'Brien.

Without looking away from the monitors in front of him, La Forge replied, "That's what I'm trying to figure out."

"Picard to La Forge." The voice of the *Enterprise*'s captain filled the room. *"Geordi, what's happening?"*

"Another glitch, Captain. Only, this one's the winner. The station's entire axial vector stabilization system is online, but we've been locked out of it."

"What does that system do?" asked Picard.

La Forge replied, "It's the Cardassian version of a reaction control system, part of what helps the station maintain its orbit and attitude. That's done with a series of maneuvering thrusters positioned all around the station, just like we have on the *Enterprise*. Normally, you'd pulse only the ones needed to make a minor attitude correction, and the station's main computer tends to handle those types of adjustments automatically."

"Things are not normal."

"No, sir. Maneuvering thrusters are firing at random intervals, with no discernible pattern."

The captain's reply was squelched by a burst of static that seemed to overload the open comm channel, then O'Brien heard nothing.

"Captain?" prompted La Forge, but there was no response. "Well, that figures."

Standing at an adjacent console, the *Oceanside*'s chief engineer, Sarah MacDougal, said, "A new security encryption scheme's been enabled throughout the system. It's Cardassian, but I have no idea what triggered it."

"It could've been anything," said La Forge. "My bet's sabotage."

O'Brien said, "Exactly." He had spent several minutes looking through the engineering files from the main computer, hoping to see something jump out from the garbled mess of Cardassian technical schematics. "There are too many redundant safety features for something like this to happen by accident. Whatever this is, it was deliberate."

The doors behind him slid aside, and O'Brien glanced from his console to see Commander Data, accompanied by Ensign Gomez, entering from the access corridor. Data was carrying a tricorder, but unlike everyone else, the android showed no sign of emotional reaction to the current situation.

"Tell me some good news, Data," said La Forge.

"I am afraid I cannot do that, Geordi," replied the android. "I have just completed a diagnostic of the station's attitude and orbital stabilization systems. If the thrusters continue to fire in their current manner, the station will eventually decelerate to a point its orbit begins to decay, at which time it will descend into Bajor's atmosphere."

O'Brien added, "Unless we can regain access to the system or find some other way to stop what's basically becoming a deorbit burn."

"That is correct, Chief O'Brien." Data turned back to La Forge. "My calculations indicate we have twenty-four minutes and eleven seconds until we will no longer be able to arrest our descent."

Gomez said, "All the people down there. What do we tell them?"

Feeling a wave of dread washing over him, O'Brien blew out his breath. "Tell them to duck."

28

———

"Oceanside *is separated from the docking pylon. We are maintaining position relative to the station's movements. The thrusters' effects are currently limited to attitude and position relative to its geosynchronous orbit above Bajor. It's decelerating and the rate of orbital decay is increasing. We can commence station evacuation, but not everyone can be taken off in the time remaining, Jean-Luc.*"

In Terok Nor's wardroom, Picard nodded to the image of Captain Hayashi displayed on the wardroom's viewscreen. She sat on the bridge of her ship, which resembled that of the *Enterprise* but lacking a few of the aesthetic choices of a *Galaxy*-class vessel. What mattered to him at the moment was the *Oceanside*'s presence and ability to help with the current problem, which was threatening to spiral out of control.

"Tamiko," he said. "I understand there are legitimate security concerns. But we must begin."

Hayashi nodded. "*Absolutely, there's no time to be dainty about it. Notify Major Heslo we'll collect the Bajorans. We can lock on to all Bajoran life signs and have them beamed into our shuttlebay and cargo bays. I can secure those areas, and we'll go from there. We can transport the Cardassian delegation to a different secure area.*"

Their dual yet separate missions had kept them from meeting, but she had acquired a reputation as a confident officer highly capable of handling difficult assignments. The types of missions *California*-class starships carried out required a deft touch and the ability to adapt on the fly to rapidly evolving situations. Their captains needed to be polished diplomats as well as experts in adaptability, improvisation, and tactics. Those who commanded ships tasked with second-contact missions were, in Picard's admittedly limited experience, a special breed, and often rubbed the top brass the wrong way.

As if sensing his concerns, Hayashi added, *"Captain, I know there are regs for situations like this when two captains are on scene, who has the tactically superior ship or who even has a ship . . . I don't care about that. You're the senior officer, but you're also the one stuck over there. I'll follow your lead, sir."*

"I appreciate that, Captain. You're doing just fine. Carry on."

Pausing to look down, Hayashi made a gesture before returning her attention to him. *"My first officer's getting things going. Is there anything else we can do?"*

"A projection for the station's most likely point of impact would be useful." Even as he spoke the words, Picard knew having that information would be of little or no help. The bulk of the station would likely survive atmospheric re-entry due to its sheer size, and the probability was it would break apart during its descent, creating a hell storm of debris that would pummel whatever area of the planet was unfortunate enough to receive it.

"I've got my science officer on it. Wherever that thing lands, it's going to be a problem."

"Agreed." There was too little time to contemplate things that were out of his control. "I'll notify Major Heslo so he can prepare the station's population. Once they're safe—"

"I know what you're going to say. Starfleet personnel will be the last ones off. But, Captain, if the situation gets to a point where we know we can't save the station, I'm yanking everyone back to the Oceanside."

"Understood. Major Heslo can assist you with keeping the situation under control."

"Outstanding." She stopped, holding his gaze for a moment before saying, *"What else can we do, sir?"*

"Carry on. Your engineers are working with mine to solve the immediate problem. I have high hopes for our success."

"I've learned not to underestimate any Enterprise *engineer, past or present. If anyone can figure this out, it's them."*

"I have no idea what the hell is going on."

Miles O'Brien stared at the portable master situation table. The mishmash of tortured kiloquads of information pulled from Terok Nor's main computer made no sense. All of the station's design specifications were now available for review, and O'Brien watched as Commander Data scrolled through pages of diagrams and their associated information at a rate faster than any living being could match.

"The fault appears to lie in several subroutines overseeing the axial vector stabilization system's emergency response protocols," said Data. "Background programs that normally review and update information supplied by attitude and position sensors for each of the reaction control system thrusters appear to be acting in conflict with one another, rather than synchronizing their efforts to maintain the station's relative position."

O'Brien said, "Sir, are you saying the thrusters are fighting each other?"

"In a manner of speaking. If all the thrusters were firing simultaneously, we would be able to use that to our advantage and maintain the station in a fixed attitude."

"But that's not how the RCS works," pointed out La Forge, moving to the portable master situation table while Sarah Mac-Dougal continued working to find a means to override the interlocked series of engines and initiate a manual shutdown. "They're designed to fire in dynamic sequences in order to automatically recalibrate the station's position above the planet."

Data said, "Precisely. The system is designed to ensure that none of the thrusters 'fight' with one another, either by canceling out their efforts or causing a diversion from the desired position."

"There are six redundant safeguards to protect against that," shouted MacDougal. "None of them are working."

"They are not working because those subroutines have been intentionally bypassed." Data swiped at the display on the portable MST so it now displayed a schematic depicting a cross section of Terok Nor. "I have detected program anomalies in seven different locations around the station. They are similar in nature to the compromised optical data network relay investigated by Commander La Forge and Ensign Gomez. I believe the same type of invasive program was used on those relays via isolinear data rods. This allowed the updates to bypass the main computer's central processor."

"Isn't that supposed to be impossible?" asked O'Brien. "For that very reason?" Trying to do something like that aboard the *Enterprise* or any Starfleet ship would trigger a shipwide alert that would isolate the compromised access point and dispatch security to the targeted location.

"The chief's right," said La Forge. "But this system doesn't take into account someone with the necessary skills to bypass them at the point of intrusion." He looked around the table. "Unless any of you have been serving on a Cardassian ship or space station prior to the last couple of days, you're disqualified—except for you, Data."

Without acknowledging the comment, the android said, "Even if we could purge the main computer system of all active instances of the malicious software, there is insufficient time to go to each of those locations and remove the data rods to prevent new versions of the code from being delivered."

"What if we turned everything off?" asked La Forge. "Trigger the station's emergency shutdown procedures. That would kill the engines, the computer core, the reactor, everything."

Data replied, "The deorbiting burn has already progressed to the point that simple inertia will push the station toward the planet surface. A complete shutdown and restart would require more time than we have available before the descent is past the fail-safe point."

"You're saying if this had happened an hour ago we could do it?" asked O'Brien. "What can we do to buy more time? Can we alter the thruster firing sequences manually? Maybe working together, we could override what it's doing and at least hold steady until we cleared the compromised systems."

"Even if we were able to gain control of the thrusters," said Data, "they possess insufficient thrust to overcome the gravitational forces now being exerted on the station. Its own mass is now working against us."

"Gravitational forces."

So soft-spoken was MacDougal's comment that O'Brien thought he imagined it. When he turned to look and saw the *Oceanside*'s engineer staring at the MST, her lips were moving, but there were no sounds.

"Commander MacDougal?" prompted Data.

Stepping up to the table, she said, "Gravitational constant. Adjust the gravitational constant." She snapped her fingers. "Three years ago. Bre'el IV. The orbit of its moon was decaying, and the *Enterprise* used a low-level warp field to change its gravitational constant. You moved it back where it belonged."

"You know about that?" asked La Forge.

"I read about it," MacDougal replied. "Your report was quite comprehensive."

La Forge said, "Did you get to the part where it didn't work because our warp field wasn't big en—" He stopped himself, then smiled. "Of course."

"This station is a damned sight smaller than that moon," said O'Brien. "Will it work?"

Frowning, La Forge replied, "Maybe. Sarah, what about the *Oceanside*? Would her engines be able to handle something like this?"

MacDougal nodded. "She may be smaller than the *Enterprise*, but she's pure muscle in the engine department. Remember, they sometimes use *Cali*-class ships when they need to tow larger vessels at high warp."

"The commander is correct," said Data. "The warp engines on *California*-class starships are larger and more powerful than those of the *Galaxy*-class. The ratio of engine output compared to total mass favors the *Oceanside* in this scenario."

"But remember what happened at Bre'el IV," said La Forge. "We almost tore the moon apart because our warp field wasn't big enough to wrap around the whole thing. Even with the *Oceanside*'s engines, if that happens here we're still talking about two different inertial densities. We could rip the station apart. That's game over."

Data nodded. "Then we should not do that."

Under any other circumstances, the deadpan comment would have made O'Brien laugh. Instead, studying the MST, he knew the talent and experience they represented. This was the team he wanted for this problem.

"Commander Data and I can coordinate with the *Oceanside*," said MacDougal. "He'll be a huge help with the calculations."

O'Brien said, "I can help Commander La Forge with the shutdown and restart procedures." His review of the process told him it would take the two of them to carry out the process in the shortest-possible time.

The next minutes were a blur as the engineers and Data got to work. With the officers occupied by all the moving parts, O'Brien directed Ensign Gomez and six other junior officers to the ODN relay hubs where the illicit data rods most likely had been deployed. He tried not to think about the possibility of other relays compromised in similar fashion, lying dormant and waiting to be triggered by the action he and his colleagues were attempting.

One crisis at a time, Miles.

"Oceanside *to MacDougal*," said Captain Hayashi over the communications channel La Forge had enabled in the auxiliary control center. *"We're ready when you are, Sarah."*

O'Brien and La Forge, standing at the console overseeing the station's primary power systems, took one last look at their respective checklists.

"Ready?" asked La Forge.

"Aye, sir." O'Brien's job would be to initiate the shutdown sequence for the station's fusion reactor. If everything went according to the specifications, the RCS thrusters would be the first systems to go offline once power flow was interrupted. In theory, this would give the *Oceanside* a chance to extend its warp field to encompass the station and begin the process of altering its gravitational constant, allowing the ship to use its own engines to pull the station back toward its proper orbit. At the same time, Gomez and her team would be removing the invasive software rods from the ODN relays while La Forge initiated a restart of the main reactor. This process would reset the main computer and return control of the station and its systems to the engineers—if all went to plan.

What could possibly go wrong, thought O'Brien. *Besides everything, that is.*

"All right," said MacDougal, taking one last look around the room. "We're out of time. Chief?"

O'Brien replied, "Aye, Commander." He began entering the necessary command string. "Here we go. Initiating reactor shutdown sequence."

The effect was immediate. An audible warbling coursed through the room, reverberating through the bulkheads and deck plating, and even the console beneath O'Brien's hands. The workstation blinked as it—along with other critical systems interfaces—made the automatic jump to auxiliary power sources. The room's overhead lighting flickered and extinguished, only to come back seconds later.

"Reactor shutdown in progress," he reported. "RCS systems are . . . offline!"

While the thrusters powering down resulted in no noticeable effect, O'Brien imagined he could feel the force ebbing, leaving the station to spin and float free in the vacuum above Bajor.

"Conditions are optimal," reported Data. "*Oceanside*, we are ready."

"*Acknowledged,*" said Captain Hayashi. "*Extending warp field.*"

O'Brien felt his stomach lurch in response to a slight yet still noticeable change in gravity. "I think it's working."

After a moment, Data said, "*Oceanside* has arrested the effects of the deorbit burn."

"Part two," replied MacDougal. "*Oceanside*, the warp field is holding steady. Begin restabilization maneuver."

Several tense moments passed before Hayashi's voice came over the comms. "*All right, people. We're pulling you back to your parking space. Starting to see fluctuations in our warp field. Get on with your restart.*"

Data said, "The fluctuations are within acceptable parameters. I recommend proceeding."

"Initiating power up," said La Forge, his fingers a blur as they entered the appropriate command strings. "We just got done repairing the reaction chambers, so here's hoping we don't break them. Reactor start sequence engaged."

Leaning over from his station, O'Brien watched the array of status indicators change in succession from red to green, indicating each of the reactor's six fusion chambers coming back online. Once all six showed as active, another status display depicted a host of primary and secondary support systems initiating their own startup processes.

"*Oceanside*, we're showing green across the board over here," reported MacDougal.

Hayashi replied, "*Acknowledged, Sarah. Our warp field has stabilized. The station should be back where it belongs in a few minutes. Nice work, people.*"

Looking away from her console, MacDougal cocked an eyebrow as she regarded the *Enterprise* engineers. "When we fix something, it stays fixed."

O'Brien was wiping his brow when La Forge slapped him on the shoulder. "This is a lot more exciting than the transporter room, right?"

"I've never plummeted to my death aboard a man-made fireball before, sir," said O'Brien. "Thanks for not letting today be that day."

The chief engineer offered a knowing grin. "There's always tomorrow."

29

—

"Panat!"

At the long table in the barracks' common dining area, Panat sat with the stew he had just ladled from the pot. It had been cooking on a low heat since the early morning, looked after by fellow Bajorans assigned to the camp's detachment of custodial workers. He had been looking forward to the meal all day, but the urgency in Ranar's voice made him look up as his friend emerged from the lavatory, hurrying along the narrow passageway between rows of beds stacked three high to where Panat sat at the table.

"What?" asked Panat as Ranar slid onto the bench next to him. His friend clutched a piece of paper on which Panat could see handwritten markings in Bajoran text.

"Yectu's been monitoring incoming communications. This was received an hour ago. It was transmitted as an encrypted data packet attached to another message. She couldn't make out what it said, but she saw what you told her to look for."

The stew forgotten, Panat pushed the bowl aside and took the paper from Ranar, flattening it on the table so he could read it by the underpowered lighting panels. It took him only seconds to see what was there. Seemingly nonsense words were the coded language he had created with his long-lost friend, Ro Laren.

"I don't believe it."

Panat read every word twice, verifying what Yectu had written from what he remembered of the naïve "decryption key" he

and Ro had devised. The message itself was short, but every sylla-
ble was like a gift from the Prophets.

"Message received," he read aloud, keeping his voice low as he
translated the original, cryptic text. "Your location plotted. Options few. Stand by. RLV2."

Her response was much shorter and carried little detail. The
length of her reply was not important.

Leaning close and speaking just above a whisper, Ranar asked,
"Are you certain it's not a deception? Some kind of Cardassian
trap to lure us out?"

"It's from her," said Panat, pointing to the message's final four
letters. These translate to *R* and *L*, that's Ro Laren, and the last
two, *V* and *2*. That's Valo II, the refugee camp where we met. Still,
your point is well taken. We need to be careful."

His original transmission and this unlikely response had
been a risk. The Cardassians learning the prisoners had somehow
found a way to call for help did not bother Panat, but the response
it might trigger from Gul Havrel did. There was nothing to suggest either message had been detected, but proceeding as if they
were was the wisest course.

"If they do know," he said, "Havrel won't wait long to get on
with whatever he has in mind for us. I'm surprised he hasn't started
already." The last report said the transport vessels en route to collect
the enigmatic project were three days away. Panat suspected they
were low-warp transports, designed to avoid scrutiny even from their
own warships. *Was there a delay?* He was not sure why Havrel would
not proceed with the final disposition of the Bajorans, excepting
the possibility that extracting uridium from the mines was a way to
keep the cadre of laborers busy. If Ro Laren had somehow brought a
ship that could help liberate him and his fellow Bajorans, how long
would it take for that vessel to get here? Once that happened, he was
certain the life of every Bajoran in the camp was forfeit.

He became aware of a commotion from somewhere outside the barracks. Shouts and cries for attention, though Panat could make out none of the words. The door opened and Panat saw Yectu's head appear in the opening.

"Come quickly! They've got Ijok!"

Exchanging matching looks of dread, Panat and Ranar followed the rush of Bajorans out of the barracks. As they moved to catch up with Yectu, Panat took immediate notice of the gallows that had been positioned at the camp's center. Night had fallen, and the exterior lights on the buildings, around the perimeter, and atop poles scattered around the compound illuminated the ground. There was also a light positioned to highlight the gallows. Standing atop the raised platform, hands secured behind her back and with a length of thick black cable wrapped around her neck, was Ijok. Her expression was one of resignation, but even from this distance Panat saw the fear in her eyes.

No.

He tried to speak the plea aloud, but the single word caught in his throat. Shifting his gaze from her, Panat counted twenty guards, each armed with disruptor rifles, deployed in a circle around the base of the gallows. It was the first time in months that he had seen the troopers with the larger weapons, which remained locked in an armory while the guards utilized stun batons and their sidearms. Upon his arrival, Gul Havrel had instituted a penalty of immediate execution for even the slightest provocative act against any Cardassian. That Ijok now stood atop the gallows meant it could only be at the prefect's order.

Hasty glances around the compound identified at least a dozen more guards, also armed with rifles. The detail accounted for nearly half of the total guard contingent, with the remaining guards out of the camp with the secondary mining shift.

This is it. Panat's mind screamed the warning.

This is how it starts.

This is how it ends.

Movement at the gallows caught his attention, and Panat saw Gul Havrel ascending the stairs at the back of the platform. A hush fell over the gathering of inmates, and when the group stepped forward as one, the guards encircling the gallows raised their rifles. The group stopped as Havrel stepped onto the platform and stood next to Ijok. After a moment spent looking at the assembly before him, the gul began talking, his voice carrying across the compound.

"Since my arrival, I have endeavored to treat you with a measure of grace and dignity. The rules have always been simple: Work hard, and you will be treated well. Respect me, my staff, and each other, and you will in turn be respected, to a degree far greater than you deserve. I believe a content workforce is a productive workforce, and every rule I have enacted during my tenure has been done with that core belief.

"I know there are those among you who cower in the dark while you conspire and plan, hoping one day to overthrow your betters. You hide your schemes, but they do not escape our notice. You act with great patience while you await the opportunity to strike. We see you. *I see you.* Inevitably, those with hatred and vengeance in their hearts cannot help but expose themselves, revealing their true intentions hidden beneath a pathetic façade."

Havrel gestured to Ijok, who stood silent. "Take this woman. Many of you call her friend. She earned my trust, and in turn I extended her every privilege. She repaid my generosity by spying on me."

"He must have found the transceiver," said Panat, his voice barely a whisper.

Next to him, Yectu muttered, "He might know everything."

"If he does," said Ranar, "then you know what this means."

This is how it ends.

From the platform, Havrel leveled an accusatory finger at the crowd. "She was not working alone. There were accomplices. There are collaborators, standing among you as we speak. Instigators. Revolutionaries." He paused, the pointing hand clenching into a fist. "Enemies of the state."

Panat tensed as he heard mumblings of disapproval rising from the crowd. Bajorans began exchanging glances and talking among themselves, and he could sense their growing dissent. The situation was deteriorating around him with every passing moment.

Lowering his hand, Havrel stepped to the edge of what had become his stage. "Now, I don't expect any of you to turn on your friends. Your companions. Your brothers and sisters. It is among the gravest of dishonors to betray one's comrades, especially among those whose bonds are forged in despair. Therefore, I relieve you from the burden of having to make such a choice. Instead, you shall all die together, and she will lead the way."

Havrel waved his arm in an obvious signal, and the next instant the floor beneath Ijok's feet gave way. Panat closed his eyes just as she started her plunge. Thus, he only heard the sound of her neck snapping before it was drowned out by cries of anguish and shouts of protest. When Panat dared to look back to the gallows it was to see Ijok's limp, lifeless form dangling from the cable. He felt rage building within him, and he imagined his hands around Havrel's neck, choking the life out of him while the gul sputtered and coughed for mercy.

His expression turning flat, Havrel once again raised his fist. "Now."

Time seemed to slow down for Panat as he watched the guards, all twenty of them, raising their rifles and aiming them toward the crowd of onlookers. They were not even aiming, at least not yet. At this distance and with the prisoners gathered so closely together, it would be all but impossible to miss.

He actually flinched as he caught sight of one guard tensing before his expression changed and he lifted his weapon, inspecting it. His companions were acting in much the same manner. Confusion clouded twenty Cardassians' faces. Panat glanced around and saw the other guards stationed around the edges of the gathering were scrutinizing their rifles.

None of them had fired.

This is how it ends.

This is how it starts.

In the face of whatever miracle the Prophets had seen fit to deliver, Panat at long last uttered the command he knew would decide his fate.

"For Bajor!"

Even as the Cardassians realized what was happening and began dropping their inoperative rifles in favor of their sidearms, nearly one hundred Bajoran men and women surged toward the gallows, overwhelming the stricken troopers in the midst of drawing pistols or batons from their belts. Before the first guard's weapon cleared its holster, five Bajorans converged on him, kicking and punching as fast as their limbs would let them.

With Ranar at his side, Panat rushed toward a nearby Cardassian, lowering his shoulder just as the guard extended his stun baton. He bowled into the trooper, sending them both tumbling to the ground. Instinct made him roll to his right as the guard swung the baton. The attack missed and his next attempt was lost when Ranar advanced and drove a knee into the trooper's face. Then other prisoners were on him, pushing him to the ground and pummeling him with boots and fists.

All around him, Bajorans were coming together to overwhelm the guards. Weapons fire made Panat drop to one knee in a desperate attempt to find cover, but in the corner of his eye he saw Yectu, a disruptor pistol in each hand, firing at the nearest of the guards maneuvering to shoot into the escalating melee. Panat could not tell if she was hitting anything, but at least she was sending the troopers scrambling for cover.

"Yectu!" he shouted over the din erupting all around them. She had stopped firing and was now looking for additional targets and finding none. Turning to Panat, she tossed him one of her purloined disruptors before pointing to where Havrel was running toward the camp's headquarters building.

"Come on," she said. "We have to catch him before he does something stupid."

They ran after him. Panat glanced around to see various fights between Bajoran prisoners and Cardassian guards. Despite their greater physical strength and the weapons they carried, the Cardassians were outnumbered. A few of the troopers were holding their own, but the Bajorans, whether motivated by the need to avenge Ijok or simply for the chance to exact retribution, had gained the upper hand.

Havrel reached the headquarters building and sprinted inside. With their captured disruptors held out in front of them to lead the way, Panat and Yectu ventured into the building.

"I can't believe that worked," said Yectu.

Scowling as he searched for threats, Panat glanced at her. "What do you mean?"

"The rifles. I hacked the armory's weapons maintenance subroutines and reversed the polarity on all of the rifle charging stations."

Realization dawned, and Panat felt his jaw go slack. "You drained the power cells of every docked weapon."

Yectu shrugged. "I thought it might come in handy at some point. The harder part was fooling each rifle's power meter to fake displaying a full charge."

Chuckling at that, Panat led the way toward a junction in the corridor. He listened for signs of movement but heard nothing. They were not that far behind Havrel when he entered the room, so he had to be somewhere close. Between him and Yectu, Panat was sure they could find the Cardassian, if only . . .

"Wait." He held up a hand. "We need to split up."

Her expression one of disbelief, Yectu asked, "Why?"

"Can you access the communications system from any workstation?"

"Of course." Then she understood. "Ro."

Panat nodded. "Contact her. Let her know she and her ship need to come get us. Chances are good Havrel's contacting higher authority. They'll send whatever they can to make sure none of us leave here alive."

"You shouldn't go after him alone. I can contact Ro, then we both keep looking for Havrel."

"I don't know how much time we have." Panat had also begun thinking about another possibility. "What if he has his own way of protecting the secret?"

Yectu's eyes widened in realization. "You're right. If he has something down there—"

"Then we're already dead."

30

—

Only when he sat in here by himself did Riker appreciate the size of the *Enterprise*'s observation lounge.

Leaning back in the chair at the head of the table, normally reserved for Captain Picard, Riker closed his eyes and allowed himself to enjoy the atmosphere of quiet and serenity the room fostered. Unlike the bridge with its steady stream of alert tones and sounds emanating from the different stations, here there was nothing but the omnipresent hum of the ship's warp engines. Riker had become accustomed to that sound. He even used it as white noise when lying in bed falling to sleep.

If you're not careful, he thought, *you'll fall asleep right here.*

Despite his desire for a momentary respite, Riker was unwilling to be too far from the bridge. Captain Picard had long ago given permission for Riker to use his ready room when he was in command and Picard was off the ship. The first officer had never warmed to that idea. He had conducted official meetings or spoken with senior officers via subspace while taking advantage of the privacy the ready room afforded, but it had always felt inappropriate. The lounge granted him the same measure of solitude when a brief respite was warranted.

His eyes still closed, Riker drew in a deep breath and released it, feeling the exercise's calming effects. *Better than the ready room.* He would never share that with the captain.

"Bridge to Commander Riker." It was Worf.

"Riker here," he said, opening his eyes.

"Long-range sensors have detected a Cardassian Galor-*class vessel on an intercept course. Approaching at warp eight."*

"Any indication they mean to cross over?"

The security chief replied, *"They are adjusting their course to parallel ours on their side of the border."*

"On my way." Riker pushed himself from the chair, crossing the lounge to the door leading to the bridge.

Break's over.

Stepping out from the alcove leading to the lounge, Riker descended the ramp on the bridge's starboard side as the Klingon vacated the command chair.

"Any change?" asked Riker.

Worf moved to take his position at tactical, relieving a Benzite ensign. "The ship has adjusted its course and heading to match our speed and direction." Drawing himself up, the lieutenant said, "Commander, it is the *Reklar*."

"Gul Lemec's ship?" Riker sighed. "You think he's still mad at us?"

The first officer suspected Lemec was still smarting from the embarrassment he had endured during Captain Edward Jellico's temporary command of the *Enterprise*. Riker had experienced a rocky relationship as first officer to Jellico, something he later decided was partly his own fault. That had not stopped him from admiring the man's tactical prowess; the *Enterprise* had prevented a Cardassian incursion without firing a single shot. Rubbing figurative salt into the proverbial wound, Jellico had forced all of the Cardassian warships, including Lemec's, to jettison their phaser coils, leaving each vessel without a primary means of defense. It was the starship equivalent of a gelding. Riker's only regret was that he had failed to think of it first.

So, mused Riker, *this should be a fun reunion.*

"Mister Worf, make sure all sensor and communications logs

and all bridge orders are recorded in the computer's protected archive, and prepare a buoy. I want a complete record of whatever's going to happen today." Riker hoped it would exonerate the crew, even if he ended up getting court-martialed over the day's events.

"Aye, sir." A moment later, the Klingon said, "Commander, we are being hailed by the *Reklar*."

"Here we go." Riker walked toward the front of the bridge. "On-screen."

The stars streaking past through subspace were replaced on the main viewer by an image of a thin, sinister-looking Cardassian. Narrow eyes peered out from a heavy brow as though trying to impale Riker by thought alone. The area behind him was blurred, an expected operations security precaution.

"Gul Lemec," said Riker.

The Cardassian nodded. *"Commander Riker. Or have you been promoted? If so, then congratulations are in order."*

Deciding not to confirm or deny the point, Riker instead asked, "What a pleasant surprise. What brings you this far from home?"

"It is unusual to see a Starfleet vessel with the Enterprise*'s reputation so close to our border, let alone twice in such a short span of time. We are naturally curious."*

Riker shrugged. "Check our course. I'm sure you'll see we're performing routine maintenance and upgrades to subspace communications relays."

"That seems a rather menial task for a ship such as yours." Lemec leaned forward in his chair. *"Are you being punished?"*

With a subtle flick of his wrist, Riker signaled to Worf to mute the connection. "You think he suspects why we're really here?"

At the ops station, Ensign Ro said, "If Panat's right about what's going on down on Satera III, I'd expect a few warships to be repositioned to provide security during the relocation operation.

If Lemec's involved, it's likely he knows the real reason for their presence."

Indicating for Worf to reestablish audio, Riker said, "I apologize for the interruption, Gul Lemec. Where were we?"

On the screen, Lemec replied, *"You were attempting to explain why one of Starfleet's most renowned vessels is conducting maintenance reviews of subspace relays."* Before Riker could answer, the Cardassian added, *"Be warned, Commander, no attempt at espionage or other activities in our territory will be tolerated. Merely crossing the border is sufficient to trigger an interstellar incident—"*

Uncharacteristically, Worf interrupted, "Sir, we're picking up a message that appears to have originated from Satera III. It is a burst transmission. Stand by for decoding."

"Satera III?" asked Lemec. *"That's impossible. The planet is uninhabited."*

He's either got a terrific poker face, thought Riker, *or he has no idea what's going on.*

"You should probably update your star charts then," he said, stalling for time.

"Commander," said Worf. "We have decoded the message. The only thing it says is 'Come now. Need help.'"

On the screen, Lemec scowled. *"A distress message?"*

"We think so." Riker was happy to provide a truthful answer, realizing he now had something he could use. "We think a transport vessel of ours may have wandered off course and crashed somewhere in this region. We've been attempting to track its movements, and this is our first clue to its location. Would you be interested in helping us?" It was a weak ploy, he knew, but it was the best card he had to play. "I'm sure the Federation would be grateful for any assistance."

"Do not attempt to cross into Cardassian space, Commander. This will be your only warning."

Riker nodded. "I'm glad you clarified that. Now I don't have to worry about wasting any more of my time. Riker out." As soon as the frequency was closed, he looked to Lieutenant Jae at the flight controller's station. "Conn, take us to Satera III. Maximum warp."

Jae exchanged looks with Riker before replying, "Maximum warp, aye, sir."

"Sir," said Worf. "I am obligated to remind you that entering Cardassian space without authorization could be considered an act of war."

"I know." Riker knew he had crossed the Rubicon. "But the Bajorans are calling for help, and we're acting to save Bajoran nationals who are being held illegally by the Cardassians." It was obvious the Cardassians had no intention of honoring the withdrawal terms. Riker would take his chances with the Starfleet Judge Advocate General.

Worf replied, "I hope to testify at our courts-martial, sir."

Smiling as he settled into the captain's chair, Riker blew out his breath.

Now it's getting interesting.

"Transmission complete."

Yectu pushed back from the workstation, leaving it active with the user profile she had forged to gain access to the camp's computer network. They were past the need to keep any secrets. She and her fellow Bajorans would either be leaving this planet or walking with the Prophets.

"Let's go," she said.

Standing near the open door with a disruptor pistol at the ready, Nesha nodded in agreement. He had followed Yectu and Panat into the headquarters building and elected to stay with her, providing cover while she burrowed her way into the camp's computer system to send the message to Ro Laren. Yectu welcomed the company and someone watching her back.

Brandishing the disruptor she had taken from one of the guards, Yectu and Nesha retraced their steps out of the communications center.

"All the time I've been here," she said, her voice just above a whisper, "and I've never been in this building."

Nesha replied, "I've been here a few times. Cleaning, meal preparation, whatever else someone wanted."

Knowing what he meant, Yectu understood her friend did not enjoy that aspect of being a covert agent for the camp's Resistance network, but he did his job with no complaints. As for her, Yectu's duties in the camp's repair bays saw to it she spent her days maintaining and refurbishing all manner of tools, vehicles, and other equipment used by the interned laborers as well as their overseers. The only things with which she and her fellow Bajorans were forbidden contact were any weapons. How tools or landscaping implements could not be considered by the Cardassians as weapons was a lack of imagination. Long ago, she had come to the conclusion that if a revolt ever took place in the camp, she would head to her workspace and grab the heaviest, sharpest tool she could find. Take out the first Cardassian, and the issue of obtaining a proper weapon would solve itself.

Like it did today, she mused.

Hefting her pilfered disruptor, Yectu aimed it ahead of her as they proceeded up the corridor and away from the communications center. The next order of business was finding Panat.

"You know where Gul Havrel's office is?" she asked.

Nesha nodded. "Second floor, rear of the building. You can't miss it. Nice, fancy furniture and a few pieces of art stolen from Bajor."

It seemed that all Cardassians in positions of power coveted the culture of the people they conquered. What better way to decorate a home or office than with stolen artifacts? Yectu abhorred the practice; even with the Occupation supposedly ending, many Cardassians would keep pieces of Bajor's past they had taken.

They found a maintenance stairwell and used it to ascend to the second floor, emerging into another corridor. Standing in silence, Yectu held her breath and listened for indications that any of the rooms on this level were occupied. She heard nothing except for the low hum of the air being pushed through the ventilation system.

"Where is everybody?" asked Yectu.

Nesha shook his head. "No idea. This building should still be occupied, and have at least few security officers." So far as Nesha knew, the uprising had not made it here. Bajorans were still outside, chasing down the few guards who might have escaped the initial assault. He decided a likely explanation was that all the Cardassians had fled at the first sign of violence.

His theory evaporated when a Cardassian emerged into the hallway, his disruptor drawn.

"Halt!"

Glinn Trina, Gul Havrel's second-in-command. Yectu realized the Cardassian was not even looking at her. His attention was focused on Nesha.

"You."

Yectu knew her friend had been cultivating Trina as an asset for months. She imagined the thoughts playing across the Cardassian's mind at this very moment. He seemed paralyzed, but with what? Shock? Betrayal? Yectu saw him raise his weapon farther, its muzzle moving in their direction.

Nesha fired first.

His pistol spat forth a bolt of pale yellow energy, striking

Trina just beneath his chin and knocking him off his feet, carrying him into the wall behind him. The glinn's finger must have convulsed on his disruptor's trigger, because it discharged a bolt of its own into the ceiling even as he slid limply to the floor.

"Well," said Yectu, "if there's anyone else around, now they know where we are."

Ignoring her, Nesha walked over to where the prone Trina lay in a heap. Yectu watched as her friend studied the glinn for a moment before raising his disruptor and firing once more into the Cardassian's head. When he turned back to face her, she saw that his expression had gone flat. His eyes appeared dull and lifeless, displaying no emotional reaction.

"Are you all right?" she asked.

Nesha nodded. "I will be."

A commotion from the corridor's far end echoed in the passageway, and Yectu was certain she heard Panat's voice along with someone else. Were they reacting to the disruptor fire? She tensed, waiting for someone to appear in the hall. No one. Then a low, steady hum broke into the corridor's near silence, rising in pitch for a moment before fading altogether.

"Is that a transporter?" asked Nesha.

"I think so." It was the first time Yectu had heard that technology's distinctive sound in years. In all her time here, she had never even seen a transporter; if one existed within the camp's perimeter or somewhere else on the planet, it was hidden from the Bajoran prisoners.

"Panat?"

Her voice echoed in the hallway, but she heard nothing in response. With Nesha following after her, she jogged the rest of the way to the open door, letting her pistol lead the way into the office.

"Yeah, this is Havrel's, all right." The furnishings were more stately than anything she had seen in the camp. There were the art pieces Nesha mentioned—an abstract sculpture and a landscape painting—both Bajoran in origin. Otherwise, the office was empty.

"Besides Panat, who else was here?" asked Nesha. "Havrel?"

Yectu said, "The most likely answer, but why would they leave together? Where would they go?"

31

—

Feeling his body coalesce from a column of energy into solid mass, Panat waited with his disruptor held out before him as the transporter process completed, and he materialized on a compact platform just like the one in Havrel's office.

The first thing Panat saw beyond the transporter alcove was the gul, aiming a disruptor at him.

Panat fired without aiming, ducking to his left as disruptor fire screamed into the alcove. He heard the energy bolts slamming into the transporter's back wall, followed by the sounds of power connections being interrupted and the sensation of sparks landing across his back. Gritting his teeth in pain, he aimed his disruptor through the door and pressed the trigger, laying down suppressive fire as he pushed his way out of the alcove and into the larger office beyond. Havrel was already gone. Looking back into the alcove, Panat saw the transporter's back panel now featured a smoking, charred hole, inside of which he could see melted cabling and rows of shattered isolinear data rods.

He would not be leaving this way.

"First find Havrel," he said, to no one but himself. "Then worry about finding an exit."

There was no reason for him to stay. If Yectu had sent that message to Ro, then anyone who intercepted it would know about this planet, and where it was. Ro would ensure the truth was made known. If she was still in Starfleet, that meant the Federation would know along with anyone else who might take an interest in the illicit activities of the Cardassian Union. So, why was he still down here?

Ijok.

Havrel needed to answer for Ijok. It was bad enough he had executed her, but to do so in such a public fashion, in a manner intended to break the morale of every Bajoran in the camp? She had risked her life for the Resistance on more occasions than Panat could count, and she met her death with a singular bravery. Panat did not know if she had endured a brutal interrogation before her murder, but he knew without doubt she had fought to the end to protect the identities of her fellow Resistance fighters. She deserved to be avenged. Panat would see to it.

The office door opened at his approach, and to his surprise, Havrel or some other Cardassian was not waiting for him on the other side. Beyond the office, he saw not a corridor but a catwalk flanked by a metal railing, and he realized he was on the second floor of a building situated . . . inside a cave. Panat's eyes traced the smooth, high-arching stone walls of an immense cavern, with a ceiling rising more than a hundred meters above a collection of dull gray buildings of varying sizes and shapes. Like the encampment, there was an undeniable Cardassian order to the structures.

"The project." Everything Yectu had described, thanks to her ability to infiltrate Gul Havrel's computer workstation, was here. Now he could confirm its existence and its location far beneath the labor camp. He was both intrigued and terrified at what he might find.

First things first, he reminded himself. *Havrel.*

Outside many of the buildings, Panat observed cargo containers of a type normally used on freighters and other transport vessels. The relocation preparations were well underway, certainly until interrupted by the chaos unfolding on the surface. What he did not see—anywhere, so far as he could tell—were any signs of life. There were no soldiers or technicians or even Bajorans visible anywhere on the cavern floor or around any of the buildings. Were they all inside?

"You're too late."

Panat turned toward the voice without thinking, firing his disruptor before he even brought the weapon to align on its target. He compensated by pulling the trigger one shot after another, sending multiple disruptor bolts arcing in what he was sure was Havrel's direction. The gul, visible where the catwalk turned a corner to the left, fired his own weapon while trying to avoid being hit, but he was a subpar marksman and possessed slow reflexes. The third of Panat's shots caught the prefect in his left thigh, knocking him off his feet and sending him collapsing backward against the catwalk railing. Havrel fired again as he dropped to the walkway, either in desperation or by accident, and his shot struck Panat in his left shoulder.

Fire shot through Panat's upper body, and his weapon nearly slipped from his fingers. He sagged against the nearby wall, maintaining his grip on the weapon. Gritting his teeth, he raised the disruptor toward Havrel, only to see the Cardassian had lost his own sidearm over the railing. Not that it mattered, as he was preoccupied with his injured leg. The gul gripped his thigh just above the wound, as if applying pressure would alleviate the pain. Panat ignored him along with his shoulder as he scanned for other threats.

He scowled in confusion. There still was no sign of anyone else in the cavern.

"I sent them away."

The voice, weak and racked with pain, next released a grunt of frustration. Turning toward him, Panat raised his disruptor until the sights settled on Havrel's forehead.

"I understand your anger," said the Cardassian. "Ijok. She was your friend." He nodded. "Well, she was something special to me as well. At least, that is what I chose to believe."

"She used you." Panat forced a smile to punctuate his words. "From the beginning. You were cultivated, manipulated, exploited. Ijok preyed on you." With the disruptor, he gestured toward the cavern's ceiling. "If not for your weakness, we might never have known about this place. Now everyone will know. You failed your leaders, and your people, and even everyone under your command, because you first failed yourself."

"Ijok paid for her treachery," said Havrel, "just as you will pay for the sin of being one of such a pathetic people. So naïve, so foolish. You never once suspected our ambitions for you and your world. We did the galaxy a favor by removing you from the interstellar stage and keeping you from contaminating it with your immaturity. If not for us, the Bajoran people would be nothi—"

Panat fired the disruptor.

The discharged energy bolt chewed into the railing less than a meter from Havrel's head, making him flinch.

"Where is everyone?"

Drawing a ragged breath, Havrel replied, "On their way to the surface. Well away from the camp. Not that it matters. Before you found me, I received a coded message from Cardassian Central Command. They've sent an armada of warships, with orders to destroy the planet and anything on it." He offered a limp wave around the cavern. "No trace of this, the camp or the mines, or you and your Bajoran friends. No trace of me and my soldiers, since we're the ones who failed Cardassia."

Was he telling the truth? There was no way for Panat to be sure.

"What are you planning to do? Sit here and wait to die?" He waved the disruptor. "I'm happy to help."

With a weak hand, Havrel gestured toward the cavern below. "Since taking this posting, I've known that my life could be forfeited at any time. That is the risk one accepts when serving the people of Cardassia."

"You're not unique," said Panat. "Soldiers in every army make the same pledge. I made a similar promise, to my fellow Bajorans, that we'd do everything in our power to kick you off our planet. We did that. At least, that's what I've heard, and that's why you've been ordered to pack up your little secret project. I've watched a lot of my friends die for the cause of liberating our world. I'm just happy I lived long enough to see it."

Shifting his position, Havrel coughed before reaching into a pocket of his tunic. The movement made Panat lift his disruptor to aim it at the gul's face.

"The withdrawal from your planet is underway," said Havrel. "That much is true, but I'm afraid you won't live to see your people be truly free." He had extracted a small, padd-like device from his pocket, which he held up for Panat to see. "It's too late."

He turned the padd so Panat could see its face. A series of Cardassian numbers was flashing in sequence, counting backward.

A countdown?

"What did you do?" he barked, raising the disruptor again.

Havrel sighed. "The only thing I can." With the padd, he waved toward the cavern. "My orders were to protect this from becoming public. A fleet is on its way to do the job entrusted to me, and which my superiors believe I failed. If I can carry out the mission and protect this collection of terrible secrets, perhaps those same superiors will see fit to spare the lives of those who were loyal to me."

"How?" asked Panat, dumbstruck.

Once more, Havrel waved the padd. "Explosives planted on the heat exchangers above each of the fifteen geothermal vents beneath this cavern. I've also increased the vents' intake systems to maximum. The pressure is already rising within the vents and the exchangers. This will lead to an overpressure that eventually will grow beyond the oversight system's ability to regulate the generators."

He paused, shaking his head. "An explosion that large, generating that much force and causing that level of overpressure, will destroy this facility, and likely bring down a good portion of the bedrock above us. Whatever survives the explosion will be pulled down into the planet's interior lava flows. The rest will be little more than debris, left behind as a reminder of what might once have been here."

The pain in his shoulder was ebbing, or was it just him going into shock? Panat could not tell the difference. He thought he might even be hearing things. A faint beeping tone sounded somewhere nearby. It took him a moment to realize it was coming from Havrel's left wrist.

A communicator.

The gul tried to keep it from him, even managing to get it off his arm before Panat reached him. He attempted to throw it over the railing, but Panat's boot on his injured leg made him drop it into his lap. Panat retrieved the device and activated it.

"Who is this?" he barked. Given the circumstances, civility seemed inappropriate.

"Hileb?"

Frowning, Panat looked at the communicator in disbelief. "Yectu?"

32

———

Will Riker was sure he felt himself coming out of the captain's chair as Lieutenant Jae dropped the *Enterprise* out of warp and the planet Satera III exploded onto the viewscreen in less than a second. Even the thrum of the ship's massive warp engines seemed to change pitch in protest at the flight controller's unorthodox piloting technique.

"We're secure from warp," said Jae.

"Shields up. Red alert." Riker rose from the center seat and moved to stand behind Ro. "Ensign, scan for life signs. Mister Worf, where's the *Reklar*?"

The Klingon security chief replied, "Closing on our position. They will be here in less than sixty seconds."

It was going to be tight, Riker knew. They had one shot to verify this crazy situation. The planet now dominating the bridge's main viewscreen was not a Class-T gas giant but instead a lush, green-brown world with an obvious atmosphere.

"Commander Riker," said Ro from the ops station. "Scans are showing one hundred seventy-six Bajoran and forty-nine Cardassian life signs on the surface. They appear divided into two distinct groups, approximately four kilometers apart. There are structures on the planet, concentrated within a small footprint in the southern hemisphere. It has to be the labor camp, sir—"

Her console interrupted her with a beeping tone. "There's something else, sir. Sensors are detecting an unusual buildup of geothermal energy. One kilometer beneath the camp."

"The secret facility mentioned in your friend's message?" asked Riker.

Ro nodded. "Possibly. Scans are muddied due to subterranean mineral deposits, but I'm still seeing a series of underground caverns where pressure is building. The rate of increase is steady." She looked up from her station. "Sir, if it blows, it'll collapse the bedrock directly under the camp, and for at least a half kilometer in every direction. Anyone on the ground down there won't stand a chance."

"How much time do we have?" asked Riker.

"Ten minutes, maybe twelve, sir."

A warning tone sounded from the tactical station and Worf called out, "Commander, the *Reklar* is dropping out of warp. Sensors show her weapons are active."

On the main viewscreen, the intimidating silhouette of the *Galor*-class warship sailed into view. The shape of its forward hull had always reminded Riker of a cobra with its hood deployed in an attempt to intimidate. Riker knew the *Reklar* was showing its proverbial teeth because its captain wanted a fight.

"Phasers and photon torpedoes on ready status. Conn, stand by for evasive." Riker turned from the viewscreen to face Worf. "Lieutenant, hail the *Reklar*."

It took only a moment before Gul Lemec's visage once again crowded the main screen. The Cardassian's expression communicated his present emotional state rather well, Riker thought.

"*Enterprise, you have entered Cardassian space without authorization. Your presence here is an act of war against the Cardassian Union. You will power down your weapons and engines, lower your shields, and prepare to be boarded.*"

"Lemec," said Riker. "Shut up." He knew he was taking a huge gamble, provoking his counterpart in this way, but there was no time for diplomacy. "Take a good look at that planet below us. Do your charts for this region match what you're seeing?"

Attempting to process what Riker said, Lemec directed his attention off-screen and said something Riker could not hear. After a moment, he returned to stare straight ahead.

"I do not understand. What is the meaning of this, and how could you possibly have knowledge of a system in Cardassian space that we lack?"

Riker drew a deep breath. "I can't speak to how, or what's taking place on the surface. Our sensors have picked up a geothermal instability beneath the only settlement of any appreciable size. Look for yourself, Lemec."

"We have conducted our own scans," said Lemec. *"You speak the truth, Commander. What do you propose?"*

"Simple." Riker knew this next part would be tricky. "You beam up all the Cardassians to your ship, we beam the Bajorans to the *Enterprise*. Mister Worf, notify all transporter rooms to prepare for emergency evacuation procedures. Non-Cardassian life signs only, transported to the main shuttlebay. Have security on site, and dispatch medical teams to assist with any injuries."

After a moment, the Klingon reported, "All transporter rooms are standing by for your order, sir."

"Deactivate all weapons systems, Lieutenant." Returning his attention to the main viewscreen, Riker said, "I'm going to lower my shields, Lemec. You scan us, our weapons are offline. You have my word we're not a threat to you."

On the screen, Lemec said, *"And what happens next?"*

"I transport to Bajor two hundred of their citizens, based on your request for assistance as a good-faith gesture toward furthering constructive Cardassian-Federation relations." Riker thought he detected a smile creeping onto Lemec's face.

"Very well, Commander. A good-faith gesture."

"Mister Worf," asked Riker, "are we ready?"

"Yes, sir."

After pausing long enough to send a silent plea to the Bajoran Prophets, Riker ordered, "Lower shields."

"What are you doing on this channel? We thought you were dead, or a prisoner of Havrel's."

His anxiety growing as he watched the display on Havrel's padd continuing to dwindle, Panat said, "Yectu, listen. Get everyone away from the camp as fast as you can. Head for the mountain range. Stay out of the mines."

"What are you talking about?" Her voice was strained, perhaps a byproduct of the stress that likely asserted itself during the revolt. *"We won, Hileb. Don't you know? We control the camp. Some of the guards are dead, but the majority of them will be all right. Well, except for the serious injuries. Ranar took a crew to the mine, but the secondary shift had already heard about what we were doing here and they turned on their own guards. It was beautiful."*

"Yectu!" snapped Panat. "We don't have time for this. There's going to be an explosion. A big one. You have to get everyone away from the camp."

"Hileb, it's over. Aren't you hearing me? It's over! The Cardassians lost. We won. It—"

Her voice disappeared in a buzz of energy piped through the open communications channel. Then there was nothing but silence.

"The frequency closed. What happened?" Panat glowered at Havrel. "What did you do?"

Havrel shook his head and offered an expression of resignation and perhaps peace. "Nothing. It sounded like a transporter. Perhaps they were taken to safety."

That notion brought calm to Panat, while at the same time giving him hope. Once more, he activated the communicator. "To any vessel in orbit who can receive this transmission, please lock on to my signal."

"It will not matter." Havrel sighed, trying in vain to move his injured leg to another position. "The minerals in the rock make an effective screen against sensors and transporters. Even if they could lock on to us, minerals in the bedrock would corrupt the transporter signal. We would materialize inside the mountain."

Panat thought about the ruined transporter alcove in Havrel's office. "Are there other transporters like the one you have? Had? The one you destroyed while shooting at me?"

"No." The reply came as the dull rumbling beneath them continued growing in intensity.

It will not be long now, Panat guessed, even as he felt the calm descending upon him once again. For his part, Havrel seemed sublimely resigned to his fate,

"There's really nothing left for either of us to do," he said as the rumbling got even louder. "Nothing to do except wait."

They would not have to wait long.

Thanks to the magnification properties of the bridge's main viewer, Riker along with everyone else on the bridge could see seams opening up in the ground all around the encampment. Flashes of blinding orange-yellow light erupted from the creases in the earth as plumes of smoke and dirt spewed into the air. It all conspired to partially obscure what Riker could see was a massive upheaval of bedrock and superheated gases before the ground beneath the camp gave way, falling in on itself. Uncounted tons of rock, dirt, and vegetation collapsed back into the pits from which they had come, taking nearly every last scrap of the surface encampment with them and leaving a gigantic kilometer-wide hole in its wake.

"Prophets protect them."

Turning at the unexpected voice, Riker saw a disheveled Bajoran woman flanked by a pair of *Enterprise* security officers, transfixed by the viewscreen. It was as if the bridge crew, or even the bridge itself, was invisible to her.

"She asked to speak to the commanding officer and Ensign Ro, sir," said one of the security guards, before he gestured to the screen. "She has information about what happened down there."

Riker directed his gaze to the Bajoran, whose eyes remained riveted to the viewscreen. When she spoke, he could barely hear her.

"Raka-ja ut shala morala. Ema bo roo kana. Uranak ralanon Panat Hileb. *Propeh va nara ehsuk shala-kan vunek."*

"What is she saying?" asked Riker.

And why isn't the universal translator working?

"Ro, do you understand her?"

Turning in her seat, Ro cleared her throat. "It's a Bajoran prayer. 'Do not let him walk alone. Guide him on his journey. Protect the one named Panat Hileb. Take him into the gates of—' Wait, Panat?" She left her station and crossed the bridge to stand in front of the Bajoran woman. "Hileb? Was he down there?"

When the woman was able to gain back a measure of self-control, she looked first to Ro and then Riker. "You knew him?"

Ro's gaze fell to the deck, but then she straightened her posture and nodded.

"Hileb was down there." Now tears ran down the Bajoran's face. She tried to wipe them with a sleeve, but they were just replaced by more.

"Damn." Riker was barely able to get the word out. If anyone had been down there at the time of the explosion, they never had a chance.

After a moment, the woman looked up to stare at Ro. "Are you Ro Laren?"

Self-conscious as always, Ro nodded. "Hileb was my friend." Now it was her turn to cry, the normally stoic, closed-off woman allowing her emotions free rein.

The woman replied, "He was also my friend. I'm Yectu Sheeli-ate. Thank you for saving us. Is it true, that . . . Bajor . . . is free? No more Cardassians?"

"Bajor is free," said Ro, tears now streaming down her face.

33

—

"While the council agrees there is value in continuing to hold these conversations for the benefit of both our peoples, the lack of meaningful progress during these negotiations compels me to declare us at an impasse. Let us not consider this a failure, but instead a beginning: the first chapter in a new history our two peoples can write together. With this in mind, we believe further discussions at this time carry no promise or guarantee of achieving the stated goals of any interested parties. Further, continuing down our present path can only serve to undermine what we have accomplished. It is therefore in the spirit of continuing cooperation and future harmony between our two peoples that we conclude our participation in these proceedings."

Picard watched Madred, alone at the table's far end, as he studied the padd he held for an additional moment. Was he verifying he had reached the end of the remarks? When he looked up from the device, it was with that arrogant, satisfied expression that Picard knew only too well.

"Legate Madred," said First Minister Kalem, who like everyone else at the table had remained silent, "is it the contention of the Detapa Council that their responsibilities in this matter are at an end? That no recompense is owed? Is it *your* contention that in the best interests of both our peoples, we focus our attentions on the future, rather than dwelling on issues of the past?"

Placing the padd aside, Madred sat ramrod straight in his chair, his hands flat against the conference table's polished surface. "First Minister, I am only the council's representative in these matters. It is not my place to infer or assign any particular meaning from their directives that has not already been explicitly communicated. I believe the council has clearly articulated its stance in this matter. They do not see this is an ending, but rather a beginning."

It required physical effort on Picard's part to keep his eyes from rolling.

"The beginning of what?" asked Kai Opaka, her hands clasped on the table before her. "Does the council believe we can move toward some imagined future in which our peoples exist together in harmony, with no memory of the events that brought us to this table in this room on this day?"

His expression unchanged, Madred began, "Eminence, the council fee—"

"Excuse me," said Opaka. "Are you about to articulate further comments from the council, or is it your intention to infer or assign meaning that has not already been explicitly communicated?"

The Bajoran leader had always paid attention. Though she had largely remained silent during the conversations, deferring to Kalem on matters that did not touch on her duties as a spiritual leader, Picard knew she was no fool. She had learned Madred reveled in the performative aspects of his duty. An opportunity to be extemporaneous was not to be wasted, particularly in those situations where he was the one in control. He therefore was unaccustomed to being interrupted, and he assuredly did not like it when it came from someone he considered inferior. In this case, that meant everyone in the wardroom. While his ability to maintain his composure and bearing was masterful, Picard could tell by the tautness of the legate's jawline that Madred was seething. A glance to Counselor Troi was enough to confirm his suspicions.

"With all due respect to the council and their contentions, Legate Madred," said Picard, "the matters before us today are anything but concluded. Rather, they are at best a summarization of the issues currently facing the Bajoran people, all of which are a result of their treatment under Cardassian rule. Their world was plundered for its resources, nearly all of which were taken in order to benefit the Cardassian Union. The lives of countless Bajorans were irrevocably altered by your presence here. An estimated ten million lives lost forever. Despite the efforts of their oppressors, the Bajoran people remain unbroken, but their tenacity and strength of spirit do not alleviate the suffering they've endured. While the council's remarks are encouraging, they do reflect one unerring truth: we are much closer to the beginning of this process than the end."

There was a noticeable beat before Madred responded, and when he did Picard thought he sensed additional hesitation, as though the legate expected to be interrupted a second time. "If there is a formal statement you wish to convey to the council, Captain, it would be my privilege to carry it for you."

"Not from me, Madred." Picard gestured to Kalem and Opaka. "From *them*. From the millions of people they represent. From the millions of voices that are forever silenced. I cannot speak for Bajor in a way that honors the lives they've lived, the lives they've lost, the sacrifices they've made, and the suffering they will continue to carry long after you and I are gone."

"Legate," said Kalem, "there is the matter of the willful plundering of our culture, as exemplified by one of your labor camp prefects, Gul Tranar. Thanks to the diligent efforts of Bajoran citizens and Captain Picard's crew, we now have proof of the concerted effort to rob us of our own history, along with deliberate acts of sabotage against our environment and our citizens."

"I was only just recently made aware of the incidents in

question," replied Madred. "Considering the orders of the Detapa Council and their specific instructions regarding behavior of this type, Gul Tranar was acting outside the scope of his authority. We do not condone his actions and he will be held to account under Cardassian law."

"That is unacceptable," said Opaka. "He must be tried here, on Bajor. Our people must see that we are committed to correct the injustices done to us and our world. I further submit it is in the interests of Cardassia to see that our system of justice treats everyone equally."

Outwardly, at least, Madred remained unperturbed. "Whereas under our system, his punishment will be seen as a warning to others who would consider acting beyond the scope of their authority."

"And what of the Bajorans being held in offworld labor camps?" asked Picard. "Who is to be held responsible for seeing to it those citizens and their property are returned?"

Madred stated, "The council's orders pertaining to ending our interests on Bajor included clear instructions that all Bajorans and their property were to be released from custody and afforded means of returning to Bajor or some other destination. There is no room for interpretation of the council's directives. Anyone choosing to act beyond the bounds of those instructions does so in violation of Cardassian law."

"That's encouraging, Legate Madred." Picard rose from his chair. "Do those directives also pertain to worlds where Bajorans are being held in secret? Where they are exploited in every conceivable manner for Cardassian gain, to include participating against their will in illegal genetic research? To be test subjects for experimental weaponry outlawed by every civilized society in the quadrant?"

"I can only speak to matters of which I'm aware, Captain," said Madred. "I—"

"You will soon be aware of a great many matters that have escaped your attention, Legate." Picard began pacing the length of the table, making his way toward Madred. "As we speak, my ship is returning from just such a planet. There are more than two hundred depositions waiting to be taken. I'm sure the council will be eager to take their testimony into consideration as they pursue justice."

Madred was moving to stand just as Picard came abreast of him. "Cap—"

"Not to me," said Picard. "To *them*."

Pausing long enough to draw a breath that also sounded like an attempt to ensure his composure was in check, Madred turned his attention to Kalem and Opaka. "First Minister. Eminence. In light of this new information, I wish to confer with the council. While I cannot speak for them, I am confident an accommodation can be reached."

Kalem, as ever, chose his words with deliberation. "That is . . . acceptable, Legate. Please also convey to the council our heartfelt desire to continue these discussions at the earliest opportunity." Picard could tell the first minister wanted to say more, but understood a victory had been secured today. In this moment, there was nothing more to be gained. Pushing the point would be inelegant. Better to retire and leave Madred to stew.

Well played, First Minister.

To his credit, Madred seemed to understand this as well and, as if resigned to playing his role, offered a formal nod. "It would be my privilege to be your messenger. Good day to you, First Minister." He turned to Opaka. "Eminence." When his gaze met Picard's, there was a fleeting hesitation. "Captain." Collecting his padd, Madred moved to the door, which opened to reveal his security escort. Picard waited until the doors closed behind the legate before expelling the breath he did not even realize he was holding.

"Finally."

Rising from her chair, Troi asked, "Captain?" Her expression told Picard she could sense his tumult of emotions: anger, uncertainty, but also relief and even satisfaction.

"I'm fine, Counselor. Thank you."

"It is we who should be thanking you, Captain," said Kalem. The first minister along with Kai Opaka had moved from their seats to join Picard and Troi. "You have done a great service to the people of Bajor."

Troi said, "Madred was right about one thing, First Minister. This is a beginning, for all of us. Know the Federation stands with Bajor."

"You have pledged that from the outset," replied Opaka, "but it is your actions for which we are most grateful."

Picard said, "I know we cannot undo our past mistakes. I can only pledge we will do better going forward. Bajor has our full support. Our efforts will continue for as long as they are needed *and* wanted."

"Perhaps there will come a day when Bajor considers joining the Federation," said Troi.

"An ambitious goal, Commander." Kalem smiled. "And one I find interesting to contemplate. In the spirit of working toward that goal, Captain, I have given serious consideration to your proposal for a permanent Starfleet presence here. I believe taking that step would ensure the Bajoran people are afforded every opportunity to regain and hold on to the freedoms taken from us so long ago."

Opaka added, "I suspect it will also be helpful as part of the ongoing effort to ensure the Cardassians uphold the stipulations of their withdrawal."

The kai reached for Picard's ear, and the captain bent toward her. He knew Opaka wanted to feel his *pagh*, a Bajoran ritual. She stood silent for a moment before releasing her grip. "Many thanks to you, Captain," she whispered to him. "I know the demands this placed on you, and your commitment will not be forgotten."

"You honor me, Eminence." Picard found it difficult to keep his emotions in check. "You honor the Federation by trusting us to be your advocates."

"After all we have endured, it is difficult to ask for help." Opaka smiled. "But that hardship is lessened when you're able to ask a trusted friend."

Picard heard her unspoken meaning and felt her grip tighten around his hand. A sensation of calm seemed to well up within him, as if a great burden had lifted from his shoulders.

"It's been a privilege meeting you, Eminence. I sincerely hope I have reason to do so again."

"Until we do," said Opaka, "I will keep you in my thoughts and prayers." Turning to Troi, she smiled. "May the Prophets guide you both."

34

—

The bustle of the Promenade was even more pronounced here in Quark's Bar, but O'Brien could not help but be swept up in the activity unfolding beneath him. Allowing his eyes to sweep the bar, he noted Bajorans along with members of the *Enterprise* and *Oceanside* crews occupying various tables or seats at the bar. Almost everyone was engaged in conversation or participating in one of the games at the room's far end. The crowd milling around Commander Riker seemed particularly boisterous, and O'Brien knew the *Enterprise* first officer was enjoying himself.

While most of the Bajorans kept to themselves, O'Brien noted a few interacting with Starfleet personnel. That was an encouraging improvement from his previous visit. While he knew it would be some time before the Bajoran people trusted the Federation, he would take any positive or hopeful sign he could find.

"You seem lost in thought," said Keiko, interrupting his reverie, and he blinked a few times, wondering if his wife had been speaking to him. Self-conscious that he may have appeared rude, he reached over to take her hand in his own.

"You caught me," he replied, making no attempt to play off his internal wandering. He glanced around. "Not exactly Ten Forward, is it?"

Smiling, Keiko shrugged. "I don't know. I have to admit it's a nice change of pace from the *Enterprise*."

They occupied a small corner table on the second level, which O'Brien had chosen, ostensibly, so he could observe the bar. It was an old habit, choosing to put his back against a bulkhead in an un-familiar establishment. The past days had reminded him of many forgotten things from what seemed like a lifetime ago. In some ways that was good, but he preferred not to dwell on the past. This station along with the people aboard it, even this bar and the patrons it seemed to attract from who knew where, in their own odd way represented the future. For O'Brien, they also signified a turning point. Not since his arrival aboard the *Enterprise* five years earlier had he felt the steady rush of anticipation at prepar-ing to face a new challenge; now he was feeling that same sense of excitement as he took in everything on Terok Nor.

No, O'Brien reminded himself. *Deep Space 9.*

The redesignation was not official, but he had already heard crewmates using the new name, now that the station fell under Starfleet jurisdiction while representing Federation interests in the Bajoran sector. Looking up and through the ports on the Promenade's upper walkway, O'Brien could see the curve of Bajor as the station orbited the planet. The Federation would, finally, help the Bajorans, and having a Starfleet presence here on the sta-tion was the first step.

He wanted to help with that mission.

"I know that look," said Keiko after a moment, and O'Brien felt her squeezing his hand. "You're thinking about tomorrow."

Offering another sheepish smile, he nodded. "Yes."

Keiko looked around. "Miles, are you sure this is what you want? Even after everything that's happened? I know this assign-ment is likely to bring back some old memories."

"It's not that," replied O'Brien, before realizing his response had come just a bit too quickly. "Okay, it's not entirely that. The truth is the Bajorans have a lot of work ahead of them: reclaiming their planet, rebuilding their government, resettling all the refu-gees who lost everything while working in the camps. You saw it yourself. That's a larger problem, and to be honest it's one I'm not really sure Starfleet is equipped to solve, or even understand."

Raising his free hand to indicate the station around them. "But this? Making this station work for Starfleet's mission in this sector is going to take a lot. What I saw down in the bowels of this thing . . . It'll take weeks just to get the station working in proper order, then will come all the upgrades Starfleet wants installed. By then, it'll be a hub for Starfleet and civilian traffic across this entire region."

Keiko regarded him with one of her knowing smiles. "You do like a challenge, don't you?"

"I do." O'Brien felt himself blushing, as though he had been forced to reveal an embarrassing secret. "Commander La Forge told me Starfleet's assigning a full contingent here to oversee everything, including an engineering team. He also said that most of those people are no more than a year or two out of the Academy. A few of them will be on their first assignment after graduation." He blew out his breath. "They'll need someone to show them the ropes, how things are really done when you're out in the middle of nowhere with no starships for backup."

The Bajoran sector was not so remote that the station would never see significant vessel traffic, but it was far enough from current Starfleet patrol routes that assistance might not be readily available. O'Brien knew there were only so many ships in the fleet, and evenly redistributing those resources to provide maximum coverage would take time. At least for now, any Starfleet crew assigned here would be on their own.

It was just one more thing that excited O'Brien about the opportunity presented to him by the *Enterprise*'s chief engineer.

"The station's incoming commander is being very selective about who he wants in key positions," he said. "My name keeps popping up in his searches for a chief of operations." He sighed.

"Keiko, the truth is that I've done more real engineering work in the past few days than I have in years. Maintaining systems aboard a starship where everything is already automated to within an inch of its life doesn't present much of a challenge, but this?" He now cradled her hand in both of his. "This place is . . . I didn't realize how much I missed *really* getting my hands dirty until I was elbow deep in *one* of the ODN conduits. There are hundreds just like that one, scattered across this station. I won't be bored, that's for certain."

Keiko cocked an eyebrow. "So, I have Commander La Forge to thank for this?"

"I know we've been talking about a change for a while," replied O'Brien. "Raising a child on a starship is fine for a year or two, but sooner or later the *Enterprise* is going to get detailed to a long-term exploration mission, and we could spend years out there. Weeks if not months without making planetfall, and there's the danger." He shook his head. "That's no place for a kid."

Squeezing his hand, Keiko said, "You can't give up Starfleet, can you? It's in your blood. Miles, I understand that."

"I gave serious thought to retiring, but if I'm being honest, I know I wouldn't be happy." Once more, O'Brien gestured to the station around them. "I thought this could be a compromise. I get to work in engineering full-time, something I haven't done in years. I get to do something I care about. We'll be together, and you and Molly will be safe. Bajor was once a beautiful planet, and there are still parts of it that are breathtaking. It'll be like having Earth right next door."

Her expression turning to one of concern, Keiko said, "Even after everything that's happened since we've been here, you still want to stay?"

"It's pretty hard to turn down a recommendation like the one Commander Riker and Commander La Forge gave me.

According to them, the commander they're sending out here to run the station is looking for someone with experience dealing with Cardassians." O'Brien hesitated before adding, "And someone with combat experience against them. Commander Riker thinks he's just being overcautious."

Keiko replied, "I'm surprised this commander's not looking at officers for his senior staff."

O'Brien smiled with unabashed pride. "He apparently has an affinity for noncommissioned officers. My guess is some salty master chief took him under his wing when he was an ensign and taught him the right way to do things." He punctuated his comments with a sly wink, which made Keiko laugh.

"I know you've given this a lot of thought, Miles," she said after a moment. "Have you given Commander Riker an answer yet?"

Shaking his head, O'Brien replied, "No. I wanted to talk with you one last time." Assuming Keiko agreed with this proposal, after finishing their dinner, they would return to the *Enterprise*, then he would inform the first officer of his decision. The ship was due to depart within six hours, on its way to Starbase 375 to pick up a contingent of Starfleet personnel awaiting transfer to the station. Once he notified Commander Riker of his intentions, O'Brien would have ten days to get his affairs in order while his request and change of assignment orders were processed. He and Keiko would finalize the relocation of their family's effects from the ship once it returned to the station.

He had given brief consideration to staying here and getting a jump on the numerous repairs and upgrades he knew awaited him. A team of *Enterprise* engineers and security officers was staying behind, assisting the station's new interim commander and other members of the Bajoran Militia with the transition. A number of Cardassians still resided on the station, awaiting transport to their homeworld, and while things had remained mostly peaceful following the conference's end, lingering tensions remained. The chief hoped the presence of Starfleet personnel would keep things calm until the full Starfleet support team began arriving.

His tour aboard the *Enterprise* had been the longest time he had spent at a single posting. It was a plum assignment, but if he was being honest with himself, he had to confess he was growing too comfortable. On the one hand, stability was desirable now that he had his family's well-being to consider, and the *Enterprise* offered more creature comforts than some of the other ships. On the other hand, the starship's primary mission all but guaranteed it would encounter numerous threats. He had no problem facing uncertainty and risk, but it was not what he wanted for his wife and child. As a civilian botanist, Keiko had accepted that reality by joining the crew, but Molly was another matter. He wanted more for her, and while a dilapidated Cardassian space station on the edge of Federation space might not be paradise, Bajor was akin to a paradise and not far away.

Then there was what he wanted. O'Brien would miss the *Enterprise* and its crew and in particular the captain, but something within the chief told him that his future lay not where the Federation flagship would travel but instead along a different path.

Keiko said, "Miles, if it means that much to you, I think we should give it a try." Pausing, she looked down into the bar. "It'll take some getting used to, but we'll manage."

O'Brien leaned toward her. "It may not be the grandest place to live, and in the beginning I'll be putting in long hours to get everything up to spec, but after that? Things will settle down and I'll have a stable schedule. It might even be a little predictable. I figure that'll be nice for us, and for Molly."

"Even though I was able to help Doctor Crusher down on Bajor," said Keiko, "they probably won't have much use for a botanist up here." She shrugged. "On the other hand, there will be plenty of other things that need doing. I'll find some way to contribute." After a moment, she nodded. "I'll make it work."

Even with their shared uncertainty about this next chapter of their lives, he knew it would be all the more satisfying with Keiko and Molly at his side. "*We'll* make it work, together. I love you, Keiko."

She leaned in and kissed him. "I love you, too, Miles."

35

The drink was as big as her head.

"You'll want to go easy with these," said Tropp, the Denobulan's face all but consumed by his elongated smile as he stood next to Crusher at the bar in Quark's, pulling a matching drink closer to him. "Beverly, they've been known to knock even the heartiest of drinkers off their stool. I once saw a Nausicaan keel over after drinking two of them." He made a show of looking thoughtful. "It might've been three. I honestly don't remember, as I'd already had one."

The glass, essentially a large sphere with an open top, sat in a cradle atop the bar. Crusher studied the orange-hued concoction, from which emanated a pale vapor. A single straw poked up from the center of the drink. "What's in it?"

"Rum from five different planets," said Tropp. "Flavored liqueur, and a couple of juices, likely sourced from fruits indigenous to Bajor."

Crusher asked, "The vapor is from dry ice?"

"That, or antimatter. I'm really not sure. It *is* called a Warp Core Breach, after all."

Unable to stifle a chuckle, Crusher covered her mouth with one hand before nodding in acceptance. "And this is a thing on the *Oceanside*?"

Tropp replied, "Sort of a tradition, following a difficult mission. Of course, we use synthehol." He nodded toward the two Ferengi tending bar. "Nothing beats the real thing, though."

"What happens if I finish it?" asked Crusher.

"You're automatically transferred to our crew, and you get a complete blood transfusion on the house."

Crusher smiled. "I was on the fence until the blood transfusion, but now you've convinced me."

In reality, downing a drink of this size and remaining capable of returning to the *Enterprise* without being transported from her seat was beyond her ability, but Crusher knew that was not her colleague's aim. Instead, it was a means of showing appreciation for their successful collaboration. Meanwhile, her counterpart's subtle flirtation was not lost on her. Tropp had made no overt comments or advances during the time they had worked together, and his demeanor remained unchanged now that things had moved to a more casual setting. Crusher had been hit on more than enough times to recognize someone with an angle or agenda, and the *Oceanside*'s chief medical officer was not meeting either criterion. At least, not yet. Shrugging it off, she decided his interplay was harmless bar talk.

As if sensing her concern, Tropp said, "You be the designated pilot. Just promise me you'll make sure one of my shipmates drags me home if I pass out, okay?"

"Deal."

Crusher watched as he leaned toward the drink's straw and took a long pull, all while ice vapor billowed up around his face. After a few seconds he pulled back, closing his eyes before shaking his head.

"That tastes divine. As one of my orderlies says, this does a magnificent job of recrystallizing your dilithium."

Laughing again, Crusher shook her head. "At what point does this become self-abuse?"

Gesturing to the bottom part of the oversized glass, Tropp grinned. "About here, I believe." After a moment, he changed subjects. "So, where's the *Enterprise* off to after all of this? Back to exploring the vast unknown? Maybe make a meaningful first contact or two?"

"Once we return with personnel being assigned here," replied Crusher, "we'll be back to our regular duties. I suspect Captain Picard will welcome that."

She knew Picard had endured his share of discomfort, beginning with his accepting this assignment from Admiral Nechayev. Crusher had wanted to be at his side, but her priorities made that untenable. She gave silent thanks for Deanna Troi, who had been with him during the conference and other activities, acting as his counsel and support whether Jean-Luc admitted to needing either of those things. He had acquitted himself well while under scrutiny of the Bajorans and the Cardassians, and Crusher knew maintaining that façade had worn on him. Despite whatever Starfleet and the Federation might think of him as a diplomat, Jean-Luc Picard was at his core an explorer, and she hoped getting back to that would help him relocate the inner peace which had always given him strength and balance.

"And what about you?" she asked Tropp. "What's next on the *Oceanside*'s agenda?"

The Denobulan replied, "Transporting personnel and cargo to the new Starbase 364. It's scheduled to be declared fully operational within the month, after which it'll be Starfleet's primary outpost in the Shackleton Expanse, beyond the far edge of Romulan and Klingon territory." Then he smiled. "That whole region is largely unexplored. Lots of new opportunities for ships like yours to make first contact, which means more work for us cleaning up the messes you'll make."

The gentle ribbing evoked another chuckle from Crusher. Emboldened by the good time she was having, she leaned forward and took a tentative sip of her drink. No sooner did the potent mixture hit her tongue than the doctor knew she was out of her depth. She was just able to keep herself from coughing while what had to be a potion conjured by demons coursed down her throat. With one hand to her lips, she held up the other one in mock surrender.

"I might need that blood transfer after all."

Tropp held up his own glass. "The first fifty sips are the hardest."

"Noted." Despite his encouragement, Crusher pushed the drink toward the bar's far side, a signal to the bartender that she was finished with it.

A voice from somewhere behind him called out his name, and Crusher looked past him to see a woman dressed in a uniform variant matching Tropp's waving to him. A group of his fellow crew members had found a table. He returned the wave before switching his glass to his left hand while extending his right to Crusher.

"Duty calls, Doctor. It's been an absolute pleasure working with you, even under these circumstances. I hope our paths cross again."

Taking his hand, Crusher replied, "I'd like that, Doctor. The feeling's mutual. Safe journeys to you and your crew."

"And to yours." Grabbing the cradle for his drink, Tropp offered one last smile before moving off to join his shipmates, leaving Crusher alone at the bar.

Almost alone.

Movement to her right reminded her of the brawny Lurian who had been seated at the bar when she and Tropp arrived and who had not said a word in greeting beyond raising his glass in their direction. That glass, Crusher noted, was now empty, and the Lurian had taken possession of her own abandoned drink. When he noticed her looking at him, his expression shifted the slightest bit, as if to communicate, "You said you were done with it."

"Well," said Crusher, "I don't know how much Tropp paid for it, but at least it won't go to waste."

She heard the sounds of laughter and cheering coming from somewhere in the bar's gaming area and saw Will Riker occupying a seat at the dabo wheel. Much to her amusement, two rather attractive and very scantily clad humanoid women were hovering to either side of him, each leaning against one of the first officer's shoulders. For his part, Riker's attention was focused on the spinning wheel, and Crusher noted the impressive stacks of gold-pressed latinum strips arrayed on the table before him. It appeared he was having better luck this time. Other *Enterprise* and *Oceanside* crewmembers surrounded the table, watching the action. Crusher started to rise from her seat, intent on seeing what the fuss was about, when another figure entered her field of vision.

"Doctor Crusher?"

She turned to see Kira Nerys standing before her, looking not like the Bajoran woman she had worked with on Bajor. Gone was the long, unkempt hair, replaced by a short cut that let it fall to just above her shoulders. Rather than well-worn clothing suitable for a life lived hiding from Cardassians while carrying out acts of resistance, she now wore a crisp new red-maroon uniform of the Bajoran Militia.

"Nerys," said Crusher. "Look at you."

Glancing down at herself as though still coming to terms with her new ensemble, Kira said, "They offered me a position here on the station."

Crusher nodded. "I heard. Congratulations, Major. And you're the Bajoran liaison to Starfleet."

"I don't know how well I'll take to being an officer," said Kira. "I spent a lot of years fighting for my people and my world. This seemed like the right thing to do. I'm just hoping I'll get along with whoever Starfleet's sending to take charge."

Crusher said, "According to Captain Picard, the new commander specifically requested a Bajoran national to be his second-in-command. That a good sign."

"You've never seen me around officers," replied Kira, a wry grin punctuating her comment. "If they think making me one will change that, they're going to be disappointed."

"They're lucky to have you."

Drawing a breath, Kira took a quick look around the bar before adding, "Listen, Doctor, I wanted to thank you for everything you did down on the surface. I know I wasn't the most receptive to your crew coming to our aid, and I'll admit I still have my reservations about a long-term Starfleet presence, but what you did will save a lot of lives."

"I understand your doubts," said Crusher. "And I can't blame you for it. The Bajorans have endured something no one deserves. Hopefully what's happened over the past few days is just the beginning of something wonderful for your people."

Kira nodded. "I hope so, too, but I'd be lying if I said I'm no longer skeptical. There are a fair number of moderate voices who want this . . . *relationship* of ours to succeed. There's also a lot of deep-seated resentment toward the Federation, and they worry what this will all mean for Bajor once Starfleet plants its flag here."

"The immediate benefit to Bajor is that the Cardassians will leave you alone. Having a Starfleet base in this sector should provide enough of a deterrent not just for the Cardassians, but also for anyone else who might seek to exploit the Bajorans. As for what's next? That's up to you. The Federation has committed to doing whatever it can to address Bajor's immediate needs." Crusher knew a full rehabilitation of the planet in those and other key areas would take years; Bajor was incapable of sustaining itself, in the short term, without assistance. "Some of the Federation's finest minds are already bringing considerable resources to bear."

"The Cardassians greeted us the same way, Doctor. Fifty years ago. They came in peace, wanting to 'help' us. They wanted to be our 'friends.' Years passed with them insinuating themselves into our lives before they revealed their true motivations, and then it was too late." Kira paused. "I've never known anything but Cardassian oppression of my people. This past week brought the first day of my life where that stopped. I don't know what freedom is supposed to feel like, because I don't have any frame of reference." She held out her arms, indicating the station and people around her. "I'm told this is it. We'll see, but you can't be surprised that we have our doubts."

"I'm not surprised, Major," replied Crusher. "Actions speak louder than words. All I can offer is that we're not the Cardassians."

"There are many of those among my people who don't—or won't—see the difference." Kira sighed. "I don't agree with that mindset either. It's more about setting realistic expectations for Starfleet and the Federation. Convincing the skeptics you *are* different from the Cardassians will be a challenge."

Crusher nodded. "Inform First Minister Kalem there is one very simple way to test how different we are: ask us to leave."

"It's really that simple?" Kira made no attempt to hide her disbelief. "He wants Starfleet here."

"Right now he does," said Crusher. "But that could change for any number of reasons. The Bajoran government can ask the Federation to withdraw, and we will." Crusher frowned. "We may not like it. We may tell you we think you're making a big mistake, but we'd leave."

Still not convinced, Kira asked, "And never come back?"

"Unless you asked us to."

Kira considered this for a beat before replying, "We'll see." Her expression was doubtful, but Crusher thought she detected something else. Hope? No, that was too strong. Perhaps what she saw was a decision to stay the course and see how the situation developed.

Holding out her hand, Kira said, "Thank you again, Doctor, for everything. I'll try to remember what you said, and see where all of this goes."

"Good luck, Major." Crusher shook her hand. "I hope our paths cross again, and next time under better circumstances."

She watched Kira make her way out of the bar before her attention was caught once again by the activity in the gaming area. As she started to head that way, she stole a glance over her shoulder and noted that the Lurian at the corner seat had drained the Warp Core Breach. She looked for some sign it had fazed him, and saw nothing. Amused, she went back toward the gaming area. It seemed as though the dabo wheel was commanding the most attention, with nearly twenty onlookers arrayed around the arrowhead-shaped table with the wheel at its center.

Maneuvering through the spectators, Crusher moved to stand next to Ensign Ro, who had positioned herself behind Riker, giving her an unfettered view of the dabo table. The doctor could see that Riker, still flanked by two attractive dabo girls, had placed a healthy bet, dividing his already impressive take between each of the table's three betting rings. There was a palpable energy around the table from those watching the action, and she could see that the first officer was enjoying himself.

"I have absolutely no idea what's going on," she said to Ro. "How's he doing?"

The ensign replied, "Much better than the first night."

"And how are *you* doing?" Crusher saw the ensign stiffen in response to the question. The doctor had heard about Ro's relationship with one of the Bajorans from Satera III.

Ro nodded. "I'm . . . fine, Doctor, thank you for asking." She drew a long breath before adding, "Actually I don't honestly know what to feel. All this time, I thought Hileb was dead. I never suspected he might have gotten off Valo II, only to be captured by the Cardassians. I just wish I'd had a chance to see him, before . . ."

"It's okay to be sad," said Crusher, "to grieve."

"I know. It's just that many of us learned at a very early age that feelings are dangerous. They can be exploited, used against you. I mourn Hileb, and I even cried for him. That's something I've never done for anyone, except my own parents. The truth is most Bajorans came to understand we could die on any given day. Not because all living things die, but because we've lived our entire lives under tyrannical rule where death is a common punishment. You become numb to the idea after a while. It's not maudlin, but simple acceptance." Then her expression softened. "I hope it's a feeling you never have to experience, Doctor."

Reaching out to place a hand on the ensign's arm, Crusher nodded in understanding. "I'm sorry about your friend, Laren."

"Thank you," said Ro, "I appreciate it."

The murmurs from onlookers intensified with each passing second. Crusher and Ro watched as the dabo wheels spun and the gathering of onlookers started to cheer. The spinning rings were slowing, with each circle's symbols coming to rest beneath one of the lights, including those illuminated to indicate a bet had been placed on that position.

Crusher felt her jaw slacken as she watched the same symbols, identical in shape and color, align themselves beneath the light in front of Riker.

"*Dabo!*"

Everyone around the table uttered the victory cry at the same moment as Riker threw up his hands in triumph. His dabo girl escorts squealed with delight, but whether it was a genuine reaction or one born from hope for a share of the winnings, Crusher had no clue.

"I can't believe it," said Ro. "Triple-down dabo. I've never seen anyone do it. The Ferengi running this place is going to have an aneurysm."

Turning from the dabo wheel, Riker grinned. "Looks like dinner is on me."

Crusher chuckled. "How much did you win?"

Hooking a thumb over his shoulder toward the dabo table, Riker replied, "About twelve bars."

Ro said, "I guess that means dinner for the entire station."

From behind, Crusher heard a new voice. "Yes, about that, Commander."

She turned to see that the bar's Ferengi proprietor, Quark, had made his way through the enthusiastic spectators toward Riker. Dressed in a colorful shirt beneath a heavy woven gray jacket with matching trousers, he looked every bit the polished business mogul. It was his expression that was far more interesting, as it was one that communicated acute discomfort.

"Quark," said Riker, his smile growing wider, "I might need help getting my winnings to the *Enterprise*."

His unease appearing to increase, Quark held out his hands in supplication. "Well, about that. You see, Commander, there's been an unfortunate mishap. My brother, Rom, seems to have misplaced the combination to my safe. Therefore, I don't have access to twelve bars of gold-pressed latinum. Would you consider vouchers?"

36

—

"You've done an excellent job, Captain. Despite the twists and turns, real progress was made, both for Bajor and the Federation."

Sitting at the desk in his ready room, Picard offered an appreciative nod as he regarded the image of Alynna Nechayev on his desktop computer terminal. "Thank you, Admiral. I know this is just the beginning of what will be a long journey for the Bajorans, but I'd like to think we helped get them off on the right foot."

On the screen, Nechayev nodded. *"Allowing the provisional government to take point on prosecuting those Cardassians charged with sabotage and the plundering of cultural artifacts during their post-Occupation withdrawal was a masterstroke, Captain. They've already requested a Federation mediator to help navigate that process. They hope it will show Bajorans aren't vindictive but seeking justice."*

Picard knew it was an important step in the ongoing process of the healing of Bajor and its people. First Minister Kalem wanted to move forward in an orderly and dignified manner. It would reinforce the idea that trials and any resulting punishments would be administered in a fair and civilized fashion. The request for Federation mediation had not been popular with all Bajorans. Leadership cadres representing several provinces had voiced opposition to the level of Federation involvement, or to the pace that involvement was asserting itself. There had been formal protests against the Provisional Government. Voices of opposition had grown even louder at the idea of Bajor joining the Federation. Picard suspected such a quantum shift in their society would be a long time coming. The Federation would of course gain the advantage of a permanent presence in this remote area of space, but that could not happen without the trust and confidence of the Bajoran people.

"Any fallout from the Satera affair?" he asked.

Her pleasant demeanor hardened a bit, and Picard noticed her eyes narrowing before she replied, *"That, I'm afraid, is a much stickier wicket. The lack of evidence affords the Cardassians the ability to—as the saying goes—be somewhat economical with the truth. Because of the unique situation surrounding that world and the activities taking place there, your crew helped expose a much larger problem. We know the Cardassians used Bajorans as forced labor on several planets. Reports are coming in of withdrawal from those worlds, and there's no way to know what they did. Starfleet has been ordered to dispatch ships to these planets, and that includes the En-terprise, Captain."*

Picard nodded in acknowledgment. "Where do you need us, Admiral?"

"Once you've completed the personnel transfer to Deep Space 9, you'll proceed to the planet Jevalan in the Doltiri system. Preliminary reports indicate the planet was strip-mined to a far greater degree than Bajor." She paused, sighing. *"There may be thousands of Bajorans there, but we have no information on their condition. You'll be among the first to arrive at Jevalan, Captain, but you'll be relieved when the flotilla of aid ships gets there."*

Picard was buoyed by Starfleet committing to the humanitarian relief effort on a substantial scale. It was long overdue, but at least they were doing something. "Is there any way to know for certain how many planets under Cardassian control may still have Bajorans there?"

Shaking her head, Nechayev replied, *"It could take years to account for everyone. Even after that effort, we may never know the complete truth. However, First Minister Kalem is talking about a special commission dedicated to locating the missing. We've offered assistance, but for the moment they're keeping that for themselves. In the meantime, we'll do this."*

"But surely Satera has put the Cardassian Central Command on notice that failure to abide by the terms of their withdrawal will bring interstellar condemnation," said Picard.

"Oh, they're on notice. The first wave of disavowals have already been transmitted. 'Unauthorized actions by corrupt officers acting in their own self-interests,' that sort of thing." Nechayev shook her head. *"It'll be an uphill struggle, for the Bajorans and for the Federation, but we'll do our best to keep them honest. After the Minos Korva incident and enduring this public embarrassment as they leave Bajor, the last thing they want is another war with us. They need to lick their wounds."* Before Picard could protest, she held up a hand. *"Don't worry, Captain. We know we haven't heard the last of them, and Starfleet won't be letting our guard down."*

"That's very encouraging, Admiral."

"Now then," she said, leaning closer to her own terminal's visual pickup. *"How are you doing?"* There was no mistaking the unspoken question now hanging between them.

Holding his head a bit higher, Picard replied, "Very well, Admiral. Thank you. I'll admit it was . . . challenging." He paused, then offered a small smile. "It did do a great deal so far as helping me get back on the proverbial horse."

Nechayev's expression softened. *"That's good to hear. I know it must have been difficult for you, Jean-Luc."*

"I have a good crew serving under me. That makes the job much easier."

Serving under me, he repeated to himself, *and looking out for me.*

"Thank you again, Captain, for a job done well. I knew I could count on you. Keep me informed about the situation on Jevalan."

"Understood, Admiral." Picard bid farewell before Nechayev's visage disappeared from the screen, replaced by the Federation seal. After ordering a course change for the *Enterprise* to the Doltiri system, he directed the senior staff to begin preparations for the aid mission they would be undertaking. Picard leaned back in his chair, closing his eyes and listening to the omniscient thrum of the ship's engines while willing himself to relax.

The attempt lasted perhaps ten seconds before his door chime sounded.

"Come," he said, straightening his posture and his uniform just before the door slid aside to admit Deanna Troi.

"Am I disturbing you, sir?" she asked, remaining at the threshold. "You said you wanted to see me after your conversation with Admiral Nechayev was concluded. With the course change, I assumed you were finished."

Picard rose from his chair. "Counselor, please." He indicated the sofa just to the side of the door and waited for Troi to take a seat. He moved to sit beside her. "We had scheduled this session prior to the admiral's call, and I wanted to keep it." He felt the corner of his mouth lift. "I didn't want you to think I was using the admiral as a pretext for avoiding you."

Smiling, Troi replied, "I would never think that, sir, but it's good to see your self-confidence returning."

"Really?" Picard situated himself so he was facing her while supported by the sofa's back. "I would've thought the past few days would have demonstrated that well enough."

"I never doubted you'd rise to the occasion," said the counselor. "Decades of training and experience make that sort of thing automatic for you. The discipline of the service is too engrained within you to permit anything less. It's one of the traits that make you an effective leader. A seasoned commander is often the difference between success and failure and even life and death. You've faced too much over the years to crumble in the face of adversity so easily, and I knew you wouldn't do that on Terok Nor."

Holding up a finger to signal a mock scolding, Picard said, "It's Deep Space 9 now."

"Yes, it is," said Troi. "Thanks to you."

"To a great many people." Folding his hands in his lap, Picard added, "The Bajorans have much work head of them. I'm optimistic about this joint Starfleet-Bajoran approach we're taking."

Attempting to forge a relationship with the Bajorans—many of whom, despite recent events, still harbored tremendous resentment toward the Federation—would be a protracted endeavor. Missions like the one in which the *Enterprise* was now engaged would further aid in that effort, but it was only a beginning. There was still much to be done, but now all sides acknowledged this fact and had pledged to work together.

"And how are you feeling?" asked Troi. "I don't mean about the mission."

Expecting the conversation to take this turn, Picard confessed, "Better, more so than before the conference." He explained his interaction with Kai Opaka and how it left him feeling buoyed.

"The kai came to me soon after your first meeting. She could sense something troubling you. Knowing I'm the ship's counselor, she asked if I would share . . . I did not, but she understood you were carrying a significant weight when we first confronted Madred."

Picard nodded. "She is a formidable woman, and a gifted leader."

"The Bajorans have always a been a spiritual people," said

Troi. "I have no doubt many of them leaned on their faith to see them through the Occupation. They'll still believe, only now they will have a promising future."

Picard knew a belief in their Prophets was woven throughout Bajoran culture and their everyday life. Free from the chains of oppression, they could use those same beliefs to help them leave the pain behind and guide them toward a better future.

"After everything the Bajorans suffered, I'd like to think I can overcome my own experience."

Troi eyed him with compassion. "Captain, that sort of healing takes time."

"I know." Picard nodded once, with conviction. "The horror is a part of me, but like the Bajorans, I'm hopeful I can leave some of that pain behind me and focus on tomorrow."

"Their path to healing will also be a difficult one," said Troi. "However, with leaders like Kai Opaka and First Minister Kalem, I believe they have an excellent chance of succeeding. The rest is up to them."

Picard wanted that to be true. "And us as well." Inroads made by the Federation in the past few days were but the first steps on a journey the captain hoped would be long and fruitful. Helping the Bajorans regain their independence was illustrative of Federation values, but it had taken too long to get to this point. That painful truth would continue to overshadow Federation efforts for a time, but Picard believed it a goal well worth pursuing.

Nothing worth doing is ever easy, he thought, recalling an aphorism his father would invoke at regular intervals throughout Picard's childhood. *Indeed, the things worth doing are damned hard.*

The Bajorans had already done the hard thing: surviving. If they had proven anything, it was that they were a resilient people. This moment represented a new beginning for Bajor. They would push forward, reclaiming their world and their heritage to emerge from the other side of that struggle as a thriving, vibrant civilization stronger than they had once been. The Federation owed them every opportunity and assistance helping them attain that goal. Yes, it would be damned hard, but together, the Bajorans would make it work.

Of this, Picard had no doubt.

A NEW BEGINNING

37

—

Alarm klaxons blared upward through the turbolift shaft, growing louder as Kira descended from Deep Space 9's operations center. By the time the lift came to a halt on the Promenade, the sound was almost deafening, heightened by the alert indicators flashing in rapid, almost seizure-inducing fashion from the bulkheads.

No sooner had she stepped from the car than Kira flinched at the report of weapons fire, just an instant before an energy pulse struck the bulkhead just to her left. Training and experience honed by chaos made her duck while drawing and firing her own sidearm in one fluid motion. Her shot, released even before she had acquired a target, still managed to strike a dark, cloaked figure in the shoulder with enough force to drop him to the deck. Gripping her phaser with both hands, Kira closed the distance, kicking away the weapon that had fallen from its owner's hand.

A Cardassian hand.

Knocked off his feet, her assailant was still conscious and attempting to stand, the hood of his cloak pushed back to reveal mussed black hair and his pale, ridged complexion. Kira shot him again, and he slumped back to the deck.

Tapping her combadge, she had to yell to be heard over the din of the sirens. "Kira to Ops. Intruder alert on the Promenade. Scramble all security personnel and shut off the alarms."

Within seconds, her last command was rewarded with the soothing sound of relative silence. Was it her imagination, or had the volume on the damned klaxons been cranked up to maximum?

"*Sorry about that, Major,*" said a voice over the open channel. "*It appears the alert system has been altered to increase audio levels as well as visual intervals.*"

Kira scowled. "No kidding. Everybody and two generations of their dead is awake now."

"*Security teams are on the way, Major. Someone's attempting to jam our internal sensors, but we're picking up multiple transporter signatures across the station.*"

"Are we being boarded?" asked Kira, her phaser in front of her and leading the way as she advanced along the Promenade.

"*Scans show individuals are being transported to a freighter holding position just off the station. We're not picking up any new life signs arriving on the station, but we are registering power and computer system interruptions in areas where the transporter signals were detected.*"

Power and computer disruptions. Those systems were already hampered thanks to the plundering or simple destruction of equipment. *What else could they be doing?*

"Keep me updated. Raise shields and put a tractor beam on that freighter. Hold them here." Ahead of her, shouts of activity along with other troubling sounds carried from around the curve of the expansive thoroughfare.

"*Shields aren't responding, and the freighter keeps maneuvering to evade the beam.*"

Identified as a civilian transport, it had now proven to be something altogether different. Kira started to order Ops to fire on the ship, then she remembered that the station's weapons were useless until missing components as well as munitions were replaced.

The controlled looting of the station had stopped with the arrival of the *Enterprise* and the *Oceanside*, and Starfleet engineers had mitigated some of the damage. The station could function at a very basic level, but anything resembling a luxury and most of what might be considered simple comfort items were gone. Now that the starships had departed, Kira and her people—along with a small Starfleet contingent—had managed, waiting for additional personnel to arrive. This meant babysitting the remaining Cardassians, including members of the diplomatic entourage who were awaiting a special transport back to Cardassia Prime. A pair of civilian haulers were transferring bulk shipments up from Bajor, as it was the only way to resupply the station until the cargo transporters were brought back online. There had been no other ship traffic until the arrival of that freighter, a vessel that appeared to be a ruse as it assisted some of the remaining Cardassians on the station who now were getting brazen on their way out.

"Ops, keep after that ship, but lock down all docking ports and transporters. In fact, secure all the airlocks while you're at it. Absolutely nobody on or off the station without my approval until further notice. Got it?"

"Understood, Major."

Kira came to the curve in the Promenade corridor that brought Quark's Bar into view. Her first impression was that she had stepped into a war zone or, perhaps more accurately, a terrorist attack. Six people, half of them Bajorans, lay strewn on the deck. Other civilians were taking cover against nearby bulkheads or in adjacent shops. Flames were visible inside Quark's Bar and from two storefronts, and a freestanding merchant's kiosk had been reduced to a smoldering pile of rubble. Smoke filled the air even as automated suppression systems addressed the fires inside the shops. Kira caught sight of two Bajorans in militia uniforms moving to suppress one of the store's fires with portable extinguishers.

"What the hell happened?" Kira demanded as she drew closer. She looked around as her people worked to snuff out the

last of the flames. Wrinkling her nose at the stench of burned veg-
etables and whatever else had been in the food merchant's shop,
she waved away the smoke lingering in the air around her.

"Some kind of improvised firebomb," replied one of the junior officers, a lieutenant whose name Kira could not remember.
"Another shopkeeper saw them light and throw it before running
off down the Promenade." With the extinguisher, he gestured farther down the spacious walkway. "He ran in that direction, wearing a dark hooded cloak."

Kira grunted in irritation. "Dark cloaks seem to be a thing
right now." She had no idea as to the identities of the Cardassians causing the current mess. She recalled from a quick review
of status and personnel reports earlier in the day that most of
the thirty-six Cardassians still on the station worked in support functions, either for officers who used to be posted here
or elsewhere accompanying the diplomatic delegation. Kira
doubted any of them were actual soldiers, or at least not actively
serving in such roles; their society's focus on martial power ensured most able-bodied civilians received rudimentary military
training.

They seem good enough for the job at hand.

She turned in response to motion from another of the storefronts, raising her phaser in time to see another Cardassian, this
one without a cloak, emerging from the shop while assisting an
obviously wounded Bajoran. The shopkeeper, an elderly man
Kira recognized, held a rag to his head where he was bleeding
from a nasty gash. He was favoring his left leg, holding on to
the Cardassian as they both cleared the store and his unlikely
benefactor escorted him to a nearby bench. Kira recognized the
Cardassian as Garak, "the tailor" who now operated a Promenade shop. According to reports, he had presented no trouble
the entire time he had been on the station, after being exiled from

Cardassia Prime for reasons unknown. Despite the obvious motive to suspect him, Odo had been forced to admit this supposed tailor kept a low profile and behaved himself. That did not mean Kira trusted him.

"You," she said, her tone severe as she aimed her sidearm at Garak, waiting for him to help the shopkeeper sit down before adding, "stand right there. Show me your hands."

The Bajoran, wincing in obvious pain, said, "Please, he saved my life."

"And I appreciate that," replied Kira. "But we're going to act now and apologize later." Until she had a handle on the situation, everyone was a suspect.

It was obvious to her the remaining contingent of Cardassians had waited for the right moment, taking advantage of a depleted station crew while exploiting gaps in security coverage thanks to the damage already done to various systems. Their only misstep in Kira's eyes was in not timing their getaway to coincide with the departure of the diplomatic envoy, as Legate Madred and his aides were still awaiting transport. If they had been involved in the current incident, Kira planned to find out.

A team of medics from the station's infirmary arrived, accompanied by another security detail. The medics started treating the wounded while Garak and the stunned Cardassian were taken into custody.

"Keep him separated from the others," said Kira, indicating Garak. A small thing, but the tailor bowed his head in obvious appreciation.

"Thank you, Major. I promise I'll make no trouble." His expression was a mask of calm and control Kira found disconcerting. In her previous interactions with him, she had always sensed he knew far more than he was letting on. She considered that a default characteristic for all Cardassians, even more so for those who had worked as intelligence agents. That was the story on Garak, and his demeanor suggested someone quite familiar with handling himself during stressful situations. It infuriated her.

Renewed weapons fire from somewhere farther down the Promenade caught her attention. Kira took off running toward the sounds of fighting. Navigating the next curve in the corridor, she spotted another Bajoran man from the militia accompanied by a woman wearing a Starfleet uniform. Each had their weapons in hand, standing over the prone form of a figure wrapped in a large cloak that all but concealed its wearer's body. Hearing her approach, both officers appeared to relax.

"Got him, Major," said the Bajoran, also a lieutenant. He gestured with his phaser to the unmoving figure. Booted feet and gloved hands were visible. The Starfleet ensign—Kira noted her rank from the pips on her collar—pulled back the still form's hood and revealed its wearer to be another Cardassian.

The ensign pointed back the way Kira had come. "He's the one who threw the bomb into the shop. There were others running around here doing the same thing."

Nodding at her report, Kira frowned. "I'm sorry, but I'm still working on remembering everyone's names."

"Lieutenant Delon, Major," said the Bajoran. "Delon Par."

"Ensign Sonya Gomez," added the Starfleet woman. "I'm with the engineering team on loan until the *Enterprise* returns."

Kira had only briefly met the detachment assigned on her arrival. There had been no time to familiarize herself with the roster of militia members and Starfleet engineers who for the moment fell under her command. She had just found her office up in the station's operations center before the litany of things requiring her attention consumed her day. Her predecessor, Major Heslo, had faced a number of issues dominated by the wanton sabotage wreaked by the Cardassians before they ceded control of the station to the Bajorans.

The most recent attempts to sow havoc just added to the list of disruptions. This ridiculous, even petty parting shot was bad enough on its own, but the damage to persons and property could not be dismissed.

"Take him to the holding cells," said Kira. "I don't recognize him. Have the constable run an identity scan."

She would let Odo, who she decided would retain his title and position as the station's chief of security, handle the formalities, such as preparing charges to bring against the Cardassian and any accomplices. Her order to secure the docking ports and transporters ensured no one was getting off the station. She supposed they might try passing through the waste disposal conduits, but they ended up at an airlocked compartment that was now shut down. The station was big, but there were only so many Cardassian still aboard. The perpetrators, however many there were, would be found.

"Major Kira!"

Turning toward the new voice, she saw a Starfleet engineer from the *Enterprise* who had volunteered to remain aboard the station and assist the Bajorans with repairs until the full Starfleet contingent arrived. Of medium build and sporting unkempt brown hair, the man wore collar insignia identifying him as a lieutenant. Along with a second Starfleet officer, he held a phaser on another Cardassian—this one a woman, dressed in a similar cloak—lying unconscious on the nearby deck.

"Where'd you find her?" asked Kira. As with her apparent colleagues, she did not recognize the Cardassian.

The lieutenant replied, "She was about to throw a grenade into Quark's." He nodded to the ensign, who Kira thought still belonged in school. The younger man held up an oblong object with blunt ends that she recognized as a fragmentation grenade favored by Cardassian ground troops. Over the years, Kira had "repurposed" similar devices for one reason or another. The expression on the ensign's face told her he had experience handling such ordnance.

Lucky him.

"Tell me it's disarmed, Lieutenant . . ." she said.

"Duffy. Absolutely." He sneered at the explosive. "I removed the charge and the detonator. It's basically a paperweight now."

Kira said, "You sound as if you've been around those things before."

With only the hint of a humorless smile, the lieutenant replied, "Let's just say I wasn't always an engineer." Then, after a pause as their gazes met, he added, "You know how it is."

"Indeed I do." Kira gleaned from the somber way Duffy made his comments that he must have seen ground combat, perhaps during the Federation's war with the Cardassians. She knew another *Enterprise* crew member, Miles O'Brien, was an experienced combat veteran in addition to being a skilled engineer. O'Brien would become the station's chief of operations, arriving here in a day or so along with additional members of the Starfleet contingent being posted here.

And that's when the hard work really starts.

Movement behind Duffy and the ensign caught Kira's attention, and she saw Odo walking toward them. Behind him was a detail of Bajoran security officers with weapons drawn as they escorted two more Cardassians. As they approached, Odo gestured to one of the security officers, indicating for her to take charge of Duffy's prisoner.

"Get them into the holding cells," he said, his voice low and rumbling with restrained irritation.

In response to his order, the Bajoran Militia members as well as Duffy and his Starfleet companion took up positions, directing both Cardassians to the holding area near Odo's office. They were interrupted by the whine of transporter energy just before matching columns of flickering yellow-orange light enveloped the would-be prisoners, and they dissolved with their guards staring in mute shock.

"Ops to Major Kira. We're registering transporter activity at sixteen points around the station. Each life sign was Cardassian. They were beamed over to that freighter."

Feeling her anger rising, Kira asked through gritted teeth, "Tell me you have that ship in a tractor beam."

There was a pause before the operations officer replied, *"Negative, Major. They got away. We never got a lock on them."*

Odo asked, "Ops, is the Cardassian diplomatic delegation still aboard?"

After a moment came the reply, *"They are, sir. Our security detail at the guest-quarters section confirms five individuals still occupying their rooms."*

"Keep them there until further notice," said Kira. Of the delegation, only Legate Madred likely possessed any information of value, assuming he had any involvement with what had just transpired. Even if that were true, the chances of him giving up anything incriminating were nil.

Her business with Ops concluded, Odo's expression told her more bad news was coming.

"I know that look," she said. "Let me have it."

Odo replied, "We have three confirmed dead, all here on the Promenade. All Bajoran shopkeepers." He grunted in dissatisfaction. "They apparently tried to protect their stores when the ransacking began. A fourth victim is in critical condition and may not survive. There are other injuries and widespread property damage to nearly every establishment."

"What about the rest of the station?"

"They used their transporters to remove key components from several systems, including life-support and replicator processing. Combine that with the damage they already did during their withdrawal, and our problems have just multiplied. We'll be eating emergency rations until the replicators are back online."

"And not breathing, if we don't fix life-support." Kira sighed. A final blow to those who had spent decades under the heel of oppression. It was maddening that the Cardassians could not just walk away from the scene of their heinous crimes. Like the insufferable cretins they were, they had to enjoy one last growl on their way out the door. It was all so petty and vindictive.

"What do you want me to do with Garak?" asked Odo.

Kira replied, "Question him along with the others." She told him how the Bajoran merchant had vouched for Garak, earning a derisive snort from the constable. She knew how he suspected the tailor of still being a spy despite the reports of his dismissal and exile. The truth was no actionable evidence linked Garak to anything untoward happening on the station, including the attack on the Cardassian diplomatic delegation or what had just transpired here. In Odo's eyes—and Kira's own—that made him worthy of more attention and observation, not less.

"I'll have a chat with him, but I doubt he'll offer anything useful either."

"My first guess is that this is Dukat's doing," said Kira. "That bastard's fingerprints are all over this."

Odo replied, "You may be right, but we'll never prove it. If Dukat is good at any one thing, it's covering his tracks and deflecting blame."

"Agreed." Kira cast a long, tired look at the disheveled Promenade. Even during the darkest days of the Occupation, this part of the station had been a thriving hub of activity. *Could it be again?* She believed it was possible.

"To hell with Dukat," she said after a moment. "We'll get past this, get past everything they left us to deal with, and get on with rebuilding Bajor and reclaiming our heritage." Then, recalling Odo, she added, "That means you, too, Odo. You're finally free to do whatever you want. Go wherever you want."

"I'm where I want to be," said her friend. "I'm doing what I want to do. This is the only home I've ever known. We'll make it better."

Kira asked, "With or without the Federation's help?" She reminded herself that the rest of the Starfleet contingent, including the officer selected to command the station, would be walking into quite the mess.

"They can't be worse than the Cardassians," said Odo.

Frowning, Kira shook her head. "That doesn't mean they'll be any better either."

After forty years of living under tyrannical rule, the Bajorans would not have patience for anything that might smack of oppression. She did not believe life under Federation "protection" would be worse, but the simple truth was Bajor was still not free to determine its own path, free from influence. For the time being, her people needed what the Federation had to offer, but this did not mean she trusted them. The Federation and Starfleet, and in particular the incoming station commander, would have a lot of work to do in order to earn that trust.

Her cynicism was the product of a life spent trying to survive while trying to throw off the cruel yoke of oppression. Kira wanted this to work, for Bajor's sake, as well as her own.

Only time would tell.

38

Alone at one of the large, oval viewing ports along the Promenade's upper walkway, Odo stood with arms folded across his chest, silent as he took in the view of open space beyond the station. For as long as he could remember, he had always enjoyed staring at the countless stars of the galaxy. There were fewer things more comforting than an unfettered view of such wonder. From his earliest days living here, he had found solace in the places where the station offered access to the sights before him. It was especially true at "station evening," when the Promenade's internal illumination was subdued in order to simulate lighting conditions on Bajor's surface. The effect acted to further soothe him as he partook in his own private ritual, which was even more welcome in the aftermath of the day's events. The practice brought him comfort, and a sense of serenity he lacked in nearly all other aspects of the odd journey that had been his life to this point.

He had long ago cultivated a preference for solitude, doubtless owing to his unique status among those with whom he shared this station. He found he preferred areas like these, away from the bustle of restaurants, shops, and kiosks dominating the Promenade's lower level. The curfew Major Kira had instituted saw to it there was little activity this evening. Several of the shops had suffered severe damage from the Cardassians' last-ditch effort to instill fear into the Bajorans who called the station home, and those businesses were cordoned off. Quark's Bar, the unofficial heart and soul of the Promenade, was also closed while its owner and staff assessed the damage they would have to repair. There were rumbles that the Ferengi was considering abandoning the bar, a sentiment shared by a number of merchants, including those whose shops had escaped the attack.

Odo knew Kira hoped to convince them to stay and participate in rebranding the station not as a Cardassian ore facility but as part of a newly liberated Bajor. With Starfleet's assistance that recovery could be accelerated, but he shared the concerns of Major Kira and many others who worried what the Federation might impose for this act of altruism. Based on his interactions with Starfleet representatives to this point, Odo could believe those in the rank and file were motivated by a genuine desire to help—to do good. What remained to be learned were the motivations of those in charge, who sat in offices far away from Bajor and eyed the system as just one piece of an interstellar puzzle they were trying to assemble while denying that same piece to other interested parties.

Those are problems for others, Odo reminded himself. His responsibilities were local. He had been entrusted with the security of the station and all who called it home. This included purview over the incoming Starfleet detachment, who doubtless would have their own personnel and notions of what constituted station security. Having already warned him about this, Kira assured him she would be speaking to First Minister Kalem to have his role and scope of duties outlined to the incoming Starfleet commander with no room for misunderstanding. Odo suspected the reality of the situation would end up being far more complicated than Kira or the first minister could ever know. As long as he was allowed to do his job, he would be satisfied.

A gradual dimming of the Promenade's illumination pulled Odo from his thoughts, reminding him that the station was transitioning from "evening" to "night." On a regular day, this meant establishments operating during the later hours would be closing soon. Power to the Promenade would be scaled back as a conservation measure, and custodial personnel as well as automated cleaning drones would be deployed to work unobstructed by throngs of people.

Odo realized he was enjoying this unexpected opportunity for his exercise in silent contemplation. Despite his marginal remove from the rest of the station's population, Odo found himself comforted by the knowledge that others were not far away. The thought made him smile with mild amusement. For someone who valued isolation, he seemed to have a dependency on the proximity of other living beings.

He conceded it was an incongruity, yet one that continued to fascinate him. The years he had lived here, on this station and in such close quarters with humanoids, had made him realize just how different and alone he was in the universe. Surely there were others like him, somewhere. Perhaps one day he would find them. It was possible he might do that on his own, but part of him knew he would need the assistance of others. There also was the possibility members of his species might one day find him. He had certainly considered the notion, even dreamed of it, while resting in his natural formless state within the privacy of his quarters. What might the planet of his origin be like? Would it be something akin to Bajor, the edge of which he could just see beyond the view port? Light from the planet's host sun reflected off its atmosphere, offering a warm glow that pushed against the unrelenting, star-filled blackness of space. In what environment might his species thrive? How far away was such a world? Could it be reached using—

"Docking control to Odo," said a voice emanating from his communicator pendant.

Though he had been expecting the call, the interruption still annoyed him. He set aside such thoughts as he tapped the device. "Odo here."

"We've cleared the Cardassian delegation's transport for departure, sir. They'll be undocking from upper pylon three momentarily."

"Acknowledged. Odo out."

The ship had arrived less than an hour earlier, the lone exception to Major Kira's orders that no vessels be allowed to dock until the unrest on the Promenade was resolved. In Odo's mind, that meant getting everyone involved off the station. At his insistence, Kira had ordered all remaining Cardassians to accompany Legate Madred and the other diplomatic representatives. After the earlier chaos, the constable wished to expend no more personnel waiting for someone else to try their hand at sowing unrest. Cleanup and repair efforts were already underway, but Odo knew it would take days for the work to be completed given the station's deficit of personnel. The Starfleet contingent from the *Enterprise* was a welcome addition, but the real work would not begin until their full complement, as well as the officer assigned to command the station, arrived tomorrow.

Still, the departure of the last Cardassians was enough that Odo could allow himself to relax a bit. Keeping tabs on the comings and goings of the uncounted vessels that made the station a port call was a duty he took seriously. Arrivals and departures carried with them a heightened risk to the station and its inhabitants. That was his default thinking whenever any ship docked at the station, but his attentiveness had always spiked when the Cardassians were involved. In the past, that meant being on the lookout for trouble between them and any Bajorans or if the soldiers decided a Bajoran was worthy of their attention or abuse. Dealing with Starfleet on a regular basis would be a vast improvement over the Cardassians.

Well, there's still one Cardassian.

That thought was interrupted when Odo detected movement in his peripheral vision. He turned toward the nearby viewing port in time to see the ungainly Cardassian transport vessel maneuvering away from the station after departing the upper pylon docking area. He did not have to orient himself to know that the ship's direction of travel aimed it in the general direction of the Cardassian border. As for the vessel, he noted it appeared cleaner and better maintained compared to other ships of this design, clearly keeping with its mission to ferry high-ranking and other important individuals. Given how things had proceeded here during the past few days, he wondered if the delegation would continue to be viewed in high regard by the Cardassian Central Command.

The transport moved beyond the station and its immediate defensive perimeter, and Odo watched its nacelles flare as it prepared to accelerate to warp speed. He was sure his eyes registered the odd effect of the ship appearing to stretch as a subspace field began forming around it, just before the vessel vanished in a blinding white flash. The ship had not jumped to warp but instead exploded. The near darkness of the observation platform was consumed by the burst of light. As fast as it happened the flash was gone, and with it any trace of the Cardassian ship. Stunned by what he had just witnessed, Odo slapped his comm pendant.

"Odo to Ops! The Cardassian transport—"

"*We just picked up the explosion on sensors, Constable,*" said a voice he did not recognize. "*Readings indicate a fluctuation in their warp core just before it happened. We tried to warn them but it was too late.*"

"Are you sure it was an internal issue?" Odo was readying his next question, wondering if another vessel could have approached close enough to attack the transport without first being detected by the station's sensors, but he stopped himself. He had caught another movement in the corner of his eye, and any further queries to Ops died on his lips. Instead, he said, "Conduct a complete sensor sweep. Notify Major Kira of the situation immediately. I'll be there as quickly as I can."

"Acknowledged," said the voice from Ops, but Odo had already set aside the conversation as he redirected his focus to the lone figure standing several meters away from him, hands clasped behind his back and staring through another of the upper walkway's viewing ports.

Garak.

The one Cardassian.

"You," said Odo, closing the distance as Garak turned his head at the sound of the voice. Glaring at him, Odo noted the tailor did not appear startled or concerned at his approach. Only when he was within a few paces did Garak pivot to face him.

"Good evening, Constable."

"It was, until a moment ago." Nodding toward the viewport, Odo grunted in irritation. "Did you enjoy the show?"

Shrugging, Garak replied, "I've seen better."

"You don't seem terribly surprised."

Instead of responding, the Cardassian returned his attention to the viewing port. Despite his best effort, Odo could not resist glancing in that direction but saw nothing save the stars which had borne mute witness to the violence of the past few moments. After a beat, Garak turned back to Odo.

"It was probably inevitable. Legate Madred had many enemies, after all." A small smile teased his lips. "Some of them were even Cardassian."

"Was he always your target?" asked Odo. "Or are you just not that discriminating when it comes to revenge?"

His expression turning to one of disbelief, which Odo was

sure was anything but genuine, Garak said, "My dear constable, whatever do you mean?"

"The bomb in the Cardassian delegation's compartment, for one thing."

Garak placed a hand on his own chest. "You wound me, good sir. I never knew Commissioner Wonar and therefore had no reason to kill him. Surely you don't still think I had anything to do with that unfortunate action when Legate Madred was here, with both motive and opportunity. You should have been subjecting him to this intense scrutiny."

Odo had considered Madred for the bombing attack based on his conversation with Garak. There was the little matter of there being not a shred of evidence linking him to the attack. Not surprising, except there also existed nothing else pointing to anyone. It was, in Odo's estimation, a rare example of a perfect assassination that only failed in its primary objective due to unfortunate happenstance. "Wonar was collateral damage. You missed Madred." He gestured to the viewing port. "So you tried again."

"I assure you, Constable, that I always hit what I'm aiming at." Garak smiled. "You really are quite the storyteller." He placed his hands at his sides, his expression remaining impassive. "Is it your intention to arrest me again on the basis of these outlandish accusations?"

There was only one answer. "No," said Odo. "But you already know that."

With no hard evidence linking him to any crime, Odo could not keep Garak in custody following the incidents on the Promenade. His was one of the shops that had suffered damage in the attacks, lending credence to his status as uninvolved. There was also an unexpected statement of support from the wounded Bajoran merchant assisted by Garak. With all of this in his favor, Odo had released him, knowing that his supposed status as an exile from Cardassian society would hamper his efforts to depart the station aboard that last, ill-fated transport.

A fortunate coincidence? An unspoken question teased Odo, but he knew better.

To his surprise, the tailor had requested permission from Major Kira to remain on the station, citing his banishment and that he had already lived here among Bajorans in relative peace for over a year. Her initial reaction was to deny the request and send him packing, but she had relented. She offered no reasons, but Odo suspected she saw some benefit to having him here in the event his story of being expelled from Cardassia Prime was a ruse covering up his actual identity as a spy. At first, Odo thought it a rather transparent attempt to engender trust from the Bajorans, and by extension Starfleet when the detachment arrived. On the other hand, perhaps Garak was counting on such a simplistic ploy being dismissed or that it was part of some larger scheme.

Odo decided if his brain resided in an actual skull, all of this would give him a severe headache.

"You've convinced Major Kira to let you stay," he said. "I'd advise against betraying the grace she's granted you. I also recommend you don't try to leave the station for the time being."

Garak had the decency to appear offended by the unspoken accusation. "My dear constable—"

"Stop calling me that."

Pausing a moment, the tailor bowed his head. "I have no plans to leave the station. If you need anything, you know where to find me."

Turning on his heel, the Cardassian moved off down the walkway toward the throng of activity still unfolding in Quark's Bar, leaving Odo to contemplate the events of the past few minutes. He would conduct an investigation utilizing all of the information he could gather along with any relevant data gleaned from the station's sensors. When that was concluded, he was confident there would be no evidence linking Garak to the transport's destruction, the bomb, or anything else. Leaving no trace was an earmark of a well-trained, effective deep-cover operative.

Exposing Garak as the spy he was would be a challenge.

Odo enjoyed a challenge.

ACKNOWLEDGMENTS

As has become my custom with these things, I offer my first round of thanks to my editors at Gallery Books, Margaret Clark and Ed Schlesinger. *Pliable Truths* is my twenty-fifth[1] *Star Trek* novel, and the twenty-first while working under the guidance of either or both of these fine folks for what now, officially, has been twenty years.[2] From the beginning, their support and trust in me have been unwavering, and I simply can't imagine doing this without knowing they're at the other end of an email or phone call.

With that said, I also wish to thank editor Kimberly Laws, who only recently stepped in to help Ed oversee the *Star Trek* novel line and also took on the task of putting this book through its final paces before publication. Welcome aboard, Kim!

Thanks also to John Van Citters, the keeper of the *Star Trek* flame at Paramount Global. He's been doing his thing about as long as I've been doing mine. Indeed, one of his early assignments (punishments?) was reviewing and approving the manuscript for my first-ever *Star Trek* novel, *In the Name of Honor*. I still have a copy of the fax! It's entirely possible he's come to view that

---

1 *Are you kidding me?*

2 *Are you freaking kidding me?!? Where did all that time even go?!?*

incident as some sort of temporal inflection point and has spent the past twenty years attempting to develop time travel so he can go back and take the other fork in that particular road. If you're reading this, then his battle rages on.

I certainly can't have an acknowledgments section without calling out my hetero life mate, Kevin Dilmore. Even when we're not collaborating, we're *still* collaborating. He might not even realize it's happening, but . . . yeah. It's pretty much always happening. Thanks, dude.

ABOUT THE AUTHOR

Dayton Ward understands and forgives readers who skip over these "About the Author" pages. It's easy to gloss right past them, as they can often be kind of pretentious, with the author listing everything they've ever written along with the names of every cat they've ever rescued from a tree. Dayton hates being that guy, even though he truly digs cats.

Instead, wander on over to **DaytonWard.com**, where you can read about all the stuff he's written and thank him for sparing you the pain of yet another long, drawn-out "About the Author" page.